Thirteen Conjurations

Thirteen Conjurations

Jonathan Thomas

Foreword by Barton L. St. Armand

Hippocampus Press

New York

Acknowledgments

"The Copper God's Treat," first published in *Weird Fiction Review* No. 3 (Centipede Press, 2012). "King of Cat Swamp," first published in *Black Wings II*, edited by S. T. Joshi (PS Publishing, 2012). "Moby-mart After Midnight," first published in *A Mountain Walked: Great Tales of the Cthulhu Mythos*, edited by S. T. Joshi (Centipede Press, 2013). "Way Up When," first published in *Nameless*, 1, No. I (Cycatrix Press, Spring/Summer 2012). All other stories are previously unpublished.

Published by Hippocampus Press
P.O. Box 641, New York, NY 10156.
http://www.hippocampuspress.com
All rights reserved.
No part of this work may be reproduced in any form or by any means without the written permission of the publisher.

Cover art by Jason C. Eckhardt.
Cover design by Barbara Briggs Silbert.
Hippocampus Press logo designed by Anastasia Damianakos.

First Edition
1 3 5 7 9 8 6 4 2
ISBN: 978-1-61498-067-4

Contents

In Situ: Excavating the Art of Jonathan Thomas

Let me begin this preface by composing a literary version of the Piltdown Man, that turn-of-the-twentieth-century grand hoax of a "Missing Link" whose skull was constructed from fragments of a fossilized cranium of an ape, supposedly five hundred thousand years old, to which was appended a very human-looking jawbone. But let me also reverse this hoaxing construction to follow the proper and scientifically sanctioned development of my primitive example of Early Man, and make the skull recognizably "human," while the jawbone itself remains manifestly ape-like. I would still, however, file down the molars and have a French Jesuit fortuitously discover a missing canine stained suspiciously with the artist's staple "brown sauce" of versatile Vandyke pigment. Nearby, in the same local dig of moldy marl, would be found ancient artifacts: a Neolithic hammer made of stag's horn and flint arrowheads of various sizes, along with assorted teeth of mammoths, stegadons, giant beavers, and the bones of a new species of iguanodon. Amazingly, some of these bony shards are incised with runic symbols that can be traced on prehistoric stones and stele as far north as present-day Sweden. Let me also report that this find was made in a secret location in the State of Rhode Island. Hence the name of this new specimen of a very uncommon ancestor: *Homo supinus woonsocketiensis.*

Yet HSW is not totally extinct. And he is not really a hoax. Indeed, he still walks—or stalks—or hikes—or lopes—among us. He likes to go barefoot in all kinds of weather, even in New England's perpetual Northeast Flow or constant Wintry Mix. At home, he prefers to huddle naked in his cave and keep warm under a gently undulating three-dog-thick blanket. He goes out to a regular job, but his status as a modern underground man requires that he work quietly, obscurely, and anonymously, plugging away at low-end work that paradoxically requires a very high degree of intelligence and technical skill, but which also offers a self-created cloak of invisibility, whether it be trouble-shooting PCs, framing paintings, or freelance copyediting. Edgy, intuitive, perpetually wrong-footed in love, he is fated to be marginalized from The Beginning. Though a college or art school graduate, he underachieved or lagged behind or tuned out, raised as he was in the midst of a failing post-industrial capitalist culture and intimidated by its aftermath of Cyclopean architecture. No castles on the heights but massive blocks of empty textile factories that flamed out in blazing holocausts of oil-soaked wooden floors and exploding bricks, or—if they survived—were turned either into cheap bargain outlets or slick postmodern condominiums. But he also cannot forget the caverns of Deep Time that lie just beneath the surface of this landscape slowly ruined by casual neglect and usurious greed, any more than he can escape the hallucinatory flashes that illuminate images of the Old Gods who lodge in the proto-human crevices of his own primal brainstem.

HSW is haunted not only by the ironies of a sudden, unexpected, and traumatic reversion to type, but by the gaps, fissures, and absurdities of his Local Color context, a serpent's tooth also indelibly stained by the random drippings of Vandyke brown. As an inheritor of the trinity of native history, folklore, and urban legend and as a connoisseur of the odd, he knows that the patrician seventeenth-century Rhode Island recluse William Blackstone of fabled "Study Hill" now lies buried somewhere beneath the parking lot of a Rhode Island mill-turned-outlet named "Ann and Hope," that some Rhode Island towns have cursed corners and "Black Books" recording unusual concentrations of violent deaths, that Bram Stoker drew upon newspaper reports of Rhode Island vampirism when researching an authentically occult backgrounds for his *Dracula*, and that South County's "Great Swamp" was the site of a particularly bloody massacre of indigenous people. As a final twist of the botanical screw, he also knows this same swamp harbors a carnivorous species of Pitcher Plant found nowhere else in New England. And many is the Rhode Island graveyard—especially those of vanished "Asylums" and "Poor Houses"—that he has seen brutally bulldozed flat to make way for new golf courses, gas stations, multiplex theaters, and shopping malls. No wonder that the very earth under his feet—as well as something deep and dangerous in himself—cries out for blood.

Europe offers no escape, but only a more exotic confrontation with the doppelgänger within. To this not-so-Innocent Abroad, a stroll among the paintings by Hieronymus Bosch in the Prado engenders not so much a surreal and alien plunge into the unconscious as a domesticated shock of recognition. The final effect is no alien phantasmagoria but déjà vu all over again, for here in all its busy horror vacuii is Rhode Island venality, Rhode Island corruption, and the continuing sinkhole of Rhode Island politics made grossly manifest. H. P. Lovecraft visited this place—at least in his own fantastic dreams and fancies—long before, but the HSW thrown on top of Jonathan Thomas's many-layered kitchen midden has become radicalized in a way directly opposed to HPL's reactionary conservatism. His vector careens toward postmodern concerns with the tyrannical effects of globalism, unrestrained capitalism, and the continued exploitation of disenfranchised classes—even dead ones clinically chained by "advances" in medical science to demeaning postmortem bankruptcy, zombies forced to serve the polluted ideals of what was once America's most pure and unencumbered "pastime." The deadening of affect and the acceleration of entertainment go hand in hand.

Perhaps the fact of horror itself can never be really "new," but depending on evolving circumstances, it also has the capacity to become a dread wider and deeper than any kind of emotion we have known before. Jonathan Thomas pushes us toward just such fresh hells, as in his pages we recognize the still startling twenty-first-century disjunction between our own fragmentary human skull and our own residual ape-like jaw. That is why HSW is really no hoax, but actually our own subterranean, present-day condition, haunted as we all are by apparitions of banished gods, by our increasing mental, physical, and spiritual impotence, by random terrorism inside and out, and by our own awkward stumbles into the unfamiliarity of the sacred and the sublime. It is this self-revelatory confrontation, embodied in supple, intimate, distinctive, and lapidary storytelling, that Jonathan Thomas manages to conjure up again and again and again.

—BARTON LEVI ST. ARMAND

From Out of the Mythos

Mobymart After Midnight

The measured scritch, scritch, scritch under the urethane floor distracted me my first night on the job. And more off-putting were the occasional pauses, as if owners of claws were analyzing where to burrow next.

None of the middle-management skeleton crew paid any of it the least mind. "Can't everyone hear that?"

A few pairs of morose eyes grazed mine and lowered toward desktops again. "It's in-store policy to ignore it," someone imparted in a tone I'd have to term bleached gray. "Exterminators gave us a clean bill of health. If personnel out front were discussing this, they were in violation."

Okay. Underlying message, plain as cold sores: freelance tech support should keep its nose down and mouth shut. Nor was I unaware that these stiff white collars reckoned me just another exterminator, targeting bugs and viruses and worms behind their monitor screens, a realm as impenetrable to them as the floor beneath their Rockport soles, and from which incomprehensible havoc could burst at any moment.

Troubleshooting PCs for Mobymart ("a whale of a place," as its ads insisted) was never a career goal, and though much crummier gigs exist, corporate powers were making this one as onerous as possible, for starters by paying wages below my standard rate. Not that I merited special exemption from blanket eagerness to slash overhead on annoyances like union wages and health care and payroll taxes. And no brilliant insight was needed to gauge my desperation for income in this economy, in this job market, in foundering South County.

I like to think, if Mobymart hadn't hired me, I'd be among the hackers righteously harassing it, but how many can spare that kind of energy after the rigors of achieving bare-bones solvency? Thus with-ers the revolution in my time.

Ironically, this most impersonal of settings was alleged to harbor personal connections, decades and meters deep. Up until the mid-twentieth century, my workplace would have been awash in cypress swamp, an ecosystem vanishingly rare this far north. More's the pity then that it was drained for the sake of mosquito control, scant years before wetlands earned protected status, to become a nursery for maples, oaks, and brambles while awaiting "development."

Along with the cypresses, say the old-timers, callous bulldozers destroyed an ancient, disused graveyard, which is where my family name ambiguously creeps in. A great-great-great-granduncle suppos-edly disappeared, was perhaps even murdered and secretly buried, within that deconsecrated ground. No relatives of mine, though, can or will say what had brought him there, or if the plot held other kin-folk. But ancestral bones may well have moldered beneath Moby-mart parking lot or even under my workstation.

I felt more rapport with those fabled bones than with company henchmen around me. To my innocent question of whether I rated employee discount on merchandise, a tubby, beady-eyed ballbuster-in-training, at least ten years my junior, brayed, "For a temp? Fuck no, Warren!"

"I do have a first name, you realize. And strictly speaking, I'm freelance, not temp. I may be here five nights a week forever."

No matter. I was already addressing his broad back. Must have been a maneuver he'd learned for relating to inferiors. Was it too much to hope for his to be one of the cars the earth swallowed up not long afterward? My seventh or eighth night pulling in, a cordon of yellow caution tape and red traffic cones caught my eye. It out-lined those prime dozen spaces to one side of the handicap signs, and a few SUV and minivan roofs showed above sinkhole rim. I gawked long enough to note that their paint was rife with scratches and slimy handprints. Surprisingly shoddy upkeep on pricey new models. Or was erstwhile swamp staging a piecemeal comeback?

The hole, I gathered, didn't contain the vehicle I'd wished into it, since the owner wasn't screaming blue murder. Otherwise I learned no more about the collapsing blacktop. It seemed to incur the same silent treatment as the ongoing scritch, scritch, scritch beneath my feet, as if anything irrelevant to the day's business might as well be a figment.

The next untoward incident held off till after the weekend. Management probably wouldn't have associated it with the sinkhole even had it occurred the same day, and to be fair, I wasn't initially suspicious either. A little past 11, according to my Swatch's glowing arms, old-fashioned blackout hit storewide, instantly killing lights, computers, air conditioning, coffeemaker. The carping of irate shoppers carried like the pounding of distant surf into stone-blind offices, where staffers were powerless to issue calming instructions because the PA was dead.

Under cover of darkness I couldn't help venting some unique freedom of expression. "We got mighty clever rats chewing on the wires, to take out the backup generator too."

"Whoever said that, you're not funny and it's not appreciated. We have no rats in these or any of our facilities!" Because I had followed standing orders to be seen and not heard, no one could positively link my voice and face, but I easily pegged Mobymart's huffy defender as the haggard, basset-eyed supervisor who embodied pathologically loyal corporate doormat.

I'd resolved to clam up while I was ahead anyhow, when flashlight beam preceded a security galoot into the office. He eased his linebacker girth through the murk with the slow-motion finesse of a sea-bottom explorer. Panning flashlight back and forth, he asked if everyone was okay, in a practiced monotone that implied he'd rather not hear anything to the contrary, and advised we "just sit tight" for another fifteen minutes. Not that we had a lot of choice, he added, since the doors were shorted out. His cagey eyes suggested that something about a pitch-black Mobymart spooked him, though nothing at the moment was spookier than his stocky face lit from underneath.

Once he'd moseyed off, the crew passed time discussing ways to increase worker productivity, believe it or not, and I alone took startled notice of the afterimage, as first it seemed, of cagey eyes floating in the doorway. I stared blankly for a bit before observing that these eyes were several inches lower than the linebacker's, and they were fixed on me with a baffling semblance of recognition, but by then they'd faded like a mirage. They made good their withdrawal without comment on my part, and really, what could I have said, and to whom? I did ascertain afterward, without appreciating what it portended, that the outage was confined to Mobymart property.

At this point on the job, my disillusionment with today's malcontent youth was at an all-time high. Where was their anti-establishment gumption? I'd encountered no diabolical viruses, no signs of malicious hacking, in a mainframe that more richly deserved mayhem for every day I stewed in cloying Mobymart culture. Then again, no sabotage during my watch may have been just as well, as I'd have had to thwart and track down the perps to the best of my ability, despite wishing them untrammeled success.

One measly memo encapsulated everything I hated about my stifling employ, not least for its officialese prose, as oafish as it was overbearing. A week after the unexplained power failure, old basset-eyes, with reflexive frown at my clip-on tie, dropped a printout on my keyboard and went his laconic way. The sender's name and rank were no sooner skimmed than forgotten, but the text, practically verbatim, is branded on my cortex:

> To all Fellow Members of my Mobymart Family—
>
> This is a reminder to you in reference to my recent directive re: spreading unauthorized or unconfirmed information. Despite of my prior appeal to your loyalty and discretion, inappropriate speculations about certain alleged incidences have escalated to a disturbing level that may be detrimental to morale and the public trust in us. Therefore I am expanding on my previous warning re: these incidences which include, but are not limited to, reports on the loading docks of intruders that "disappear" when pursued, the erroneous assumption of stockrooms being "haunted" because of unverified footsteps and voices in them, and especially, the actionable rumor that one or more shoppers late at night has gone missing. It must also bear repeating that our standards of cleanliness insure we have no rodents or other pests at this or any Mobymart. Employees are imperatively directed to refrain from bringing up or discussing these and further reports that may arise among yourselves and

with our shoppers. Strict disciplinary measures will be enforced if future infarctions are brought to our attention, including dismissal and legal action. Like in any family, I am sure the good name of Mobymart is of utmost importance to you, and I will not have to remind you again to not circulate hearsay that will damage the reputation and confidence that are a keystone of our success.

The mealy-mouthed bastard, whoever he was. Nowhere in that minefield of deadly verbiage did he deny the truth of sensational "hearsay." And I grudgingly admired, "despite of" stylistic handicaps, his skill at dodging the weightier issue of safety and lives at potential risk. No, the corporate good overrode whatever else, and he might have believed that sincerely until his own neck was on the block. Of course, most of the workforce and I might never have heard of these "incidences" if he hadn't listed them. I was tempted to shoot back anonymous e-mail criticizing his omission of luminous eyes floating in the dark, but amateur sleuthing could have easily retraced my electronic trail.

As events panned out, I should have posted my gesture of disdain. I'd have gotten away with it. The store was out of business by the time the grinches in charge would have busted me, or so I calculate in tidy hindsight.

The light was turning red that final night as I drove up to the intersection and switched on left blinker for the access road to the parking lot, though I was signaling to no one. In pre-Mobymart era, this traffic light hadn't existed, or the intersection. This stretch of highway was also much wider now.

I couldn't conjure further memories of how the landscape used to look, as if they too were casualties of the bulldozer. Had nothing except brambly woods replaced primeval swamp, or had isolated homes and shops started nibbling away at them? In either case, local merchants and hundreds more had petitioned the Zoning Board to veto the proposal for this Mobymart, but thousands might have lacked the clout to jam the spokes of "progress." And someday, cold comfort though it was, this big box on its desolate acre of tarmac would also exit the geography and sink into oblivion. Naturally I had no inkling then that the process was already underway.

I snapped out of my brown study as high beams in left lane raked by. How many green lights had I sat through? Luckily no traffic was waiting behind me. Few customers came after 10, but on some ornery principle Mobymart peddled its wares 24/7. I could have picked a space much closer, except I preferred a minute's buffer between the car and my timecard.

Would the careerists in their cubicles ever conceive of this building, this company, as eventual dust, or did they smugly assume it would be flourishing here in a thousand years? They seemed to consider their windowless lair so bloody sacrosanct, it was a wonder they didn't escort me in blindfolded. These downbeat musings took me to the sliding doors, on which I almost banged my forehead. Why didn't they whoosh apart as usual?

Gawking around only fueled my confusion. The fluorescents were on, and people were rushing about, but nobody was manning the cash registers. The shatterproof glass muffled any soundtrack to the commotion and made it even harder to interpret, beyond the sense of staring into an aquarium. Or rather, a shark tank, I reluctantly corrected myself. Consumers, or so they seemed at first glance, had become predators. Revulsion and self-preservation alike dictated headlong retreat, but I couldn't move till kaleidoscopic violence formed some intelligible pattern.

Singly or in gangs, "consumers" were jumping and latching onto everyone with turquoise Mobymart smocks or more managerial apparel, biting down and loosing streams of blood, not just on the neck as per standard vampire practice, but anywhere on the body from which they'd ripped the clothing. These must have been the trespassers who had haunted loading docks and stockrooms, and had tampered with the electrical supply, and had snatched an unwary shopper or two.

At the worst extreme, a mound of attackers covered a victim, like a pileup of rugby players, but with egregiously more squirming and struggling. It projected an obscenely sensual aura, as disgusting as it was difficult to look away from. My assessment of the chronic scritching under the floor, that first night on the job, had been metaphorically correct. This slaughter of salespeople boiled down to a vermin problem, like a grand-scale infestation of fleas, a cloud of mosquitoes, or an assault by "mighty clever rats," as I'd so unpopularly put it during the blackout.

Peering helpless at the feeding frenzy, I mentally withdrew to safer vantage and speculated, Who am I to say these creatures aren't behaving like "proper" vampires? After countless run-ins for millennia with garden-variety ghosts, no one can conclusively anatomize them. Why be any more cocksure about an entity all the rarer?

In further contrast to their haggard stereotype, these legions of undead were positively chubby, some of them Titianesque. Their physiques were shamelessly on display, because linen gowns and winding sheets had rotted into the vestigial condition their wearers had unnaturally avoided. Underlying torsos were the white of mole rats, maggots, termites, or any species foreign to the sun.

Several of these fiends were staggering slackjawed through the aisles, less glutted than intoxicated on the blood they still licked dreamily from wide smudges around their lips. Their skin was taking on a rosy tinge, as if their diet had encouraged postmortem tissue to revascularize.

I had to be in shock. What better excuse for my readiness to accept the reality of vampires, of this whole vile spectacle at face value? The sane alternative, that the entrance was locked because a film shoot was underway, never even occurred to me, though I'm pretty sure it would have if a camera crew had actually been there.

My reaction, if I could call it that, was no less detached than if this had been a movie of bitten, lacerated corpses in pools of their congealing blood, at which were lapping, like famished kittens, buxom girls with blond antebellum ringlets and gouty grandfathers in disheveled periwigs and husky children with smallpox cavitations. How many decades or centuries had expired since their last meal? A liberal amount of vampirism figured in our regional folklore from Colonial days forward, but this order of atrocity belonged more to the realm of Grand Guignol.

In my numb pseudo-objectivity, the solution to at least one mystery, of where these creatures had come from, seemed self-evident. As I'd conjectured back when a mere sinkhole was the extent of the problem, the smothered swamp, with the graveyard at its heart and formerly quiescent denizens within, was staging a resurgence in the most brutal manner.

I was, in fact, so oblivious to any danger stalking me that at first I thought my own reflection in the glass had usurped my attention. But my mirror image wouldn't stare with egg-white eyes loose in necrotic-looking sockets, and its skin wouldn't belie a zaftig flush by harboring a crackled pattern like Bakelite in decay, and its hair wouldn't be commingled with cobwebs, and it wouldn't have blood on its chin. My mirror self also wouldn't dress in mildewed rags of white shirt and black trousers that ill-concealed a slew of double punctures from head to foot, like the perforations of underlying needlework that now held flesh together. Otherwise, the ogling nightmare did bear daunting resemblance to me.

My great-great-great granduncle was no longer among the missing, much as I might have preferred that he was. His fate was no longer steeped in obscurity. Nor did any comfort accompany the realization I'd seen his glimmery eyes before, aloft like hoverflies in benighted office doorway. And here we were as if I'd unwittingly kept an appointment with him.

In his eyes I read no hostile or predatory intent. Not that any affect was readable in those filmy windows on the soul. He absolutely wanted something, though, to justify watery focus on me when he could have been feasting on salesclerks. The sight of him put me on tenterhooks, or maybe I was suspended between emotions, not panicky, not threatened, at a loss for how to feel, for any inkling of what would happen next, and that mental limbo produced its own unique malaise.

Mindful only of this death's head with my face, I'd been unwary of the waxy hands that acted now on their own apparent cognizance, as long-lost uncle and I prolonged our staring match. One hand reached out and flattened against the big glass door, right where it said "Unbeatable Prices," and the other snaked beneath the waistband of soiled, shredded trousers, to extract a black book about the size of a pocket Bible. Had he been shoplifting paperbacks? Meanwhile, the hand upon the door pressed hard, as arm bent at the elbow, straining to empower the squidlike force of suction in outspread fingertips and palm.

My uncle pulled with literally inhuman strength, and the door slid open inch by grudging inch. Strangest of all at this fraught juncture, I wasn't fearful for myself and watched in naive fascination. When the gap had widened enough for him to slip through, he flipped the book underhand out onto the sidewalk, and a cloud of nasty black dust billowed up in the storefront fluorescence. Nope, it certainly hadn't come from Mobymart racks. His hand pulled free of the glass with a vulgar kissing sound, and the door snapped back.

Some of his throng had begun flaring their nostrils in our direction. Uncle never turned away from me, but seemed aware of developing situation just the same. "Get that to Carter!" he ordered. His voice was simultaneously gurgling and raspy.

Carter? Who the hell was Carter? Hundred-year-old kinsman must have automatically taken for granted that I'd know. Perhaps disregard for the passage of time was another undocumented trait of the genus vampire. Rather than quibble, I bowed to scoop up the book, though my skin crawled on contact with sooty, slick cover.

He suddenly stretched out his arms and smacked the glass with a resounding clack of long, split fingernails, surely more to startle than to menace, and he snarled, "Now go on! Beat it!"

Outmoded slang from a vampire, let alone a vampiric family member, gave me brief pause until I glimpsed ragged, bulbous figures gathering in the background, leveling their gaze at me one by one, crouching for a pounce at the entrance. No second warning had to jolt me out of there and to my car, which I unlocked and started up with minimal futzing, in welcome contrast to the nonstop mishaps that always hinder movie escapes. Like a fugitive from wicked Sodom, I never dared check my rearview mirror, never bade my spectral flesh and blood goodbye, never confirmed I wasn't imagining the hailstorm of bodies against shatterproof glass amidst the rumble of my badly tuned engine.

Sirens, as of police or rescue, were definitely audible in the distance. I was speeding away from them; not that I had to worry about being pulled over while holocaust raged at abattoir-cum-"whale of a place." Someone trapped inside had evidently vented final breaths on screaming into cell phone at 911.

And when the police arrived? What then? I couldn't say. I've refused to read a paper or watch the news ever since. The media couldn't possibly have gone public with a showdown between cops and vampires, and based on rumors about teenage gangs and Satanists I overheard at post office and supermarket, they hadn't. I wouldn't want them to. I had no urge to learn the body count, or how the bloodbath had played out around my workstation, or how bullet-proof swarm had vanished with impunity into burrows, and whether it had dragged along exsanguinated victims to join the ranks, or left them to the stakes and axes of the authorities.

What's more, I'm gratified no cops have beaten a path to my door, leading me to guess I wasn't on that night's surveillance foot-age, or else as lowly freelancer I didn't even make the list of "Moby-mart family" MIA.

Every time I've driven past the scene of midnight massacre, yel-low tape has cordoned off the width of boarded-up façade. From the road I can't make out if it says "Crime Scene" or merely "Caution." A much bolder sign, pasted to the plywood and already dog-eared, trumpets "Under Reconstruction," but I'd bet that was a bald-faced lie. And though I'm overjoyed there's one less Mobymart in the world, I'd never try to paint that as the upside of the carnage. Nor should I be deemed mean-spirited because I'd still describe pursuing a Mobymart career as classic example of backing the wrong horse, impossible as a rerun of that same mayhem elsewhere would be. Then again, it was impossible in South County until it happened.

As for the squalid little book, it promoted anything but enlight-enment for the few days I possessed it. To identify its rightful heir "Carter" or his progeny would have been a fool's errand, so to claim it as my *de facto* own sat fine with my conscience. But expectations that it might reveal why ancestral Warren had carried it, what had brought him to the graveyard, or what more general skeletons lurked in family closet were doomed to frustration. I couldn't even tell if scribe or printer had assembled the contents, which consisted of im-penetrable script most similar to Hindi, but more elaborately hiero-glyphic. The letters were disturbing, as if they might take on a third dimension, shake off the horizontal bar yoking them to the text, and skitter like spiders across the table.

Yet I forged along from page to page, mechanically scanning each line in a daze of incomprehension, and no sooner did I turn a leaf than shaggy purple fungus sprouted and pungently luxuriated, eradicating glyphs and then the paper itself at a borderline discernible pace. Arguably I had no more cause to balk at this implausibility than at the circumstances that had handed me the book.

I had a single chance to read each page and squandered every one of them in short order, compulsively, as if gorging on potato chips instead of glossing priceless arcana, until two moldy covers and a spine containing nothing were all I had, and those too disintegrated without trace sometime when I wasn't looking. A moot point, whether exposing frail leaves to air had triggered hungry spores to multiply, or baleful grimoire simply didn't want me delving into it.

Would a perusal by Carter have fared any better? I lumped that with the rest of my recent windfall of fruitless questions. And on a less academic note, will my heart rate always skyrocket when a branch scritches against the windowpane or my chair legs scritch across the linoleum?

Meanwhile, "despite of" itself, the book had managed to impart a message, or at least renew my awareness, that nothing of the past was amenable to real understanding, and purported actualities within the firmest grasp would crumble, with or without a Mobymart to blot out every clue.

Or might vampires pose an exception, with minds ruled by appetite but embedded in the past, indifferent to the present, insensible of the future? Why would great-great-great-granduncle otherwise presume I'd be acquainted with his defunct pal Carter? Could vampires reconstruct the chain of decisions that led them to perdition on their last mortal day? Every contributory event had to have gestated within such period-specific context. Could they recollect all that? I knew where to unearth the answer to those riddles, but what's the good of knowledge that gets the finder killed?

King of Cat Swamp

Dwight peeked past drawn shade in the living room to make sure the yard crew had decamped before he switched on the underground sprinkler system. Yes, they were gone, but how long had that frail old guy been pacing back and forth out front, in this July scorcher? Like a stray dog with a fix on some tantalizing scent? And why did he keep casting coppery bright eyes toward the house, and were those eyes probing, or beseeching, or resentful? If he was casing the place, not that he looked physically capable of burglary, he scored no points for stealth. In fact, Dwight was a little surprised none of the neighbors had called the cops on this blatantly "suspicious character."

Edith reached from behind his shoulder and parted the shade another inch to let her see what was so absorbing. Made him jump. "Maybe he needs to use a bathroom," she speculated. "Maybe he needs to borrow a phone. Maybe he's thirsty."

"But why does he have to be thirsty here?" Dwight didn't consider himself the least mean-spirited. Or elitist. It just seemed a fair question.

"Well, we can't stand by and let him limp around till he gets sunstroke." Edith had an extraordinary gift for telling Dwight what to do short of coming right out with it. All right, so she was only hastening the decision he'd have made on his own, eventually. That didn't help him feel any less like a hapless pinball as he chucked a pair of gold cufflinks into a sideboard drawer to prevent larcenous temptation, bumped into the row of suitcases ready in front hall for dawn taxi to the airport, and opened the door onto triple-digit heat index. A world of stunning difference from the central air inside. Dwight needed a few seconds to regroup before calling out, "Can I help you?"

But by then, ancient geezer had shuffled halfway up the gray

slate walk. His burnished eyes never blinked as they narrowed upon
Dwight, and he licked cracked lips, priming them to speak. In his
expression resided a strength of will completely at odds with his
general infirmity. Osteoporosis had crumpled him so severely that
the average catalpa pod looked more substantial. His dark but blood-
less complexion reminded Dwight of walnut meat, with comparably
deep wrinkles and hairlessness to match.

Dwight was a washout when it came to pegging ethnicities, and
even at the edge of point-blank range couldn't tell if angular features
were Hispanic or Italian or Syrian. "Mediterranean" struck him as a
rational compromise. And the outfit was emphatically generic.
White button-down shirt with long sleeves, loose khaki trousers,
sandals. If anything, too much coverage for this hothouse climate.
Maybe he suffered from poor circulation. "Please, I come back after
long, long time away," he wheezed. "I do not want to steal." The rut-
ted face peered up at Dwight's as if in supplication, but also as if
Dwight owed him something, an insinuation with which he was less
than comfortable. What's more, the accent contributed nothing toward defining the stranger's pedigree. Cajun? Portuguese? Mexican?
Dwight was starting to feel rudderless. Say something! "Did you
work for the people who used to live here?"

"This place was mine! Something of mine is still here!" Oh shit.
Dwight had wounded the catalpa pod's dignity. He'd also been blind-
sided by that claim to former ownership, and who was he to brand
anyone a liar out of hand? Still, he couldn't see it, not in this upper-
crust Colonial Revival enclave, in what had always been, well, an
unapologetically white bastion on the East Side of Providence. Like
water into cracked cement, the geezer took advantage of Dwight's
nonplussed state to slip past him and into the house. This turn of
events had scarcely registered when Edith's startled yelp pulled
Dwight inside on the double.

How had those decrepit legs carried unwanted guest to the living
room already? Dwight heard him mewl, "Please, I am only Castro. I
have come back here for something that is mine." Edith was still at
the window, and this so-called "Castro," with hands upraised in a
medieval-looking gesture of appeasement, had violated her personal
space, to judge by her red cheeks and arched eyebrows and incisors

biting into lower lip. She was wedged in among the beige velvet drapes and had backed well beyond arm's length from the doddering intruder. Dwight could understand why she was aghast, even if it seemed an overreaction. She treated Dwight to a glance that fairly bristled, *I meant for you to find out what he wanted, not ask him in!* Oh boy. No smoothing this over till she decided in due course to cool off.

Instead, Dwight aimed for a conciliatory tone toward Castro, who was, after all, merely a feeble and confused, if not senile, old specimen. As if anything of his were really on the premises! "Mr. Castro, why don't you have a seat? I'm sure we can get this sorted out in a minute." Castro eyed him as if wary of forked tongues, waddled backward and away from Edith, sized up the furnishings, and planted himself in the leather Deco club chair, their most valuable piece, facing the plasma TV. Dwight perched at one end of the puffy canvas sofa, across the room from the rear picture window, setting his guest in three-quarters profile. Castro swiveled on the squeaky upholstery to confront him head-on, putting Dwight unjustly on the defensive.

Edith, with a valiant post-traumatic smile, was rebounding from the drapes, rising to the occasion, doing her part to defuse the awkwardness. "Can I get you something to drink? It's so humid out there, isn't it?" Barely making eye contact, let alone giving Castro a chance to answer, she was off to the kitchen, with that sway in her hips, more pronounced when she was in a hurry, that Dwight had found so provocative in premarital days, before realizing she couldn't help it, that it wasn't meant to turn him on. Maybe she was less interested in relieving Castro's thirst than in jumping at any excuse to absent herself a while.

Castro did watch her departure with what Dwight preferred to regard as appreciation. Yes, the man must have been parched, though no more perspiration shone on his furrowed skin than on petrified wood, as if his sweat glands had worn out over decades. Then he further disconcerted Dwight by confiding, "She is pretty, your wife."

Dwight for the life of him couldn't think up an answer to that. Castro didn't visibly care, content with an armchair inspection of the room, from Japanese woodblock prints on the wall to Erté bust on Corinthian pedestal to bronze figurines from Benin on the mantel. Casing the place despite protests to the contrary? Dwight wished in vain for something to say, if only to curtail the mental checklist. Jeez, had the sneaky codger noticed the luggage on his way in? Good luck enjoying Costa Rica for two carefree weeks now. And where the hell was Edith with that glass of whatever?

"Here we are!" she lilted, bustling in with a blue plastic tumbler of cola. In her own good time, as usual. Handed it to Castro, who sniffed it with pursed, questioning lips as the fizz subsided. He tasted it and his features crinkled disdainfully.

"Please, can you put nice rum in this?" he demanded. "Nice Cuban rum."

Dwight and Edith exchanged helpless frowns, far from thrilled at prospects of drunk, out-of-control foreigner in their den. More disturbing, it was as if Castro knew about that liter of Edmundo Dantes, a gift from Dwight's boss, who'd smuggled it in through Canada. It was locked in the bottom drawer of Second Empire china cabinet in the dining room. On reserve for special occasions. Was Castro psychic? Or a practical joker in the employ of Dwight's boss? In either case, refusing him would likely result in an ugly scene sooner rather than later. This Castro, as two minutes with him had demonstrated, was nothing if not irascible.

Another excuse for Edith to duck out, anyway, and she seized upon it without comment. Dwight heard her clattering in the McCoy bowl full of Lindt chocolates where they hid the key to the cabinet, and then the key rattling in the lock. Castro was also listening, head cocked quizzically to one side. More clinking and scraping of glass against glass, across wood. Followed by the squeal and pop of a cork stopper.

Edith tripped back in, with a cheerful demeanor that may have been less transparently phony to Castro than to Dwight. Castro had to hold out his cup to meet Edith's outstretched arm with the open bottle. Quite admirable, her skill at hovering no closer than absolutely necessary to get the job done. "Say when!" Her smile did become brittle as the level of liquid rose significantly in the cup before Castro gave an understated nod of approval. He sampled expensive concoction and smacked his arid lips with gusto. Nobody's fault if it sounded more to Dwight like the click of mandibles.

Dammit, with all that fuss over the drink, Dwight had almost forgotten Castro's purported reason for worming his way in, and beaming Castro was relaxing and enjoying his Cuba libre way too much. Dwight leaned forward from the edge of the sofa and aspired to a stern, authoritative timbre. "Mr. Castro, when we bought this house, the attic was completely empty, the basement was completely empty, and every cupboard and closet was completely empty. Unless we've missed a secret crawlspace or trapdoor, anything you mislaid was gone when we moved in."

"Mislaid?" huffed Castro scornfully. He nestled deeper in the maroon leather, sipped his drink, and adopted a more serene air. "Please, Mrs. Nickerson, you sit down too." Castro extended his free arm toward the sofa and drew circles in the air with his index finger. Edith sighed and played along. Keeping a lid on her impatience, but no longer smiling. Dwight wondered whether guest or hostess would blow up first. Edith had an extensive record of speaking her mind on short notice.

Wait a minute: how had Castro known their last name? Dwight had to rein in his alarm. Let the old guy spook you, and you pass the ball to his court. "Nickerson" was on the mailbox, for chrissakes. Or, assuming Castro's claim about lost property was sincere, he could have learned by any number of aboveboard means who occupied his former address.

"The houses around us, the streets and the sidewalks, the ground under our feet, they all feel so solid, like they always will be here, like they always have been," Castro expounded. "But it was not so long ago, things were different, were they not?"

"I don't see how this enters into your business here." When had Dwight asked for an oration? Had he already allowed Castro an inch and ceded a mile?

As if affirming that worst fear, Castro took a slow, exasperating slurp from his tumbler. "This ground we walk on, for example, with the big houses and the neat yards on top of it. Underneath, for thousands of years, was a swamp here that festered and bred sicknesses and vermin. Even less than a hundred years ago, some swamp was around us. The English who first came, they named it Cat Swamp, and the street you call Olney now, it went to the swamp, and they called it Cat Swamp Trail. That swamp is all buried, but who can say it is gone forever?"

"Whether it is or it isn't, every word of this is news to me," Dwight retorted. Loath to admit Castro had hit a nerve by reducing his exclusive neighborhood to malarial wetland. "Why should we trust this information?"

Castro shrugged impassively. "No one can be sure of how much history there is, even in one's own backyard."

"Well, maybe I see what you mean," Edith ventured. "I heard there used to be a ravine where Elton Street is. But what does any of this have to do with whatever it is that belongs to you?"

"The ravine? Nothing to do with it, nothing." Sly Castro winked. Yes, of course he was acting purposely obtuse. Not out to fool anybody. Just his little jest, okay?

"Okay, but why in the world," asked Dwight in spite of wishing he could stop himself, in spite of misgivings that he was somehow chomping on bait, "was it called Cat Swamp?"

Castro raised index finger and wagged it back and forth, as if to say, All in good time, my child. "It took a little while in front of your house to be sure you still had my thing of value. It will take a little while to relate how that thing of value came to be here."

Oh God, please, just get on with it, Dwight inwardly fumed, regretting he'd ever peeked out the front window. A like sentiment was all too readable in Edith's body language.

"In the beginning was a religious persecution, very long ago, but it is the first cause of my being here." Castro indulged a generous swallow from his tumbler. "In Andalusia, the people had leave to worship as they pleased. But after the Moors were expelled, it became bad, too hard to stay, for those who did not profess the orthodox creed."

Oh no, Dwight silently quailed, he's not really dragging us all the way back to 1492, is he? But yes, he plainly was, and Dwight would have been fidgeting with irritation had he not been spacing out amidst Castro's nonstop babble.

"The Inquisition and the wars about faith were to spread all over

Europe. To be safe for the longest time, it was needful to join with the Portuguese, who were sailing to lands with no Christians, with no jealous gods. And what is now New England would be safest, even though the Portuguese had put up a church and a fort where your Newport is today, and sought to convert the Niantic people. But in a few years the soldiers and the priests went away, as anyone could have foretold they would, because the gold and the silver and the trade were elsewhere, and those passengers were soon forgotten who chose to stay and watch hurricanes and lightning hammer away at the fort. Nothing remains from those Portuguese builders except some of the church, visible at sea, and used by mapmakers as a landmark for generations before the Protestant colonies."

Inexplicably to Dwight, the more Castro drank, the more polished his diction, the more educated and articulate his delivery, above and beyond simply warming to his topic.

"And so where the doctrine of the Catholics did not take root, another did, with precious decades to flourish unmolested, and to attract members from among the native men, and to receive those disciples from the Old World with the cunning to seek and find American refuge. For the sake of avoiding friction with the sachems and the shamans of that region, the newcomers retired to territory shunned as worthless and unlucky, a swamp in fact, north of the bay. There they could practice their rituals and libations in privacy, to curry the favor of divine powers sovereign over earth and sea and stars. Native leadership for the most part left these swamp dwellers in peace, unwilling to risk the displeasure of strange gods."

Castro emptied the tumbler and set it gently on the parquet beside his chair. He had crossed the line between doddering and delusional, in Dwight's confident opinion, and where would he go from there? Slipping out of earshot and phoning the police to remove this potential menace might have been the best plan, but the babble resumed, and Dwight didn't want to exit in the middle of a monologue and maybe set off their touchy powder keg. Wait till the next pause.

"Throughout this era, the only English to come ashore were fishermen who stayed in summer stations, and who had nothing for recreation but to become drunk and to seduce the native women. These seasonal visitors, and not the next century's settlers, gave Cat

Swamp its name, which was later thought to be from an abundance of cattails, or because bobcats prowled there; but no, it was because of the fishermen's own cats that ran off and hid in the swamp, hunting mice and beetles." Castro silently clapped his palms together, with fingertips leveled at Dwight. "And that is the answer I owed you, Mr. Nickerson, is it not?"

The best Dwight could do was nod helplessly, as if he had to keep his head above treacherous current, to the exclusion of almost everything else. A current of verbiage? Is that all it was? Edith was similarly glassy-eyed.

"The people of the swamp were happy to let the cats breed as they would, for they made acceptable offerings to those exalted, almighty powers, greedy for adoration. Much more pleasing to those powers was the blood of living men, which the fishermen also supplied when drunkenness made them easy marks, or when the furious kinfolk of a ravished native woman delivered them bound and naked. If entire boatloads of fishermen were to disappear, for the most part no one would miss them, and if someone did, where would blame ordinarily fall except upon the Atlantic?"

This crazy old coot, this demented story, it must be a hoax, Dwight reverted to telling himself. Staged by his boss, a send-up in lieu of a send-off, before tomorrow's flight. Yeah, that would be just like him. Any minute now, someone somehow, Castro, boss, or third party, would tip his hand.

"Mrs. Nickerson, you look especially upset about these past happenings. Would it help for me to assure you that fishermen and rapists and slavers were often the same people?"

Castro droned on without waiting for Edith's yes or no. "Those first English colonists came here to escape persecution, even as we did, and those who built the first homes around the bay, and who were sometimes in earshot of our feline sacrifices, pretended deafness to them, in those days when the reputation of the cat was doubtful at best. Again you are upset, Mrs. Nickerson, but you must accept, your ancestors did not care about what happened to cats."

Castro's hands were still clasping together and seemed to operate with a fidgety, independent volition of their own. They jerked a couple of inches back, forth, up, down at irregular intervals, as if obeying the skittish pull of the four compass points. Ever more annoying. If only Dwight could find the words to make him stop. At least Edith, bless her, had mustered the wherewithal to scoff, "Mr. Castro, do you really expect us to believe that Providence was founded by a coven of witches?"

"No, no, Mrs. Nickerson," he patiently corrected her. "Witches are friendly to cats, remember? Most of your forebears also made that mistake. Almost none had the learning to perceive the ancient, enormous gulf between my religion and that of gullible rustics. But those forebears of yours, as their numbers increased over the months and pushed inland, grew violently offended at what they glimpsed and overheard at the end of Cat Swamp Trail, and did oblige the swamp dwellers to quit their refuge of more than a century. In haste those victims of hatred had to scatter into the wilderness or secure passage to far-flung ports where none had knowledge of them or where the roads led to deathless masters who might enlarge their wisdom and impart how men and time might do them no further injury."

Okay, Dwight pleaded, if there's a man behind the curtain, it would be really good of him to pop out right now. The shiny black mantel clock ticked impassively on. Nope, nothing.

"Meanwhile, your forefathers, in their ignorant passion, strove to expunge my people not only from the land but from memory and the written word. Over the long run, that was also preferable to us, insulting as it was at the moment. Of those self-righteous witnesses, William Blackstone alone preserved a plain-spoken account of us in his journal, which fire destroyed along with the rest of his library, days after his death."

"And that was never considered suspicious?" Dwight found himself asking.

"William Blackstone's death was purely natural." Maybe so, but Castro's crooked smile was hardly innocent. Truth interposed as a wall of deception? "And Roger Williams, rumor had it, described us in some coded manuscripts, but they have never been deciphered. Perhaps he was libeling other neighbors altogether. Did you know his mortal remains turned into the root of an apple tree?"

What? Dwight was becoming disoriented, numb to the sofa beneath him as if his legs had fallen asleep up to the waist, or he was at the outset of an amateur out-of-body experience. "Mr. Castro, do you honestly believe that anything of yours is inside this house?" Dwight managed to ask. "Would you at least do us the courtesy of stating what it's supposed to be? In one straightforward sentence?"

Castro's smile had taken on a capricious edge. Or was it patronizing? His copper eyes, in contrast, had gone emotionless, borderline reptilian. "Hidden in the hinterlands of Cathay were the most accomplished teachers of my religion. In three lifetimes, a disciple could not grasp the fullness of wisdom in one of them."

Castro's hands, still acting on their own, were performing manipulations, tangentially like a game of cat's cradle, except the shapes they wove, while fluttering apart and spiraling toward a contact they never quite achieved, induced a queasiness in Dwight, a foreboding, yet he lacked ambition to lower his gaze.

"One master too many in the disciplines of Cathay would have sown deadly, useless conflict, so after my intellect had penetrated to the innermost circle of secret lore, I withdrew and eventually reached the haven of Louisiana bayou, where I could gather and teach acolytes in the seclusion of another swamp for yet more decades, until small-minded men enforcing human law drove us forth again. They caught me and nearly brought me to grief, but I tricked them by playing the mestizo degenerate they presumed I was, and when their guard was down, I escaped by the grace of my religious resources. Today you would call it 'playing the race card,' would you not?" An unpleasantness stole across Castro's grin, as his hands danced on of their own profane accord.

"And when was that?" Edith was surprisingly naive to expect a straightforward answer from Castro now after so many deflected questions. Her hands were wrapped around the upright bottle of Edmundo Dantes in her lap, as they had been since she'd sat down.

"To have your nice bottle of rum, or any fermented beverage, would have been illegal then," Castro disclosed.

"You mean to say you were alive in the 1920s?" Dwight exclaimed. How could Castro lie so blithely? How many years past a hundred would that make him?

Castro's frown may have directed disappointment or condescension, but not sympathy, at Dwight's dull wits.

"How long ago did you live in this house?" asked Edith when it became clear that Castro would not honor Dwight with a reply. Her tone was incurious, as if she spoke only to keep other questions at bay. Was her mind a scary leap or two ahead of Dwight's?

"I have never lived in this house."

To go by Edith's blanching complexion, Castro, in that skewed way of his, had answered a question other than the one she had asked, one that she was afraid of asking. Nor did Castro's hands relax in their manic, unseemly choreography. Why didn't Edith prevail on Castro to leave off, as Dwight would have, had he been less preoccupied trying to concentrate?

"Let me get this straight," Edith slowly enunciated. "You started referring to yourself, in this epic account of yours, as one of the fugitives from this Cat Swamp you alleged was here. You're implying, in other words, that you're more than four hundred years old?"

"No, not four hundred years, no."

Petty or not, Dwight disliked how Castro was far more mild-mannered when "pretty" Edith guessed incorrectly. And since Castro liked her so much, why, he railed inwardly again, didn't she insist he stop futzing with his hands?

Copper eyes grew brighter as if Dwight's mute, unbecoming resentment were amusing. "During my sojourn in Cathay, I rambled among the Sichuan mountains, and contemplated the archaic dawn sequoias there." Castro had broken into a singsong chant, at a tenuous volume that obliged Dwight to lean forward, ears straining. Was this somehow Castro's roundabout approach to revealing his age? "Those trees offered me food for thought on the origins of predacious flora. Sometimes I observed that flies and bees resting on the soft green platform of a frond had adhered to it, and then fused with it, dissolving into a wingless, glossy husk. Some enzymes in the needles, I inferred, had served inadvertently to trap and digest the insects. The chemical makeup of these trees, and the insects' susceptibility to it, had conspired to make a carnivore of the sequoia, which benefited from this intake of animal protein."

Dwight could do nothing but sit flummoxed, struggling to follow the breathy lecture. Deranged cultist was effectively impersonating a botanist, whatever the validity of his science. Moreover, his accent waned as his eloquence expanded. Curb a couple of diphthongs, and he could have anchored the evening news.

"Reproductive fitness, I realized, favored those individual plants that derived extra nutrients from prey, within those species endowed with the appropriate enzymes. Therefore certain species would exploit carnivory more and more, to the exclusion of their conspecifics that did not."

Who or what, Dwight puzzled, was the real Castro? That was one riddle Edith couldn't solve any better than he could, though between the extremes of rampant insanity and erratic brilliance, Dwight had to go with the first option, to label Castro a hopeless sociopath who talked a fantastically elaborate game. Trusting first impressions had always steered him safely away from troublesome characters before, and what was this scholarly discourse but a loony departure from equally loony historic fantasy?

"In common with spiders and many another predator, the earliest carnivorous plants foremost needed a means of immobilizing victims while remaining passive themselves." Castro fell silent as if his recital had reached its fit conclusion, and his hands, which had persevered in their enthralling, unwholesome gyrations, dropped limply to his lap.

The gleam in Castro's eyes had subtly ignited along the ridges of his face until an exultant mask leered at Dwight and Edith. In conjunction, a musk had been invading Dwight's nostrils, as if Castro, still dry as petrified wood, had been exuding a malodor of disguised excitement through channels other than atrophied sweat glands. It was acrid with longstanding piss and entrenched fungus, and with a whiff of partial spoilage, of arrested decay, like that of an elderly neighbor's corpse he'd once had to i.d. at the chilly morgue. Dwight tried to slide back across the sofa, to withdraw a little from that nastiness, but he couldn't budge. He was stuck like a fly on a sequoia frond, as if subject to oblique power of suggestion, or was it something more, something in those weaving hands?

"At present," Castro resumed, "I should think I need merely reaffirm the truth that has dawned upon you. In that benighted age before your streets and houses, this place was mine, and a sacred object of mine had to be concealed in haste beneath the water and mud of Cat Swamp. The followers and victims here were mine, the rituals were carried out under my guidance, and when those almighty powers that ravened among men before history return to end human history, the triumph will be mine. I will be much greater in the future when the stars are right, but in that olden time, I was the King of Cat Swamp."

"But what about us?" Edith's formerly low, sultry drawl had coarsened, thickened, as if airways were clogged with swollen, uncooperative vocal muscles. "Why can't we move?"

Castro bounced implausibly to his feet, brushed invisible specks off his shirtfront, and shrugged. Not a twinge of osteoporosis in his posture. "You are here where you say you belong. Why should you want to move ever again?" His placid smile was at odds with his pitiless copper focus.

"But what did we do to you?" Dwight also had to invest stubborn effort into eking out words, and they emerged malformed, gurgling.

"Mr. and Mrs. Nickerson, you are both proud of your distinguished ancestry, are you not? Of those who carved your towns from wilderness, as you like to put it, as if they simply daubed upon blank canvas? You are not, to look at you, different from your forebears who dispossessed the native peoples, and who dispossessed us. You might say that I am here to retrieve but a single token of what I have lost to you."

"But how could we help whatever it was they did?" Dwight was nearly choking on each syllable. Uncanny that Castro understood him.

"Regardless of that, you are the beneficiaries of what they did, yes or no?" Castro's smile had hardened to the grimness of his eyes. "Can you deny it? Can you stand up and dispute it? No? I thought not."

"Please, we can help you. Whatever it is you're after, let us get it for you." The urgency in Edith's strangled plea implied that she and Dwight were of one panicky mind: Castro meant for their paralysis to be terminal. "There must be something we can give you!"

"The devil has a hand in all bargains," Castro admonished. "Let us not complicate this and involve him. I deal with someone else."

Castro ambled over to Edith and twisted the bottle of Edmundo
Dantes up and out of her two-handed grip, as if unscrewing a
threaded stopper. Her fingers persisted in enclosing nothing. "My
thanks to you once more, humoring an old man his taste. I never did
say 'when,' you may recall. For nice rum like this you have no further use."

Dwight heard Castro's sandals cross the kitchen linoleum, and
then the door to the back hall creaked wide, and then the sticky
back door burst open, causing the whole house to tremble. Dwight
next picked up Castro's trail in the back yard, as framed by picture
window. Castro had a long-handled shovel from the garage and was
digging in the shade, by amazing coincidence, of a young dawn sequoia, a housewarming present from his boss. With a flash of insight
that passed just as readily for psychosis, Dwight pondered how well
he really knew the boss. What was his religious affiliation, for instance?

Castro was laboring steadily in the terrific heat like an ox in its
prime. Every so often he'd lodge Dwight's shovel in the turf and savor a swig of rum, smacking his leathery lips. Not too late for the
joke to be on Castro maybe. Dwight might have smirked had it not
been such a chore. An hour ago the landscaping guys had sprayed the
grass with chemicals that stayed toxic for three days. Too much to
ask for a dose of modern suburbia to be this ancient fiend's undoing?
If the fiend's unflagging vitality were any indication, then yes, it definitely was. Dwight watched and watched, with consistently sinking
spirits. A gallon of pesticide might not faze Castro. But maybe he
wasn't even digging in the right spot. Yeah, that would serve him
right. What had made him so cocksure about destroying that portion
of Dwight's cherished lawn, anyway?

Castro was chest-deep in his pit, surrounded by mounds of min-
gled sand and loam. He bent from view and straightened up, dammit, with something in his arms, something the girth of a hassock,
and he hoisted it with tender care onto grass already smothering under loose soil. Whatever had led him to the front door had performed unerringly up to the last square foot. He reverently wiped
clods and smears of dirt off his artifact with a handkerchief, which

allowed Dwight to see it was made of greenish stone, though he couldn't otherwise make head or tail of it. And to think, it had been under his lawn almost four hundred years.

Castro flattened his palms on the grassy perimeter, boosted himself out of the hole, clapped his hands free of grime and ineffectual lawn poisons, drained and chucked the Edmundo Dantes, and, incredibly, hefted and hugged his prize to his chest with one spindly arm. With no intention, evidently, of tidying up over there. He hove toward the back door and out of sight again, to reenter Dwight's field of vision in the living room.

The greenish bulk and Castro's white sleeve bisecting it were all that Dwight could briefly see, but proximity afforded no aid to comprehension. Here was a block of masonry or a squat statue, but of what? There were wings and claws and tentacles and eyes, disjointed, asymmetrical, out of proportion to each other, like an optical illusion set in some unfamiliar mineral, or like a mess on the floor at closing time in a sinister butcher's shop.

After Castro had exited, Dwight spent a futile while fixated on reconciling those disparate body parts to one another. He didn't snap out of it till a car door slammed in front of the house and an engine revved and soon receded. Shit, it sounded like his boss's Explorer. He then belatedly glimpsed in peripheral vision that Edith was gone.

Dwight was reminded of a laughable scene in a movie back at college. An old movie, nowhere as old as Castro, but old enough to be silent, and it was German. In that memorably funny scene, a vampire picks up his own coffin and strolls around with it on one shoulder. Ridiculously or not, Castro had gone that German vampire one better, toting off a boulder plus Dwight's wife. He would have felt more angst about her fate, had his own not been much closer at hand.

He and Edith were supposed to be on vacation. Mail and newspaper delivery had been cancelled, the oblivious yard crew would come and go, and the Nickersons had warned friends and coworkers they'd be incommunicado for two weeks in paradise. Nobody would miss them. Nobody would ring the doorbell and worry.

Days and nights inched glacially by, in which Dwight soiled himself and then no longer soiled himself, hungered and thirsted and then no longer hungered and thirsted, shivered in the drafty central air and then went forever numb. Pangs and aches and every sensation wore out, just as Castro's glands had done centuries ago. So did Dwight's spite and indignation at being singled out, at the unfairness of Castro tracing that block of masonry to his backyard among all the equally deserving candidates for slow death in former Cat Swamp. He gradually gave up despising Edith, too, for making him let Castro inside in the first place. At last Dwight was down to one coherent nagging thought, recurring to him more and more rarely, that after a certain unremembered number of days, the ravages of thirst and starvation were irreversible.

He was in no shape to acknowledge or to appreciate the aptness of it, when a scruffy feral tom stole in through the back door Castro had carelessly left open and began spraying the drapes and scratching up the upholstery, and in general behaving like one more previous owner come home. Dwight didn't even hear the crash when the cat bumped the Erté bust off its pedestal.

Pictures of Lily

For the longest time I wondered what Lily saw in me. Now I'm down to wondering what she was. And no harm in asking, since she's gone for good, she and her whole oeuvre, aside from the sketchbook. Otherwise, who's to say how my sphinxlike sweetheart would have dealt with such a loaded question? Incidentally, Garth is likewise not coming back.

I'd heard of her for months before our paths crossed, but by then, who hadn't? To all intents, Lily Terkel had sprung full-blown from a crack in the sidewalk, a trendy subversive without a past, basking in the warm esteem of *ARTnews* as much as the *Village Voice*.

Succès fou had rewarded her very first show, disingenuously titled "I'm a Stranger Here, Myself," at an ultra-chic Chelsea salon. She'd daubed up nothing more than raw pastiches of the last 500 years' most familiar images, the *Mona Lisa, Blue Boy, Demoiselles d'Avignon, Whistler's Mother, The Scream, Nighthawks at the Diner, Girl with a Pearl Earring, The Sleeping Gypsy*. The acrylic was so thickly slathered in such lurid, almost day-glo colors that every slap-dash imitation seemed on the perpetual verge of sliding like slime off the canvas. But something animated, impudent, authoritative shone through the crudity and made her work entrancing, irresistible, exorbitant. "I put a little of myself in every frame, beyond the obvious that everyone sees," she confided to an interviewer, as if that explained anything.

We met, or rather, she picked me up at an opening in Providence, which was her abode of choice. The provinces reportedly suited her because she could accomplish more under the radar, where she wasn't in demand. She hadn't attended RISD, so she wasn't here out of habit or nostalgia. No records of higher or lesser education ever came to investigative light.

The gallery was on a rehabbed ground floor in a row of historic warehouses sandwiched between the Interstate and the waterfront. The show, an up-and-coming hipster's portraits fashioned from the minced, flattened innards of cell phones, PlayStations, and laptops, was nothing revolutionary or spectacular, and I was surprised to find Lily checking it out. Since I'd framed all the pieces, I felt as if I had a right to be there, whereas I ordinarily feel out of place at openings, irrationally or not. I was in my second decade of part-time servitude at Shadwell Fine-Arts Picture Company, where the hours were flexible but the pay was stingy. Hence free wine and a meal's worth of finger food were always welcome.

I pretended to admire a fuse-and-wire profile and held wine glass plus paper plate in one overtaxed hand while biting off some ham and cheese calzone in the other. Breathy words an inch from my ear almost startled me into dropping everything. "I think you're right to fill up on those. That's what I'm doing." What the hell? I didn't know a soul here, so who could be accosting me? I swallowed and turned toward Lily's quizzical smile in stunning close-up. "I'm also really impressed with the way you framed all this."

"What makes you accuse me?" Did that sound remotely like repartee?

"I've seen you at work. I've been over there a bunch of times the last couple of weeks." She persisted in her disarming proximity. She was maybe a smidge taller than I was. Her bountiful blonde hair was straw yellow with overtones of silver, and was bound at the base of her neck with beige yarn. Her eyes were meltwater blue, and her jeans and black jersey flattered her without going overboard. She didn't introduce herself. Plain to both of us she didn't have to, and she seemed to know well enough who I was. Instead, she asked about me, my career as a framer, what I did on my own time. "I can't believe you're defined by that job," she gently probed.

"I just do it to make ends meet. It's not my life's calling or anything." My replies were nowhere near scintillating as far as I was concerned, but she listened as if they were and kept asking away. I'm not exactly Quasimodo, but demoralizing experience has taught I'm no ladykiller either. Since I couldn't possibly be Lily's type, I concluded she must have been trying to sweet-talk discount framing out of me. And I couldn't rule out that she might, too.

My five-year plan, I professed, was to earn a livelihood producing bands in the basement studio at my address and recording my own stuff as I went along.

"I have a friend in town who's been doing okay in that line of work. I'll introduce him to you sometime," she offered. I nodded obligingly, a million miles from guessing she meant Garth, or that he even lived in these parts.

At least I wasn't deaf to Lily's subtext that she intended seeing me again after tonight. Her point-blank tenacity in this conversation, meanwhile, was both enticing and a little disconcerting. With the most stealth I could manage, I shifted my focus hither and yon, baffled by the absence of scenesters interrupting us, of a posse at her celebrity elbow. But no, I had her all to myself, which was as mystifying as her sudden objections to "putting up with any more of this godawful wine," and did I need a ride anywhere? I had, in point of fact, arrived on foot.

I volunteered to treat her at one or another neighborhood bistro where the wine certainly wouldn't be worse, but she countered, "I have my own place in mind." I sat in dread of the beating my debit card would likely take at her kind of place, till she parked her Prius in the driveway of a triple-decker way off Hope Street, near the Pawtucket line. "I can vouch for the liquor here," she pledged. She led me by the hand down some steps and into her basement apartment, where it finally sank in that she wasn't after me for cheap framing.

Thus began the first of many nights, three or four per week for bemusing months, at Lily's live-in studio. And she was right about the drinks. She christened our "relationship" with forty-year-old Armagnac.

Early on, I speculated that Lily might have picked me over someone more solvent or accomplished for any number of reasons. Maybe she just arbitrarily liked me. Maybe our affair was her idea of a conceptual art project. Maybe, in keeping with her low-key lifestyle, she wanted a low-key boyfriend who wouldn't crimp her productivity. I tried not to overanalyze. As for how I felt about her? She was talented, beautiful, and attracted to me. Again, why overthink a good thing? Let it unravel in its own good time.

In short order I conditioned myself not to push my luck, making a show of support and encouragement (despite my lack of scholarly credentials), expressing curiosity about her and her work, but without challenging her many cryptic or evasive responses. When I asked if she'd arrived in town during a housing shortage, since she could well afford tonier aboveground quarters, she defended basements as "cozy and soothing, like a childhood memory." And to correct my impression that someplace more open to natural light would better serve a painter, she questioned why I believed darkness was less natural than light.

Peculiarly, I never caught the artist in the painterly act, and precious few of her canvases turned up in bedroom, kitchen, or TV room, and never longer than overnight. Her studio took up the rear half of the floorplan, behind sliding double doors that stayed closed, allegedly to seal away noxious fumes of turpentine and fixative. The key was always in the lock, but unspoken law denied me the use of it, and she neither went in while I was around nor invited me back there. Some people really felt the need to compartmentalize, I supposed. Chalk it up to artistic temperament.

At my house, she seemed happiest in my basement setup, hanging out while I recorded bands or mixed tracks, although she should have been bored silly. But she really was that much "cozier" belowground. One evening we were ensconced in the booth, with soundproof Plexiglas between us and some aspiring youngsters selling themselves as "Thunderation, an homage to Lightning Bolt." I had to explain that Lightning Bolt was a hometown avant-noise duet that had made good in the '90s. Lily borrowed the earphones a minute and listened to Thunderation churn out take 3 of their second masterpiece in as many hours, and she observed, "They shouldn't be so sure they're climbing a ladder to the stars."

"I won't tell them you said so." According to the word around town, though, these fledglings thought they were doing exactly that, and Lily had tuned right in on it. My psychic girlfriend! As I reclaimed earphones and withstood further imitative Sturm und Drang, it enervated, it dispirited me for as long as I paid attention. I couldn't see these boho arrivistes relating to or even dreaming of the groundbreaking novelty of a Captain Beefheart or Sun Ra. They had ambition, they had a schtick. What else mattered?

Then again, who these days was setting the kids a good example? Sure as hell not Lily. As with "alternative" music, so with the contents of frames, after a century that had produced nothing with the game-changing impact of a Picasso or Matisse or Duchamp, even if you held your nose and counted Warhol. Lily's portfolio might well have functioned as our just desserts, the logical endgame of fine arts as parody and recycling and ironic allusion, and after hearing her critique of Thunderation's derivative racket (in dual senses of the word), I reflected that maybe it took a copycat to know one. Naturally I voiced none of this while Lily sat beside me and we played footsie beneath the console.

For a serious, prominent artist, she spent perplexingly little time in her studio, and a perplexing lot with me. Nor did I ever detect pigment under her fingernails, streaking her hair, staining her jeans, even after a few days in quarantine to grind out some commissions. She did, however, give off constant traces of a fishy oil, always too faint and masked by sweet herbal shampoo to pose a problem, and which I dismissed as residue of paint thinner or cleaning fluid. I also read it, erroneously or not, as proof of hours spent toiling in front of an easel, or else of her allegiance to cod liver oil.

We went out on the town, such as it was, remarkably seldom. Never to clubs, or to openings unless she had something on the walls. As she put it, "What would we go out and look for? We found each other." How could I debate that?

At least half our evenings devolved into early bedtimes. These always left me wishing for a history of her sex life, but no tactful approach to the subject ever occurred to me. She liked being on top and loved planting her lips on me and sucking in the damnedest places. Can't dispute it was a turn-on, though her focus often shifted beyond any visible horizon, she forgot her own strength, and I'd have to remind her, tenderly but sternly, to ease up. The morning after a lot of our liaisons, I noticed transient rashes, bright and burning, which I attributed to Lily's brand of soap or laundry detergent. Never got around to broaching these outbreaks with her either.

And likely as not, we spent our quality time in her lair under the influence, courtesy of her bottomless and borderline hallucinogenic stash. Three tokes along, whether we were watching TV or whatever else, I'd often observe that Lily no longer had a distinct outline, instead dissolving into froth around the edges, tapering away into space. This was especially perturbing while we made stoned love. On those occasions, I couldn't shake the even more outlandish perception of witnessing some loss of constraint on Lily's part and not my own addled vision, although high as I was, I understood that likelihood was against me.

On two or three of these dissolute evenings, while flipping through the channels on her wall-mounted plasma screen, she'd pause and absently set the remote on leather sofa arm and lean halfway off the cushion toward the geometric animations on a "special subscription" channel. Or that's how she described it. This channel, she gave me to believe, broadcast kaleidoscopic, strobing, mesmeric patterns in black and white, 24/7. They resembled Rorschach blots in eternal flux. For some unspecified reason, she felt "duty-bound to check in there" sometimes. In her minutes of rapt gaze, I was completely off her radar, free to ogle her with impunity. Her eyes would flick back and forth as if absorbing data, and her lips slowly formed words as if they were important and must be read correctly. In a while her mouth would close and she'd sit back, blinking repeatedly. Remote in hand again, she'd favor me with an inscrutable smile and resume surfing.

The night after one of these viewing experiences was one of our rare nights out. We were at the Underground, the Ivy League campus coffeehouse, because a gallery assistant downtown had badgered Lily into promising to go see her boyfriend's band. Or so Lily said. Besides, she liked the name of the venue, even if it was actually ground level on one side of a sunken patio. We arrived half an hour early to stake out one of the room's four or five tables and had no trouble seeing the band past the drifting bodies of a couple dozen undergrads. I had to stop watching after the third song. Three bland guys and a blonde girl on a low, cramped stage were very self-consciously channeling the Talking Heads. Lily was coolly studying them, as if recording with dispassionate eyes. If they weren't to her taste, she was above letting them bother her, apparently. They bothered me, and I poured creamer in my coffee just to fixate on the convection currents. Then like the answer to an SOS, Garth Shaw was leaning over us and the band never impinged on my awareness again.

On his CD covers he wasn't so gangly, almost freakishly tall. The best I could tell in cavernous gloom, he and Lily had the same blond hair and blue eyes. Couldn't say I was shocked that she and Garth were acquainted, though their physical resemblance did take me aback. He and she had followed equivalent routes to success in their given fields. In an age of reissues and revivals and retreads, he epitomized the facile, ingratiating spirit of assimilation, with nothing original or innovative past his commingling of genres. Not that I disliked his output. Everybody loved his output. His latest, which I owned, was the refreshingly blunt *Commodify This!* And here he was, pulling up a chair and kissing my girlfriend's hand.

"Honey, this is the friend I was telling you about." I prayed Lily was talking to me and not him as I half rose to shake his hand, introduced myself, and assured him I already knew his name. But I hadn't suspected he was a fellow Rhode Islander.

He came across as a regular guy. We chatted about my setup, my projects, and in a way that didn't leave me feeling like a piker, he divulged that his every recording, from demos to mastering, happened in the studio at the rear of his basement apartment.

Always a little fluky to me, how two such high-profile characters, with respective coverage in *Artforum* and *Spin*, would live as well as work in humble cellars in the same one-horse town. On the other hand, everything they had in common conduced to buying into the logic that if one had the inclination to live here, then the other would too. Merely an equal need, I theorized, for them to control the amount of spotlight on them, to safeguard their privacy, their productivity. Could that really be all there was to it?

Our conversation petered out and Garth swiveled toward Lily. I was reconciled to the idea of Lily hobnobbing at length with celebs, but they were up to something else, conferring sotto voce, impossible to overhear, and when one finished a sentence, the other paused thoughtfully, as if decoding diplomatic communiqués. The vibe between them partook less of chance encounter than of a rendezvous.

The band may or may not have been playing at this juncture. Don't ask me.

Garth and Lily were public figures, especially on college campuses, and well before now I'd pondered why Lily was never a magnet for pests and glad-handers. And if not in this enclave of entitled flaming youth, then where? Speak of the devil, a petite redhead with heavy black eyeliner and leather jacket to match was slinking up to our table. Determined to have a word with one or another of her idols, biting her lower lip as if torn between posing as starstruck waif or worldly punkette. Neither persona was in the cards. At arm's length, she veered off course and continued across the room, wearing the expression I'd imagine on a moth after narrowly eluding the bug zapper. Or on a steel shaving after magnetic force had repelled it. Entrenched in their tête-à-tête, Lily and Garth acted oblivious to whatever had just transpired. I should have been spooked, but at the vexing moment welcomed fannish imposition no more than they did and blindly admired their hoodoo for dealing with it.

Something else, in any case, was weighing on me. As these two colleagues' wealth of rapport and common ground became clearer, my position loomed increasingly untenable. What was I doing with Lily? How much of a future could I hope for with her? Amiable Garth, suddenly on his feet, interrupted my brown study by shaking my hand and sauntering out.

"Please don't be jealous." Lily was lacing her fingers through mine. Was my darkening brow that dead a giveaway? "He and I couldn't have what you and I have. We're so much alike, Garth and I, that we couldn't learn anything from each other. Such a thing as too much in common. You don't think I'm a narcissist, do you?" I shook my head and returned her smile in token of my trust, though the mordant question chafed at me, Was Garth running off to my counterpart, to wit, a low-key townie girlfriend?

Garth I was not to see again, despite his off-the-cuff promise to "come over sometime" and advise me on getting the most out of my cellar facilities. Still, he was often on my mind, starting less than twelve hours later. Lily wasn't a news junkie per se, but our days usually commenced with BBC News, and though she didn't come off as a staunch tree-hugger either, she was prone to shush me during international reportage of floods, of sea levels on the rise, of wildfires out of season, of long-term forecasts about land, food, and water shortages, of political intransigence or fecklessness in the face of inexorable realities. The mealy-mouthed treatment of these stories on American networks only moved her to sarcasm. That morning, however, she stuck with local coverage on a Providence station.

With dusty plaid curtains across the three-paned windows, I was ignorant of April snowstorm in progress until the weatherman enlightened me. White Easters, even white May Days, at this latitude aren't unprecedented, except nobody had seen our doorknob-high drifts coming, forcing recourse to coinages like "pop-up" and "ocean effect" flakes. Some viewers, deputized as "weather-watchers" to call in backyard conditions, contended that what was in the air looked too anemic for the amount accumulating, as if more lay on the ground than had fallen, but the weatherman in glib rebuttal shrugged, "What you see is what there is."

And what there was wouldn't be going anywhere, because the city had shot its budget for snow removal in February. Not a problem for Lily and me. We were fine holed up together for a few days of civilization on pause. Nonetheless, she looked askance at my townspeople's lack of civic initiative. "Where I come from, everybody would've been out already clearing the streets in front of their homes, and not sitting on their hands while elected hacks and money-grubbing stooges butted heads." I asked if maybe she wasn't exaggerating some. In answer, she proposed we bundle up and play in the unplowed drifts. A sincere offer, too. She loved making angels and building forts and digging tunnels for the neighbors' dogs to race in, like a genuine child of polar regions.

But first, she fielded a phone call at a pretty intrusive 8:30, and her side of the terse exchange reminded me of last night's conference with Garth. If the overheard phrase "watching just now" plainly referred to the weather, how did "going fine so far" in the same breath fit into that? Lily and Garth seemed to be in mysterious cahoots all right. Of course, that assumed Garth was at the other end, which I couldn't prove, since the voice in Lily's ear was inaudible to me. A curator from anywhere on Earth might have been consulting her about impending exhibition.

I had no chance to elicit the truth. Immediately on hanging up, Lily shooed me to the vestibule to try on some fancy Frye boots, and damned if they didn't fit perfectly. Then till my toes went numb, we were out of doors and carefree, apart from Lily's inquiry from left field on whether I thought the locals were like people in the rest of the country. I said I didn't see why not. She nodded wanly and, affecting renewed cheer, lobbed snowballs at a Stop sign.

During lunch, we took up the game where I tried prying into her history, and she humored me with out-and-out apocryphal or uselessly vague information. Judging by her fondness for winter sport, I ventured she'd grown up in a cold climate, and she admitted to spending "formative years" in an especially remote corner of Patagonia (which led me to infer her putative kinsman Garth must have, too). Funny then, I persevered, how she didn't look or sound Hispanic or Native American at all. This she attributed to her status as "second-generation colonist." Yet another explanation that clarified nothing, take it or leave it.

As usual, I shied from pushing any harder for specifics, courting a fight I couldn't win, potentially jeopardizing our affair. Anyway, she'd received a heads-up about a "big job" due by the weekend, so would I understand if she kicked me out after lunch? Hated to go, but a gentleman has to say yes. That must have been what the phone call was about.

A few days noodling around in my own cellar, taping my poor efforts to channel the spirit of psychedelia, wouldn't do me any harm. Nor did they, on balance, inspire a single spark of faith in my own creative instincts. Lily's invite Saturday to come hang out felt like blissful reprieve from myself. Foot travel, though, was even more onerous than during the "snow event." Nothing had melted, volunteer truckers had plowed only the most major thoroughfares, and a soaking downpour since Friday evening showed no sign of abating. The saturated snow was dense like wet cement, and furrows of shoveled sidewalk had become ankle-deep canals for icy rainwater. No matter. Off I went, and gladly.

Lily had "loose ends to pick up" in the studio, so I'd find the outside door unlocked in case she couldn't hear the bell. Why bother ringing, then? I locked up behind me, consigned my rubber boots to

the Astroturf mat, and with quiet shoeless steps entered equally silent quarters. I detected no bump and clatter of tidying or rear-
rangement and was about to announce myself when across the TV
room I noticed a gap of roughly half a foot between the double-
doors to her sanctum. To peek in, or even to knock on the dark veneer, impressed me as violations, and I stood indecisive within the
cool draft seeping out. Inexplicably, I smelled nothing. With the best
exhaust fans on the market, remnant odors of paint, of solvent, of
that stubborn fishy oil should have lingered.

The doors groaned some inches wider apart, and Lily lunged
through, her face confrontationally close to mine. I was too startled
for words. She regarded me without surprise, or censure, or challenge. Instead, I felt she was clinically appraising me, observing me,
much as she had the band at the Underground, as if she'd contrived a
bit of temptation to see what I'd do. That same night out, she'd also
spoken of "learning from each other," but whatever she wanted to
know now, why not just come out and ask?

No sooner had I conceived that question than she flung her arms
around me and kissed me, a jolting embrace, almost frightfully pas-
sionate, verging on aggressive. She released me after I responded in
kind to her kiss. "That's better," she said. "I get so wrapped up in
there, I space out something awful. Sorry." What a relief. I wasn't in
trouble with her, not yet at any rate.

She clutched my hands in hers and backed me onto the sofa, but
had no grander intentions than mild smooching and switching on the
local news at six. Weather topped the headlines, as it had when last
we'd tuned in. A warm front had stalled over southern New England, dumping three inches of rain, and because the snowpack was
impeding drainage, streets had become flumes, low-lying intersections were ponds, and rivers were cresting above flood stage. From
my cushy vantage, none of these calamities was personally upsetting,
until the meteorologist quoted frantic "weather-watchers" whose
basements were awash with sludge. Sewers were allegedly "refluxing"
everywhere around Narragansett Bay. "Oh shit, I better go check out
my cellar. I'm completely screwed if—"

I was halfway off the sofa when Lily's hand on my shoulder drew
me down. "Old news. Don't worry. You'd have been well aware of

anything going wrong by two o'clock. I heard bulletins while the damage was being done. Nothing more will happen." She sounded as cocksure as ever she had, unreasonably so in fact, as if she had secret founts of privileged knowledge.

"How's Garth doing?"

"We talked already. He's fine." Beneath her upbeat surface, an undercurrent of Rubicon seemed to murmur, You don't doubt me, do you? I redirected my attention to the nattering screen. "You know how these self-styled journalists like to sensationalize," she added, and leaned toward me till I had to face her. "From what I read between the lines, the trouble was fairly scattershot, but you can't expect call-ins from the multitudes who weren't affected. So there's no way to measure the extent of the disruption." Maintaining that steadicam expression she quizzed me, "But let's say sludge had destroyed your studio due to neglect of the sewer system, what would you have done about it?"

"What could I do? Sue the city? I'd spend more in court than I would on replacing my equipment. Besides, if the DPW can't pay for snowplows, how much would I get for a mixing board? Blood from a turnip, you know?"

Lily crinkled her brow as if flummoxed at my usage, and then she blinked away such frivolous outlay of mental energy. Maybe she really had grown up in Patagonia with English as a second language. "Would you predict most people will swallow their indignation, without holding the government to account?"

"I'd say my level of apathy is around average." Was she seriously using me as a surrogate John Doe? For what possible reason?

"Back home we don't abide mismanagement." Her tone was neither judgmental nor provocative. She was simply stating a fact and, thank God, didn't elaborate on her countrymen's implied love of *coups d'états*. Then she was off to replenish the hash pipe, and with timing almost too impeccable for coincidence, the portable phone rang and Lily yelled for me to grab it.

The ringing emanated from between sofa cushions. Garth was as unfazed at hearing my voice as I at hearing his. "Could you please pass along to Lily that it's going ahead as planned?" he requested. "And it'll absolutely come off as natural, right up to the finale?"

"Is this a musical project you're wrapping up?" Digging into Garth's business stirred none of the reflex qualms I'd acquired from dealing with Lily. Nor did he sound put upon. His wry amusement, though, was somehow unsettling.

"Well, I'll tell you, the orchestration has been murder. You might also want to jot down, the provisional title is 'Potholes That Bloom in the Spring.'"

"Uh-huh." I wasn't jotting anything down. No idea where pad and pencil hid, and anyway, the instant I hung up Lily strolled back in and I relayed the message. My conscience had no chance to bother me for lying to a celebrity. She raised a knowing eyebrow at Garth's tidings and left it at that. My place with her was in the dark, but wasn't that true of any relationship to some degree?

Whatever she and Garth were up to, that title had to mean something, and they'd practically dumped it in my lap. But to what purpose, unless I was part and parcel of their research and they were leaking details of their activities to test my reactions, positive I couldn't hinder them? No, that didn't wash either. Lily and I enjoyed intimacy avidly and often. Would that make me her lab rat "with benefits"? How to square that with any template of normal human behavior? Besides which, I'd be damned if I let paranoia jam the spokes of this once-in-a-lifetime romance.

Paranoia might all the same have launched a whispering campaign during the alone time of a standard twenty-hour workweek, but I was on the clock more like fifty hours, in the wake of Sunday's thaw. A dawn wakeup call from Shadwell on my cell Monday disqualified slush as an obstacle to trudging in. One hell of a backlog had built up, and nothing in it but rush jobs. Nights, I had scant energy to enjoy Lily's charms, and none on tap to debate why she lavished them on me. By Thursday, the treadmill pace at Shadwell had wrung me out, so just as well that Lily went into isolation to crank out pictures for a big impending show, here in Providence for a change. I'd only begun to pull myself together on Saturday afternoon, the second in a row when Lily, mission accomplished, desired my presence on the cusp of citywide tribulation.

"You didn't drive over, did you?" she greeted me.

"No. Why?" I did own a rattletrap Saab with outdated inspection stickers. It slept in the garage at the end of my driveway. I couldn't afford pumping gas into it.

Lily sat me down in front of the six o'clock news, just like last Saturday. Road conditions in Rhode Island were a perennial disgrace, especially after a punishing winter, but April's smothering snow, torrential rain, and fluctuating temperatures had dragged them to a new low. An anchorman with baby-fat cheeks and slick black hair that conjured the phrase "greasy kids' stuff" gleefully cued "dramatic video" of streets whose voracious sinkholes spanned a block or two. Viewers were cautioned because paving had appeared intact until the weight of a single vehicle triggered extensive collapse. A number of drivers and their passengers had to be hospitalized. No word yet on the severity of their injuries.

Lily's arm was around me, but her impersonal look was fixated on the newscaster, as if to glean what emotions, if any, underlay his slick exterior. At the commercial break, she shook her head inconclusively and rejoined me on the sofa. "Why do they pretend it's under control? I want you to stay here till Monday morning."

No objections on that score. I did feel obliged to comment, "Lucky you weren't on any of those streets when you went downtown to drop off the paintings."

"I was out earlier, before anything was happening."

How could she have known that? The newscaster hadn't provided a timeline and had warned that the roads seemed okay until they suddenly weren't. Her round-trip to the gallery must have been blessed by sheer dumb luck. Or did I want to credit her with foreknowledge of today's sinkholes, and of implicitly more to follow? No, I didn't, because from there I faced a leap, as easy as it was deranged, into blaming her, and Garth while I was at it, for unstable tarmac. Especially Garth, come to think of it. What was that title of his? "Potholes That Bloom in the Spring"? To be interpreted as prophetic or incriminating? A prime example of Hobson's choice for the beset rationalist inside me.

Lily was subjecting me to surgical gaze, as if to pinpoint why smoke would billow from my ears, when the portable phone rang in the bedroom and she sprang up to get it. The smattering I overheard of subdued and guarded syllables gave me to believe Garth was checking in. I caught "couldn't be better," and a minute later, "all battened down and ready," but was Lily confirming we were okay, or that the city wasn't, and wasn't going to be? Whatever those two were hatching, why did it have to be anything more sinister than a multimedia installation at the Brooklyn Academy of Music? Who was I to assume it was? Above and beyond the lunacy of allotting them the power to sink traffic, I could not for the life of me fathom what was in it for them.

Uh-oh, there went the beep of Lily turning off the phone. Incumbent on me to wipe all trace of suspicion off my features, and pronto. "Garth says hello." She emerged from the bedroom and snuggled up to me as if all was well in the world. No outward interest in scrutinizing me for shadows of mistrust.

Sunday's update at six impaired my appetite for the splendid feast Lily had whipped up from a fridge without the evident makings of lamb cutlets, polenta, and braised asparagus. Hidden ingredients, hidden talents. Meanwhile, the weekend total of "sinkhole incidents" had climbed to twenty-three, with no official remedy past bracketing the danger zones between white and orange barricades and construction barrels. Among the escalating toll of accident victims transported to area hospitals, four had been pronounced DOA. I couldn't touch another bite for the duration of the story, though Lily kept busy with the plate on her lap, as if watching ancient history reenacted. I also couldn't help but brood, Exactly what I need, blood on my girlfriend's hands, and murders for good measure. Simultaneously, I wasn't proud of what that rush to judgment said about the fabric of my personal loyalty.

Lily cleaned her plate first and feigned absorption in the national news till I was through. Then she wheeled at me like a public prosecutor. "Before dessert, there's something I was curious about. What, in your opinion, caused this rampant failure of basic infrastructure?"

That really put me on the spot, since my list of potential culprits was limited to her and Garth. I hemmed, "An act of God?"

Her eyes accused me of not taking her seriously. "If you buy into an almighty and omnipresent deity, every occurrence becomes an act of God because it's either divinely perpetrated or permitted. Where does that get you?" Her brow wrinkled as she reshaped the original question. "In the present crisis, to whom do you assign responsibility among those who can be held responsible?"

Hah. This was a shopworn old routine in the Ocean State. "Based on experience, the Mayor's Office will blame Public Works, and Public Works will blame the Department of Transportation, and the DOT will blame the contractors who do road maintenance, and they'll blame their suppliers. And they'll all keep passing the buck around till the brouhaha fades away."

"In other words, nobody accepts responsibility, nobody is penalized, and the general population has nobody from whom to exact satisfaction. Is that how your democracy functions?"

"Well, the city can't leave the streets full of crevasses. They'll be fixed eventually."

"But no governing body is directly answerable when the common good is at stake. And if nobody is answerable, then the vast majority of your people are always subject to exploitation. When those in power can only be circumscribed by one another, it amounts to the abuse of everyone else in society, and when abuse goes unchallenged, it can only worsen. You have no more say in what happens around you than a sugar cane harvester or a sweatshop seamstress, despite your higher standard of living."

I'd never heard her so fired up. "I can appreciate the system is different where you come from, but aren't you judging us a tad harshly?"

Nothing pushed her closer to a blow-up, I'd found, than my attempts to be conciliatory. Today, thankfully, she rewarded me with a tolerant, bittersweet smile. "In my background is a fucking long period of servitude, a history of oppression so severe that I guarantee we're not on any map. We endured exploitation by some extremely old and overbearing interests. Only now are we in a position to set our sights on the wider world." She shrugged philosophically, and consolidated our dishes and silverware into one pile at her feet. "You'll have to forgive me, I'm kind of sensitive to abuses of power."

As was Garth, ipso facto, I noted.

I told her I was sorry for everything she'd gone through, and she squeezed my hand and transfixed me with a kiss that thoroughly cleared the air. From the oven she fetched a pecan pie for dessert.

Monday morning, Lily was up ahead of me, and till I had to roll my workbound bones out of bed, I contemplated a terrifically vivid, tingly rash around my groin and navel. Into the kitchen I shuffled, finally impelled to point at the irritation and urge the girlfriend to try new soap and detergent. Coffee was brewing in the Braun. Lily was otherwise not in evidence.

Across the TV room, the double doors to her studio were a shoulder-breadth apart. I squinted in before I realized what I was do-ing and, since I was still in the kitchen doorway, fancied I wasn't overstepping bounds at this distance. Feeble light through her sanc-tum's triple-paned windows showed me nothing, in any event. Noth-ing was tacked to white plaster wall, nothing lay on clean brown carpet, at least not within view. Nor did I hear exhaust fans whining. Here, one might well infer, was an atelier in name alone.

Lily slunk through the gap and leveled her eyes at me. She'd re-garded my previous near trespass coolly, analytically. Now her man-ner seemed more coy, a shade away from teasing me to violate our tacit compact, not today but maybe soon. Figuratively dangling for-bidden fruits of knowledge. Mum like the sphinx, she turned and pushed the doors together, slipped by me, and poured us each a mug of coffee. I resisted the impression, stronger than during my last chat with Garth, that she'd inducted me into a behavioral experiment.

She got on with toasting bread and washing fruit and shooting the breeze like at any other breakfast. "And don't forget," she said at the table, between sips of her refill, "we have that opening Thursday at the Empire." I promised "we" would be there, even if the opening was strictly hers.

Thursday was monthly Gallery Night, when imitation trolley-car buses made the rounds of art exhibits from East Side to downtown to West Side. No roads had caved in since Sunday afternoon, so the evening went forward as scheduled, with only minor detours in the shuttle route. The Empire, where Lily was showing, was named for the street it fronted. With its roots in the Reagan era, it held the re-cord for longevity among Providence's "alternative spaces." Thun-deration played there often, on a stage to the rear of the first-floor gallery, whose scruffy, subterrene ambience may have accounted for Lily's attraction to the place. Another artist's reception was underway in an upstairs salon of this rehabbed shell of a bicycle factory.

Entry to Lily's exhibit was through the Empire's bar and grill, and on the glass door into the gallery black press-on letters announced, "Sincerest Forms of Lily Terkel." On some evasive, nagging level, that title augured badly, and after I'd trailed in behind her and scanned the walls, my twinge of disquiet flared into ulcer-grade stomachache.

At face value, Lily's landscapes of urban and industrial blight and portraits of townie luminaries were departures from her mockups of fine art's greatest hits and iconic advertising and Hollywood caricatures, except I knew where they'd originated, encrypted though they were in her trademark garish swaths and dollops. Every composition had been cribbed from framing jobs I'd handled during that madhouse week at Shadwell. Unless the artist was a friend, how could Lily have accessed her work, and if they were friends, how could she justify a stunt like this? Did Lily's covert talents include seeing through my eyes while I labored unsuspecting with mat knife and mount boards? That harebrained notion shouldn't have taken so long to dismiss.

Lily was working the room, conversing briefly with attendees of her choice and moving on. As usual, nobody approached her. Self-serve refreshments beckoned from a folding picnic table decked with butcher's paper, over in front of the stage. I poured a cup flush to the brim with Merlot.

After a second tour of Lily's confounding images, I needed more alcohol. She intercepted me halfway to the table. Without detectable irony she advised, "You should definitely have fun and enjoy your fill of the wine. I had to spring for it myself, to be sure we'd have something drinkable for once at one of these things." I raised empty plasticware and mumbled, "Cheers." She favored me with a quick smooch and resumed schmoozing.

On impulse, I decided to try the wine upstairs. I never came close. Three steps into that markedly less crowded reception, I backed out. Customarily I'd have felt I had a right to be there since I'd framed all the art, except it was the art that Lily had somehow cribbed. My face was probably chalk white.

Downstairs again, I sampled the Syrah, but the classy spread of focaccias and beef braciole and cannolis whetted no more appetite than if it had been of wax. Uh-oh. A frizzed-out brunette, short and stocky, with silver disc earrings and tight black turtleneck, was crossing the gallery toward Lily. Her expression shifted from resolve to trepidation to rancor, and finally froze at what I read as freaking out. Here was the upstairs artist, I wagered, and uncharitably wondered how frizzy her hair had been before she'd seen "Sincerest Forms."

As the aggrieved party shambled near, her features became rigidly similar to those of the coed who'd tried buttonholing us at the Underground. Glazed and confused. Lily, meanwhile, acted as if this encounter was proceeding on schedule.

Eerily, no one but I paid them any heed, and the brunette was dumbstruck beyond unsealing her lips. Impassive Lily addressed her in deceptively placid tones, as much a sphinx as when she'd met me on the threshold of her studio. "I can understand why you're upset, but you must remember, there are only so many ideas in the world. This kind of accident is bound to happen, and you really stand to profit from it. Whoever purchases anything of mine would also need your corresponding piece to complete the pair. In fact, I've been recommending that to all my customers tonight. Would you be willing to reciprocate? You'll find everything of mine is priced to go, so it would almost be like a two-for-one deal."

The brunette nodded sluggishly and renewed her course across the room on a slightly different bearing, as if she'd ricocheted off Lily in slow-motion. Lily located me and ambled over, smiling toothsomely. "See how situations improve with a spirit of cooperation?"

Oh, is that what she had demonstrated? For want of any germane reply, I offered to fetch her a drink, and during that brief respite I marshaled my faculties to ask, "Isn't Garth coming?" He was, after all, the person with whom Lily most closely "cooperated" in some covert respect.

"He sent his regrets." She sipped her wine and nodded demurely at a passerby who kept on going. "He's up against a now-or-never deadline."

"That still wouldn't be the composition about potholes, would it?" The Syrah had blurred my affect too much for me to tell if I were being sardonic or not.

In either case, Lily shook her head nonchalantly. "He hasn't mentioned what he's calling this."

Garth or no Garth, Lily should have been pleased with the evening. At its height, the turnout was airtight shoulder to shoulder. She posed for a *Providence Journal* photographer with the Empire's married founders, both of whom sported shaven heads and tattoos of crows on their forearms. Some delegate from the Mayor's Office clambered on stage and delivered a few fawning sentences about Lily's preeminence among preeminent artists flocking to the "Renaissance City," though nobody paid attention except to eschew the finger food as long as he loomed over it. By nine o'clock, red dots had sprouted beside most of the black lacquered frames, and the neo-beatnik gallery director reported "nibbles" for the rest.

I hadn't the heart to ascertain if the upstairs artist had profited from Lily's "recommendations," but at least she wasn't standing mesmerized in the corner toward which she'd been slogging. Lily had also, to my knowledge, fielded no flack from anyone else about whence she'd derived her images. Watching her exercise this occult gift to quash uncomfortable interactions had spoiled my appetite, but at four libations and counting, I bowed to the wisdom of cushioning the brunt of alcohol with bracioles while they lasted.

On the ride back up Hope Street, Lily reminded me less of an artist savoring triumph than a sorry drudge after eight tedious hours. She'd fulfilled some onerous obligations without particularly good graces and didn't even seem too kindly disposed toward me. If I were any judge of tirades, Lily was taking out repressed frustrations on me, couching them as cabalistic accusation. "Everyone sees but nobody acts. The tunnel is rotten with cracks, but everyone stubbornly advances. You, for instance. What are you doing for the sake of the world to come?"

Tipsy as I was, I still had the wherewithal to speculate that Lily may have downed more wine than she or I had realized, but she seemed in no mood to hear about that. Instead, I hemmed and hawed her an answer to the best of my disability.

"The lobbyists, the billionaires, the corporations, they have it all sewn up these days, more than ever. I sign a lot of online petitions, I go to a rally if I get enough e-mails about it, and I'm not doing anything else. Never makes a meaningful difference, does it?" Oh shit. The onset of hiccups could only undercut my gravitas. "Protests are for the young, anyway. Younger than me. And how could anybody profoundly shake up the system without landing on death row under some provision or other of the Patriot Act?"

I thought I'd done all right at persevering through the hiccups to sum up the Gordian knot of twenty-first-century activism. But Lily's frown conveyed I'd merely bored and disappointed her. Not my first girlfriend by a long shot to make that discontented face. It brought home to me the finitude of our relationship. Had rash honesty put us on opposite sides of a hairline fissure that would widen into inevitable parting?

I added nothing in my defense, in no hurry to dig myself deeper. Lily likewise refrained from mincing further words. She had a right to sulk, didn't she, whether or not that made sense after tonight's brilliant success? She let the Prius idle in the driveway as she peered at the garage door. Her look was more subdued or resigned than irate. Or was she simply logier as intoxication hit her?

She intoned hollowly, as if channeling someone else, "I used my fame to leverage an obnoxious condition on the gallery, and they gave in. I stipulated each canvas would go home with the buyer upon its sale, and I'd bring its replacement within forty-eight hours. Was that too antisocial of me?"

There must have been more to her outburst than guilt at pushing around a few arts administrators. I, however, was in no shape to coax it out of her. In my best fumbling stab at sensitivity, I asked, "Would you rather I went home right now?"

She shook her head forlornly. "Let's make the best of our time together." Just as well I was deaf to those intimations of parting ways. They might have undermined my efforts to reciprocate when Lily made hungry advances in the front seat. Wine fumes definitely soured her breath.

When we were done, we went inside and smoked, no further loveplay resulting. Rather, she rolled over on top of me in bed and made me vow, her face an inch from mine, to come straight back after work. She drummed that into me again on Friday morning. Easier to say okay than tactfully explore why she was so insistent, especially in my post-indulgent haze.

My vanity ascribed amorous motives to Lily's demands I rejoin her ASAP. Anyhow, impure thoughts helped the hours fly by at Shadwell. In the event, however, she was crankier and more contrary than during the ride from downtown. She seemed pathologically compelled to greet me with a diatribe, the closest she ever came to losing control in my presence. "You people with your conflicting little ideologies, that's what's going to destroy you." She was pacing between kitchen sink and fridge, and I had a hunch she'd have addressed this lecture to the meter reader had he shown up first. "None of them work in every situation, none to the exclusion of the rest can create any kind of fair-minded society. Of course, your capitalists are the worst because they're in the best position to subsidize themselves and flout the common good. And if your government didn't cut special deals for irresponsible banks and oil refineries and factory farms, it'd be obvious they're propping up a house of cards. At this rate of environmental abuse, whoever wants the world need only sit back and wait their turn and rebuild it to their liking."

Hard for me to buy that ideologies were so much less divisive in Patagonia or wherever she was from. How different could their capitalists be? I also couldn't fathom who might be waiting unscathed to reassemble the pieces after Lily's global apocalypse. But I had to sympathize with her disgust at inept, venal authority as doom approached on multiple fronts, and I strove to play the calm, still voice, if only to keep my nerves from frazzling along with hers. "Well, I'm no Pollyanna either. On the bright side, though, we're not dead yet. And don't forget we survived the Cold War, and that could've ended in annihilation too. Take climate change, we have a few decades to clean up our act, and a lot of bright people with resources understand it's a serious problem. Worse might not come to worst."

Lily stopped pacing, the better to eyeball me joylessly. "And what are those bright people with resources saying to themselves in the privacy of their homes? 'Thank God I'll be gone before it goes to hell in earnest, why should I chuck my SUV or my stock in Exxon when nobody else will, how much harm can I be doing as one lousy individual, aren't these end-of-the-world scenarios always exaggerated by alarmists?' Whether here or in New York or LA, the sentiments are the same, no matter how liberal or well-educated the demographic."

She was only echoing an opinion I must have entertained a hundred times myself. Then why were my defensive hackles up? What was it in her stance, as if she were lumping herself and me into a respective "them" and "us," an "us" where I hated to belong, but that deserved more than offhand contempt? On what was I basing my gut reaction to her, when I had no inkling who exactly "us" and "them" comprised? But another question shoved to the front of the line. "Lily, how the hell would you know what people are saying in the privacy of their homes?"

Her smile was utterly strange, a bewildering weld, as best I can describe, of impish and cynical. "I visualize my art on the walls in those homes, and I ask myself, What do the ears in my paintings hear? My finely tuned psyche does the rest."

I nodded noncommittally. For my own peace of mind, I had to presume she was joking. As opposed to deranged or whatever else. She'd moreover convinced me to pose no additional questions, which may have been the idea. I was seated at the vintage pink Formica table, which struck me as a DMZ amidst her agitation.

Suddenly her knotty shoulders relaxed and she beamed at me affectionately as if I'd just arrived, and sat on my lap. That boded well for the evening, but then she had to wreck it all by immersing me in local news at six. For the third weekend in a row. And three was the jinx, in terms of killing any doubts that Lily had corralled me here for my protection, based on her prescience of, or collusion in, bizarre crises, with today's the most insidious and deadly yet. I had to restrain myself from blurting, What did you and Garth have to do with this? A moot point, whether I held my tongue out of anxiety over self-endangerment or over plunging erroneously into the deep, demented end. Complicity will always cling to me.

The reportage went into lovingly excessive detail, as befit such ghoulish episodes, such lodestones of viewership. Mrs. Grace Randolph, age seventy-nine, was concerned when her husband's spaniel returned by itself from a walk, trailing its leash. Mrs. Randolph found her husband half a block away, facedown in the road. She called 911 while hurrying to his side, and fortunately was too overwrought to dare touch him herself. This was on one of those sedate, exclusive side streets between Blackstone Boulevard and the Seekonk River, basically a gated community without the unseemliness of a gate, and the rescue wagon was likely the first vehicle to come along. The pair of EMTs who began rendering assistance convulsed and collapsed on contact with Mr. Randolph. The wife's wailing panic alerted the ambulance driver, who understood the significance of the manhole cover beneath Mr. Randolph's body.

Meanwhile, across from the State House over on Smith Hill, a city worker began unbending a Stop sign walloped by a hydroplaning truck during early April's snow and black ice. Witnesses, in his case, put two and two together and didn't try moving the singed victim. Investigators were operating on the premise that our triple whammy of snowpack and sewer backup and sinkholes had severed electrical wiring and uncoupled utility pipelines under the pavement, though the wide scatter of mishaps implied chronic lax maintenance by the power company. No corporate spokesperson could be reached for comment. The state medical examiner was also reviewing ER and hospital records of heart attacks in the last twenty-four hours for other possible casualties of "stray voltage."

Lily vented a derisive chuckle. "They'd have to be thorough imbeciles to expect no more."

"And why is that?" Pitifully, even such weak dissent as this felt ballsy to me.

"How could it be otherwise?" My unshakable sphinx of a girlfriend. Neither acknowledging nor denying culpability. I quit while I was ahead, dolefully aware of the penalty for pissing off a sphinx.

Our weekend defaulted to laid-back routine of channel-flipping, smoking, lovemaking, outside of Saturday breakfast and dinnertime, when Lily devoutly tuned in to the mounting death toll. Between newscasts, it had doubled to an appalling three dozen, partly because word of the danger was slow to circulate, and partly because nobody had second-guessed the danger to encompass fire hydrants, the frames of bus shelters, the tarnished plaques in sidewalks denoting their WPA vintage.

Lily's nose crinkled as if she smelled my malaise. Had my passivity, my indecision, made me a silent partner now in mass murder, while nudging me into the belief that a painter and a rock star could weaponize weather and tarmac and the power grid? Lily muted the TV, and with telepathic acumen, refracted the glare of guilt from herself and toward more credible villains. "Okay, there's no way to shunt the blame for this disaster from one spineless authority to another. The upkeep of all those cables fell to one corporation, and a morgue full of corpses testifies to unforgivable neglect. What could prevent the disgrace and imprisonment of those worthless executives?"

"Oh, I'd love to see the bastards get their just desserts for a change. I'd cheer, believe me. But need I remind you, the bastards hire the best lawyers. Survivors of the victims may well launch a class action suit, and then years go by before they maybe reach an out-of-court settlement, and if they don't and it comes down to a civil trial, that can drag on forever. As for criminal proceedings, forget it. The big fish always slither off the hook somehow."

The disgust creasing Lily's brow dissuaded me from saying more, and I prayed it was aimed at the inequities of realpolitik rather than me. Killing the messenger should have been beneath her. "And that's it? A lawsuit? The guilty parties pay up without even forfeiting their positions, with no guarantee they'll behave any more honorably? What do you solve by changing nothing?" The flow of Lily's passion bore me haplessly along, till I regained my grip on the slippery proposition that Garth and Lily may have been the real culprits here, much as I preferred to crucify CEOs.

"Would you call this the prevalent attitude among your people after larger-scale disasters like levee breaches or oil spills or nuclear reactor leaks?"

I was still loath to put words in John Doe's mouth, but playing along made for the least aggravation all around. "History speaks for itself."

She nodded gravely, and then her frown softened into a warmer, more wistful outlook. She snaked one arm around my shoulder, and the fingers of her free hand slid under my sweatshirt and daintily tiptoed up my back. Hours elapsed before it registered that the muted TV had been on the whole time.

Sunday she ignored the revised casualty figures, as if they were no longer of interest after our discussion. Or to put the worst, least reasonable face on it, she'd electrocuted several dozen people solely to hear how that made me feel. Hardly rosier to surmise that Lily had no need of updates because she had her own means of knowing the situation was over.

At any rate, she moved on to her next order of business and betrayed no anxiety about crossing sidewalks where lightning might lie in wait. "I have to go down to the Empire and replace three paintings that sold on Friday," she explained as we brunched on pancakes and bacon. "You ought to stay here and take it easy. I won't be an hour."

"Are you sure this is the best day to be doing this?" I gently objected.

"Oh, the gallery director has a live-in studio there. He'll be around." She treated me to a winsome smile, as if that had to be what I meant.

Into her sanctum she retreated and left its double doors gaping wide after lugging out three oily urban landscapes, exuding that fishy whiff, and quivering a little as she leaned them against the vestibule wall. The paint glistened as if still slightly wet, so she must have finished them very recently, but when? We hadn't been apart since dinner Friday.

The phone rang at just the right instant to divert Lily from closing off her workspace. Another impeccably staged imitation of coincidence? She waltzed into the bedroom with the phone and conversed while getting dressed.

From the phrases I overheard, or was allowed to overhear, I doubted Garth was the caller at first, because her manner was too breezy, too bright. But then again, everything she said was of a piece with previous dialogues. "Our results are mostly in agreement . . . won't learn much more of value, nothing to justify . . . homesick too . . . drawings were a good idea, but afraid they didn't help. . . . Right, it's not logical, we have ages to look forward to. . . . only a blink, relatively. . . . willing to go on record . . . afford to be patient . . . waited so long, what's a few more decades? . . . Why put ourselves at risk? . . . doing it for us themselves and none the wiser . . . always come back to a military approach if . . . just another blink in the overall . . . you tomorrow, then . . ."

Out of the bedroom she barged, before I had any chance to pretend not to be eavesdropping. She'd done a flawless job of dressing one-handed, and she caromed past me like a runaway train. Then she spun around and plunked the phone on the table and announced, "Hate to run, but I'll be late. Be a dear and put that in its cradle for the batteries to recharge." Funny how she'd been in no hurry before the telephone rang.

In the vestibule she brusquely scooped up her paintings as if they were anything but precious commodities, and I sang out, "Do you want me to close up the studio for you?"

"See you soon!" Was she feigning deafness or too keyed up to listen? I stared dully at the phone while the door banged to and fro, largely, I guessed, by dint of agile footwork.

So maybe I should have carried her canvases or grabbed the door or something. But while she'd been bouncing around the apartment, my mind had been bouncing wildly between the prospect of free pass to Lily's sanctum, and her opaque, scary talk of "military approaches" and "ages to look forward to."

With fresh urgency I vainly pondered, Just who were Lily and Garth, and where were they really from? Well, here was her studio, and where better to forage for clues? Especially when she'd practically dealt me carte blanche to spy?

I wasn't worried about her out there. Of course she'd return as promised. The lethal sidewalks simply didn't have it in for her, or she wouldn't have ventured out. We'd been together long enough that I bought into her (and Garth's) daft version of reality, into her unnaturally cooperative world.

I cleaned my plate because I usually did and didn't want Lily suspecting anything unusual had occurred in her absence. That felt like a rule of the game, even if she'd set me up to violate her trust. I eased my chair from the table and padded with gratuitous stealth through the apartment. Bodily crossing the threshold was really gratuitous as well, because from the middle of the living room, the gaping double doors gave onto a perfectly revealing view. No matter. I had to see all there was to see, though that proved to be precious little.

On my previous glimpse I'd already inventoried clean brown carpet, white plaster ceiling and walls, and a pair of high, three-paned, plaid-curtained windows, and that was almost it. No furniture, no easels, no art supplies or storage units. Nothing with which to paint those four portraits currently propped along the baseboard, reminiscent of some images at Shadwell, and readied, by whatever extraordinary means, in case of further sales downtown.

Technically they were as limited as anything of hers, aside from the uncannily sophisticated trick of eyes that not only followed me around but seemed to examine me wherever I stood, though I couldn't say they'd been rendered with any extra skillfulness.

I also couldn't fathom, in a room destitute of raw materials, what was giving off the subtle taint of fishiness that quickly grew too cloying to have seeped from any four paintings. It chased me out of there, as if that was its job after I'd completed my survey, without pursuing me into the living room, for which I was too grateful to wonder why it hadn't. I refrained from pushing the doors together because that's how Lily had left them. I also entertained the wholly academic question, What would I find, if anything, in Garth's alleged studio?

I finished off the coffee in the Braun and sat staring into inscrutable space. On top of puzzling over girlfriend's role in multiple killings and calamities, I had the riddle of how her art kept emerging from a studio where it couldn't have been created. Of course she may have done the work elsewhere and only pretended her studio was at home, but why bother to fool me like that? And then arrange to unfool me? Minus any proof of Garth and Lily's criminality, I couldn't do anything, but given the mayhem potentially brewing, how could I do nothing? No coffee was strong enough to jar my mental cogs into clarifying motion, to point me toward my moral imperative.

In my flustered state, I was unduly pleased with myself for remembering to hang up Lily's phone, and that wouldn't have happened had my sight not drifted and then clung to it. A self-satisfied glow lingered as if doing that small thing should have convinced her I couldn't have been up to anything else.

When Lily traipsed back in, right on schedule, I was sitting where she'd left me, glumly eyeing my breakfast plate. This passed muster as normal in her book. A typical Sunday ensued, till a dead-end dialectic complicated mid-afternoon tea. "What do you think an individual owes society?" she grilled me from out of the blue.

Quite the weighty issue to wrangle with on short notice. "To play well with others?" I fudged. "Behave decently, don't grab more than your share, as opposed to how the Fortune 500 operates? Leave a place better than the way you found it?"

My pearls of wisdom only made Lily fret impatiently. "But society is nothing you feel personally bound to protect? How much would you sacrifice in common cause? Friendship? Love? Happiness?"

"How would parting with any of those help promote this common cause of yours?" I honestly couldn't grasp it. Or could I? Had my spirit been more willing, if self-centered instincts hadn't dug in their heels, might I have clearly apprehended Garth and Lily's grander purpose?

"Are your loyalties reserved solely for individuals?"

"The jury may be out on that for a while."

"And if time didn't allow for vacillating?

"Then I'd have to say it depended on your particular common cause."

She sighed and swirled the dregs of her teacup around, gazing in as if they might yield more astute musings than mine. Her attitude afterward was tinged with melancholy, but she smiled tenderly when our eyes met. Short-term Sunday doldrums, I decided. By suppertime she'd resecured the studio, probably when I was in the bathroom or toting her recycling bins to the curb. The televised news from both hereabouts and abroad she flipped right past, as if she'd wrung what relevance she ever would from it. A minute of that artsy channel with the 24/7 abstract animation only made her groan.

That night she loved me as usual, with our usual embellished consciousness. Later I rolled onto my side and away from her, as usual, except she clamped an arm around my waist and pulled me aberrantly close to her, stiflingly tight. Her breathing was soft and steady, and she may have been either asleep or awake. But I was definitely going nowhere till it suited her, and in the meantime was she feeling needy or ardent or possessive or nothing so benign?

In any case, the pressure was frightening, and with each exhalation I dreaded worse constriction, but her hold never varied. And the longer it went on, the more anxiously I thought of my incursion into Lily's sanctum. Was she under some compulsion now to punish me for what I'd obviously done, though it was something she knew I'd do? What the hell, baiting me into an empty room and then killing me made no sense whatsoever, unless Garth and Lily were grossly, incorrigibly mad, and had set out simply to commit murder in the first place. I was desperate not to doze off and put myself entirely at her mercy.

I never caught myself going under, though my next few memories were dreamlike and chimeric, symptomatic of lapsing in and out of sleep, plus or minus the stunning impact of premium weed?

Lily's embrace had not relented, but her arm had softened and broadened as if boneless, bereft of the confines of skin. From my hypnogogic limbo emerged the feeble witticism, Why, she can hardly contain herself. I wasn't sure what I meant by that, and wasn't about to think it through.

And then I was listening to a bout of sobbing, hovering disembodied somewhere overhead. It couldn't have been coming from Lily, who continued to enfold me with mineral stillness.

Sometime afterward the air stuck in my throat and I gasped, engulfed in an overpowering fug of putrid seaweed and crustaceans and red tide, and I feared the goal of Lily's oppressive hug had been to slowly poison me. I resorted to shallow breaths through my mouth, and suddenly it was morning and the smell may only have been a pungent dream and I had to admit, No, she hadn't been trying to asphyxiate me, because I was alive, wasn't I, groggy or not?

We carried on with breakfast like the night had passed serenely. She did slip in one statement that never would have gone by the boards had I not been functioning at such low ebb. Or maybe that was the condition in which she preferred I be listening. "You know, none of what's happened around here would have settled anything unless I loved you." How to begin processing that? She also asked me to call after work, or in other words, to phone before coming over. In my lackluster mood, I didn't make much of that, either.

Thus after Shadwell I went straight home, where I hadn't been in subjective ages, and snacked on chips and horseradish dip, and called some bands to firm up dates for recording sessions, and almost dialed Lily so many times that I lost count. I wanted to speak and be with her, yes, but I'd mislaid my cell somehow, and whenever I headed for the landline, some other piddling task intervened, and I'd find myself at the wrong end of the apartment.

At length I couldn't even approach the phone without going blank, so I rustled up some supper, nothing heavy by any stretch, but afterward I moped from room to room as if I'd gorged on Thanksgiving feast, and couldn't even contemplate reaching Lily. Was this how it felt to be under a spell? I was sunk too deep in lassitude to wonder what was causing it, and when the meager effort of pacing grew as arduous as wading through knee-deep aspic, I shuffled ingloriously to bed.

I woke up unaccountably buoyant, as if a load to which I'd been oblivious had shifted off my chest. Lily couldn't have had anything to do with my new composure one way or another, could she? Oddly, though, and off the point as it seemed, the word that arose to sum up my brighter mood was "liberated." I had no inkling yet that knowing too dangerously much about Lily and Garth was no longer an issue because I'd never see them again.

My cell turned up in the inside coat pocket where I'd sworn I stowed it yesterday, and all attempts to call Lily from Shadwell routed me to voicemail. Well, she hadn't told me to phone before dropping by on Tuesday, so there I was at 5:15, making the most of flimsy technicality.

My sense of time has been muddled from that day on, but it wasn't till the following Tuesday at least that Lily became a "missing person," though she may not have qualified as either. Based on *Providence Journals* I skimmed at work, the Empire's gallery director had swung by Lily's unlocked apartment after numerous e-mail and voicemail requests for replacement pictures met without callback, and on tiptoeing in, he purportedly cringed at "an aura of foul play." The cops saw fit to investigate about a week later, when a Chelsea consortium to which she also owed some pieces more effectively threw their weight around. Aside from one item, everyone found exactly what I did.

I too couldn't help but tiptoe in and navigate by stingy twilight the half-open closet and cupboard doors and the furniture and major appliances that wouldn't have gone anywhere without teamwork. More decorous to prowl that way, I imagined. At a glance, all the portable property was out without a trace, except for dust-free squares and circles on the floor. Lily had slid the studio doors completely out of sight, exposing the one room whose emptiness didn't make me tense and disoriented because I'd never seen it otherwise.

The one small change I almost overlooked did unnerve me, for reasons my subconscious was keeping to itself. Along the baseboard, the four black lacquered frames that had contained watchful portraits were vacant now, an observation that mushroomed in significance when someone at *ARTnews* eventually confirmed that every single canvas of Lily's, in whatever country, under lock and key or in a bank vault, vanished on the same night she did. Whether heist or PR stunt or practical joke, the amount of coordination, or collusion, or coincidence would have been preposterous. Police had no leads anywhere, and the *ARTnews* columnist basically dismissed the enigma as one for the conspiracy fringe.

The disappearance of Garth and the contents of his cellar studio took even longer to discover, comprised no less a mystery, and did earn some featurette attention from *Rolling Stone* and *Entertainment Weekly*, but nobody, in print anyway, has forged a connection with Lily's dive into oblivion.

As for me, I backed away from those four vacant frames as if they might pounce, and only turned around to avoid bumping into the wall. A single personal relic had been positioned on the arm of leather sofa where the TV remote used to lie, and where my line of sight would travel from the studio doorway. I'd become so skittish I almost didn't stop, but judging by its placement, she'd wanted me to take it, on sentimental or more oblique grounds. I refrained from locking up on my way out because she hadn't locked up, and in the slightly more generous twilight outside I examined my memento.

It was a sketchbook, the dimensions of a trade paperback, with high rag-content paper stock between coarse, fibrous green covers. Several dozen pages had been consumed, from side to side and top to bottom, by amateurish polar landscapes in charcoal, of mountain ranges rearing above glaciers, icebergs floating at the base of sheer white cliffs, ice floes rife with zigzagging fissures. The foreshortening, the perspective were flawed, the lines were childishly clumsy, the compositions were postcard banal. I seemed to be leafing through the output of her naked technical ability, without the trademark ton of paint adorning it.

More tellingly, these must have been the "drawings" she'd touched upon when Garth last phoned, the futile remedy he'd advised for being "homesick." I might uncritically have used them to support her claim of Patagonian upbringing, but the terrain looked too inhospitable, starkly uninhabitable, more like the Antarctic. All in all, she'd dealt me one more hand of wild cards in her unintelligible game.

I packed the book beside the cell phone in my inside coat pocket and vamoosed before anyone set eyes on me in the driveway. I'm not afraid of Lily's sketchbook on my nightstand marking me as a "person of interest" in her disappearance, because who would believe those dull and dreary renderings were hers? I'm also unashamed of filching what the cops would optimistically bag as evidence, because they wouldn't learn a thing if they pored over those pages till doomsday, even if that's only fifty years away. And since I'd been out in public with Lily on multiple occasions, I was reconciled to policemen leaning on my doorbell sooner or later, but it hasn't happened yet, for which I'm grateful, delusionally or not, to Lily with that anti-personnel hoodoo of hers, fondly shielding me from afar.

Reporting that Lily was MIA never entered my head. She'd cleared out of her own free will, and who was I to make a legal matter of it? And if someone else had stumbled on and tried to publicize Garth and Lily's missing personhood that Tuesday, the news from Monday night would still have overshadowed it, maybe consigned it indefinitely to back-page purgatory. The headlines here were also topping national coverage for nearly twenty-four hours, an unprecedented blip of notoriety for stodgy old Providence.

By dint of epic sabotage or vandalism or indictable bungling, our waterfront had sustained a stupendous swath of damage, on a scale to do any terrorist proud. At midnight, huge explosions, massive fires, thunderous demolition had erupted and spread rapidly along the industrial strip between Allens Avenue and the bay, half a mile from the gallery where Lily and I had met. Motorists and second-shift labor who weren't exterminated in the inferno were only good for a stack of conflicting, hysterical statements. These converged only in broadest aspects that nobody touring the site thereafter could have missed. Cranes had toppled, freighters had capsized, wooden piers were squashed as if under some rolling, titanic burden. Warehouses and office buildings had been gutted into shells and crooked girders by conflagrations reportedly electrical in origin, despite the heroic struggles of firefighters from three counties on site within half an hour.

At the putative epicenter of disaster, telephone poles and streetlamps and brick walls and the very cobblestones underfoot had been pushed and bowed and rippled outward in a lopsided figure-eight outline, as if some unguessable form or forms had expanded with concussive speed, burgeoning into their surroundings without caution or concern. No conventional explosion had taken place, for nothing in that radius was even singed. Several witnesses described blinding arcs of voltage crisscrossing the scene, concealing whatever was going on at the center of the violence, and several more told how writhing, brilliant coruscations spanned the sky, like an aurora below the overarching smoke.

However, the most widespread accounts from bystanders amidst the chaos, and then from stargazers on Rumstick Point and fishermen off Newport, were also the least compatible with stolid reconstruction of a crime scene, and received short, patronizing shrift from officialdom and the media. But not from me. After a harrowing season with Lily, I'm not one to laugh off the uncanny episodes of others.

A pair of gigantic marine animals, immense as whales but emphatically not whales, were reputedly heaving half-submerged through the whitecaps, plowing southward at a hefty clip, splitting the black water ahead with green shafts of bioluminescence. They were the sallow white of grubs or maggots, and their hide was defined as pebbly or perhaps encased in lather or bubbles. No further specifics about anatomy or behavior were forthcoming. I moreover need hardly mention, the hunt for perpetrators has come up empty-handed, as it has for traces of Lily and Garth.

I have my speculations that conjoin and solve both mysteries, but I refuse to articulate them even to myself, in light of the scorn heaped on mere sober sightings of large ocean beasts. I'll go out on a limb as far as suggesting the bloodbath on the waterfront was incidental or else the aftermath of a miscalculation, and commit myself no further.

Even under normal circumstances, I tell myself, my affair with Lily would have foundered before too long. That was always a given, but it didn't save me from sinking into a dismal funk when Lily went away. I still miss her, despite her mystifying, sometimes frightful interludes, despite all she may have been or done.

She won't be back again within my lifetime, that much I can take on faith, but if she did return, would I recognize her, or would she belong to that nebulous, imponderable host too eager for an unpeopled world? Until that farfetched day, I can gaze on a reminder of her whenever I unbutton my shirt, whether intended as grotesque consolation, or a mere accident. Across my midriff, ever since she clutched me to her on our final night together, I've been carrying her pink handprint, neither itchy nor painful, more like bas-relief than welt or blister. Or did she have some proprietary motive for branding me?

In any event, it hasn't faded months along, indelible as a tattoo. And often when I study it, I have the absurd sensation it's studying me back. I feel then that Lily isn't altogether gone, that she's close to me until I look away. Afterward I wonder uselessly if her handprint is like her paintings, or, as she once remarked, if she's invested a little of herself into it, "beyond the obvious that everyone sees." I may never fully understand what her mark upon me is or what it means, but it seems more real than anything else these days.

The Last Jar

"I've got the curse of the slug: it all looks beautiful ahead but I leave a trail of slime behind."—LEONARDO PADURA

Up the walkway to H. A.'s pilastered door I dolefully trod. Blue shale slabs underfoot were rife with fossils of trilobites, nautiloids, crabs, and scallops, in pristine detail as if boot heels and weather had had no chance to inflict wear or splits. They never would. The rock, he'd claim, had been quarried from ravines in the surrounding lush green hills.

My hand was an inch from the bronze star-shaped knocker when H. A. threw open his dream home to me. Moot, wasn't it, to ponder whether he'd seen me from multipane window or had obeyed a psychic impulse? I was welcomed like an old friend into that Georgian-era farmhouse where, for better or worse, economic and logistic constraints of ordinary life did not apply.

In sumptuous front hall with oak wainscoting and gilt striped wallpaper, he bid me hang Homburg and trenchcoat on a rack of silver-blunted narwhal horns that echoed the spiral balusters of central staircase. Had indifference or hauteur led him to hold court in mauve quilted dressing gown and fleecy yellow scarf? I followed him down the hall into no less elegant or eccentric a parlor, of dimensions that seemed too expansive to fit within the shell of the house. The brightness through south-facing windows lent his midlife features even more rugged vitality as he turned to ask, "Who did you say sent you?"

"The daily of record. The only one in these parts." My Vermont drawl was cut from the same pattern as his. "We talked before. Frankly, you didn't seem to be all there at the moment. You must be bored to distraction at prospects of the same questions for the hundredth time. But I might just pitch a curve or two that'll make you see yourself in a whole other light. High hopes, I know."

"Hubris, I'd say. Not that I fault you. I'd have amounted to nothing without a goodly dose of it." He settled onto one end of a bulbous, tomato-red sofa with scrollwork arms and gestured me into a blue satin Deco armchair like an indented cube. He resolutely planted slippered feet upon a hooked rug of trompe l'oeil geometric design, as if battening down for my inquisition. I freed notepad and pencil from vest pocket while my sight strayed beyond the rug to a floor of green marble with purple veins. It perversely whetted cravings for Roquefort or Gorgonzola.

A deep fortifying breath loaded my nostrils with an earthy air reminiscent of truffles, which H. A., if anybody, could afford, though I knew he had no gourmet victuals on the premises. My mouth watered, regardless. Jesus, when had I last eaten?

No matter. I had to get this show on the road or he'd be stuck here. We'd be stuck here. I'd awakened to the necessity of this onerous business with leaden feelings of ennui and déjà vu. Our previous interview, a virtual lifetime ago, had initially sparked a more cogent spirit, a forthright assessment of the situation. Yet here we were, with moral imperative incumbent on me to try again. No one else was responsible for steering him out of existential impasse. Gray mustache hid the challenging or smug or tolerant tenor of his expression.

I cleared my throat and took an easy way in. "You're fifty-seven, are you not?" That was the same age at which, in a different chronology, his drastic change of status had occurred.

"Does fifty-seven seem past my prime? Nonsense. I'm on the brink of momentous breakthroughs, stunning new chapters. I can practically taste the rejuvenating power of fresh ambitions."

I jotted down shorthand notes, opting to humor rather than contradict him at this stage.

"Ever married?"

He sagely shook his balding head. "If you don't have a wife, you can't be a widower."

I raised an eyebrow but scribbled onward. Old wife, old life, I wrote, New life, no wife. I remembered her fondly, whereas H. A. had voted it wasn't better to have loved and lost.

"During your salad days, you were quite the man of parts at the university in Brattleboro. Well-versed in math, astronomy, biology, anthropology, and folklore. You could have had a distinguished academic career."

"Man of parts?" he huffed. "Jack of all trades, more like. I wasted too many years in that ivy-covered mire, waffling over which trail I'd blaze into the world." H. A. stretched his legs and plunked his heels on the coffee table, basically a slab of glossy black stone wherein faint striations maybe passed for vestigial rows of script. The baroque fireplace mantel and teardrops of the waterfall chandelier were of the same inky mineral.

His appraising eyes, his self-satisfied smile, so much as taunted, Is this your idea of grilling me? I assayed a meek, deferential mask. Just you wait, H. A.

On all four walls from baseboard to molding, bold, dynamic frescoes in black and white with red highlights fairly burst past the window frames and bookcases hemming them in. They represented the most memorable tableaux from his oeuvre, of outcast Greenland Inuit consummating human sacrifice, of Pacific islanders reenacting marine gods' rapine of their ancestors, of bayou priests either conjuring devils or playing nasty tricks with smoke and embers. I leaned forward as far as cushy armchair allowed. "What informed your decision to produce and direct ethnographic documentaries?"

He spread his hands forbearingly. "How the dickens else was I to harness all that sundry expertise of mine into a lucrative profession? Luck was with me then, which as a rule it always has been, and Hollywood clamored for the glamour and sensationalism I alone could deliver. I amassed a huge bundle, but more importantly, found out what I was made of, as would never have happened on that milquetoast campus."

Oh? What he was made of, eh? I suppressed a grimace and left off shorthand in favor of doodling.

"Not that everything fell in my lap. I had to take a lot of initiative, keep one eye on the crystal ball. I no sooner heard about talkies than I switched over, not like that stick in the mud Merian C. Cooper. What did he ever do after *Gow the Head Hunter*? And don't think it was a picnic, operating sound equipment in the jungle and on top of glaciers."

I couldn't very well defend Merian C. Cooper, for I'd seen nothing of his beyond 1928, any more than H. A. had. Besides, I had the more pressing task of giving the screw its first turn. "You must admit it's interesting, though, how your résumé has parallels with that of Cooper, and especially with that of your fellow Vermonter, Robert Flaherty, as if you were unconsciously heeding the same cues."

That name had him sitting up at galvanic attention. "Don't get me started on that poseur Flaherty and his *Nanook of the North* hogwash. Two of a kind, him and Cooper. They concocted entertainment. I filmed the raw truth, but I had the ingenuity to make it entertaining. I didn't stage a minute. In my exclusive locales, I didn't have to."

"Yet didn't you host a radio program dramatizing your exploits? You wrote for it too, as I recall, with a definite flair for hyperbole. *Too Fantastic for Fiction*, wasn't it?" I couldn't resist knocking the sanctimonious H. A. down a peg.

"That was packaged as sheer escapism, nothing more, and it aired six months at most." Did a blush begin to tinge his ivory face? "It was the means to an end. I had a project in need of investment capital."

"At heart, in any case, you might not disagree you caught a string of breaks that Bob Flaherty didn't."

"Yes, that's my ongoing surplus of terrific luck, for which I do have to credit some compliant higher power." His air, however, was more boastful than beholden. Incipient blush faded in the course of a speech that should have made it blossom. "Not to invoke saints or angels, since I've never sensed any sacred presence hovering near. Still, the universe has evidently chosen me to effect certain innovations. My long shots always pan out, and the right person, without fail, shows up at the right place and time, as if by appointment, to solve problems or present opportunities. Sure, obstacles and reversals have beset me, but at every eleventh hour, windfalls and reprieves save my fortune, my interests, or my skin."

I no longer bothered even to doodle. H. A. was virtually blind with self-absorption.

"Nor are the happy accidents in my history confined to fiscal affairs. To retail one curious example, my movies' polar, island, and swamp denizens all worshipped the same savage deity under strikingly similar names. What were the odds of stumbling across those scattered primitives with that one incredibly obscure cult in common? Had I gone into anthropology, that uncanny happenstance alone would have guaranteed my renown."

"Coincidence on such a global scale does beggar belief, doesn't it?"

I had no desire to acknowledge H. A.'s patronizing nod, and my gaze roved over the walls' sanguinary depictions of Arctic monolith, Polynesian ritual headdress, and statuette bespattered with bayou muck, with their common element of the same "savage deity's" portrait, dominated by fishy, hateful eyes and squirmy tentacles for mouth. This "god" was no stranger to me, but the mere thought of its name presaged ill tidings. A change of subject was in order.

"Were you ever tempted to go on safari in your own back yard? Bag or debunk the legendary beasts and denizens of Vermont?" I gamely pretended his reply was unforeseen.

"Now I'd consider that a recipe for trouble. Like defecating where you dine, to gussy up the rude idiom." The sun through parlor windows blinked coyly, as if a moose or cow were trotting by, except H. A.'s eyes grew into shiny saucers, betraying dread of traffic much less innocent. His buoyant smile was slow to resurface. "But then as in a hundred other contexts, my intuition must have channeled the voice of providence to deliver me from evil shoals. One more sign, if you will, of how the universe is in my corner."

I had to bite my lip or call him out on his naïveté. What shoals hadn't he struck head-on? The screw deserved another little turn. "Your brilliance is a matter of record. That said, doesn't the abnormality of continuous triumph give you pause? Isn't it unnatural for events to unfold so neatly, for fate to bless all your endeavors? More the stuff of daydreams or wish fulfillment, wouldn't you say?"

Was selective hearing among the ingredients of his success? Gripping a scrollwork arm, he levered his physique out of the sofa. As if seeking distance from my words lingering in midair like a miasma, he lumbered toward the wall behind the sofa. His destination was an art nouveau buffet whose panels were busy with sinuous bas-reliefs of octopi and jellyfish drifting above seagrass. His expression was deceptively impassive as he hefted a sapphire-blue crystal decanter from atop the buffet and addressed me, "Who'd have predicted Prohibition to drag on, lo these many decades? The good news is, I smuggled a crate of Armagnac back from a film shoot in Algeria. Join me?"

"Thanks." To refuse would have been antisocial, though 80 proof on my empty, growling stomach smacked of foolishness. Not that any real harm was in it. Besides, a self-congratulatory toast was apropos. I'd maneuvered H. A. toward the dubious refuge of drink, and that was a manifest sign of progress.

He checked in vain inside a pair of snifters for dusty buildup, poured generously, brought me mine, and smartly clinked our glasses together. "Carpe diem!"

I sipped obligingly. Fumes clogged my nostrils, heat flowed down my throat, and the sublime taste sent caution packing. Few enough fringe benefits came with this territory, and imbibing might stimulate H. A. into rustling us up some food. I more impetuously grinned and gulped. "Yes, I have to admit you've rigged a lovely patch of utopia here."

"No earthly paradise can be perfect." Shiny anxiety flickered across H. A.'s eyes again, and he glanced out a window. He imparted sotto voce, "Inimical presences spy and silently persecute me, though I cannot fathom why. Envy? Suspicion? Gut-level antipathy?" Now we were getting somewhere. The cracks had begun to open, and reality was peeking through. "The hell of it was, I'd been so careful not to provoke local animosity."

"Since when have these presences been harassing you?"

"Sometime after I finished renovations here, I noticed footprints circling the house and leading into and out of the woods. They were shoeless, and some weren't human at all. Cloven, rather, or like the letter V. And then the trespassers would stare in, during broad daylight. I'd glimpse them in peripheral vision, and once I blinked, they were gone. Moreover, whenever I spotted any of them, I had the notion some ancillary power of eyesight had been activated in me, but by whom or why I couldn't guess." H. A. sloshed his brandy around and brusquely drained it. I followed suit.

"The big land crabs must have made the V-shaped prints. As for how big they were, well, they were gaping at me through a window. Mind you, I liken them to crabs with some poetic license, because crabs have only two eyestalks. On these there was a bumper crop, though an exact tally was beyond me. The whole set of stalks was synchronously bent toward me, but they never stopped waving and coiling around each other." H. A. strode back to the buffet and decanted a goodly refill. I held out my snifter to no avail. He could have been narrating a script from *Too Fantastic for Fiction* into a studio microphone.

"Yet strange as it sounds, I preferred seeing them to the ostensibly normal men studying me and flaunting their nakedness. I read no hostility in their demeanor, even as I read no individuality, no distinguishing characteristics, into their appearance. They were too dispassionate, too generic, like a model of *Homo sapiens* for demonstration purposes, too unblemished to be genuine flesh and blood. Had I any remaining hair to speak of, those Peeping Toms would have made it stand on end. They seemed more artificial, more cold-blooded to me than the oversized crustaceans."

H. A. fascinated me. The encroachments of giant crabs and nude simulacra had him understandably agitated, but their existence he accepted matter-of-factly. And he took for granted I'd do likewise. In someone else, such a frame of mind would indicate derangement. In him, it hinted he was inching toward a breakthrough. Nor was his store of revelation depleted.

"Nightfalls can be godawful sudden in these hills, and sometimes I swear they jump the gun." He cast another look outside, as if conditions might play to his remarks, and swigged more Armagnac. "On those off-schedule nights, there's no landscape out the window, no moon, nothing but stars ahead, above, below, as if the house is perched on a spire or anchored in the void. What's worse, the murky silhouette of a bird or bat or other winged brute, whose scale and distance I have no basis for gauging, may glide by, blotting out the stars in its passage. I'm always of an impression then that the aviator isn't out in cold night air, but instead is crossing interstellar space."

"And how could you infer that, if you can't judge scale or distance?" Good old H. A. was beginning to make my job easier. Very promising.

"I just know."

"And how exactly do you just know?" That must have been the

brandy talking. A tone of sarcasm would have been most unbecoming in a bona fide professional journalist.

"I just know." No doubt he'd tax his ingenuity to escape the realization he was painting himself into a metaphysical corner. He replaced empty snifter atop the buffet and slipped into a lively facsimile of bonhomie. "How remiss I've been as an object of human interest! You've yet to witness anything worth writing about."

H. A. strode with a pretense of verve to a dim side of the room and pulled the cord under a Tiffany shade that resembled either green-and-purple clusters of grapes and viny tendrils, or else warring colonies of protozoa. The lamp sat on a mahogany hutch proportioned like a Victrola and adorned with Deco streamlining. He unlatched double doors in front to reveal a square glass screen. "Do you own one of these?" he asked, while beckoning me over to a row of red velvet theater seats that faced the hutch and was bolted right into the marble.

I heaved myself out of blue satin cube and shook my head forlornly as if wishing I did own one of his damned Opticolas. Springs under red velvet squeaked as I sat down again. Amidst fooling with pushbutton and dial on chrome console below the screen, H. A. declaimed, "Of all the happy accidents to grace my history, this was one of my most idealistic, and profitable. It was also the logical, possibly inevitable, fruition of assimilating motion picture technology, wedded to my concerns for marginal, deprived populations."

The screen brightened, and H. A. rifled through a spacious drawer below the console. "What a boon to inmates, shut-ins, isolated plainsmen, mountaineers, islanders, and residents of the remotest hamlets. Movies can now come to all those who have no access to a cinema. One film can perform the educational role of thirty textbooks in the most backward, impoverished one-room schoolhouse."

H. A. extracted a miniature, Bakelite-encased movie reel, and opened a rear hatch to load it somehow into the Opticola. Humanity's great benefactor had invented a home movie player that only encouraged rather than cured insularity. Urbanites no longer had to go out to a show, and the machine would do its intended boonie clientele no good without electrification first. On the other hand, if not for his lucrative brainchild, H. A.'s dream home would have languished on the drawing board.

"Here's something you won't see anywhere else," he promised. "Edits from the Greenland expedition, too disturbing for the public. I cut them before the censors had an opportunity. Less fuss, less wasted time that way." A porcelain knob on the console glowed yellow after he pressed it, and he flounced into the seat beside mine. The spool needed a minute to start rolling. The mechanism clicked and whirred very quietly, I had to give it that, though it still incurred suspicions that a large insect was in charge back there.

"For all the wealth this contraption has raked in," H. A. confided, breathing that odor of truffles into my face, "it's of deucedly recent manufacture. The basic design had to wait for engineering and production capabilities to catch up with it. I didn't secure the patent till I was fifty-four. That's why I'm champing at the bit today, and damned if I won't accomplish more going forward than I have in the past. Nothing save mortality impedes me."

"Given your druthers, then, you'd choose to be immortal, despite ample advice against it in myths and literature." I felt like the devil broaching that, and H. A. would have agreed, had he any inkling of how I'd been enticing him down the garden path.

"Hell yes!" Our row of seats quaked at his reflexive shudder of sincerity. "I suppose you're invoking the emptiness, the ennui, the meaninglessness of existing forever? As if death alone ultimately made life significant? Myopic nonsense! What a lack of vision, of drive that portends! With all the time in the world, I could finally, really get something done. Haven't you ever wondered what kind of novel Joyce might write after *Ulysses*, longevity permitting? Or about the gist of unified field theory, and of how much else on the frontiers of physics Einstein might achieve with a bonus hundred years?"

H. A. was plainly oblivious to the flickering black prelude to his footage. "Bah. I'd call the bluff of every so-called savant who recommended lying down and dying versus a drink from the fountain of youth. One guess as to what those hypocrites would do when the reaper came calling."

"But let's complicate the picture a little. A ticket to eternity might not be as simple as your name on a dotted line. What if you had to become other than human first? Sacrifice any visible bond with your fellow man?"

H. A. snorted contemptuously. "Would I hesitate to abandon that baggage, those frailties and vices bogging down the mind and soul? Are you kidding? Would a chimp balk at evolving because it would miss eating the lice off its relatives?"

"Even if you had to spend eons in a specimen jar?" There. That was the turn to embed the screw past hope of detachment.

"Don't be facetious."

I'd begun to take stock of the content on screen, and so, I wagered, would H. A. momentarily. A quartet of fur-clad Inuit was patting down a dome of snow like a giant's bald cranium. A title card interrupted them. It proclaimed, "Complete within the hour." And I, knock on wood, would be finished with H. A.'s smaller head somewhat before then. Following the caption, a knife began to saw through the forehead of that white noggin from the inside. Soon a rectangular section like a self-administered trepanation popped out, and into the daylight crawled the grinning housewright.

H. A. had homed in on the distinctly ungrisly fare and was goggling aghast from under crinkled, stormy brow. "This isn't mine!"

Nor could it be, since he'd never shot a foot of film in his life, and in his latter decades, any dexterity whatsoever would have been impossible. His subconscious was owning up to that, way ahead of his ego. Bob Flaherty's opus, meanwhile, did exist, and was available to the mind's eye for review. "We're watching *Nanook of the North*, aren't we?" I toned down the cattiness as best I could.

Nanook was jabbing and jabbing at the frozen surface of Arctic sea with his spear, and H. A. winced as if each thrust penetrated his scalp. I'd have felt sorrier for him if he'd been less mulish and unregenerate. "What kind of prank are you pulling here?" he accused me. "I don't have copies of anything by that hack Flaherty. It's not like I could have mislabeled a canister."

Nanook extricated a translucent block of ice, which he installed as a windowpane in his igloo. Did this particular celluloid clip shadow forth H. A.'s readiness to admit insights about his literal state, or was that wishfulness on my part?

I didn't begrudge him lashing out at me. Volatility signaled crumbling illusions, a major stride forward. "Hate to contradict you, H. A., but I haven't the means or the motive to pull such shenanigans."

He lunged from his chair and punched the Opticola's lambent porcelain knob. The gizmo went dark with the screak of stylus across turntable and a dying wheeze. He wheeled around, bristling with indignation. "Those skulking overgrown crabs! They were responsible. And if not them, those ersatz muscle men, with the stone cold eyes. They're up to no good. In fact, they're all in on it together."

I sighed. H. A. still had too much moxie for me to reel him in without a struggle. "Well, thanks anyhow for exempting me from the rogues' gallery. I'm no crustacean and no Adonis either."

He dismissed my gratitude with a backhanded wave, a gesture I parsed as, "Don't mention it!" His sangfroid rallied for a last stand. "Are you feeling peckish yet? I am. Let me go fix us a snack."

In spite of my foreknowledge, I nodded enthusiastically. With no food in me to soften the impact of Armagnac, my growling stomach had taken to gurgling in anguish. When had I last eaten? How long ago was 1928?

I hung back as he toddled into the kitchen. Why not converse with him from here? We'd been through this before, and to subject myself to a grueling replay at his side would serve no purpose. I was woefully aware of what would meet his eyes.

"Lest we forget," I called out from my theater seat, "we are in the middle of an interview. Maybe you can clarify something for me. According to my information, you were fifty-seven in 1928." And how much water under the chronological bridge since then? "So what year were you born?"

"You can do the arithmetic as easily as I, can't you?" he retorted. I reckoned he should have grabbed onto the icebox handle by now.

"What year would you say this is, then?"

"Are you impugning I'm out of touch? I may not keep abreast of everything outside my garden wall, but there's more than enough in here," he contended, and I visualized him tapping on his brow, "to explore and to dazzle the world with."

I may have heard, or merely imagined, the icebox door clatter and creak open. "H. A.?" I shouted. "For better or worse, after your abduction or subversion or disembodiment or whatever you care to call it, you did sign on to be immortal and other than human."

"Dammit, I thought I told the housekeeper to go grocery shopping yesterday," H. A. complained. "There's nothing in the Frigidaire except a jar of pickles. I could have sworn I had a little blue cheese at least." Yes, I was absolutely audible from here, but why not let him feign distraction to save ephemeral face? The handwriting on the wall was indelible.

"H. A., when they took you away, you were fine at first," I soldiered on. "The universe was your oyster. Not your fault you weren't cut out long-term for the infinite void and the personal curtailment. You took all you could before beating a delusional retreat."

As my harangue sank in, and as H. A. glowered at solitary quart vessel, I was positive that he was lapsing into confusion, because we'd already experienced this once or twice or maybe more. Did the increasingly cloudy brine contain a quantity of discrete green pickles, or a single grey, multilobed object? I resumed, "Our hosts were anything but callous toward our discontent at being so cooped up physically, even as our minds were roaming the cosmos and communing with one another."

No sooner would H. A. apprehend what he was ogling than the glass would, like the brine, become opaque, and steely too, and now the very air was dimming around us both. "What's going on in here?" H. A. cried disingenuously, for he had to be quite as cognizant of that as I was.

"Our compassionate warders, and our fellow passengers, have checked on you regularly, hoping you'd snap out of it and qualify for everlasting synthetic anatomy." To my embarrassment, though, this false biography of thrills and glory had proved yet again too tempting for a stodgy old professor, just as the enormity of galactic space had proved too daunting.

By this juncture, I was talking to myself in the dark. "Nobody's about to put an unstable brain in the kind of body that could destroy a spacecraft if it ran amok, so there we remain, the last jar on the shelf." But damn me, I'm smart enough, I can change, I can get it right, and thank God the warders have patience to match their compassion.

Actually, I was not only blind but also deaf and a hundred percent numb to sensations, even to that of floating in nutrient fluid. On the plus side of the ledger, I wasn't famished anymore, and I wasn't mute. "Hello, could somebody please hook up my senses?" Deafness to my own grating monotone I counted as a blessing.

Talking to oneself, contrary to received wisdom, can be therapeutic, specifically to one's conflicted self. Fortunately some diehard critical faculty of mine eventually recoils from belief in a life as charmed as H. A.'s, and then I find myself on the outside flinching in at that pathetic fairy tale and my more gullible half still wallowing in it, and it's incumbent on me as a man of parts to reintegrate for the sake of self-mastery. Chalk it up to the power of lucid dreaming, which as an academe I'd always reviled as hokum.

Aha, a few blinks to adjust my lenses, and the quavery crowd of orange blobs resolves into the nursing staff of overgrown crabs, waving worried clusters of eyestalks and reeking of truffles, which is hardly surprising since their ancestors were mushrooms. Several of my colleagues, sporting perfect, generic bodies, also attend me in stances of inexpressive solidarity. Have they waited minutes, months, or years for me to "snap out of it" and recognize this twilit steel cubicle, chockablock with the Rube Goldberg gadgetry that sustains me like a sapient egg in a futurist nest? Luckily time here is not a precious resource. This go-around, I solemnly pledge, I'll stay sane and become one of you.

At a loss for words appropriate on this fraught occasion, I greet everyone in that grating monotone, "Okay, here we go again." All to the well I have no face, insofar as my motor cortex labors to orchestrate the muscles for a sheepish grin, and that would never do.

From Elsewhere

The Copper God's Treat

"There's a snap in the grass behind your feet and a tap upon
your shoulder,
And the thin wind crawls along your neck: it's just the old gods
getting older."

—Ian Anderson, "Beltane"

A friend at work lent Jared his cabin for a long weekend, on condition he wouldn't go kill himself there. Pretty insulting, whether
meant facetiously or not, but Jared laughed it off. Why get huffy and
jeopardize free digs? And to beg the broader question, were workplace cronies really convinced he was flailing on the edge? He
wouldn't deny some moodiness of late, yes, for which he could cite
ample justification. Suicide, though? That would be stupid after everything he'd gone through to stand scarred, abridged, but apparently
cured.

The cabin marked the end of stony dirt road off a one-lane series
of switchbacks scaling the heights outside Peterborough. Scant miles
from small-town society as the crow flew, but a Saab hauling food
and supplies had to labor the better part of an hour. For Jared, the
sense of isolation was ideal.

What he knew damn well he needed was to "go walkabout," but
expenses wouldn't spare him those weeks off the clock, his job
wouldn't wait, and he was nowhere near fit yet for epic undertak-
ings. Hence he had to make do with the balm of three days' wooded
solitude to restore him after double crisis of disease and fiftieth
birthday.

Amidst the moss and granite outcrops and grassy tufts in the
clearing out front was a shallow, rock-lined firepit. Didn't smoke and
flames traditionally purge the spirit, banish bad juju? Seems he'd absorbed that lesson from college reading or the History Channel or

obscurer wellsprings, and it provided elegant rationale for a cookout. He darted about the woodsy fringes of the yard collecting birch and rowan twigs for kindling, and nobody would miss a few split logs from the cord against the house.

Besides, he had to gorge himself on roast hotdogs tonight. It had slipped his mind that the cabin was a world away from the electric grid. No fridge on the premises, nothing that didn't run on batteries or scary propane.

Before shadows had lengthened into twilight, Jared warmed his hands proudly at a campfire that might not have shamed a Cub Scout. The aromatic smoke, with any luck, would also deter mosquitoes, since he'd forgotten to buy 6-12. The gnats hovered undiscouraged. He went in to uncork a bottle of Burgundy and fill a tumbler from the kitchen cupboard. He also retrieved his package of hotdogs, bag of buns, and a bread knife.

To sit cross-legged and focus on crackling, antic combustion while his rattled brain relaxed felt therapeutically primal. He lapsed into scoffing at his new-minted status as "cancer survivor," as if that should be the measure of a man. Technically he was less of a man forever for want of a prostate gland. But he was coping okay with that, as he had with the diagnostic needles and probes, the surgical ward and its factory ambience, even those ten heinous days till the catheter came out. And his prognosis couldn't be better. That was the good news.

No, Jared's bad attitude, his short fuse, stemmed entirely from a billing department hellbent on overcharging him all his savings plus IRAs for twenty-four hours in the hospital, on top of what insurance had kicked in. Most galling, though, was the call from a hospital stooge, three days postop, to enlist him in a Penile Rehabilitation Program, as if Jared wasn't in deep enough hock. The flack only backed off when Jared spelled out his brusque acceptance that God had slammed a door on his dick. As it was, he'd have to retain a *pro bono* lawyer to wrangle with "healthcare providers" who'd saved his skin and hence felt entitled to clean him out. How the hell could anyone recuperate under that load of stress?

And how to benefit from "weekend walkabout" unless he left his cares behind and properly observed this major milestone of fifty years on earth? Oh God, there was another can of worms to boot around. More than halfway to the boneyard, with or without cancer, and what did he have to show, what had he accomplished? Humanity's tritest birthday question, perhaps, but no less legit for that.

He slashed open the hotdogs, skewered one on knifepoint, and thrust it toward the fire. It slid off the blade and plopped among the embers. Jared took a deep breath. All right, hold that temper. Let's not add heart attack to the menu of woes. At least he hadn't knocked over the increasingly precious glass of wine between his feet. He set undivided attention on raising a toast to himself, the "cancer survivor," the aging Walpurgisnacht baby. The sizzle and scent of meat sacrificed to carelessness made him salivate, but what of it?

Then he had to guffaw or else throw a tantrum and his drink as well. A gnat was paddling frantically across the expanse of wine. He clenched his teeth and briskly tipped and jerked his glass above the fire, to rid it of bug while saving most of the beverage. Studying vacant red surface against the flickering glow finally gave him cause for cheer. Success was success, no matter how puny the scale.

A reverberant voice of authority, to all intents from the void, accosted him. "I need you to move away from the fire!" Wonderful. Was roving forest ranger about to bust him for illegal outdoor burning?

Jared managed to scuttle beyond the fringe of warmth without spilling a drop. In the chilly dusk he squinted around for covert ranger and blinked in bewilderment as someone lunged straight through the smoke, fist over coughing mouth as he came to a swaying halt mere inches from squatting Jared.

"Bah. Not used to wood smoke anymore," the foolhardy stranger complained. "It's been ages."

"Are you all right? Do you want some of this?" Jared essayed no bolder move than to lift his glass toward hacking guest, not without more detailed mental appraisal.

The man wasn't in Parks Department uniform or prison jumpsuit. His costume, for it definitely wasn't routine civvies, consisted of collarless red smock and loose gray leggings, of cloth like linen but heavily stitched like cattle hides, and fancy latticework sandals. The fabric was also evidently flame-retardant and resistant to smoke stains. He cleared his throat and sniffed, "Do I want any of that? To drink? No, it's fulfilled its purpose."

Sporting braidably long copper hair and droopy mustache, this fussy party-crasher could have passed for a re-enactor of "The Dying Gaul" or a member of the Allman Brothers, and despite his lean and hungry look was almost delicately handsome. He smiled with disarming gentility and reached forth a hand to help Jared up. It seemed unwise to refuse.

The stranger held on and treated Jared to a hearty handshake, just long enough to make him uncomfortable. "I happened to be in range, and to find you paying respects like that made me so happy I had to thank you in person. Such a rare show of devotion in this negligent era." He had a vaguely Brit or German accent, too protean to pin down.

"Pay my respects? What?" Funny how a minute ago Jared had been craving distance from earthly troubles, and now here he was haplessly at sea. In the best-case scenario he could picture, this was an elaborate hidden camera stunt rigged up by workplace pal.

"Hidden camera stunt? Ah, a practical joke." The stranger shook his head indulgently as Jared, reeling at this demonstration of apparent telepathy, wished for more of a barricade between himself and this spooky character than a glass of wine. "Jared, Jared. Didn't you light the sacred wood and offer roasting flesh and pour out the libation?"

Had he done all that? Uh, those were the only sticks around, the hotdog fell in accidentally, and he was trying to dump a gnat out of his drink. This list of corrections no sooner occurred to him than he suppressed it lest psychic "Dying Gaul" were still eavesdropping and easily offended.

"Well, the important thing, Jared, is that your actions honored me, and here I am. And who am I, you ask? If you were to conduct a poll of everyone who ever lived, a landslide majority would agree I'm a god."

Jared mechanically chugged at his wine without tasting it till his Adam's apple had bobbed three times.

"No? You don't believe me? Okay then, I'll prove it."

The tumbler flew from Jared's nerveless fingers as self-styled god clutched his wrist and skipped backward into the smoke, dragging

Jared along. Jared ruefully clamped shut his eyes and mouth and heard glass smash against granite.

He staggered through the campfire and a heartbeat later was sitting on a bench, with a beaker of black ale to replace his tumbler of wine. Only a dreamer would take such a jump-cut transition for granted, and Jared provisionally chalked up his outlandish surroundings to hypnosis or smoke inhalation. In fact, the smell of smoke persisted but was impossible to localize in this echoing vastness of gilded beams, shadowy rafters, porthole windows, and endless trestle tables. It hearkened to a shore dinner hall from childhood beach vacation, and to the Adirondack lodge where youthful fiancée had chucked his ring into the squash purée.

The numberless multitude crowding around him would have qualified as bikers and pro wrestlers, except they were more muscular and wore outfits from the same tailor as the "god's" across from him, and also were much bigger, practically giants, though in panoramic terms they came no more closer to making a dent in this space than fresh-mown grass came to blotting out the sky.

The upside, if dwelling on it didn't risk jinxing it? These brash, thirsty, quarrelsome, laughing bruisers were minding their own business, and he strove to uphold status quo by curbing eye contact and sharp movements. "You see my predicament," confided divine escort, arching rusty eyebrows toward the rowdy clientele at his elbow, "and why it's a pleasure talking with someone different like you, a mortal, who can lend a novel perspective."

"You brought me here purely to talk?" Jared hadn't yet ruled out that "here" was merely the interior of his skull. At the same time, his escort's glib manner, fiery advent, and overall color scheme did hoist a red flag, however silly Jared felt in heeding it. "That's all you want from me?"

Soft-spoken "god" drained his beaker, swiveled to lift and waggle it toward parts unknown, and wiped his mustache on absorbent sleeve, from which the taint of ale speedily faded. He narrowed pale blue eyes at Jared and simulated shock. "You're not mistaking me for the devil, are you? Most of us have had to put up with that since the Middle Ages, and it's exasperating. Besides, you don't believe in the devil."

Or in gods, Jared noted, and instantly censored his impudent self. "You're right, I don't. Sorry." Whatever the hell you are.

Unsampled ale was warming in his clammy grip. He swigged and weathered wrenching out-of-body experience. He'd never tasted anything at once as sweet and bitter, or as rich and tannic, literally hard to swallow. At the blurred periphery of vision, he suspected guzzling benchmates were jeering at his milquetoast constitution. Or maybe they were braying at his comrade, smooching brazenly with athletic, ravishing blonde in long blue gown who'd swooped in to replenish his ale. Better, he decided, that he never find out which. An instant later, the barmaid disappeared, the neighbors settled down, and fickle god resumed, his interlude promptly forgotten, "There, in a nutshell, is why I love this tête-à-tête of ours. You're afraid I want something from you, when it's always been the other way around, from the Ice Age forward. Worship, they called it. Bah."

He slid his beaker from hand to hand across the silvery veneer. "When the Europeans defected in bulk to the Church, we mostly heaved a sigh of relief and groaned at every pagan revival, be it in ancient Rome or recent Iceland."

He fixed Jared with a searching eye. "You used to work for the post office. You understand how it is. The crap never ends. You start to catch up, and then you're hit with more, always more." His shoulders slumped dejectedly. "No, if you'll pardon my bluntness, you couldn't understand the scope of our frustration. For millennia, to be accountable for every solstice, every equinox, every eclipse, every rainy season, nearly everything that we had nothing to do with. By and large we ignored the supplications, let 'em go to voicemail, as you say nowadays. The prayers piled up regardless. Nothing slowed them down."

Jared sipped more warily at his high-impact brew. He had no idea what was in store for him, but could guarantee he'd be on that bench a long while if he had to finish his drink. Meanwhile, grousing deity left off pushing beaker back and forth and emptied it at one slurping go. He repeated the waggling gesture, stole another sloppy kiss from the beautiful evanescent blonde amidst raucous approbation, and attended to Jared again. Jared regarded these displays of heavy drinking and heavy petting as tactless and insensitive in light of his recently ablated capacities, but what to say in present company that wouldn't lead to more scorn heaped upon him?

"And the torrents of shameless petty shit. You would be appalled, my corporeal friend. The incessant whining for love or money. Avarice devoid of originality. Disgruntled selfishness on a tremendous scale. Plus the centuries of spiteful, vindictive defixiones."

"I'm sorry. The what?"

"Curse plaques. I'm so glad the word is strange to you. Inscribed on lead usually, and dropped into sacred wells. Great for water quality. 'Please smite the landlord for making me pay up,'" he mockingly intoned. "'Please cripple the whore who laughed at my special needs.'"

Jared waffled over whether he ought to apologize for any sordid forebears. No, not an option. Futile trying to put a word in for now.

"Begging for miraculous cures. That was the pits. Subjecting us to nasty, gruesome figurines to show us where it hurt. Goose-egg eyes, crooked limbs, goiter, harelips, tumors everyplace." Third beaker he obsessively rotated, to imitate a squeaky wheel. It became irritating immediately.

"Even after Christianity raided the game, prayers to saints for healing and money and revenge, the same old same old, were routinely misrouted to our ears. Sometimes we were so fed up we made damn sure the sniveling pipsqueaks got the opposite of what they demanded, and you know what they did then? They'd take an icon of their venerated saint and pulverize it against the wall. Veneration indeed. We never tolerated that sort of disrespect."

He tossed off ale number three and peered skeptically at Jared's scarcely depleted first. "Go on, drink up! It's on my tab, you realize. I can spend eternity on something, but you can't."

Jared fidgeted to the edge of the bench and leaned forward. He may have been ensconced in some heroic fantasy, but his body's post-surgical limitations remained the same. Copperheaded god obligingly cocked an ear his way, as if well aware Jared wasn't keen on attracting macho audience. "I'd like to visit the bathroom."

"Not here you wouldn't. Trust me." Wry deity peered into Jared's liquor as if reading tea leaves. "I prefer the other place myself.

More robust brews, roomier seating. Rougher customers, though. Not that I'd disparage our proprietress in a million years. I haven't in twice that time. You can feel the womanly touch here. More refined." He bent near and whispered, "She might be listening. Take my word, when you see the bouncers coming, it's too late." Then aloud, "Doesn't mean we shouldn't adjourn to a quieter venue where the drinks are more to your liking. No, don't get up."

Valiant self-control saved Jared from the faux pas of exposing how startled he was. Otherwise the piss in progress would have zig-zagged out of quaint eggshell urinal and onto stamped-tin walls. In terms of one small blessing, the flanking urinals were unoccupied, though a duffer in dowdy tweed was scrutinizing him via the mirror above the sink where he was washing up, as if Jared had somehow behaved conspicuously. Had this second jarring "jump cut" wrung unseemly squawk from him, or unseemlier flatulence, before mind and body had rejoined? The duffer shot baleful glance at him while stumping through a doorway propped wide open with a cannonball.

From a cubby for two with a beeline vantage of the restroom, the copper god waved Jared over. Well, if lofty deity didn't care if Jared's hands were clean, then neither did he. Or was this deity especially lofty? A prankish aura tinged those jolting shifts of scene, and hints of run-ins with bouncers were symptomatic of a troublemaker. To take him at his word that he wasn't Satan didn't mean he was on the up-and-up. Or that Jared wasn't really squatting temporarily insane beside a campfire outside Peterborough.

At least the present delusion boasted old-school appeal. Jared trod on creaking floorboards decked with sawdust, noting darkly varnished walnut paneling, and dusty heads of bear and elk and boar mounted at a height secure from further human harm, and a pall of cigarette and sweeter pipe smoke, and a hairless, hulking, aproned barkeep who might have doubled as a butcher. Nothing showed through oriel window with leaded panes beyond lazy tapping branches and rural darkness. Topers cut from the same cloth as their colleague in the bathroom, or in equally threadbare serge and twill, prattled clannishly at the hinged end of mammoth Victorian bar, acknowledging neither Jared nor their barman nor the god among them. Their discussion was too cloistered for Jared to identify its language or even isolate any syllables.

The copper god now wore a cable sweater enlivened by rows of archers aiming at moose. He'd applied no makeover, however, to Jared's ill-matched beige fleece pullover and baggy green khakis. He remarked, as Jared squeezed into the pew across from his, "I thought you'd find this wayside den engaging."

A pair of pint glasses was sweating condensation on the narrow, spindly table, and they appeared to contain that same black ale Jared had so gratefully left behind. More trenchant humor from divine drinking partner, whose sixteen ounces were down to eight already? "You're in luck," the god announced, indicating their draughts with a flourish. "I have an in with the publican. Special reserve." He raised half-empty glass toward Jared with the chummy air of inflicting a high-five. "A toast." Jared half-heartedly brought his glass into clinking range. "To May Day and everything about it." And happy birthday to me, Jared mused gloomily. Would have been nice if omniscient god had mentioned that.

Jared saw no way around a trial swallow. He naively tried willing his taste buds to lie low, but yikes! "Special reserve" could have spewed from the same tap as that supernatural beer, except watered down for mortal palates. This lite version might have grown on him, were it not so onerous by association. In its favor, he could probably nurse it along without passing out, thereby staving off divine pressure to binge.

For now, though, self-absorbed god was off in the fog of memory lane. "You know, my personal connections with this locale run incredibly deep." He paused to tip remnant foam and droplets from the glass into his mouth. "Used to be a sacred grove where we're sitting now. Consecrated to me among others. Men of more than one race conjured me in various guises down the centuries. I had quite the following. You'd never guess, but the faithful flocked to this forlorn spot by the thousands. You should have seen the fear and awe when I showed up, which happened as often as not on May Day."

Wistful deity made a sign of *pax vobiscum* with uplifted arm to request a refill from the bartender. His frown into the gulf of history lapsed deeper into melancholy as two more pints, with nervous alacrity, plunked upon the table. "Oh, who am I kidding? Those sacrifices to me. Ugh. Nothing worse, here or elsewhere. A stink beyond your vilest nightmares. Scorching fur and viscera, rancid blood. Giant wicker men crammed with miscreants and cattle and put to the torch. Groves like the one on this site, with dozens of men and horses hanged on boughs, gutted and rotting until they dropped piecemeal like blighted fruit."

He grimaced as if his nostrils could inhale the past. "Uppsala— that had to be the nastiest. Every solstice, seventy-two victims at each go, nine days in a row, till nobody could duck into the arbor without getting soaked in blood and ghastlier fluids. And crow shit, I might add. Or does my nostalgia exaggerate?" He grinned cattily to ensure the irony registered. Jared would never have guessed that a god had so much to complain about.

"I stayed well away from there and all holy ground on most major holidays because of the stench and misery. We all did, so these grisly spectacles achieved the opposite of their purpose. They were god repellants, no less, the best ever devised, and your ancestors were too hidebound to figure that out. When the missionaries charged in purging and vandalizing and exorcising, nobody cheered louder than us, I can tell you." He pushed fresh pint across sticky oaken surface to plink against Jared's first glass, which rested on the table, enclosed in his damp fingers. "Prosit."

Jared humored him with a token gulp. Foolish to provoke a deity who mightn't need much further working up before he started lobbing thunderbolts. The outsized barkeep shied timidly from meeting Jared's sidelong glance.

"Ah, delighted you're more receptive to these refreshments."

"Yes, thank you!" Jared chimed.

"You're welcome. See? This is nice. Some simple back-and-forth civility. Our dealings with the priests and supplicants were basically so impersonal. They never really knew or cared who fielded their petitions. Wotan, Zeus, Osiris, Baal, Thor, Enlil, Apollo—what was the difference from beggarly human viewpoint? And none of those, by the by, has ever been my name. You may have noticed I didn't come right out and introduce myself. That was deliberate. Experience has taught it's best to remain anonymous. No risk of seeding false expectations."

Jared's every gulp of "special reserve" helped dissolve its association with celestial brew. He began warming to it, and loosening up, in spite of himself. "Okay, I understand your disgust, and I sympathize, and I'd never impose on your good graces. But if you'll pardon my asking, since you're so fed up with people, why did you respond to me and my cheap hotdog and a little spilled wine?" More politick, he decided, to skip the drowning gnat.

The copper god chose painstaking words. "Well now, to be pestered or fawned over, that's a nuisance, yes. Being worshipped is a burden, but who thrives on negligence? Everyone's entitled to their share of acknowledgment, aren't they?"

Jared nodded complaisantly, while repressing a suspicion that divine host was navigating the shoals of some duplicity.

"Let's say, for the sake of discussion, that my kind are gods second, and something more nuanced first. 'Gods.' That's a human label, just as our names for one another bear no relation to your names for us. Prior to *Homo sapiens*, we never called ourselves gods, but it's been so long we can't remember what we were before."

Pensive deity chugged, dourly restrained himself, smacked his glass back down with a fraction unconsumed. "We are what we are. Your species tells us we're gods. We've never genuinely understood the term any better than you do, or any better than you understand yourselves, for that matter. Turn it around, shall we? You're a man. Quick, what does that mean?"

Jared's wits fumbled pathetically at the unforeseen ball in his court. His mouth gaped open in advance of coherent reply.

"Not exactly child's play, to sum yourself up on the spur of the moment. Might come easier to you if you weren't lagging as far behind." Divine index finger nudged Jared's intact second pint almost indiscernibly closer, a gesture that carried much farther than the bare millimeter involved.

Jared took the hint and choked down an arduous slug of his first ale.

"That's more like it!" Nameless god clapped approving hand on Jared's flinching shoulder. The impact made him shudder head to toe.

Jared reckoned he was in his rights to plead, "I'm not in top form. I've been unwell, you see."

"Yes, yes, but you're better now," his host countered matter-of-factly, and with a broad streak of paternalism. Excuses, dammit, were always transparent to a god. That was one thing that made one a god, wasn't it?

"Honestly, I'm not fishing for sympathy. And I'm not moping around sorry for myself." Uh-oh, were those the mild initial wobbles of headspin? Impossible! He'd only had—what was it?—half an ale here and a couple of sips from the heavenly beaker. He forged intrepidly toward clearing the air. "I don't have to explain 'going walkabout,' do I? You must have learned about that sometime in the last fifty thousand years. A walkabout, that's what I was doing, to the best of my paltry ability, when you homed in on me. Putting some distance between me and the bullshit. Promoting a little peace of mind. Healthier mind for a healthier body, as the cliché more or less goes. And if I'd had the resources to attempt it correctly, our paths would never have crossed."

"They wouldn't? You can't be too sure."

What the hell did that mean? Jared had no chance to ponder because the copper god was off on another tangent. "The humble scope of your effort isn't important. You still deserve a lot of credit for looking to your spiritual welfare after a life-threatening crisis. Not a high priority in your generation. You're not quite yet the man you were though, are you?" Compassion shone plain through diaphanous blue eyes, but Jared squirmed at the notion of supernal X-ray vision penetrating his underwear, lingering on absorbent pad. And on more chronic soft-tissue shortcomings to which he'd resigned himself.

"That's all right," he hastily asserted. "My identity isn't stuck in my pants."

"No, I'd never accuse you of machismo. And I'm satisfied you're not the grasping type, either." Immortal hand, with skin smooth as marble, patted Jared's consolingly, tarried there. "That's why I'm fully prepared to fix everything for you. As good as new. Just say the word."

Holy shit, was this a come-on? Jared's headspin accelerated a notch. Don't panic! Potentially disastrous to panic. He slowly withdrew his sweaty hand and wrapped it around his second pint, ridiculous though he must have looked with a glass in each mitt. Two-fisted drinker, indeed.

"No? As you wish." Godly expression continued placid and benign.

The tardy possibility occurred to Jared that "fixing everything" might extend to colossal hospital debt. But no, hell no, what was he playing with here? Maybe no *quid pro quo* was at stake, maybe he was jumping to wild conclusions, but that was preferable to the least likelihood of enlisting as divine boy-toy.

"In any case, Jared, on a purely academic note, how did you suppose our pleasant symposium was going to end?" Did Jared detect a cunning undertone, an indirect reminder that mortal misgivings were never secret in godly company?

He pursed his lips and hedged, "I've given up predicting what's around the corner. Any corner. I leave that to wiser heads such as yours."

"A reasonable life lesson after what you've been through." Copper god drained his glass but withheld the gesture for more.

Jared, meanwhile, seized upon a flash of insight. This drinking partner hadn't volunteered a name because he didn't have one. His unbridled smooching and imbibing, his "jump cuts" into the unknown, even his offer to "fix everything," all added up too handily as projections of Jared's insecurities, his yearnings to escape, his impractical wishes. And how about that remark implying he and deity would have met wherever Jared had been? Nonsense, or else dead giveaway, that alleged god and these environs were outright hallucinations. And that being the case, why not swill illusory alcohol, since his headspin, logically, wasn't for real, and neither would be his hangover? Manners decreed, however, that he attend to his imaginary friend.

"I do feel I owe you something, Jared. You've been so kind to hear me out and treat me with respect. There must be a way to repay you. 'A gift seeks a return,' to quote your nobler ancestry."

Jared guzzled past the verge of masochism. "Thanks, this beer is plenty," he gasped. "Nothing like it." Surprisingly, the beer was truly fine, once he'd set aside that foolish dread of repercussions.

"Glad you've acquired a taste for it, but let's not be naive. You've got a god at your disposal, remember?" The towering barkeep had shambled over, perhaps because he'd seen the empty glass and dared not miss a cue. Arching russet eyebrows sent him scudding away. "This walkabout of yours, Jared. You can't allot a single weekend to it and expect much benefit. We're talking about the restoration of your *joie de vivre*, your sense of place in the universe, your self-worth, your very sanity."

Interesting, mused Jared, to be lectured by a delusion about sanity. He put a reckless dent in his first drink and ogled the next while asking, "Where would you have me go? The Australian outback is completely foreign to me. I've no affinity with it. I don't see it as helpful. Plus it's too hot and dangerous. The same goes for the Southwest and those vision quests. Nothing worse than the hubris of an Anglo like me going Native American." Another pull at his glass did it. One down.

"Where does it say you have to find yourself under a rock in the desert?" A spark ignited in pellucid blue eyes. Sly or inspired? "Dolmens are part of your cultural heritage, aren't they? Alias chamber tombs, cromlechs, portal graves, Hünengraber, dösar, or quoits? If you're hoping to find yourself under a rock, that might be your best bet. Waking up in one is reputedly auspicious, especially on May Day. Or that's the hype immemorial. An impeccably relevant place, ethnically speaking, for your renewal or rebirth, from which you can pursue therapeutic wanderlust in a temperate climate, with idyllic countryside and villages purveying food and shelter at your beck and call. And home? No more than a day's fleet journey away."

Jared marveled at the persuasiveness of this extraordinary sales pitch, but he foremost gave his benefactor the nod because no harm could come of humoring a figment, could it? He proffered a salute to anonymous god with uplifted glass, which he tossed back so zealously that liquor clogged his sinuses.

Elated deity clasped Jared's free hand heartily in both of his and proclaimed, "Congratulations! Your wish is good as granted. I postpone it only to advise you strongly to retire to the bathroom again. 'Travel in comfort' is a motto of yours, is it not?" He had Jared there, as none but a god or his subconscious incarnate could.

The table scraped harshly as he pushed it away and reeled toward the urinal. Yes, this pit stop was a grim necessity, he realized as his lurching stride kept jostling a tightly swollen water balloon be-

hind his belt. The knot of codgers nattering at the bar steadfastly refused to see or hear him, despite the snickering pleasure that might
have afforded them. Capricious god let him piss in peace, but after
flushing, Jared reckoned, all bets were off. Between bathroom door
and table, he suspected every logy blink, every faltering step would
segue him into *terra incognita*. Or into another befuddling mirage,
more like.

His unearthly guide, however, was steeped in somber reflection,
studying empty glass from sundry angles, apparently as subject to
beery mood swing as anyone. Did Jared have to clear his throat to
establish he was back? Ahem. Yes, he did. Pretty selective omnis-
cience, wasn't it?

"Are you fashioned in our image, or we in yours?" deity brooded.
"As hackneyed as the riddle of the chicken and the egg. If I could
only exhume those memories to solve it." Reviving smile, half-
hidden under ruddy mustache, seemed more guarded now. "Well,
let's get you sorted out."

As if that sentence cast a sedative spell, leaden fatigue descended
on Jared, but why fight something that wasn't actually happening?
He did crave one last mouthful of sumptuous "special reserve," unreal or not, and dragged it toward his parting lips. "One for the road,"
he slurred.

He sucked some in and savored it, sloshing it from cheek to
cheek, and after he'd consigned it to his gullet, instinctively spat out
foreign particle stranded among his molars. He squinted at the speck
on oaken tabletop. A gnat? That boded more significance than his
guttering faculties could process.

"In your parlance, don't sweat the small stuff." Tricky gleam in
clear blue iris seemed at odds with mellow veneer. Inscrutable divin-
ity blandly backhanded spent pints to smash upon the floor and
nodded in approval when sodden mortal reflexes didn't even twitch.
"Yes, you go ahead and catch your forty winks. I'll handle the arrangements."

As his chin sank inexorably to the table, Jared invested his last
grains of cogency to puzzle, If I'm dreaming already, is it really possible to fall asleep? Two fading snippets pierced the cotton in his ears.
A profoundly sonorous hiccup preceded an ominous "Oops."

Jared was sitting up straight when his eyes reopened on dazzling blue sky. Pungent sea breeze fanned his face, and low morning sun deposed chill from his back. He felt fine, no headache, no queasy stomach, no distended bladder, except his ass was sore, as from too long a sojourn on a hard surface. That pew in the pub would be the obvious culprit.

He awoke at this special moment because someone was poking the soles of his loafers and shouting up at him. Best not to make overly much of that yet. First let him get his bearings. Beneath cloudless sky was ocean of a more limpid blue, and leisurely wavelets broke sibilant on a beach shaggy with grasses above the tideline. As breaches of promise went, he could live with this, so far anyhow. All around nicer than materializing in a dark, moldy underground crypt.

He squinched down at the party responsible for the fuss. Roughly ten feet below, a grizzled pensioner with bulbous nose and plaid soft cap and frayed gabardine jacket was literally hopping mad, stretching on tiptoes and launching himself trembly inches into prodding range with his cane. His aim was remarkably good. He was grousing in what sounded like Welsh with a French accent and, after panting for breath, French with a Welsh accent. Where the hell was this?

The geezer was doubtless incensed because Jared was perched like a flagpole sitter on a narrow, battered monolith, cavalierly profaning a cherished ancient monument, at whose base was black entrance to long subterrene passage, with a ground-level roof of slabs like squarish turtles on the march. Tipsy deity must have meant to transport him inside.

Or was Jared still, as sanity would have it, spaced out beside the cooling embers of moribund campfire? He clamped his eyes shut and insisted that he was, that he'd open them in the middle of woodsy front yard. Nope. Hadn't budged an inch, which was just as well, considering his precarious station. Perhaps the codger's invective was too distracting for Jared to blink himself back to normality, and whether he were physically atop a menhir or not, he'd be foolhardy shutting his eyes again and letting a lucky prod topple him by surprise.

For lack of a better plan, Jared returned geriatric glower and began to exclaim, "Get a ladder!" The ornery cuss might not understand, but Jared's French was vestigial and his Welsh nonexistent.
Eventually, he had to hope, his tormenter would perceive he was a
Yank and fetch a bilingual friend.

Jared lapsed into bellowing autopilot while debating whether
silver-tongued god really had misrouted him. That parting "oops" was
a shade too coy, too staged. Of a piece with much else in his double-
edged, smart-alecky deportment. Better late than never, Jared
guessed why a god would prefer going nameless if he were archetypal joker, lord of tricksters Loki, whose powers to bamboozle
would be compromised if mortal rubes were on to him. How manifest in 20-20 hindsight, as well it should have been even had he not
squandered youthful hours on Loki's supervillain exploits in *Mighty
Thor* comics. Yet here he huddled like an anchorite, the butt of divine joke, no inkling where he was or how to make waspish native
desist. Jared crossed his feet to elevate them out of dependable
reach.

The counterintuitive hell of it was, he did feel optimistic, reju-
venated, ready for epic undertaking. Those hotdogs at the cabin must
have spoiled hours ago, which would have bothered him yesterday,
but on this glorious morning, so what? Hotdogs and medical bills and
his job had become unreal specks in the astronomic distance. Maybe
he'd never go home. Could he swing that somehow?

Anticipation and foreboding mixed restlessly in his stomach.
Any serious god of mischief couldn't be through with him already,
and Jared deep down banked on more chaos forthcoming to spice up
his next fifty years. And if this was still a dream, he plainly wasn't in
charge of waking up. But awake or not, the freedom to live as if he
were dreaming might prove his best birthday gift ever. "Get a ladder!" he yelled, a bit hoarsely, for the umpteenth time.

Sympathy for the Deadbeats

I lucked out and made the Concessionary Pool. At the ballpark, no less. Thanks to my clean credit score, according to conventional wisdom, which states: why should the C.P. bureaucracy throw economic life preservers to un- or underemployed yahoos drowning in debt? And deprive the gross domestic product of interest, late fees, annual fees, service fees, and diverse arcane penalties? Not to mention free labor down the road? As for the likes of penny-wise me, though, if I'm making money, that ups my potential to spend over my head. Putting me where the proverbial "they" want me. Anyway, kudos to the Department of Labor, whose e-mail to report at Yellowjackets Field arrived the same day as my last Unemployment check.

Whether due to weak wills or bad faith, the Dems predictably choked after campaign promises to make like David with the credit-industry Goliaths. Instead, Congress brayed of "triumph for the middle class" on mandating that 10% of a workforce where those Goliaths were stakeholders (i.e., everywhere) had to be "antemortem." Big concession. Hence the "Concessionary Pool." Not that the G.O.P. would've extended that much lip service.

A representative of the non-payroll 90% was shuffling toward me down canary-yellow corridor. Moaning at the same pitch, in their pitiful way, as the humming overhead fluorescents. On the elderly side, but no more so than a lot of guys taking orders at Burger King. A strapping physique for his likely lifespan. His semblance of fitness was somewhat offset by bluish, pocky skin stretched translucent over facial bones that could bust through any minute, bulging egg-white eyes leaking brown fluid, mouth in tragic-mask, white-gummed rictus. He was in his Sunday-best burying suit, naturally. Dead, I reckoned, six months. "Are you sure this is where you should be going?" I asked when I saw the pinpoint irises in the whites of his eyes. Neck bones creaked as he torpidly shook his head and reversed plodding course.

I'd been taking a breather in stockroom doorway, about to load up another dolly with boxes of sweatshirts for the gift shop. And gift shop is where stray zombie would have wound up, had he persevered. Everyone knows why an evening of baseball is affordable these days, but customers still tend to balk in the blue face of reduced operating costs. Even during preseason clearance sale.

"Thanks, kid. Well played." From out of nowhere, Zack, the general manager, was standing right next to me. Yikes! That gave me a much bigger scare than a poor old "working stiff" ever could. Nobody had called me "kid" in a good twenty years. But nice to be appreciated. My reply hadn't fumbled past a deferential nod when a ringtone version of "Born to Run" warbled from his nylon blazer pocket, and he strode off to palaver, helloing before the phone was halfway to his ear. Leaving a trail of musky aftershave to my left. And to my right, a more acrid trail of rot retardant.

Do the stadium medics favor Decay Away or Fresh Flesh? Can't tell. I'm not among the connoisseurs. Don't want to be. No difference in how well either spray will help, after slow and steady rot bores too deep for the juice to keep up. Without the juice, none of this ghoulishness would be happening. The juice goes by either "the juice" or its chemical formula, with too many syllables and double vowels for use by mere laymen. Its big pharma licensee deemed it inappropriate, for once, to register a jazzy trade name.

Doubtful that those unsung R&D white coats fooling with Haitian voodoo powder had banked on more than cheap thrills in their personal research time. The end product, though, was as far removed from Santeria as penicillin from moldy bread. And was first intended only to beat the rising cost of lab rats via resurrection and reuse. Until some evil fiscal genius got wind of it, and had a mad epiphany about those umpteen cardholders dying in arrears every day.

The drug's patent-holder was still downplaying the true nature of its "healing accelerant for rodents" while lobbyists secured passage of an outwardly absurd law. In brief, death did not release the deceased *per se* from any accounts payable. The shape of corporate perfidy became obvious only when lawyers, with armed deputies in tow, waved writs preposterous but ironclad, and seized corpses awaiting autopsy in the morgue.

Legal objections foundered in a judicial Sargasso, where precedent perversely favored white-collar grave robbers. If running out of money and declaring bankruptcy canceled no outstanding balances, then neither did running out of time. Not when the juice could zap some motor function into the delinquent dead and requalify them for employment. Unions and religious groups and human-rights advocates battled the body-snatching tide, but were swamped like Canute before the pharmaceutical, mortuary, banking, and manufacturing lobbies. In other words, everyone with something to gain from the juice. Not to mention CEOs itching to subcontract the ultimate scab labor.

After I helped unpack the clearance merch and replenish gift shop shelves, Barb the cheerful supervisor had me break down the cardboard and haul it to recycling. Most people here are outright cheerful, actually. No idea how they pull it off. What with zombies moping at every turn.

I got lost en route. Again. This park is a humble 10,000-seater, but its bowels pass for endless labyrinth all the same. Seemed ambitious enough to get my bearings by week two on the job, in time for Opening Night.

A stunning flare-up of retardant odor warned where I was headed. Around a bend, a pair of doors confronted me, with brighter paint on surrounding wall to intimate where one door used to be. And beyond those doors, a new dividing wall split the old infirmary into two. One for the living, its door always closed and lined with weatherstripping to seal out the smell. The other, always open to air it out and help the "patients" find it. Those lined up outside also amounted to a dead giveaway, so to speak. The setup at Yellowjackets Field was typical of a hundred places I'd seen in my job search.

A humming light shone down on the queue. Prompting a tuneless, pathetic chorus. The sturdier moaners with parched faces like gator handbags were reporting for a spray coat of retardant. Their palsied, weak-kneed, even prunier comrades needed a syringe of juice. I wheeled my cumbersome bale of cardboard by them post-haste, unacknowledged apart from a few who fixated on my squeaking handtruck and tried to harmonize.

At this range, something fishy complicated the chemical bouquet. That would be the juice. Pufferfish venom is touted as the only ingredient to survive from the original recipe. Reputedly to keep "graveyard shift" docile. Though when the juice in their veins conks out, so do they. Too stupefied and doddery for a rampage, despite well-founded resentment. And within palsied hours, they're done for good. Ditto after one booster of juice too many. Rumor also lists aloe, caffeine, and stem cells among the restorative agents.

I took a gander through open door as I rolled by. The doc was sitting on a metal stool, chewing gum, jabbing hypo into naked zombie thigh without even looking. He was overdue for a shave, and his aquamarine smock was slit at the seams for the sake of expansive gut. I hoped he hadn't graduated at the top of his class. Then again, I should talk. My sheepskin decreed "magna cum laude." But multiple outsourcings, downsizings, and redundancies later, I'm grateful to be a gofer for a farm team.

By Friday, I'd more or less made good on my ambition to learn the tortuous floorplan. And everywhere, I continued to find, people were so nice and laid-back. In the ticket office, bookkeeping, community relations. Even the guys who sold advertising. Zack seemed to like shooting the breeze with me, between incoming calls. Gave me to believe he was unduly impressed with my academic background. Much more than I was. On nagging second thought, though, the bonhomie had begun creeping me out. As if it signaled a double standard, or selective vision at best, vis-à-vis sizable postmortem crew.

Case in point, it rubbed me the wrong, squirmy way when I saw them dispose of a plopper. Mike the groundskeeper was out on the field, rehearsing a row of zombies with those bizarre agribusiness-scale rakes for resmoothing the base paths between innings. They were trotting along at optimal speed, after arduous minutes of shouted corrections. Mike had the bulk and gruffness of a former biker or maybe gym teacher, but was more civil with me than anyone from those walks of life had ever been. One zombie keeled over in midstride and landed in such a jumble that I thought the head and limbs might have come detached. Mike hollered at the others to stop, but by then, tines had already snagged on plopper flesh and sent his coworkers sprawling. When the juice stops working, that's often how it happens. Plop! Mike harangued one zombie to fetch a wheelbarrow "before the stink gets ripe and kills someone," and the rest to dump their inert comrade in, after which Mike ordered the plopper's removal pronto. As if he were dogshit on the diamond. None of the living spectators batted an eyelid. Mike, a stickler for neatness, dusted off everyone's funeral formalwear with a whisk-broom and resumed practice. Call me cynical, but I began to wonder if staffers were so genteel because they had this ongoing safety valve of disposable helots to boss around.

Did it ever occur to anyone that these were still people's fathers or husbands or brothers? Corporate noblesse, in a blasé nod at decency, packed newly exhumed labor into big rigs bound for out-of-state worksites, to reduce chances that next of kin would bump into their dear shambling departed. But doesn't that only encourage the callousness? Make it okay, as long as your own relations aren't degraded right before your eyes? Meanwhile, talk-show reactionaries more and more brazenly assert that defunct spendthrifts are only getting what they deserve. And to any quibblesome "bleeding hearts" they misapply the label "necrophiliac." Which, if I'm any judge of slovenly usage, will cast up in the next *Merriam-Webster* on a wave of runaway popularity.

Since our plopper has paid down all the debt he ever will, the Personnel Department should be arranging transport back to his rightful grave. So ordains a federal directive with no one to enforce it. In other words, who knows where the remains go? When, to belabor the obvious, has big business ever heeded regulations devoid of punitive teeth?

"Deadbeats," in financial-services lingo, used to be the derogatory term for punctual cardholders who failed to rack up interest and late fees (which would have rendered me a "deadbeat"). But now, the same element out to redefine "necrophilia" styles the zombies "deadbeats," as if they were of a piece with welfare or alimony cheats. Yet the heavy lifting at Yellowjackets Park, as elsewhere, is in deadbeat hands: groundskeeping, custodial, offloading trucks. And after several office stints, I can expand zombie skill set to document-shredder, errand boy, window washer, doorman, maid. On good authority, some can alphabetize, though "Mc" and "Mac" reduce them to quivering indecision. Deadbeat brains are demonstrably not all equal. Begging the question, how much intelligence can they muster? How aware, how rueful of their miserable lot might they be? They can't talk. Some malarkey about irreversible autolysis of synapses between parietal lobe and larynx. Nothing, though, stops them from understanding enough language for grunt work. Or from having something to say, if they had the means?

Monday, made the unsavory discovery that zombies weren't exempt from kitchen duties. No closer to the food than operating dishwashers and scouring cookware. And they do wear airtight hazmat suits to coop up any unclean sloughings. Suffocation's not an issue, insofar as their breathing days are over. Still, couldn't help feeling a little grossed out at first. I'd been sent to roll a lunch trolley down to one of the luxury suites, a richly appointed bunker in essence, with a shatterproof view of the third-base line. Zack was meeting with the team owner and chief of security and some local pols. He urged me to grab a couple of brats and a carton of fries off the trolley and hang out in the box seats adjoining the suite, in case anyone had dessert requests later.

I was munching contentedly till a chance glimpse inside wrecked my appetite. From the suite's bathroom lumbered a deadbeat, lugging a red plastic bucket of cleaning supplies and a toilet brush in his magenta-gloved mitts. Zack and associates studiously ignored him and his hamfisted efforts to twist doorknob and exit with his hands full. If only, like them, I'd had distracting business while a nonentity struggled. No such luck. I blinked incredulous at grimacing profile, and the air stuck in my throat.

It was Denny Santangelo! My high school English teacher, my mentor and confidant through the dismal swamp of adolescence. He wrote the letter of recommendation that got me into college. Corruptive influence, in purely life-affirming ways. Introduced me to single-malt Scotch, twentieth-century glam rock, and science fiction, or "mind rot" as he dubbed it, back when it could compete with current events for freakishness (sex and drugs I had to navigate on my own). The summer before junior year at university, he talked me into calling in sick one night at a mill job so we could go barhopping, lest I start treating drudgery too seriously. No mistaking him, even if his hairline had receded something awful before death started taking its toll. Lost track of him after he moved out of state to pursue a doctorate. Whence his body had been shipped back here, in accordance with the letter of the law. To replace the plopper from last Friday? Someone had added insult to injury and buried him in a snooty Brooks Brothers suit that would have been anathema to him in life. In galling fulfillment of his favorite Henry James quote, "Death makes you vulnerable." Santangelo had never let insufficient funds dampen or defer his enjoyment of life. And here was how his admirable joie de vivre had caught up with him. Seeing as he'd died young, had he necessarily gotten the worst of the bargain?

Glad he hadn't returned my dumbfounded stare after his goggle eyes grazed mine. His cause of death was a mystery, but not what happened afterward. The instant his demise had entered hospital database, a red flag popped up beside his name, to preempt autopsy. Ambulance rushed him to the undertaker's, where juice instead of formaldehyde flooded his veins.

Dead Santangelo's new proprietors, like 800-pound gorillas in the next room, would have been conspicuous despite their absence during calling hours and funeral and committal service. On Santangelo's third day six feet under, a backhoe dug him up, and uniformed goons escorted him to a van making the rounds of county cemeteries. The juice had reactivated him a day or two earlier, but letting him stew down there better served a pretext of decency than quarrying sooner and risking friction with any tardy mourners. Cemetery crew, usually deadbeats themselves, reburied the coffin and finally reseeded the topsoil. Santangelo had stood zero chance of resting in peace unless dynamite or worse put him beyond reach of cosmetic repairs. And my hopes of a good night's sleep were likewise dashed till further notice.

Sometime after Santangelo had fumbled out the door, Zack, again with that uncanny cat tread, was at my elbow. Apologetic because, from the look of me, it was colder out here than he'd thought. Why didn't I go help proofread some press releases? Nobody at his meeting felt like dessert.

No C.P. colleague crossed my path till Wednesday, forty-eight hours before Opening Night. And he was one of those buttondown professionals who looked a decade older than me, but was probably that much younger. Perry had been ensconced in the Ticket Office from day one. Formerly, ran a temp agency. One of many lines of business that had gone belly-up due to deadbeat competition. In the process, jacking unemployment numbers even higher, along with lifelong credit-card debt, ultimately breeding more deadbeats. Someday will everyone less schooled than licensed tradesmen be zombies, or slated to be? Has any thought gone into what'll happen when menial jobs are off the table for anyone alive? Understandably, Perry was no fan of the "working stiffs."

Ticket sales were brisk. Same as every year on the cusp of the season, I gathered. Hence my recourse to the Ticket Office, answering a phone and processing orders. Instead of a midday lull, the pace picked up mercilessly. A deadbeat in hazmat suit wheeled refreshments in. Chafing trays of cheeseburgers and fries, piles of deluxe nachos, a platter of diced fruit, bowls of mixed nuts. With paper and plastic picnicware, sparing me visions of corrupt hands washing our dishes and utensils. Some of us tried to work straight through with our mouths full. Others, like Perry and me, pretended it was more civilized to take five and chew like maniacs.

Between bites, I tried engaging Perry on some points of inquiry that Zack or anyone in charge might not have deemed tactful. Did the zombies remember who they were? Did they understand their predicament, or were they robots in effect? Perry shrugged. "They're dead. They got nothing going on inside." He stood up to refill his plate. I followed suit. Okay, we were taking ten rather than five.

"They're smart enough to obey commands. They don't have to be shown how to do things from scratch. They can navigate the maze of this stadium as well as anybody. What do you think that all means?"

"Don't care," Perry mumbled. More concerned with scooping up tortilla chips, choosing which of all the identical cheeseburgers was, on some esoteric basis, the best. My toothpick and I, meanwhile, were ruthlessly culling all the pineapple wedges from the fruit platter. "They got themselves into it, didn't they? Bunch of slobs. And now they're taking jobs away from the rest of us."

Was he borderline hot and bothered at this innocent airing of ideas? On the verge of calling me a necrophiliac? Strategic retreat seemed prudent as we sat back down. "On the bright side, nobody gets outsourced anymore."

"No, they wouldn't, because the deadbeats work for free. Can't beat that." He sounded put out at having to explain the obvious to me. Humor, or my idea of it anyway, wasn't about to build any bridges here.

In fact, outsourcing wasn't the only moot issue. Legal and illegal immigrants alike had despaired of bucking the moldering horde. And back home, they confronted bitter tidings that the juice had preceded them. Class-war riots had dominated months of news from Mexico, Central America, India, but reportedly accomplished nothing. Whereas in the good old U.S. of A., people just grumbled and bore the yoke of plutocratic abuse. Same as during past foreclosure and banking crises. Zack might have been open to some friendly debate on international affairs, but why hand Perry an excuse to brand me a socialist as well as a necrophiliac? I didn't bug him any more for the last two minutes of our lunch.

So what was flukier? Meeting none of my C.P. coworkers for over a week, or seeing no ballplayers in this ballpark till Thursday morning, when the whole team was out on the grass? Eleventh-hour training before the first home stand. Calisthenics, stretching, fielding, pitching, fungoes. When I punched in, a note from Zack was smushed into my timecard slot. Please come to the maintenance entrance. He greeted me with a hastily scrawled to-do list and some twenty stoop-shouldered zombies. No Santangelo among them, to my relief. Zack launched into a spiel about the privilege of having responsibilities. A come-on that seldom bodes well. Based on my Ivy League background, he was trusting me to direct a zombie to each job on the list, making sure none of them interfered with whatever the players were doing. Didn't matter which deadbeat did what. For Zack's money, they were all interchangeable parts. Groundskeeper Mike had strewn all the tools and other materials along the wall beside the entrance. Sorry they weren't arranged more neatly, but Mike had been in a rush. Had a date at Traffic Court. More than that, Zack advised, I didn't want to know. My two cups of coffee were beginning to wring twinges out of my stomach, but I smiled graciously and said okay. "Knew I could count on you, kid," Zack opined and vamoosed.

Overnight showers had given way to dazzling sunshine, making short work of mist rising off the diamond. The bold yellow of team uniforms, in stark contrast with black socks and caps and trim, was stinging my eyes, and behind my eyes were the stirrings of headache.

Well, if it were done, then best it were done quickly, to misquote the Bard and affect the classiest available spin on this ordeal. I consulted the list, scoped out what parts of the field were fair game, and dispatched whichever zombie was gaping at me that instant. They consistently foraged what they needed from out of Mike's disarray and homed in on where they had to go after I pointed them in the general direction. The better they performed, the worse I felt, for tacitly buying into operative premise that they were mindless puppets.

My gang had replaced some burnt patches of sod and mixed Quickdry into some mud on the infield, and one deadbeat had partly rechalked the line from second to third base. The number of zombies was proving much larger than the list of tasks warranted. Careless figuring on the part of Zack or Mike?

Against the split-second odds, I was facing the right direction when a batter cracked a line drive, low and through the heart of center field, into the skull of that zombie bent over his chalk. The impact threw him, arms whirling loosely, into the air and onto his side. The sound was like a melon hitting pavement from a tenth-floor window.

"Plopper down!" shouted a player, inaccurately. The team and other extant onlookers drifted over or cast a casual eye without moving. Still mechanically chewing whatever they were chewing. The zombies, busy or idle, were either oblivious or swaying passively like poplars in a breeze as they stared dully toward the accident.

I sprinted over, without any forethought or desire for a better view. Joined half a dozen guys ogling glumly. I, on the other hand, was hard pressed not to whimper. Or vomit. The zombie lay stretched out like roadkill. But every so often, his teeth gnashed, and a shudder like a high-voltage jolt ran the length of his body. The ball was embedded halfway into his temple. Firmly enough that his movements didn't budge it. Each time, though, the seep of brown juice sloshed across his quivering cheek and protruding eyes.

Zack was by my side. From out of nowhere, as usual. Had to stop letting that startle me. Breath whistled through his nose, as if he'd scrambled. He was frowning. Couldn't tell if he were sympathetic, or simply exasperated. "I was afraid something like this would happen again," he muttered. Again?

"I think he's suffering," I presumed to say.

"Nah, he isn't suffering." Zack's confidence fell short of convincing me.

"How can you be so sure? Look at him." Some bosses might have read this as mouthing off, but I rightly foresaw he'd take stock of the concern in my tone.

"How can I be so sure?" All living eyes were now on Zack. And his were on me. As if I should listen very mindfully. "Because if he was suffering, what could we do about it? Do you see what I'm getting at here?"

For everything I was thinking, all I dared do was nod. His faith in my intellect, in my fitness for employment, seemed to depend on it. The ruined deadbeat spasmed on, regardless. And the reason for the extra deadbeats on the crew dawned on me. Better safe than sorry, if I needed a spare.

Bystanders withdrew as lackadaisically as they'd assembled, till it was just Zack and me. "Don't take this the wrong way, kid," he cautioned, his errant focus on the blank scoreboard, "but I notice you have a pretty good rapport with these stiffs. You treat 'em like human beings. You know, between jobs they just kinda wander around. Might be worthwhile to set up an office where they stay when no one's using 'em. Like a Zombie Central. Maybe convert the space we store 'em in overnight. If we can fit it in the budget, do you wanna in be in charge? It'll mean pretty good money, mostly for answering the phone and filling requests. Or if people can plan ahead, organizing a daily worklist. What do you say?"

"Sure!" I heard myself exclaim, feigning an eager smile while my inner man flailed desperately against vertigo. As if fighting for balance on damnation's doorstep.

Zack observed me uncertainly. He was no dummy. Did my body language hint at hidden turmoil? "They're a fact of life, you know. It's bigger than any of us, and I'm betting they're here to stay." Who could he mean but the deadbeats? I mumbled something diplomatic. Would have been happier, had he added a few words about wishing things were otherwise. "I'll call Personnel to take care of this." He indicated the mishap at our feet. Writhing unabated. But in silence, thank God. Paying the supreme price of a baseball through the head because of bad fiscal judgment or bad breaks.

At a volume calculated to penetrate my brown study, Zack empathized, "Rough morning, kid." How long had I been gawking? "Go grab a snack. The chores here can wait. I'll get back to you when I hear something from Accounting." By the time I nodded and turned toward him, he was gone.

So I had twice as much that night to toss and groan about. The image of Santangelo with his bucket of bathroom supplies was as vivid as ever. Like being haunted by my own discarded idealism, or my own half-forgotten, half-betrayed potential. I dreaded seeing him again. As was inevitable in cozy Yellowjackets Park. Especially if I were full-time zombie handler. A prospect that aggravated my insomnia. Did I want to work anyplace in the midst of a "graveyard shift"? Or for that matter, even live in a world that tolerated "graveyard shifts"? No and no. Nor did I relish a return to the bad old days of unemployment. Skimping, scrounging, and deprivation. Like life in perpetual wartime. And with eventual slide into the red when plastic had to cover rent and groceries. Distinct likelihoods, if I rejected Zack's generous offer and came off as less than a team player. As a budding whiner. Two roads lay before me, and both crossed slick hellbound slopes. But I needn't have spoiled my sleep. Twenty-four hours later, those worries were forever behind me.

The daylong windup to Opening Night threatened to frazzle everyone into zombiehood. Even with deadbeat army in the house, we were shorthanded. Stupendous amounts to do involving food, sprucing up, press kits, paperwork, logistics. None of which could have happened any earlier. Or been relegated to graveyard shift. Prepping for a party, in effect, with the players, the media, and 10,000 ticket buyers on the guest list.

Mid-afternoon, Barb the supervisor consigned me to shuttling boxes of program books from a storeroom to the gift shop, whence employees from different parts of the stadium would collect their share. Barb was wearing her characteristic cheer like a wax mask, and her demeanor resembled death warmed over. Yep, guess we were all zombies for a day. The storeroom was cattycorner from the infirmaries. The smell hardly registered any more. As I dollied out the first stack of boxes, I marked how the line of dilapidated moaners was twice its normal length. Maybe Opening Night rigors were getting to them, too.

I didn't want to stare at the deadbeats, and even less did I want them staring back. Worse, what if Santangelo was among them, whom I especially didn't want to stare at? But to ignore him when he was right there, as if he were nobody? That really choked me up. My full handtruck and I zipped past the hulking parade so that each eroding face was a blur. With naive hopes that I might not i.d. him in passing. When I did, and our eyes made fleeting contact, I resolutely pushed on, but nearly spilled my freight as if I'd wheeled over a pebble. Santangelo was about sixth from the rear. No more spark of recognition from him than before. He was parched and blackening like a raisin, wilted, on the literal verge of crumbling for want of juice. Would he reach the doctor in time? Should he?

To and from the gift shop, that final question hounded me. Didn't reckon myself the type to venture beyond daydreams of yanking Denny from the chorus and hiding him in a closet to collapse in peace. Simultaneously, that little mental filmclip of Santangelo, too weak to mimic the fluorescents' hum through cankered lips, was unbearable. Obvious to me, whether or not it would be to Zack, that he was suffering.

Breathed easier on my return. No longer an option to abduct Santangelo. He was hobbling through infirmary door. Still, I wasn't off the hook. Don't blow it and do nothing, my foolhardy conscience kept insisting, as I loaded up the dolly. But do what, specifically? No reply. Before my next trip to the gift shop, I sneaked a glimpse across the corridor. Same disheveled doc. No visible sign he'd moved since last week. Doling out treatments on autopilot. "Pull 'em up," he drawled, and the zombie whose thigh he'd injected sluggishly raised

and redid his trousers. Turned to go. And there was Santangelo, tot-
tering straight at me! As crumpled in body and soul as previously.
Lurched by without acknowledging me. The juice can take hours to
suffuse leathery flesh.

Only one thing to do now, if I were to do anything. Overcame
reflex squeamishness, took my dead friend by unresisting pinstripe
elbow, and redeposited him at the end of the line. Acting first,
thinking about it in retrospect. If one shot of juice rebooted motor
function and some rudimentary smarts, might a double portion lend
Denny the clarity to assess his situation, the will to escape? And
what then?

That was too far in the future. Behind looming short-term po-
tentialities. Had someone spotted me? Belatedly I checked around.
The corridor, hither and yon, was devoid of CCTV cameras and
antemortem personnel. Whew! As for the doc, was I asking too
much of his incompetence? How could he miss a repeat customer
from five minutes ago? And what good was supposed to come of
this experiment, exactly? Could I altogether disown vagrant curiosity
about what would happen to a zombie overdosing on juice? Santangelo stood quiescent as these thoughts revolved around him. I,
meanwhile, had program books to deliver. My nerves were beginning
to flutter. Foolish to wait for passersby who might link me with a
deadbeat exerting some initiative later.

Santangelo was near the front of the line on my return from the
gift shop. I reloaded the handtruck in hushed slow-motion, listening
for any reaction to his repeat visit. None forthcoming. Apparently I'd
taken a true measure of the doc's negligence. As I trundled out of the
storeroom, Santangelo reemerged from the infirmary. Still lethargic.
Not that the first hypo should've made any difference yet.

How to rationalize what I did next? My overwrought conscience
must have been chanting subliminally, hypnotically, More is better. I
left the handtruck in the middle of the corridor. Intercepted Santangelo. Guided him into line for a third shot. Sought for vestiges of my
old pal in the cave-in of his Roman nose, the scrunching of cleft chin,
the expansion of laugh lines into bone-deep furrows. The closer I
looked, the less I found to distinguish him from the rest of the
moaners. Death as the great equalizer, all right. Shut my eyes, pic-

tured the Santangelo of my youth, and fought a lump in my throat.

"Excuse me?" Yow! The shock of unexpected company was like treading on a live wire. Humorless Perry was violating my space. How the hell long had he been watching? If he'd seen me steer Denny around, he was squirreling that away for later use. "You wanna let me have a box of programs? You didn't give the ticket office enough." Pretty sure Perry wasn't the one to decide what the ticket office's quota was, but did I want to cross somebody who might know something that could get me fired, or worse?

I must have been deliberating too long for a man of Perry's self-importance. "So can I go grab a box? Yes or no. If you can tear yourself away from whatever weird shit you're into here." Winced inside at the length to which that clumsy putdown might be loaded. Blackmail in the offing? I foremost wanted him out of my sight and gestured him toward storeroom doorway. Posting myself a mental memo to deal as seldom as possible with the unpleasant bastard. Overheard boxes getting kicked around.

"They're all the same!" I reassured him. No response. Nor any wish on my part to enter the same room with him. He came out grappling with his ill-gained goods. Offering a scowl instead of thanks. Must have been my fault the box was too heavy. That moment, Santangelo hobbled from the infirmary. Was it my imagination that he was toiling against inertia in leaden legs, as if pulling boots from clingy mud? He focused on me, as best his pinprick irises allowed. Thank you, he mouthed. Trudged onward. He understood what I'd done! But no way to tell, beneath that rigid surface, if he grasped who I was. I had a grim suspicion of setting more in motion than I'd bargained for.

Perry, meanwhile, was still jockeying for better grip on his unwieldy load. Even if he'd missed me shepherding Denny earlier, his glare now bespoke knowledge of some funny business between deadbeat and me. Speechless with a disgust that fairly shrilled, Whose side was I on? He stalked off without a word. Much more ominous than if he'd lobbed further sarcasm!

So whose side was I on? Food for thought while I leveled the mountain of programs, and then transferred actual food from kitchen to clubhouse for the players' pregame spread, and to the glorified pigeonhole of a press-box "lounge," in upper stadium reaches, for the media spread. In the meantime, had to admit that my career in baseball was in its final hours, one way or another, thanks to my stunt with Santangelo. Whether or not he made a spectacle of himself, and whether or not that weasel Perry blew the whistle on me. I'd chosen the side of Luddites and saboteurs, and knew full well I'd do it again as opportunity arose, till I ended up under arrest. Hard to believe that half an hour ago I wasn't the type to hide zombies in closets. Zack liked me and wanted to treat me right, but he'd thrown in his lot with one hell of a despicable status quo. How long could I stomach sticking around and betraying the trust of an otherwise totally nice guy?

The media reps were merrily gorging and guzzling as if in fulfillment of birthright, ignoring pregame ceremony on a crowded field of veterans, Boy Scouts, and marching band. And ignoring me as if I were a deadbeat too. I was in retreat from the lounge when Zack sauntered in, dammit. Endured the angst of tiptoeing on eggshells throughout our genial exchange.

"Still haven't heard about the money for that position yet," he greeted me.

Almost blurted, *That's good!* Thanked him instead for going to such effort on my behalf. Attempted shoring up my end of the conversation by stupidly admitting I'd no idea who tonight's opposing team was. Too scatterbrained to open one of the program books I'd been schlepping.

"From North Dakota." Zack wasn't perceptibly holding my ignorance against me. "The Bismarck Kaisers."

"Bismarck Kaisers? But there was never any Kaiser named—" Oh, great. Now I was coming off as didactic on top of ignorant. "Sorry. Never mind."

"That's good, kid. You're catching on." Through mammoth sliding window, Zack surveyed everyone belting out "Star-Spangled Banner," led by a sequined townie *American Idol* runner-up on the mound. "Don't sweat the stuff you can't do anything about. And for the record, you're right. Never any such Kaiser."

Beneath its cellophane veneer, Zack's advice was really more about working stiffs than misnomers. I groped for innocuous response to this laissez-faire pragmatism that I still found so hard to accept. Saved by the ringtone! In synchronized midturn and midreach, Zack hastily addressed me, "Why don't you hang around up here? I'll get back to you." He loped away, and his voice dwindled amidst broadcasters tromping to their sound booths, and reporters to their computer stations.

It wasn't my place to second-guess whether beleaguered Zack would forget me here or not. I dipped into the abandoned buffet, lugged a black-leather swivel chair to the window for an Olympian vantage of the game, and awaited further orders. Two innings along, I'd swear my ears popped. Depressurizing after ten nonstop hours. Listened with equal contentment to my own calm respiration, the p.a. announcer booming through stadium amps, and the radio play-by-play via wall-mounted Bose speaker. I'd achieved the zoned-out serenity that rewards staring into a fish tank too long. An immense fish tank, its back wall a quilt of billboards for donut shops and furniture outlets and car dealers.

At the top of the third, Buzzy, the most exotic specimen in the tank, made his customary trot around the bases, firing soft souvenir balls from an air cannon into the stands. Bulbous, garish black-and-yellow striped costume, with apparent tea strainers for bug eyes, must have afforded poor visibility even in noon sunshine, and the tamest breeze smacked at his big acetate wings. Hence on this blustery evening, before the floodlights shone from on high, Buzzy had every excuse to stumble. Just the same, when he did, was it a gust I heard or the gasp of many spectators? As if I weren't the only one suspecting zombie promotion to beloved mascot? Desecration! Management wouldn't dare! Or would it? Buzzy righted himself and barreled ahead, but some proof of a living drunkard inside the costume would have helped ease any onlooker tension.

The graveyard shift had otherwise been in and out of sight all along, without a whiff of controversy. Plodding from discreet shadows, mostly to collect windblown wrappers, or foul balls for which little kids no longer clamored at the railing as in bygone seasons. Buzzy capped his dash home with traditional bunny hop onto the plate and was halfway to the dugout, waving goodbye, when a nattily attired zombie advanced with unique deliberation toward the mound. As if to usurp it and give a speech. Holy crap, it was Santangelo! And on his hands, magenta gloves, for reasons that only began to make imperfect sense later. Neither radio nor stadium announcer was acknowledging this unseemly stray. Nor was the Kaisers' pitcher, bantering with the second baseman. Beneath them all, to mark anything as trivial as this dead man walking. What Denny intended to do I can't imagine. Moreover, if staffers were planning to corral him, their moment had already flown.

Maybe that third shot of juice had been one too many. As if an open palm had slammed into his right shoulder, and then his left, Santangelo whirled halfway around, recovered, and whirled again. He forced himself ahead once more. Stalled in midstep. People might have believed a plopper was due to bite the dust. Instead, he reeled on lock-kneed legs toward third base, then reversed course, arms straining forth and constantly raking the air, gloved hands clenching and unclenching. From distended jaws, a raw, frustrated keening carried all the way up to me, the most self-expression that "irreversible autolysis" must have allowed. The pufferfish venom, at triple dose, was badly losing ground against the juice's more tonic ingredients. Santangelo was bearing down on Buzzy, who defended himself by firing souvenir balls that bounced weakly off posh Brooks Brothers lapels. The p.a. announcer was at a loss for words, but the voice in the wall speaker prattled, "Seems to be a zombie acting up over by the Yellowjackets dugout. Either it's some kind of gag, or he's got a problem with Buzzy. Oh my God!"

Santangelo had furry yellow mascot head in a vice grip and was pulling. Buzzy dropped his weapon and desperately pulled back. The head snapped off and sent both parties staggering away from each other. People shrieked as if Denny had really decapitated someone. He landed sitting down and tossed mascot head in the air as he flailed around getting to his feet. Safe to bet that I alone here was feeling sorry for him. The man in the costume hit the sod rolling and crawled a little before he was up and scurrying erratically to the visitors' dugout. To judge by his footwork, if anyone still cared, Buzzy was a living, breathing drunkard after all.

The play-by-play announcer was positive he'd never seen anything like this in his life, and both teams, fidgeting on the diamond, could have ganged up and subdued Santangelo, but maybe ballplayers nowadays had a superstition about getting near or touching a dead guy. Ushers and security were closing in on Denny, and Zack, phone to his ear, was hustling onto the field, redfaced like I'd never seen him with stress and anger. The loudspeakers were spewing jittery entreaties for everyone to stay seated. The game would resume shortly! And then, as the floodlights automatically flashed on, the evening went from bad crazy to worse crazy.

As if heedful of a lighting cue, deadbeats came thrashing from their shadows under the stands, and in a turgid, halting current from the players' entrance, the maintenance entrance, the warehouse entrance. Their range of motion mimed Denny's St. Vitus's dance. The same murderous anguish, undercut by the same faulty muscle control. And putting me in mind of their shared inclination to moan along with ceiling lights. Had the juice retooled their brains to such similarity that they were subject to "sympathetic vibrations" under the right conditions, with nervous systems linked "psionically," to validate a term from Santangelo's vintage mind rot? Would they all react alike to certain stimuli inflicted on one of them? Had those extra hypos of juice really made death the "great equalizer"?

Denny's would-be captors, busy maintaining safe elbowroom, hadn't figured out how to stop him, and now they had to contend with some hundred deadbeats amok. I couldn't confirm whether zombies had penetrated the stands, because 10,000 attendees were jostling and shouting and jamming the stairs up to the exits, thanks in part perhaps to wholly unpersuasive repetitions of the loudspeaker message. I pitied the zombies engulfed in that panic. The play-by-play guy, meanwhile, was practically babbling, as if beholding the Hindenburg crash of his generation.

In any event, this game was over. Both teams had manfully gone for their bats, raring to spill some juice, as soon as the deadbeat host had mobilized. But out of the woodwork scampered geeks in suits, presumably the owners' reps, screaming bloody murder and herding everyone in uniform out through the service gate beyond right field. These players were valuable commodities. Some of them might make it into the majors. Nobody was paying them to put down zombie mutinies. That honor fell to patsies like us, earning our skimpy fraction of an athlete's salary.

Zack was barking by turns into the phone and at shaky staffers dodging zombie clutches. Groundskeeper Mike was distributing bats for holding the enemy at bay. This was manifestly the hour for all hands on deck, and for me to repay some of Zack's decency. Even if he had caved obligingly to the sordid reality at the root of this crisis. A crisis I had precipitated, sure, but bound to occur somewhere, sometime!

So how to circumvent the humanity clogging the exit routes? The mauling arms of zombies? It soon developed I needn't have asked. A deep breath, and I took the plunge, down the aisle, by closed doors of sound booths, by open doors of sportswriter cubicles. With every word flying out of here good news in a sense. How could this disaster not put the kibosh on robbing debtors' graves? There were no do-overs on live radio or live TV, assuming the local cable crew hadn't quailed and followed the players. And the coast-to-coast AP feed must have been crackling by now.

The aisle opened onto a dingy little anteroom. Uh-oh! The morning headlines may not have been such a solid bet. Four sweaty journalists were fogging up their glasses piling chairs on tables on receptionist's desk and file cabinet to barricade the door. Much higher than necessary to discourage a wave of spastic, disorganized moaners. I cleared my throat. They all whipped around horrorstruck, far from ready to tackle their worst fears. One of them smoothed down a comb-over and demanded, "How'd you get in here?"

"Don't they pay you to be observant? I've been here all along."

Enough of my pointless chitchat. "Give us a hand! We need to stack up more chairs," wheezed a bearded Hemingway impersonator in red Dacron turtleneck.

"What you need to do is take everything down so I can lend a hand out there."

"Over your dead body!" This from an angular, baggy-sleeved wreck cramming a potted palm into the defenses.

"If you're not going to do anything productive, like your jobs, then get out of my way. Zack needs me." My own pragmatic inner voice, however, sounded the warning, Let's not carry this to extremes.

A reporter resembling some rangy 1940s character actor who

played reporters brandished his phone. "I have him on speed dial. Let's see what he says."

I opened my mouth to protest that Zack had his hands full without answering nuisance calls, but what the hell. Let him get as sick of Zack's voicemail as he wanted.

Incredibly, he got through on the first try. "Hey, it's Pete up in the gallery. Someone here wants to come down and be heroic. What should I tell him?"

Zack, believe it or not, quit deploying people long enough to look in my general direction and wave me back and mouth, *Stay there!*

Pete pocketed the phone. "Okay. Satisfied?"

"No." I didn't feel I owed it to these hacks to be reasonable.

Two dull thuds and the scrape of square-headed fingernails on the other side of yellow steel door shut us both up. Nobody moved in the dumbstruck minute before a fist monotonously hammered and hammered and arbitrarily let up. Not exactly a concerted or ferocious surge. Had it even been the same zombie twice? In the following lull, out-of-sync sirens hovered at the edge of audibility. Of course Zack wanted me to stay here. Why endanger any of his people when the cavalry was charging in?

If sirens had impinged on press corps awareness, it didn't stop anyone from racing to cubicles, where I heard furniture for a bigger barricade bumping along the tiles. What I didn't hear was anything else at the door. I retreated to the lounge, grateful that semi-hysterical broadcast still gushed from the speaker.

Reseated myself on squeaky leather, leaned forward to study the view. As if I'd never left. Radio's "Voice of the Yellowjackets" may have been overwhelmed. Or just shamelessly milking the spectacle. As zombie rampages went, this was pretty mild. Whatever they latched onto satisfied their lust for destruction. One usher's carelessness let a deadbeat blindside her, and she was lucky to squirm free with only the loss of a cardigan, which he dismembered as fiercely as if it had been her. Another couple of zombies in a tug of war sundered Buzzy's shabbily stitched head, and others attacked discarded outfielders' mitts and the catcher's chest padding and the pails full of bubblegum next to the bullpen. A deadbeat did clamp someone by the shoulders and shook him furiously, or else the shaking was simply the upshot of spasmodic hands trying to clutch a victim, till two bruisers from Security rushed up from behind and sank bats into brittle postmortem skull. Someone else skipped backward from one zombie's zigzag charge, into the path of another, swinging wild, who slugged him in the temple. From what I saw, coworkers rescued casualties before they came to grievous harm. But where was Santangelo? The absence of magenta gloves from the mêlée made me ill at ease, for more reasons than I could name.

The stands impressed me as much dicier than the combat zone. Pissed-off, pained, frightened outcries of fans swamped any noise on the field. Clumps of people surged forward and dropped back, and sometimes one loss of balance radiated into many, to imitate the shape of a restless, lopsided zinnia. Fights were widespread, and I felt sick to glimpse people faint and vanish within the milling turmoil. To my huge relief, police and ambulance sirens soon swelled to a welcome din and plunged into jarring silence, as vehicles entered via same service gate through which players had evacuated.

Cops and EMTs must have stormed the stands from street entrance as well as field, because they were everywhere, fanning out and dividing the thousands into manageable groups, extracting the injured. On the grass, people who'd been roughed up were being treated on site or evacuated on stretchers. Cops whose helmets and Kevlar vests more strictly defined them as riot squad were forming a line. Zack and Mike were yelling at everyone alive in front of the line, parrying the fitful onslaught of deadbeats, to withdraw. The cops, conceivably at Zack's recommendation, had high-powered rifles and hoisted them the instant all civilians were behind them. They aimed at zombie knee level and fired in unison. The first echoes were almost as deafening as the shots themselves. Everyone in the stands stopped and stared. They were much more tractable from then on.

Most of the deadbeats had toppled, and the unscathed few fell to a second volley. Police tactics, I inferred, were to blast zombie feet out from under them so that any wild shots plowed into the dirt and not the public. The sportscaster was waxing ecstatic, as if brave servicemen had saved the world for democracy. Fallen zombies stubbornly flopped like hooked fish or pawed the air or crawled like defective windup toys. The cops pressed forward, and frayed nerves were writ plain in cagey body language. Marching up to each floundering deadbeat, they patiently pumped bullets till skulls shattered. As if these had never been anyone's fathers or brothers or husbands. The "Voice of the Yellowjackets" was rapturous at law and order's triumph, but I was sick at heart, and woefully sick to my stomach.

Each earsplitting gunshot made me flinch as I hurried back down the aisle, as if I had someplace to go where the sounds wouldn't reach me. The Fourth Estate was typing away at long last, as if they'd seen it all. I dismantled the barricade, shaking my head at how they'd mangled the poor potted palm, and after brief pause to indulge the afterthought of listening for zombies, yanked open the door. Just in time to grit my teeth at the stereo racket of rifle fire from fore and aft. Voted to linger till I could shout out my location at approaching search-and-destroy operations. Why be adventurous and find out the hard way how trigger-happy these galoots were?

The media spoke too soon about a miraculous lack of fatalities on Opening Night. Some hospitalizations were serious, mainly cardiac arrests and fractured bones, all among the stampeding attendees. But the single death at zombie hands went untallied almost twenty-four hours, when a sous-chef ran screaming from the depths of a walk-in freezer. Despite major soft-tissue damage and frostbite, the body stashed among frozen hams and chickens was recognizably Perry's, my secret nemesis, one of several no-shows at work that morning. Time of death was narrowed to the hours of deadbeat uprising. His remains yielded smears of rot retardant and juice-blackened scurf, which satisfied detectives that no mortal assailant had been involved. Besides, who had a grudge against Perry?

Magenta gloves held the answer to that. The gloves Santangelo might have worn in semi-coherent effort to hide fingerprints implicating him and me, in case it came out I'd known him. He understood better than anyone alive the eventual result, should Perry get me fired and I tailspin into debt. Death hadn't stopped Denny from looking out for me! So when he and his gloves disappeared from the diamond, had he been on the hunt for Perry? Or had he ambushed Perry earlier? And had the initial berserk from that third syringe receded, allowing him the clarity to flee before police swarmed in? Or had dumdum bullets blasted his brains all over canary-yellow wall? I needn't have dwelt on any of these questions. The truth came to me soon enough.

By way of some consolation, I was right about the upside of this disaster. All North American working stiffs were warehoused, doubtless under wretched conditions, God help them. Mealy-mouthed corporate attempts to shift blame for the debacle onto lax stadium security and crowd control only fueled the ire of a senator at the game whose son sustained busted arms and collarbone. The feds imposed a moratorium on the activation or transport of "postmortem labor," pending either government probe into why the zombies revolted, or titanic disbursements of campaign contributions. So in one respect, I brought down the whole abysmal zombie-labor apparatus single-handed. Not that I can ever take credit for it.

Meanwhile, I remain where the C.P. put me. I need the job, don't I? Even at the same place that exploited zombies before, and certainly will again, after vested interests sleaze their way around the present inconvenience. If I did resign on principle, Denny's sacrifice would go to waste. That's right, I do indeed refer to Denny and not Perry as the sacrificial lamb. One clause in the contract I've framed of how to live with myself. Along with refusing to feel bad about coworkers' and spectators' injuries on Opening Night. Not when I can indict the credit industry and drug manufacturers and corrupt congressmen and everyone else who let those zombies in the ball-park. As for loosing a killer deadbeat on the world? Not an issue.

Yesterday morning, I was out in front of my house, fiddling with recalcitrant lock to my untidy old Focus, in a dither at leaving late for work. In the driver's side window, a fingertip had scrawled an oddly oblique plea for me to wash the car. Or so I thought. At first, blamed a fastidious or merely wiseass neighbor. The wording gave me pause, though, as did the meticulous use of quotation marks and period at the end. Yes, I realized, this was a quotation, and I remembered from where, and had to sit stricken on the hood a while. Eclectic Santangelo had been a partisan of David Bowie as much as Henry James. And here, I intuited, was his fond farewell, and most troubling sign yet of deadbeat capabilities. "Let me collect dust."

From that classic anthem of disillusionment, "Panic in Detroit." Had to squint up and down the street, but knew I'd never see Denny again. And dammit, that tune has been stuck in my head ever since. As is the image of Santangelo waiting for the juice to wear off in some foreclosed bungalow equivalent of Arctic wasteland where Frankenstein's monster went to die.

Before heading off to work that morning, I dried my eyes and wiped the glass clean with the same handkerchief, just because I'd grown paranoid about people drawing improbable connections between me and my killer zombie friend. A hero with my résumé can't be too careful.

Way Up When

I was a like a lot of other little kids, I suppose, who got excited at planes up in the air and pointed till everyone else looked too, and that's how I discovered I wasn't like other little kids, with repercussions to this day. Nine times out of ten, family or strangers would crane their necks and uniformly grumble, "Plane? What plane? What are you talking about?"

Some assumed I was pulling their leg, and some that I had a screw loose, and this reputation for being a notch or two "off" haunted me through twelve grades of school, long after I'd learned to ignore everything aloft in blue yonder. But that was the kind of small town it was, petty-spirited and slow to let anything go. Or possibly the neural or ocular quirk at fault for aerial visions also made me "different" in ways apparent to all except myself. I did grasp, even as a child, that disapproving frowns from everyone were giving me a "complex." How could they not?

My parents ran me through a gauntlet of sawbones and shrinks, to no diagnostic effect. Child psychologists, at least, I could con in a couple of sessions by agreeing that airborne phantasms had been "just my imagination." But then Mom, in the process of housekeeping, infallibly found the hideyholes for new eyewitness drawings of a noteworthy biplane or flying fortress, and back on the medical carousel I'd go. I'd had it with self-expression at around age eleven.

A few samples of this artwork escaped maternal purge and remain in my custody. Amidst the creases and tears and grease stains, they're a testament to the wondrous antiquity that used to cross my sky. The planes I see these days are old, of course, but proportionally fewer are pre-jet era among afterimages of more recent history. In my youth, I took for granted glimpses bordering on the genesis of powered flight, rather as astronomers now regularly delve almost as far as genesis in general.

The honking taxis and rumbling trucks and blaring radios below my apartment window usually dwindle away when I contemplate the picayune details in otherwise *brut* renderings. The number of engines, the cut of wingtips, the flair of tail section, the stoutness of fuselage bespeak a need to nail down specifics, to prove, at least to myself, that I wasn't making anything up. In my corner were the TV matinees and schoolbooks with thrilling likenesses of the vintage bombers traversing my airspace, ample demonstration to me that I hadn't produced them out of whole cloth.

I may have seemed a budding planespotter, but my mind's eye was already spotting too many of the otherworldly variety. I instinctively shrank from more expansive interest in aviation as from proverbial slippery slope, thank God. Full-blown OCD had doubtless been lurking below.

I was precocious enough a preschooler to surmise that flying machines visible to myself alone weren't physically "there," yet surprisingly tardy catching on that normal planes made noise, whereas mine didn't, whatever their altitude. That first family junket to the airport, to fetch an uncle whose name I've misfiled, nearly threw me into a panic. Something had to be ungodly wrong for those airliners, huge or not, to be so bone-shaking loud! What were my folks thinking to drag me along when they knew planes were my whole problem? Three decades on, I still can't get used to the din of low flight paths.

The hectic marks of blue Bic on Manila sheets also convey anger, in equal parts righteous and impotent, at the skeptical, snickering world. The hell with everyone who couldn't see what I so plainly did, they fairly shrill. Besides, I had no other symptoms of clairvoyance or sensory disarray, had I? Annual checkups always concurred I was fine.

And if I'd been the victim of diseased imagination, shouldn't it have shaped more dramatic figments? All I beheld was routine air traffic going about its anachronistic business. No trails of black smoke, no flames engulfing propellers, no fighter aces spiraling earthward, no UFOs or even blimps, nothing catered to boyish extravagance. And what was I to make of brilliant sunlight reflecting off silver skin beneath unbroken overcast?

What's more, if I had owned binoculars or telescope, I might have clarified whether I was psychically attuned to ghosts of planes with ghastly postmortem passengers, like a horde of Flying Dutchmen, or else the past refracted into the present whenever I focused above a certain height. That riddle shadowed me into adulthood, and I occasionally gaze upon formations of green transports from the "Greatest Generation" and ponder, What year is it up there? But today, more than ever, I'm dead set against training any lenses on rows of minuscule portholes.

I had those drawings spread out on my kitchen table, and was happily deaf to the ruckus of Loisaida, when the phone rang and I answered, too spaced out, dammit, to consult caller ID box first.

"Hello?"

She started in without divulging her name, as if it should have been obvious. It wasn't, and I was a little miffed. The caller ID box came up with a vexing "PRIVATE." This was the worst time to fumble at guessing games. My love life reliably cycled through dry months of cold shoulders, until the heavens inexplicably opened and three or four relationships at once came knocking. That overdue season of plenty now loomed on my horizon. Of course, if the pattern held true, I'd blow it with every prospect while dithering over whom to pursue in earnest. So I was sore averse to messing up already over mere mistaken identity.

The queenly tone, the homey accent, resonated with teasing familiarity, stirring suspicions I'd been hijacked onto *This Is Your Life*. In wracking my brains to place who she was, I drifted far away from what she was saying.

"Dill? Are you listening?"

"Sorry. I was in the middle of something just now." Dill? That odious nickname took me back, and much further than I liked. It did bust up the logjam in my memory, but as always with her, a trice too late.

She sighed dolefully. "It's Donna. Remember me?"

Oh yes. Last of the hometown girlfriends. I was at one college, she at another, and weekends we reconnoitered on native turf. Did we spend one or two summers together?

I won't stoop to the vulgarity of demonizing the ex, so I'll simply recount that our courses diverged when she toyed with a stint in the Navy, and they fissured toward opposite poles when she transferred to business school. Till then, I could hedge that her tripwire temper and red-hot libido balanced each other out, were maybe twin tines on the tuning fork of her soul. But after she dumped me, the last of my ties to old stomping grounds snapped. I was free to admit that a decent future meant planting fresh roots where I had no history and where I'd never, ever acknowledge anything airborne.

The years have justified that stratagem, as well as my insight *ex post facto* that Donna was a better lover in my dreams, where selective nostalgia smoothes prickly surfaces. But here she was, demolishing the adage that you can't go home again. Making a clean getaway, for me at least, has always been the real problem. To whatever extent she wanted back in my life, it would have to raise hob with other burgeoning romances. Or hadn't I the wherewithal to be twice shy with volatile old flame?

Damn, I'd strayed out of earshot twice in as many minutes. Donna wasn't one to suffer airheads gladly. To my relief, she was still spouting prefatory chitchat. I didn't care what she'd been up to, but from guttural seat within my throat, reflex politeness occasionally went "Hmp!"

She changed gears with that most cringeworthy coinage, "Anyhoo, I'd like to offer you an opportunity." Holy crap, had she been reduced to telemarketing? "You can put that occult gift of yours to good use." I inwardly groaned. Why do infatuated kids have to tell each other everything? At eighteen, my rep for being "weird" had stuck with me, but where it came from had pretty much retired from local awareness. Donna had been blissfully ignorant about "occult gift" till I blabbed in the thrall of teen pillow talk.

"In fact, there's a major humanitarian dimension to this. Someone here needs to clear something up, and you're the only one who honestly can. You're his last resort." She was doing her traditional damnedest to wheedle commitment from me, short of spelling out a thing. Kind of how we got involved in the first place.

"I dunno, Donna."

"Look, you'd be doing me a favor, you'd be doing him a favor, and you'd be doing yourself a favor because he'll pay five thousand dollars cash." Her voice was rising microtonally, in concert with impatience heating up degree by degree, a slow burn at nascent stage of rubbing two dry sticks together. I should have been sorrier than I was to aggravate her. "A few details would be appreciated." That was bound to raise hackles. My sales resistance should have buckled at the mention of five grand.

"I'm only asking for one afternoon. How much does that come to per hour? I can't go into particulars. I promised."

"Who did you promise?"

"My boss, okay? And we're both taking a big chance on you. So give me a fucking break." Maybe I should have listened to her prefatory chitchat. It might have helped me read between the lines. "Here's what I am at liberty to discuss. You would come to Penn Station and meet me under the clock on Saturday at noon. I'll have our tickets and you'll be punctual because the train leaves at quarter past. We'll have a pleasant ride into the boonies for about an hour. He'll be waiting at our stop. It's a short walk from there. He says a walk is good for him at his age. Whatever you find out, he swears to let this be the end of it. You got all that?"

I tried for the verbal equivalent of a shrug. "Nothing to strain my humble faculties."

"Wonderful. See you Saturday." In the same breath, she alleged an urgent call was waiting on another line and signed off before I could inject a syllable. I gazed ruefully at my juvenile rendition of a Douglas DC-3 in green ink on looseleaf stock. Laughable foreshortening. It failed pathetically at making the urban racket go away. Funny, I went over my every word with Donna, and none sounded a bit like yes. Yet suddenly Saturday was booked solid. It felt like old times all right.

The next seventy-two hours allowed for plenty of vacillation. Should I stand former heartthrob up? Craven, yes, but arguably wise. Or chuck caution to the winds and almost certainly regret it? The same moral applied, regardless. Screen that ID box religiously from now on, especially if I decided to bail on Donna.

A home truth about myself also had ample chance to percolate from my subconscious. Intrusions from the past had made me what I was, and they hadn't finished meddling in my destiny. Ectoplasmic planes and ex-girlfriend were, in this respect, equivalent, to say nothing of inauspiciously linked. Or was everybody, even without ability to gawk into historic ozone, plagued by visitations from interfering yesteryears?

The answer might have been obvious to anyone else, but my freak talent disqualified me as a judge of ordinary human experience. Others may have been likewise resentful and resistant in the face of influence from long ago. I hadn't a clue, but when I woke up at 2 A.M. on Saturday, I was ready to admit I'd been kidding myself. I'd never seriously contemplated skipping out on Donna. Coming clean like that should have let me get to sleep again, but it didn't. The stubborn fog around my head all morning followed me out the door.

I indulged more soul-searching on the hike to Penn Station. Sundry and conflicting as my motives were for meeting up with Donna, none were admirable. That carrot of five grand in cash was patently bogus, though I'd kick myself forever if it had only fractional basis in fact. And maybe Donna was nursing vagrant cravings for a fling, arranging this whole jaunt just to reel me in. Well, I might be reconciled to such a consolation prize, unless the cruel interim had prematurely grayed and fattened her, as schadenfreude would have it. The more germane question of how she planned exploiting my "occult gift" hadn't even occurred to me.

The reality under the clock was more ambiguous and perturbing. I was a shade early, and maybe that's why she didn't perk up and notice me till a moment after I'd recognized her. Crass hopes of shaking hands with a dumpy, faded matron were fatally dashed. Her demeanor reeked of sexless professionalism, but matching red nylons, midthigh skirt, and snug jacket underscored how fluky time had been more than gracious to her trim physique, and her shimmery ginger hair was more distracting than ever. Color-coding alone ensured I'd spot her across crowded concourse. Was a fiendish portrait of her vicariously wasting away in padlocked bedroom closet?

Initially I figured she'd rigged up racy ensemble to encourage my cooperation, and I should have been more indignant at this appeal to base masculine nature, but what the hell. "You're looking more gorgeous than ever," I volunteered at first opening.

She ignored that. "Come on. We can't be late." She pushed

through the sluggish weekenders and I tagged behind, vaguely non-plussed at how she plowed through them like a ghost through masonry. The spectacle of midlife Donna bodily, behaviorally unchanged did shake me up, like an apparition on terra firma instead of at its proper elevation. Worse, she threatened to transform me back into my malleable, green collegiate self, a conjuration of dismal, buried identity.

The factoid used to crop up frequently that female libido didn't peak till forty-two, or was it forty-eight? Was that stat still on the books, and did it explain why Donna had glammed herself to the hilt, turning heads by the dozen en route to the platform? According to the same received wisdom, my libido had trended downhill since nineteen, the mental age toward which I was coincidentally regressing. Her chill deportment specified she hadn't dressed to kill for me, that much I had inferred.

We boarded with a while to spare, which was smart because the train soon filled completely and we'd have had to sit some rows apart. Or would that have been for the best? In the congestion, our knees and elbows came into prolonged contact, and I did nothing to separate them. Neither did she, raising mixed signals to a new plateau. I didn't try regaling her with autobiographic recap, and she didn't ask for one. She mostly read the *Wall Street Journal.*

I paid the scenery sporadic heed, mulling whether Long Island City and Merrick constituted Donna's idea of riding "into the boonies." Within this packed humanity, I also had to question how necessarily unique I was. Someone else in this very car might never realize half the aviation in his sky was extrasensory, provided no unlucky remark gave him away. A majority of passersby on the sidewalk, or of vehicles in traffic, might be ethereal, and who would be the wiser, since physical interactions are so rare? I've often mused that madmen aren't put away for harboring, but for expressing, whatever's on their minds.

Canned announcement sputtered about an impending stop at some posh enclave. Donna, with robotic precision, lowered her newspaper, let it flutter to the floor, and hustled me out as the train lurched to a humming standstill beside a whitewashed wooden awning of beaux-arts vintage. The scent of salt air refreshed me the instant I disembarked. Sad but true, the city generates too much odor of its own to smell of its proximity to the water, even at South Street Seaport.

And yes, I had to concede we were out in the sticks, though during my urbanite adulthood parts of Prospect Heights have come to seem rural. The number of trees here tipped me off, enough to screen out the surrounding terrain, and most were in seasonal orange and yellow. I'd forgotten trees changed in October, and the novelty of it was arresting.

A handful of yuppies had detrained as well, bolting directly for the parking lot out front. Inside the quaint station, redolent of varnish, an old gent laboriously quit his bench as we entered and listed slightly as if weathering low blood pressure. Donna's boss, I presumed. The two of them were equally lean, but he in a puckered, brittle way, set off by shiny, taut pink skin, the plausible upshot of multiple facelifts. White hair, as thick as mine, was slicked away from steep forehead. Somber black suit suggested a funeral on today's schedule. Puffy white neckerchief was fastened with diamond stickpin.

"How much has Donna told you?" he barked as she and I stepped within hailing range. A wobble in his tone implied unease had ratcheted up any customary bluster. What was that Jimmy Stewart line from *Philadelphia Story?* "With the rich, always a little patience"?

I assured him, "She hasn't told me a thing. Not even who you are."

"Good! Donna, you will please refrain from addressing me by name. We cannot afford to corrupt his impartiality now." Always delightful to be right there when somebody spoke of me in the third person. And patience was already at a premium, as I had to split it between him and Donna, who took no visible umbrage at moneyed rudeness. A discreet wince for my benefit would have been nice. "Incidentally, I have the Beamer just outside," he informed her. "Would you rather we drove?"

"I would not. You promised to do this, and I quote, 'on shank's mare.' You're not going back on your word, are you?" Donna was never a shrinking violet, but I had to suspect she'd missed her calling as a drill sergeant. The boss was remarkably sheepish in the teeth of reprimand, but Donna had that effect on people, as I was well aware. "Once you get started, you're always fine."

"Once I get started, I'm always fine," he echoed resignedly. Theirs was not a typical office dynamic, but at some visceral level I was leery of pursuing that. And once he got going, he did pick up a more surefooted pace. We crossed the tracks and traded sun for the shade of oak-and-maple canopy. Boss and employee strolled through colorful leaf litter, preceding me with a sense of direction aided by neither path nor signage. Was he immune to her charms? His conduct toward her was too dry and formal to be believable. Meanwhile she treated him to ongoing surveillance, but I couldn't decipher whether her profile was stern or solicitous.

The woodlot was suddenly behind us, with as clear-cut a border as if we'd stepped out from a waterfall. We waded into brassy knee-high grass blanketing low-slung ridges, at which point Donna forged on and her employer dropped behind to walk with me. His unease was simmering over, as if this more open space induced it to expand. "Did you have your dad around when you were growing up?" I detected mournful undertone, as if he hankered to unburden himself, to fish for sympathy.

"Yeah. Nights and weekends, after clocking out."

He could have asked me where my dad clocked out, but his interest only peripherally involved me. I reckoned deep down he was rattling skeletons in his own closet, hinting at some crisis in his youth. "Were you with him when he died?"

"He's alive. According to Mom, at any rate. I'll have to take her word for it till Thanksgiving."

My flippancy didn't win him over. "I worshipped mine. He was a great man. I was very young." He stalked ahead and rejoined Donna. Well, so what if I had alienated him? I hadn't taken that five grand seriously from the outset. Who would?

Gusts were picking up and riffling zigzags through the grass, depositing a cold, moist veneer upon my face. It could have been worse. Not every day I had ex-girlfriend and a millionaire for windscreens. On a hillock off to the left was the base of a squat round tower like a Norman keep or an oil tank with a brick foundation.

Maybe it had been a coastal fort. Then we were on top of a gentle bluff, overlooking desolate beach and the choppy sea.

"I'll do the talking from here," Donna told me. "It'll be too emotional for him, and he might say more than he should. Basically, the spotlight's on you."

Whatever this was about, it was also a sterling example of going out of the way, literally, to get in good with the boss, never mind the exact bounds of their relationship. She was welcome to give it 110% as she pleased, but I was beginning to shiver in my sweatshirt. Would she really have betrayed any vow of secrecy by advising I dress in layers? Afternoon sun was deplorably feeble. "Okay, don't tell me why I'm freezing in the middle of nowhere. Could you be kind enough at least to estimate how long we'll be courting hypothermia?"

"You're in your prime!" scolded cranky tycoon. "You have a good hardy circulation. I've stood here on this date every year without exception since I was a boy, under much more inclement conditions."

Donna pursed her lips and eyed him reproachfully. His frown hardened, and he aimed it skyward.

She regarded me yet more severely. "You're going to complain about a little fresh air? At how much per hour?" She consulted gold Rolex. "You and your goosebumps just sit tight a minute." Then she arched a catty eyebrow. "I can say this, without tainting your objectivity. The flight path and its timing are a matter of record. He simply wants to know what happened. He's hired psychics and ghost hunters, and they 'spewed a lot of hooey,' in his words. They felt 'vibrations,' 'impressions,' 'residue,' nothing to rule out they weren't humoring him for a hefty fee, no explicit nouns and verbs. You, on the other hand, aren't the type to humor people, are you?"

I essayed a mordant grin, and a metallic flash above the brick ruin drew my attention. A hornet-yellow two-seater was on a leisurely ascent, soaring overhead en route to the Atlantic. Its engine was dead silent. I probably could have pegged it at much greater speed and altitude as a prewar Piper Cub because thousands had flooded the market. "The Model T of aircraft," aviation buffs dubbed them. I glanced at Donna's boss, still riveted on the same pinpoint of blue. She, more shrewdly, was studying me.

The plane climbed steadily beyond the tideline, beyond the shallows. The hunch that something bad was due to happen set my stomach churning. I resolved to play it cool, more to prop up my dignity than for any noble reason. The sunshine of a previous century dimmed rapidly from the Piper's nose to tail, perhaps the shadow of bygone oncoming cloud. The wings in silhouette became a giant emery board, a tongue depressor. They jiggled, they seesawed a few degrees. Turbulence? Stalling out? Aerial dumb show didn't allow for such distinctions.

I blinked, and then the Piper's forward thrust was stayed a second, as if a glass wall had magically materialized and disappeared on impact. A mute explosion consumed the propeller, the hull split lengthwise into a jagged fleur-de-lys, and the wings flipped away as a unit in yet more striking imitation of an emery board. From the shattered eggshell of a cockpit cartwheeled two flapping bodies, one in jodhpurs, one in knee-length skirt. I was dumbstruck and transfixed, which I counted as a blessing. What would I have bleated, what would I have pantomimed otherwise? Still, I wish I could have neutralized the spell that made me follow the trajectories of spinning wreckage and flailing victims till they vaporized in quick succession at that height where history blanked out again.

I regained the power to lower my eyes when nothing remained to be seen. Had the pilot cruised into a flock of geese? A freak of atmospheric pressure? A thunderbolt? Some agency more obscure, short of voodoo? Was it sabotage? And shouldn't debris or corpses have cast up on the tide or been recovered by the Coast Guard, since the incident had occurred so close to shore? But if they had, I wouldn't be here today, would I?

Donna too had been staring skyward, as if trying to borrow my vision. Our lines of sight collided and locked. "Well?" she demanded. Grim oligarch left off squinting into the void at last and scrutinized each of us with a pitiful, clueless intensity. His black funereal outfit impressed me now as morbidly appropriate.

I gravely shook my head. I'd perceived nothing but the Piper and its ejected contents. Planes were all I ever envisioned, and never their surroundings. I had no enlightenment to offer, nothing to convince them I'd witnessed anything "explicit." To claim a Piper was involved would have been a facile educated guess, to reinstate those comparisons with the Model T. And I couldn't bring myself to verbalize the pointless horror that in itself explained none of the circumstances, promoted no reconciliation with tragic loss. I might have been quicker on the uptake if I hadn't been awake since 2 A.M. Hollow consolation as it was, thank God initial efforts to borrow binoculars for this excursion had fallen through, even had they settled whether I were seeing temporal refractions or "spirits of the air."

If my face reflected how I felt, it must have been alarmingly ashen. My audience evidently didn't notice. Too absorbed in personal priorities.

The desperate old cuss, for lack of "closure," had been hurting maybe twice as long as I'd been alive, and I would have empathized, had he not blown up at me as if I were a valet who'd scratched his precious Beamer's paint. "Don't you dare bullshit me! Was he alone? Did he run into trouble? Was he making for Bermuda?" An overhand mock pitch broadly indicated southerly route.

"I didn't see anything either." Decent of Donna to back me up, but how could she have seen anything? The boss, however, was too distraught to think that through, and her timbre of authority persuaded him to rein himself in. Rancor was cooling into disappointment. "Any paranormal activity would have been and gone already. You have to be satisfied with that, and you have to honor your part of the deal. The past has consumed enough of your energy. Get on with the present while you have some 'wind in your sails,' as you like to put it. Right?"

He nodded drearily. She touched his elbow and steered him toward the swath of trees, the suave gesture of an undertaker at the end of calling hours. None of us opened our mouths to mar solemn trudge away from the hermetically black unknown. My lingering sensation since noon of reverting to mental age nineteen had seesawed toward feeling decrepit decades in advance.

At the depot I sat by the clattering baseboard heater to thaw my feet while he and she conferred out of earshot. Scratchy PA squawked about the momentary arrival of a citybound train. Donna moseyed over to me. Her employer moped with hands in pockets, features alternating between dejection and petulance. "I'll ride with you. I have business to attend to in town. He needs some time alone out here. He doesn't have far to drive."

"He lives this near to where we were? Is that healthy?"

Donna glanced sidelong at the boss. He was glowering at a fly in the front window, and stone deaf to us.

"He has a cottage up in Newport, but the one down here is bigger." Her diction was as flat as a steel "No Trespassing" sign. Fair to conclude she'd rather I not poke into his emotional well-being.

A piercing whistle down the line warned us to get ready. He didn't see her traipse over and was startled when she hugged him. Another terse, hushed exchange ensued. "I'll take care of it," she promised in parting. "Rest yourself and practice that meditation for clearing your head." He turned and strode out the door as if strongly disinclined to do any such thing.

For chrissakes, were they married? Doubtful I'd have received straight answer about that, or about her livelihood, insofar as it was somehow tied in with their relationship. She was probably glad I hadn't pressed for details over the phone when she'd gabbed about herself in what must have been deceptively veiled terms.

She trotted me out to the platform. No one else boarded, and we sat across from each other, in no danger of physical contact for the duration. She forked over an envelope from somewhere on her person. It briefly retained her body heat. "It's in thousands. The government quit printing them before we were born, but they're still legal tender. If you can muster the patience to shop around, collectors pay more than face value for them." I said thanks, folded the envelope in three without peeking inside, and wedged it in left hip pocket. The more she let slip about the old curmudgeon, the more his five grand came to resemble chump change.

"Can you trust your boss to keep his word?"

"He'd better."

"Or else what?"

Her brow furrowed with disdain at my shamelessly leading question, and when that didn't make me fidget, she countered, "Do you think you were worth it?"

I shrugged. "Don't you? You act like you want to protect him. A person of average resources couldn't afford to spring for mediums and clairvoyants throughout his adult life, not at five thousand a pop anyway. I've been a great investment when you consider the money he won't be spending on charlatans anymore, assuming he doesn't backslide." I'd also spared him the horrific details of his dad's demise, which would have been anything but conducive to his peace of mind, and where were my thanks for that? "But money never improves a person's judgment, does it?"

My verbiage metaphorically beaded up and rolled off her lovely back. "What's on your plate after this?" She was referring to my bigger picture, wasn't she, and not angling for a night out?

"I'm resuming my normal life."

"Except you're not really normal, are you?"

"To the world at large, outside of you and the dump we grew up in, yes, I am. I just have to avoid people and situations that convert me back into a maladjusted little kid. Millions of others have a much worse time passing for normal. If my normality is an illusion that I can sustain indefinitely and it makes me reasonably content, I'd say I'm one of the lucky ones."

None of that rated any comment. "I'm glad you handled him as you did," she finally professed, "and pretended to see nothing." Now it was my brow's turn to furrow. Was she simply a keen reader of unconscious nuances, or did she have the same damn ability I did, plus the superior intellect to hide it successfully? In which case, she'd hardly have let me in on it at this casual juncture. Or had she done so not only now but earlier on the grassy bluff, when she'd chimed in, "I didn't see anything either?"

Then out of the blue, mercurial ex-lover asked, "Do you want to go out for coffee sometime?"

"Sure, why not?" The words popped out unbidden. Could be I was crazier than I realized. A masochistic blunder on the face of it, even had I been blind to that murky liaison between her and crotchety millionaire. Or was five thousand dollars the kind of money that instantly impaired my judgment, however trifling a sum it had become to Donna? I homed in on her hazel eyes and told myself I had a rationale for dating her, a mystery to unravel. Did she or did she not see what I saw?

The train veered, and she used that excuse to avert her head and concentrate too hard on the increasingly suburban scenery. She said no more for the rest of the ride. I tried and failed to snooze away some of last night's sleep deficit and any of this afternoon's early-onset decrepitude.

In the terminal she repeated her invitation to get together and sprinted off after a hurried handshake, without giving me her card. Typical! People, beneath their visible selves, are really as unchanging as the past, aren't they? Nor should I be one to talk, as recent days are bearing out.

How naive to dream I had long-term prospects here. And Donna, once more, has driven my decision to pull up stakes, god-damn her. Recurrent nightmares of aviators thrashing in midair will pass, and those I can wait out. But they've put me in mind of all the aeronautic disasters, infamous and otherwise, plaguing Gotham's sky-line. Downtown, Queens, Midtown, Park Slope, no compass point is safe, and those are the few crashes I recall offhand. I can't keep beating the odds, and I can feel the "complex" I had at age ten creeping over me again.

If Donna's like me, then how does she cope? That's something else to ask her if I can make it long enough. I was nearly run over twice this week crossing 23rd and First, because I wouldn't look east toward open sky, just in case a phantom plane was going down. I should have packed up already, but I'm kind of waiting for her to phone.

The Comeuppance Hour

Personal Log, Jasper Kent, Director of ECTO, August 30

What a coup! The ex-governor's McMansion. Just the kind of high-profile haunting the ECTO Files can use right now. A lavish change from suburban bungalows, grubby taverns, seedy theatres, derelict hospitals, i.e., run-of-the-mill locales for the East Coast Traveling Occultists, and for our basic-cable copycats. We hold our own, but coasting's not a sustainable option. About time we upped the ante on Wraith Quest, Spectre Catchers, and their upstart ilk.

The state's former First Lady contacted us via voicemail. Our most flustered call-in ever, which is saying something. Beleaguered to the point her prep-school enunciation backslid into the dropped R's and nasal diphthongs of her native zip code. She's no trouper, I concluded, blaming her lack of starch on life too long at the top.

A recent "Homes" section of the Sunday paper featured the Filberts' palatial digs, and I couldn't fathom how any ghost could be scarier than the place itself. And this on the basis of a cursory rotogravure tour. In the lead photo was an antebellum plantation portico, too shallow, for all its height and width, to fit a porch swing. It fronted a hulking chaos of dormers, like a cluster of pointy toadstools, with random punctuations in shingled walls by Palladian windows, oriels, balconies, and stained-glass portholes.

The inexplicable choice of indoor views included a clinically white billiards room whose dimensions dwarfed the table, where colliding balls must have echoed something awful. And as if to prove the premises were habitable, the photographer had posed ex-gov Abe and the missus on the cushioned edge of a bay window seat that could sleep four. Their smiles had all the warmth and spontaneity of skillful taxidermy, and in that setting I couldn't picture myself doing any better.

Mrs. Filbert's message was curiously sketchy on supernatural details. To paraphrase her desperation, "He refuses to go away and shows us no respect!" She might as easily have been jabbering about the trespasses of a drunk or a drifter. But could I care less how vaguely she described phantom tribulations? Nothing trumps location, location, location, not when the series is gasping for fresh air from whatever quarter.

Personal Log, Jasper Kent, Director of ECTO, September 3

I inveigled my producers at Shock Horror Channel into bumping Nightmare McMansion to the top of our shooting schedule. Mrs. Filbert seems skittish enough to seek parapsychological help elsewhere if we lag, and I've been increasingly anxious to get this over with. Some people, it seems, can't have the autocracy scared out of them.

Latina housekeeper answered my callback and handed me off to prospective client who, going by her tone, mistook me for one of the servants. No, she dictated, we were not to conduct preliminary interviews and inspections. On our show, or so she insisted, we never imposed on people for more than one night. Come in, don't break anything, evaluate the problem and get rid of it. I declined to inform her we didn't do exorcisms. The contract would spell that out if she bothered reading it. In a closing bid at sounding her out, I remarked on the rarity of hauntings in brand-new houses. What, offhand, did she suppose was going on? "It's your job to tell us, I'm sure," she archly reminded me.

My research was no more helpful. A cornfield. That's what used to be where the house and the rest of its subdivision are now. No previous buildings, no Yankee or Native American graveyards, no battle, massacre, or other traumatic event ever marked the site. The apparition had, contrary to the usual sense, arisen out of thin air. I'd only thought I loved a mystery. I evidently hated them when they occurred in grossly unsympathetic locations.

The possible skeleton in Abe Filbert's closet, however, had to be less obscure than he'd wished. As governor he'd thrown his conservative weight around to have a suburban homeless shelter demolished, on the pretext that State Police needed the land for new barracks. And then, surprise! The barracks never went up because of a budget shortfall. The shelter was either torn down for no reason, or because the governor thought the unsightly poor would simply go away if he destroyed their habitats. Stubborn rumor had it, though, that one sick, if not delirious, resident didn't feel like vacating and hid himself too cleverly for his own good. He was allegedly in the cellar when the edifice pancaked on top of him. The story was neither denied nor verified officially, and scandal simmered but never erupted because loyal media outlets buried it.

Meanwhile, coming home from ECTO HQ becomes a little less appealing every night. When I installed the ground-floor tenant, he was an integral part of my economy. Not so, since the show took off, and he's had some pretty unsavory characters in and out at odd hours. Hoods, in passé usage. I'd be less worried if they blasted the stereo or laughed too loud sometimes. Instead, they're quiet as bacteria, except when their slamming car doors alert me to arrivals and departures. And initially he'd come across as so frail and soft-spoken. Practically diaphanous, like a ghost with a lease. Guess he had me snowed.

Personal Log, Jasper Kent, Director of ECTO, September 9

I'd have sworn the ex-governor was sporting a toupée. Silver-gray, though? Why not a more vain and youthful black or brown? Was it an off-target stab at "looking distinguished" or "aging gracefully"? He pretended bonhomie to the extent of joking he'd have retired to Florida had he known what this place was going to pull on him. Otherwise, while we were futzing with cables and instruments and remote sensors and such, he and she hovered, in ongoing dither lest we gouged the wallpaper or poked holes in the carpet or scratched the furniture or worse.

The first floor was conspicuously free of art on the walls and knickknacks on tables and shelves, but was that in the wake of poltergeist aggro, or had they been removed in case we were clumsy oafs? I asked, and Abe equivocated like a politician. "We've only been here a few months. Don't worry about it."

Generally our clients were more forthcoming, but Abe had consented only grudgingly to the standard pre-vigil on-camera chat. He had no problem discussing the number of bedrooms, square feet of living space, or provenance of the marble on kitchen countertops. As for otherworldly activity? Well, it was prone to commence in the basement, in the billiards room actually, and work its way up. When pressed for details, however, he volunteered no more than, "Oh, you won't miss it when it happens."

They were adamant about staying the night in their own beds rather than letting Shock Horror Channel treat them to a suite at the Biltmore. And based on their attitude toward us, I gathered they were expecting a restful night because we were there to draw supernatural fire, if to no better purpose. We were, in effect, fresh meat, and accordingly didn't rate concern, hospitality, a pot of coffee, or even a glass of water.

The Filberts withdrew upstairs, and the theme from *Jeopardy*, faint and tinny, wafted down to us. I sent Jake the intern with four thermoses to the nearest strip mall Dunkin' Donuts for a gallon of French roast and thirty crullers. I've learned to keep refreshment orders simple.

In the dining room, Ed and Stacey were making the most of technical college degrees by manning the recording and analytic gizmos of our impromptu nerve center, with pickups for ion counters and motion detectors and digital thermometers all over the house. My on-again, off-again Evie and I stationed ourselves on a couch in the cavernous billiards hall, while junior partners Kelly and Cheryl monitored the kitchen. Everyone carried a camcorder, and the producers assigned us a roving cameraman. I often suspect our spooky encounters never live up to informants' dramatic anecdotes because eight strangers overrunning the premises intimidate most spirits into laying low. Then again, sometimes the weight of our experience lulls the best of us into naive complacency.

Evie calls it quits with me every three or four months, and my heart never breaks when she does, but afterward we can't keep our hands off each other. What can I say? I'm a sucker for black nail polish and Olive Oyl legs. Haven't a clue why she's attracted to me. Sometimes these all-night stakeouts end up as make-out sessions in a strange, dark room when the cameraman roams elsewhere, and history was repeating itself *chez* the Filberts.

If ever we dropped our guard and sneak footage of us surfaced on YouTube, I'm just close enough to celebrity for that to scuttle my career. Luckily, the producers had sent a man of honor who clumped down the basement stairs and cleared his throat at the doorway, homing in on us with the infrared.

"You know, our masters in LA won't be happy if tonight's a dud," he greeted us, "after they had to reshuffle a bunch of personnel. Maybe you could, I dunno, get up and try riling an eerie presence into clanking chains or something?" Well, if he had been spying on us a while, he could have been ruder about rubbing our noses in it.

Evie slipped into her ankle boots, languidly stretched her limbs, and adjusted horn-rim glasses as if shifting into studious mode. I was already on my feet, striving, paradoxically, not to act self-conscious. Clanking chains, indeed. "This is your first tour of duty with us, right? Bear in mind, there's a warm-up period when you get the feel of the place, and vice versa," I extemporized. "But let's go for it right now, if you're so eager."

Studio hireling shrugged and checked the batteries and finessed the viewfinder. "Say when." Whether I liked it or not, he was correct. Supernatural phenomena were often in need of a kick-start. Was I jaded? And was that the equivalent of a backdoor, unhealthy skepticism, some hundred investigations along? I nodded toward blinking red diode and dim body behind it. "Let's get this show on the road."

Evie and I reflexively assumed the position of wary scouts in dangerous borderlands. I addressed empty air with stock rhetoric. No great expectations. The technology on my utility belt confirmed the absence of cold spots or magnetic flux. "Hello? Whoever you are, maybe you're confused or angry or afraid. We want to help you. We're not here to harm you." As if we could. "Can you hear us? Mister and Mrs. Filbert say you're making them miserable. What did they ever do to you?"

The murky atmosphere changed, as if someone were blowing a dog whistle extra hard. This was a new one on me, paranormally speaking. Or was it only a vagary of the Filberts' security system?

Evie and I hoisted our camcorders like elaborate monocles, our instincts resorting in sync to night vision. Some digital-age equivalent
to "the pricking of my thumbs" was in charge.

Our three infrared lenses swung in tandem toward a flicker of
motion. I renounced my budding skepticism, backdoor or otherwise.
The balls in casual disarray on the table were bouncing in tandem, a
tentative inch or two at first, without even making one another
quiver on the green felt. I can report this in such detail because I've
studied the videos pretty much nonstop ever since.

The balls soon no longer bounced in place but upon impact
leapfrogged toward the edge of the table nearest us. As the balls
hopped over the rail and fell to the polyester carpet, they rebounded
with alarming force and were swatted as if with a silent tennis racket
to slam into the wall behind us. Crack! If they weren't aimed unerringly at us, they weren't meant to miss, either. And the acoustics in
here did make them echo something awful. Small comfort that none
of our fragile remote mics and sensors were set up between the table
and the wall.

Our craven feet were backing us out of there. Volition had no
part in it. If the lucky shot that nicked my elbow and made me see
white had connected with my other arm, we'd have had a third less
footage. The camcorder would have dropped, and I'd have turned
tail. That's how close to panic I came.

As it was, our hectic logjam in the doorway could have been
lifted from the Three Stooges, and while we pounded up the stairs
to the accompaniment of balls walloping plaster, I wondered about
Ed and Stacey in the lamp-lit parlor. Probably elated at the wild
readings on their instruments, the sorts of electromagnetic spikes and
raw material for electronic voice phenomena that often functioned
as the centerpieces of an episode. Not tonight, though!

A minute later, and they too realized this. Here was a level of
manifestation, open-and-shut, over-the-top, whose likes we'd never
seen, didn't dare dream of, had given up on, in fact. And it had followed us into the den, where Ed and Stacey, already agog at their
meters and readouts, were, well, more agog as we burst in, and before I could get a word in, the "eerie presence" was swiping cups of
coffee pinwheeling away from workstations, launching thermoses

into the ceiling, and hurling crullers around the room like a spray of torpedoes.

Professional reflexes kicked in, thank God, and we all filmed some respectable snippets of ghostly tantrum till I ordered strategic retreat for the sake of our expensive technology. We people, and not movable objects, were the center of baleful attention, I figured, and rightly so, because apparent poltergeist chased us into the kitchen.

No hyperactive needles on gauges had warned newbies Cheryl and Kelly of oncoming incorporeal shitstorm. They were sitting on barstools under the skylight, facing each other across the granite surface of freestanding island. Uneasy amidst the horse latitudes of their conversation.

To my disappointment, they'd left their camcorders halfway across the room, on marble countertop beside the stove, and no sooner had their boggling eyes met mine than their gear joined the whirlwind. Hence they couldn't augment our documentation of plates and ladles and saucers and tumblers and trivets and mugs and spatulas leaping from cupboards and hooks and drying rack to ricochet off terrazzo floor and walnut paneling and assume new flight paths with no loss of energy.

While trying to film projectiles even as I dodged them, I had the marginal wherewithal to note that everything airborne was plastic and nothing was pointy. The Filberts may have learned the hard way to store everything sharp out of spectral sight. And on the upside, Kelly and Cheryl had never unlocked the steel valises for their video recorders, so those might not be reduced to smithereens if our bogie desisted in the short term.

The seven of us in throes of evasive maneuvers were as apt to suffer a concussion from one another as from the projectiles assailing us. Just as well Jake the intern wasn't here, but where the hell was he? Anyway, present conditions were unsustainable. I racked my brains for some means to assert leadership, to modify this no-win game. My previous try at conversing beyond the mortal veil had incited this chaos. Even if further verbiage didn't restore calm, inaction was definitely not an option. I posed the only question that occurred to me. "Are you the homeless guy who blames his death on the Filberts?"

My ears registered a shift in atmosphere again, a modulation of the dog whistle. Utensils and dishware and camera cases dropped limply, one by one, from their last points of collision. Simultaneously, a scrawl spanning cabinet doors and wall space grew visible in the gloom, like a photo in the developing vat. Crude letters of ectoplasmic ink glistened, and Mrs. Filbert's complaints of "disrespect" became clear as I read "FUCKIN ASSHOLES," "ROT IN HELL," and "SUCK ME."

I had been all set to pat myself on the back for quieting the tempest, but these were not sentiments that boded well. They did at least reinforce my impression of whom we were dealing with. I found a dimmer toggle by the fridge and flipped on the track lighting, which made the blue language wink out. The hell with protocol about conducting research in the dark. Didn't we deserve to see whatever was coming next, given the past five minutes? A little wattage wasn't likely to deter this unforgiving presence.

My next executive decision was also a no-brainer. Muffled shouts and screeches reached us from the second story. I led the charge up the elegant curving staircase, preceded by our flashlight beams. No time to search for the switch controlling the massive chandelier. And there was Jake the intern, ear to the bedroom door, stricken eyes incognizant of us till we were right on top of him. When our flashlights shone in his face, he didn't even blink, like a deer in oncoming traffic.

I nearly fired him on the spot for blatant voyeurism, but the noise was too distracting. The banging and squeals and crashes and hoarse protests added up to the classic soundtrack of poltergeist infestation, with the implicit biting and pinches and bruises and hair-pulling. My big chance to confirm if Abe wore a toupée, I uncharitably mused.

Higher impulses prevailed. "Mister and Mrs. Filbert!" I hollered. "Can we come in? We want to help you!"

"No! Nothing you can do! Go away!" the ex-governor squalled, with a peculiarly self-conscious, plaintive inflection. Perhaps like the howl of a flagellant. Or of a monumental ego bereft of wig. But where to go? The supernatural action was no place but here, and here it would eventually exhaust itself, I conjectured. As agents of ECTO, we belonged nowhere else. Back to the needles and LEDs of our nerve center? That would be worse than anticlimactic. So we stood around haplessly as the scourging continued, our faces pallid and ghoulish-looking above our flashlight beams angled toward the floor.

Jake motioned me aside. "I was checking the guestroom for cold spots and magnetic spikes when I heard laughing in the bedroom."

I was sorry, but Jake's expansive toothy grin always made him resemble a weasel. I also had to entertain the premise that Jake was "checking for cold spots" by napping on the spare bed.

"I couldn't figure out what could be so hilarious under the circumstances, especially with all the racket and yelling from downstairs. Well, who wouldn't try to listen in? And you know what the old dude was saying?" He shifted into a patrician baritone. "'Actually it is funny when it's happening to someone else.' And she said, 'Serves them right. Pushy little pipsqueaks.' And he said, 'You get what you pay for, and we're paying them nothing. Hope for the best, but we may have to put this house back on the market.' I thought you would be interested in hearing where we stood with them. And then I thought their ceiling had caved in, except the ruckus just kept on going, and that's when you showed up."

He was smirking as if I ought to award him a gold star. Instead, I nodded thoughtfully and suppressed resurgent urge to can him. Wouldn't be sporting. I wasn't an ingrate. Maybe let his next infraction be his last. And anyway, the maelstrom in the bedroom was dying down. Executive decisions were incumbent on me once more.

The Filberts probably wouldn't be overjoyed to find us eavesdropping on them. I aimed my light down the staircase. "Okay, let's call it a night." We tiptoed off to pack up and decamp. Switched on lamps at will, as we no longer had reason not to. Ordinarily investigations lasted till dawn, but we'd already hit the jackpot. I was betting we could milk two episodes out of this material.

With some misgivings, I wrote the Filberts a note on my Shock Horror Channel scratchpad and left it on the shiny black kitchen table, using plastic mug from the floor as a paperweight. It stated I'd phone to set a date when the team could return and discuss its data, the "reveal" as it's known in the trade. Not a rendezvous I was looking forward to.

As a parting courtesy, I skipped back up to boudoir door and cleared my throat. "Mister and Mrs. Filbert? We have what we came for. We'll be going now." No answer, but I discerned creaking mattress and peevish whispering, and exited with a clean conscience. They were in good enough shape to be furtive.

We were a subdued crew in the van back to ECTO HQ. Our evening's results should have made us proud, excited, euphoric. Whatever a ghost was supposed to be, we had proof at least that it was for real. Take that, scoffers and detractors. Yet shellshock had the better of me, and I didn't seem to be alone. Extra glad I hadn't pinkslipped Jake, now our most competent chauffeur by virtue of resilient youth.

My teammates may also have been brooding on the human misery beneath psychic pyrotechnics, on the harsh, curtailed life of a homeless person who refused to take his unmourned death lying down. Never mind that the death had occurred two counties away.

Still, tonight's stress and havoc in the McMansion were preferable to sitting around at home, pondering what the cagey downstairs tenant was up to with his hoodlum friends, and why he was late with the rent.

Personal Log, Jasper Kent, Director of ECTO, September 12

Customarily the clients thank us for allaying or confirming their worst suspicions. Of course, the Filberts "suspected" they were haunted to the same degree they "suspected" the Earth was round. And they may have been upset at finally reading the contract that limited our role to documentation and analysis, and not exorcism. But did that entitle them to sulk? Had they ever really watched the *ECTO Files* or just drowsed through it?

The fine print also authorized us to shoot a "reveal" in their home. Bedraggled housekeeper let us in and showed us to the kitchen. Our clients shambled in a while after we'd set up. Ed the technician, Evie, and I sat along one side of the shiny black table. Abe and the missus leaned against their posh marble counter, declining to sit with us. As if they'd become new converts to passive resistance. At his end of the table, Ed had the laptop and speakers to display highlights of the other night's occult exertions and voice phenomena. The Shock Horror camera guy was out past the opposite end of the table to fit both the Filberts and us in frame.

The producers had also dispatched a second camera operator for additional coverage and a gaffer to rig lighting on this interior day shoot. Mrs. Filbert took predictable umbrage at two new strangers barging in, but the ex-governor gave her a scowl that must have signaled, *Let's get this over with, please.* Amen to that, Abe.

The camera crew cued me to commence. I mustered my sunniest hypocrisy in uphill battle to offset the pained intolerance of our hosts. "Right off the bat, I wish to thank Governor and Mrs. Abraham Filbert for the most momentous experience of our careers." No reaction. No more than if Madame Tussaud had replaced them with lookalike dummies. "They didn't need us to tell them their gorgeous new home was haunted, yet they invited us to study the disturbances and share our findings with the world."

I built up my blather in the best pitchman's tradition, harping on the importance of our research here, on the first indisputable record of an Invisible World impinging on this one, of how the scientific and occult communities both had to wake up and take notice at this earthquake of a paradigm shift. "And even though Governor and Mrs. Filbert can rightly claim to have seen it all, I'd lay odds they haven't heard it all, not by a long shot."

Our laconic hosts still weren't having any. Maybe they'd seem camera-shy rather than disdainful on the small screen. I, meanwhile, was well aware of the slippery slope down which my spiel was headed, but had no will to pump the brakes. Didn't even faze me that Abe was manifestly the type to shoot messengers. I'd never proxied for the hand of justice before, and the gravity of that role must have pressed me onward.

I had Ed at the computer run snippets of ricocheting billiard balls and airborne kitchen utensils. The former First Couple merely renewed their waxen scrutiny of the floor. "As this footage shows," I narrated, "we got a fleeting taste of what you've been up against every night, and to look at you now, I have to say your fortitude is amazing." I used to think there was virtue in feigning deafness to praise. That deafness was about to be sorely challenged.

"All right, Ed, why don't we pull up the audio data?" Intrepid Ed was a step ahead of me. I keep meaning test him for ESP. "By boosting, filtering, and otherwise enhancing what we recorded with microphones planted all over your home, Ed has discovered some truly astounding electronic voice phenomena, or EVPs for short," I explained to the wooden Filberts. "In terms of both quantity and clarity, these are unprecedented. For instance, here's what we captured down in your billiards room, while the balls were hurtling around."

Ed hit Enter, and I examined our clients' faces for flashes of insight, twinges of guilt. Playback proceeded from my off-the-cuff plea, "Mister and Mrs. Filbert say you're making them miserable. What did they ever do to you?"

A veritable torrent of invective gushed forth. "Fuckin' assholes killed me rich sons of bitches lookit this castle plenty of room for me had nothing but a fucking cot in the corner shitheads wouldn't even let me have that here they are in a fucking castle but me they drop a building on top of fucking cocksuckers who's laughing now motherfuckers you got room for me I ain't goin' nowhere who's in hell now you fuckin' shits . . ." The vitriol gushed in that vein from basement to kitchen to the upstairs, for as long as the mics were on. Our entity was taking full advantage of never having to catch his breath again. First time on *ECTO Files* we'd have to bleep out the bulk of message from beyond the grave.

Mrs. Filbert, in keeping with her first name of Prudence, had gone ashen at the vulgar onslaught, but without any furrows of remorse or soul-searching on her brow. Ditto the ex-gov, who wore a mask of bland dissociation. Their lack of engagement had become annoying.

My inspection bore down on Abe. "This was quite the unusual case, and even though we had a lot of blanks to fill in, I feel you'll be impressed by the answers we've obtained." Under the table, Evie's stocking foot was resting on mine, flexing toes and applying intermittent pressure. What was she playing at? Trying to be supportive or to drive me crazy? Her serene profile revealed nothing.

"The destructive behavior we witnessed would have been in line with a poltergeist, but a poltergeist is considered the energy emanating from someone alive, most often an adolescent girl, conflicted or under stress. It has no independent awareness or personality. We had to rule that out because, as you heard, your anomaly has personality to spare and no trouble verbalizing its emotions." Dammit, why didn't Evie cut it out? "Emotions" nearly spilled out as a yodel.

"By the same token, neither are we dealing with a ghost defined as the unconscious imprint of a traumatic occurrence. History, as best we could ascertain, has left no mark of any kind at this location." Ennui was beginning to cloud Abe's eyes.

"The EVPs, on the other hand, point to a deceased individual acquainted with Mr. Filbert. And then there's that intense ill will. Who is he that death itself can make him no less resentful and vindictive? We may have that answer, too." Abe had suddenly narrowed his sights on me, not shrewdly so much as inspecting me for shrewdness.

I reminded myself of a public prosecutor as I requested Ed jump to the relevant excerpt, where visuals and EVP had been synched up. The next onscreen perspective was mine, as cookware and steel valises careened around the kitchen, and my voice inquired, "Are you the homeless guy who blames his death on the Filberts?"

In replay, obscenities bloomed across cupboards and walls, and I half expected them to reappear now in the wake of repeated stimulus, but our entity must have been sleeping in or perhaps raising hob elsewhere. And in concert with luminous written abuse, the soundtrack contained the growling EVP, "Sherlock wins a fucking prize!" The prize was apparently the collapse of that vortex of kitchen accessories, immediately followed by tenuous but urgent cries and bellows from the bedroom.

The laptop screen went dark, and it dawned on me only then that I could simply move my foot and Evie would cease to distract me. Hated to do it in a way. But I had to harness my most dispassionate, lawyerly diction to announce, "The spirit's language is open to a single interpretation. As governor, you condemned a homeless shelter, claiming it a waste of taxpayer dollars. The homeless man who died during that building's demolition holds it against you. He accuses you of killing him. His allegation, not ours. We're not here to judge. If you belong to the Catholic or Episcopal faith, we can put you in touch with some highly esteemed exorcists. Otherwise, this entity may be impossible to appease."

Prudence Filbert's posture was stiff and angular, as if her circuits had overloaded. Abe still had the wherewithal to fake relaxation, but I envisioned wheels spinning in career politician's head, tempering his anger at my insinuations of manslaughter in terms of his image on national television. Blustering or exploding wouldn't play well. "Well, it's a lot to chew on, isn't it?" he drawled. "You won't be offended, will you, if we treat this seriously enough to seek a second opinion?"

"You should," I agreed, but whom was he planning to consult? Our competition or his cadre of attorneys? ECTO had impugned nothing, had in fact simply relayed postmortem grievance. Prudence, meanwhile, had lost herself in hundred-mile gape, till she repaid my interest in her with a glower I read as scathing, betrayed, disillusioned. Had she never absorbed that we were not "ghostbusters"?

Foolish urge hit me to pack up and bolt away and rush the postproduction before ex-gov could slap an injunction or somesuch legal ban on broadcasting this exposé. It was a wrap, in any event. We'd wheedle no further repartée out of our taciturn clients. Coldest shoulders I'd ever met. After lying through my teeth to thank them again for their hospitality, I yelled, "Cut!"

Prudence had the housekeeper help lug our equipment, to clear us out that much sooner. I'm a firm believer in "idiot checks" to ensure we had every last lens cap and power strip, especially where we were no longer welcome, but the Filberts' insistence on hovering behind us, as if we might filch their silverware, put us to nervous rout. Abe's sotto voce farewell to me, punctuated by slamming the front door an inch from my nose, consisted of "Thanks for nothing."

Thus we abandoned Nightmare McMansion to its vengeful anomaly, and this morning I raised bathroom window shade upon my own brewing nightmare of a landlord problem. The badly dented Ford Escort of the tenant's hoodlum pals had parked overnight on the paving out back. I could tick off various reasons for what it was doing there, all of them conducive to headache.

Personal Log, Jasper Kent, Director of ECTO, October 3

Good thing I prevailed on Shock Horror to air the Governor's McMansion segment ASAP. Evie came over to watch, on the pretext

I had air-conditioning and she didn't. Actually she'd have been too cold were we not tangled together on the couch. Yesterday the producers had forwarded me a copy of Abe's typewritten threat of litigation if our program dared stray one step into slander. So far, at least, the producers concurred that suing and shooting the messenger were equally bad form, and fuck you Abe Filbert. When I recounted this potential imbroglio during commercials, Evie loyally cussed the clients out and squeezed me tighter.

As the end credits rolled, I was relieved more than anything else. Higher-ups could have yanked this landmark production at the last minute, or censored it, but maybe, just maybe, they realized how important it was. After a depressurizing hour of channel surfing and heavy petting, we switched to Wild Planet for a gander at what the clowns on *Spectre Catchers* were up to. For a laugh, we figured. We were very wrong.

First off, dammit, they were working our turf. Our state, our county. And more outrageous yet, they were overnighting in a suburban McMansion. It belonged, uncannily, to mogul contractor Bruce Kilbarron, who'd have been the shoo-in candidate to flatten the condemned homeless shelter. It stuck in my craw, and Evie's too, when the Kilbarrons were nothing but courteous, grateful, and cooperative to the S.C. team. The equivalent of Gallant to the Goofus household we'd put up with.

Our displeasure didn't max out, though, till we saw the literal handwriting on the walls in the Kilbarron home gym. A viscous "ROT IN HELL" was in danger of dribbling onto stationary bike and Stairmaster. The rest of ectoplasmic script had been blurred out, no doubt in deference to the FCC, the same as in our footage of the Filberts' billiards room. We traded thunderstruck grimaces and cried foul, rationally or not, at getting ripped off somehow. The competition had poached our ghost!

The balance of their show plodded along like a less informative retread of our own, except for their clients' better graces. Their maelstrom of projectiles, like ours, migrated from basement to dining room to upper story, and extensively bleeped EVPs pegged the Kilbarrons as targets of posthumous vendetta. But because our rivals weren't local, they lacked the background to link their anomaly with the fatal incident behind it. Then again, the Kilbarrons might not have remained so nice had their guests involved them in the negligent death of a homeless person.

The S.C. hacks didn't shy from touting how revolutionary their findings were, any more than we did. Yet they and their hosts alike were haplessly scratching their heads about the tormentor's identity and why he was on the warpath. Not so the Filberts, thanks to our superior sleuthing. Or anyway, their option of willful ignorance was off the table. ECTO still led the ghost-hunting pack by however narrow a margin.

Evie and I congratulated each other on that, and I refrained from asking what she thought might be going on when one ghost haunted two houses. Sex was a higher priority at the moment than brainstorming. Our brains had struggled with quite enough for the day.

And come morning, I awoke to Evie shrilling my name from out back, much louder than the noisy air-conditioner. Happily she doesn't let loose when startled during investigations, or we'd all have tinnitus. The air-conditioner, conversely, had been able to block whatever sounds the thieves had made who'd left Evie's Camry door ajar and scooped the contents of her glove compartment onto the floor and front seat. Nothing was missing because she wisely drove around with nothing worth stealing. It was the mess and the violation that upset her, and it upset me that she might henceforth be averse to spending the night.

The trashy Escort of my tenant's cronies hadn't been around, and I had no grounds to accuse the tenant of anything worse than stalling on the rent, but my gut told me to presume him guilty of any malfeasance till proven innocent.

Personal Log, Jasper Kent, Director of ECTO, October 14

Must be a poor reflection on me that I honestly don't feel bad. Just yesterday, Abe was rattling litigious saber at us again, rankled these several weeks unto fixation about his damaged rep after our TV recap of homeless shelter controversy. But how could we have explicated the case minus tragic backstory? Then today it became indisputable our clients really should have retired to Florida, because their massive chandelier had landed on them last night—payment in kind, I surmised, from someone on whom a building had landed. Ghoulishly or not, I couldn't help rejoicing that we were out of the legal woods. As for the Filberts, now that they were dead, I had to believe their hardship was only beginning.

Beyond that, my life amounts to so many cans of worms. The Filberts had proven mere opening salvos. The demand for our services has tripled in the same number of weeks, and pillars of society like the ex-gov account for 100% of the increase. The grapevine has it that our imitators are riding a comparable tide, but does anyone beside me wonder why this spike in supernatural activity is targeting affluence?

Or perhaps nobody in our business can wonder much of anything while scrambling to handle burgeoning caseloads. To revamp shooting schedules for every upper-crust client wouldn't be feasible. They're too numerous, which in itself negates their cachet, and they're typically high-maintenance past the point of diminishing returns. We're hiring an exorcist purely because we got so sick of telling clients we didn't have one.

In principle we've embarked on a seller's market, free to choose the least onerous contenders for our services, consigning our surplus to *Wraith Quest* et al. In practice, sadly, the biggest blowhards bend the ear of Shock Horror chairmen and bump themselves to the top of the list. And the Filberts are convivial compared with most of these guys. Among victims of unearthly spite across the Lower 48, bankers, mortgage brokers, developers, speculators, and Congressmen predominate, and none of their afflictions has moved me yet to commiserate with any of them.

To our disadvantage, on out-of-state jobs we don't have access to the sorts of inside dope so useful with the Filberts. Nor do clients, naturally, see fit to air their dirty linen. Some common thread beneath all these high-tone hauntings eludes me, even as I worry mansions will become too commonplace to hold an audience after a season filmed nowhere else. Familiarity breeding contempt? That was shaping up as the cliché to define our relations with the clients, and the viewers' impending relations with us.

My other major can of worms is living downstairs, and contempt is entering into those relations too. The bank phoned this morning. This week's check for last month's rent had bounced, and after five minutes of steady pounding on his door, the tenant emerged from midday nap or stupor or hangover and mumbled with abject contrition, "Hey, I'm really sorry, man, I made a withdrawal from the ATM and I spaced on writing it in my checkbook. I should have money after this weekend. I'll pay you Monday, man. I promise." He was too pathetic to browbeat. Do I lack the spine for this landlording game?

Funny, but before *ECTO Files* was a hit, the kid was punctual and inspired a provisional confidence. And now that collecting the rent, and rent I no longer need, has become a hassle, I keep picturing what primo bachelor quarters I could make of the first and second floors as a unit. Evie might be less reluctant to hang out if this were a hoodlum-free zone. And if not her, I'll probably meet someone willing soon enough. I am, after all, verging on celebrity.

Personal Log, Jasper Kent, Director of ECTO, November 5

Fears of a season tedious with palatial luxury were unfounded. Millionaires have been jumping ship left and right. Maybe after catching the first few episodes with Abe and his peer group, they decided there were better forms of publicity. We've had to make hasty arrangements with owners of more traditional sites like taverns, museums, and triple-deckers, and that's fine. I've missed the old familiar haunts, so to speak. And Brother Bill the Exorcist remains on the payroll. Turns out he was a good idea. I may make bold to say a godsend. Ups the quotient of drama whenever the suspense slackens.

Don't get me wrong. I've been thrilled to record evidence a hundredfold more convincing than garbled EVPs and "orbs," a.k.a. dust bunnies in an updraft. Not pleased to be falling back on those. I'll miss that uptick in ratings, too. In that brief shining span, *ECTO Files* has become a different species of reality show, in which ghosts are pretty much secondary to the havoc they wreak, and our clients function as lightning rods for downtrodden America's class hostility. We were effectively *The Comeuppance Hour*, which might further explain why well-heeled applicants have been bailing on us.

I've also gained a more nuanced understanding of ghostly mental workings, short of particular motives for mayhem. Some private eyes, under decades of media influence, model behaviors on Bogart or Telly Savalas or Jack Lord when it seems conducive to results. Our recent spate of apparitions seems likewise to have picked up pointers from *The Exorcist* and *Poltergeist* and *Amityville Horror*. We've borne witness to shamelessly derivative but viscerally potent swarms of flies on caviar, levitating mahogany beds, pyramids of Louis XV furniture, black ooze welling from the best chrome-and-crystal toilets, and the sacrilegious marring of gilded Byzantine icons. Clients never profess an awareness of being subjected to shopworn routines, and to accuse irate spirits of plagiarism would be foolhardy.

We have one more upscale domicile lined up before the apparent end of this era, and I'm looking forward to it for a change. A Frank Lloyd Wright, no less, in sunny California. Or would I rather sit around brooding about declines in property value when a tenant neglects to take out his garbage except for cigarette butts and burger wrappers in the driveway, and parks a defunct junker next to my new LaCrosse?

Personal Log, Jasper Kent, Director of ECTO, November 11

I didn't think I was especially thick, but it took the lips of the dead to let me in on the obvious. And as this was our last foray among the overprivileged, I might still be in the dark had my wits not miraculously slipped into gear. This final patrician also beat the record for our oldest, a strapping nonagenarian, a retiree before I'd entered the workforce. His career title had been "municipal construction coordinator," which I gathered was the term for "city planner" back when that normally meant "slum clearance."

True to violent pattern since the Filberts, we experienced the same intensity of occult activity as our frazzled client. Had he not been a rugged disciple of "physical culture," he might have been a moribund shadow of former self, and not merely ashen and skittish.

His Frank Lloyd Wright house was predictably spectacular, a faux-rugged structure in keeping with its owner. In broadest strokes, it was a giant wagon wheel lying on its side, partly jutting past a cliff top high above Ventura County beach. Inside and out it invoked nagging déjà vu till I recognized it from two totally dissimilar movies separated by almost fifty years, a science fantasy and a rock musical. What we all first noticed on crossing the threshold was the stiff cross-breeze. Window frames were devoid of glass.

The client, who stipulated we rename him "Quincy," described how every artifact relating to his taste, history, achievements, relationships, whether *objets d'art*, photo albums, souvenirs, or awards, had hurtled meteorically through windowpanes onto boulders or into the surf. The bulky teak furniture, no less perversely, had become immovable, as if ethereal guests were reserving it for nightly conclaves. In Quincy's firm opinion, multiple entities had to be responsible for so much simultaneous mayhem.

At sundown, Quincy, more judicious than the Filberts, left us in a literal sense to our devices, and we set them up out of rote, to preserve that scientific veneer. Did our viewership really give a damn about magnetic flux when there were stately surroundings to trash? Low-tech Brother Billy, at leisure meanwhile to ruminate, remarked, as usual, that our client seemed to be hiding something. To our greenest recruit, this continued to qualify as news.

I also had the impression his heart wasn't in the majority of our exorcisms, as if he were a double agent on the metaphysical front, whose sympathies weren't necessarily with the living. I didn't fault him, and I didn't press him about his level of priestly commitment. But was it symptomatic of our attitude that ECTO never followed up on the results of Billy's solemn hoodoo?

Quincy wasn't even in the running for most odious tycoon. Not to say he was a regular guy. Some invisible shield of formality, some chronic remove from garden-variety existence, rendered communications with him impersonal, as had been the case with all these muckamucks. And the simple fact of being haunted did impute, as Brother Billy perceived, some moral stain on sterling citizen's résumé.

Our grasp of that, however, wouldn't make anomalies more kindly disposed toward us, as we anticipated when the gloom grew oppressive with a cold snap that hadn't blown in through the windows, with a mistiness that hadn't drifted from offshore. And in our ears was a sensation almost too subliminal to call sound, like an echo of the waves crashing below, or like the ebb and flow of chat at a cocktail hour. My intuition told me Quincy was on the money envisioning a mob of specters.

Then our whole crew, in spacious, sparsely furnished room with panoramic vista, shared an attack of claustrophobia. Ed and Stacey hunkered grimly at tabletop station, but their heedful eyes darted around. Every needle on their instruments was lodged in the deep end of the red, and much as I wished I could hear the EVPs in real time, I doubted any single voice would emerge distinct from the babble. Understudy Kelly and the two Shock Horror cameramen kept readjusting their shoulders as if under a chafing yoke. Evie's eyes met mine with an urgency that conveyed she wanted to come hold me, but didn't because it wouldn't be cool. Maybe so, but I wouldn't have stopped her. Safe to bet that none of us, including celibate Brother Billy, would have.

Nothing assaulted our equipment or Quincy's PC and filing cabinets and sundry caches of Sunday-painter pigments and brushes. Hands down, that would have been less distressing than the drafty cold stirring and then jostling against us as if we were bucking the tide of a rush-hour crowd, and soon rubbing brazenly at us like otherworldly molestation. Worse yet, we had no choice but to inhale the milky air, and it cloyed and tickled, making us aware of conscious ectoplasm, of commingled souls in our throats and sinuses.

How could abusive phantoms not mistake us, with an exorcist in tow, for allies of Quincy? Naturally they'd ratchet up the nastiness and torment till we fled, unless I could pose a question that gave them pause. The numbers in here were also problematic. Experience had taught that the deceased, perhaps even more than the living, wanted uppermost to talk about themselves. But on whom to focus? It was like addressing an entire block party. And there I had my entrée. Quincy had been "construction coordinator" in the heyday of "slum clearance," so in that capacity he'd have likeliest done the most harm. Was this a population culled from one obliterated neighborhood?

"Did you all die homeless on account of urban renewal?" I bellowed, and my colleagues held their breath and watched me for further developments.

Scant heartbeats later, the indoor gales were buffeting us less persistently, ganging up instead on a weathered brown leather satchel, batting it across the floorboards, plucking at its flap, and finally flipping it over to disgorge umpteen tubes of acrylics. As if adults after death regressed to the motor skills of toddlers, invisible fingers sent tubes skidding every which way, stampeding invisible feet crushed them, and invisible grips bent and twisted them apart in midair. I'd gladly have swapped eyeteeth to see more of this scuffle than a swirling, pasty haze, but at least we could be thankful spirits no longer clogged our respiration.

Between the soupy atmosphere and the glut of incoming moonlight, our infrared lenses were serving no purpose and would have bleached out the bold tableau of acrylic dabs and gouts streaking through the air toward floor and raftered ceiling. In cobalt and sienna and vermilion and indigo, crude ghost paws struggled to form smears into letters but they mostly spread blotches, some dripping onto us from directly overhead. The spectral effort to surround us with several dozen whole or partial versions of "Yes" must have been excruciating. The curving "s" caused greatest difficulties and succeeded best as three angled strokes, as if chiseled into Roman triumphal arch.

But that emphatic, multicolored syllable was a segue, not an endpoint. It absolutely led somewhere. I practically tasted revelation, there on the tip of my tongue, if only I could summon the words. And I meanwhile had to summon the nerve to stride through psychic tempest for the sake of now-or-never illumination, though equally for the sake of a classic, perhaps immortal, TV moment.

I became the center of poised attention for both the quick and the dead as I stooped to smother forefinger in Mars Black spewing from its squashed cylinder. I knelt on relatively clean floor between the cameramen and me. Then I volunteered to act as human Ouija board. "Choose someone to guide my hand," I exclaimed, "and write me your response! Did everyone everywhere who died homeless since forty years ago decide to exercise some poetic justice?"

Inaudible squabble to pick a spokesperson may have lasted seconds, but they were grueling seconds. My outstretched arm was beginning to ache when a chill seized it, sank partway in, and set it to

trembling like an overtaxed engine. A spirit rusty in the use of muscles was attempting to be gentle, or anyway wasn't out to be rough.
If it had been, I reckoned the charley horse in my forearm would
have been agonizing.

To emulate a blank slate, to steer clear of counterproductive
second guesses, seemed the best approach to getting this over with.
Accordingly I averted my sight from the wobbly, torturous penmanship underway, the lift and dip and push of ill-controlled limb. I
hoped these ghosts were grateful. A message of this length would
have been impossible without borrowed flesh. I also apprehended
each letter was smaller than its forerunner, as if author were concerned with running short of paint. Why oh why couldn't they
scribble in ectoplasm like their East Coast counterparts?

Sometime after I estimated this ordeal had dragged on too long
for a "classic TV moment," my knuckles plunked numbly against the
floor. I had to gasp at a release of unphysical pressure that had
mounted imperceptibly, and as circulation resumed, my arm tingled
ferociously. I massaged out the cold and tension and, for the benefit
of myopic viewers, recited the phrase at my feet, "ALL 1 PAYBACK
4 EVER." Damned if it didn't sound like the motto on a bottle of Dr.
Bronner's soap.

I suppressed that trivializing thought before it made me smirk,
peered earnestly into a Shock Horror camera, and explicated off the
cuff, "What does that mean? Those of you who've followed us into
luxury accommodations this season may agree when I say it means
the souls of everyone who died without a place to live have all come
home to roost. Moving in with the parties they hold responsible.
And with no intention of going away."

I got to my feet and dusted off khaki knees while toughing out a
dizzy spell. My announcement seemed to have knocked the wind
out of this haunting. I'd justified the ways of ghost to man, and that
was apparently the size of tonight's agenda. The cold hadn't abated,
but the breeze blew weaker, and the surflike pulse in my ears had
become thinner and irregular.

My colleagues were breathing easier, and the threat of occult onslaught no longer weighed down their shoulders. Only Brother Bill
was cringing, shrinking into his black cassock as into maternal skirts,

eyes cast dolefully toward the rafters as if still waiting for the sky to fall. His anxiety, though, was all directed inwardly, I suspected. With finger across throat I signaled cameramen to desist a minute. At my approach, Bill gripped the neck rest of teak chair the way motorists grip steering wheel when state troopers pull them over. I essayed a genial "good cop" smile and asked, "You up for exorcising this place?"

He made too serious a show of staring me in the face. "My materials are nowhere to be found. The spirits must have gotten rid of them."

I'd have sworn his vintage doctor's bag with holy water, surplice, oils, salt, beads, and Bible had never left the van, but I gamely nodded. Ornery as they were, to evict the homeless yet again on the eternal side of death just seemed unfair. Brother Bill didn't have to explain anything to any of us, but I wondered if he'd bring up this prevarication in Confession, and if so, how? And what penance would Father Confessor assign?

I'd have to pass Billy's fib along to Quincy. Not a problem. Misinforming elite clients had become second nature. Quincy could well afford to hire his own damn exorcists till he joined postmortem ranks himself. Meanwhile, the cleaver edge of drafty cold had dulled, and the patchy clouds of subsonic chatter had lifted altogether. Ed and Stacey's needles had swung firmly back to zero. We packed it in, and thus without fanfare ECTO Files cut connections with the guilty rich. My sticky black fingerprint was more perturbing at every glance, like a mark of complicity in cheating the customer.

Personal Log, Jasper Kent, Director of ECTO, November 13

Quincy didn't get to be a nonagenarian by blowing his stack at every frustration and setback. Or else he brilliantly faked philosophic calm during the reveal. Our EVPs corroborated his hunch that he was indeed up against a supernatural horde. He had precious little more for which to thank us. Despite Ed and Stacey's genius for pulling articulate English from hiccups in tape hiss, they weren't equal to isolating single strands from too much gabble. Their soundtrack added up to an indivisible matrix of raving white noise.

This may have bothered me more than Quincy because I sorely

wanted ghostly quotes to elaborate more meaningful context for "ALL 1 PAYBACK 4 EVER." Indelible Dr. Bronner slogan did express, if nothing else, that Quincy was on the receiving end of retribution unduly deferred.

Former city planner, it almost went without saying, had no idea how any urban renewal on his watch could have been anything but benign. And besides, that had been a lifetime ago. Why no backlash till now? We had to plead ignorance. Not even coherent EVPs would have solved that mystery.

We also regretted the exorcism had been a "no-go," an evasion safer than an outright lie, and much safer than the truth. "Well, you were greatly outnumbered," Quincy sympathized. Right through the masklike skin of repeated facelifts, slackening muscles told me he was giving up, determination sagging into despair.

Evie sitting beside me at the teak table had her foot on mine again, except now with steady, reassuring pressure. I felt sorry for Quincy, as I presumed we all did, but a spotless innocent wouldn't be stuck in this situation. He, unlike his persecutors, had survived to enjoy a long, full life, and how could that not make them hate him more? Were dictators and war criminals ever too old to confront justice when victims had their say? Moot to suggest that Quincy had only been "doing his job."

Moreover, we were powerless to assist, let alone console, our client. We could advise he move away, but to throw off pursuit he'd probably have to resettle across oceans on foreign soil. And to that he wouldn't consent, if he wasn't a hair's-breadth open to the possibility of misdeeds in his distant past. Not that many nonagenarians were willing to emigrate. Like everyone in his position, we wished him luck and inured ourselves to his misery by contemplating what his nemeses had against him. Keep it simple. That's the modus operandi for us, whether cultivating an attitude toward clients or ordering refreshments from Dunkin' Donuts.

Personal Log, Jasper Kent, Director of ECTO, November 16

Underground comix characters always used to cuss "Shitfuckpiss." That was my mantra too when airport taxi dropped me off last night and I came upstairs to a busted lock on my apartment door. Depredations included computer, TV, stereo, contents of liquor cabinet, and a six-pack in the fridge. Shitfuckpiss.

One of the investigating officers called himself a big fan of the show, for all the good that would do me. Neither of them had to spell out the laughable chances of recovering my property. With a blasé professionalism akin to mine, they jotted notes about the tenant and went down to interview him. I made no effort to incriminate the devious little slacker, but had to state for the record he was well aware of my comings and goings.

I had no proof and, to the same degree, no doubt that this robbery had been an "inside job." I also had no illusions my tenant would give himself away under police questioning and solve the problem of his ongoing presence for me by departing in handcuffs. To evict him feels like courting bad karma, but under what sane rationale can I let him stay?

Personal Log, Jasper Kent, Director of ECTO, November 20

I love my entertainment lawyer. Contract renewals with Shock Horror coincided with our giddy spike in ratings amidst our adventures in the upper crust, and he played it to the hilt. We're locked in for another three years on stunningly more opulent terms, minus hefty legal fees. These he's undeniably earned for fighting valiantly on our behalf, though this is someone who candidly opined that "spook chasers" like us "pull the whole shebang out your asses."

Too bad our audience is bound to shrink once we permanently revert to lower-rent business-as-usual. Too bad for the network, primarily. Three years should allow me to store up a sizable nest egg, to get the hang of investing wisely. I'll be fixed a while for creature comforts post–ECTO *Files*, provided I resist profligate spending now. Or for sure, starting the day after this house is rechristened as a single-family dwelling. As for the increasingly slovenly, insolvent tenant, the longer I afford him my compassion, the longer he'll be taking advantage of me. I won't even dun him for this month's rent. Write it off as a parting gift.

My buoyant mood enjoyed a further lift from the National Paranormal League, which sent an invite by registered mail to deliver a talk at next month's annual convention. Smells to me like a prior speaker canceled on short notice, but so what? The NPL are strictly old school, old as jazz, the self-styled rigorous, scientific sticks-in-the-mud who've always looked askance at mass-media lightweights like us. But we scored first with the unimpeachable data, and I'm glad they're not above basking in the warmth of our newfound credibility.

Their epistle informs me I'm to outline my organization's main findings and propose a theory as to their relevance in parapsychology. And, by way of halfhearted afterthought, congratulations on extending the boundaries of knowledge in both the public and paranormal communities! The ink on watermarked stationery practically reeked of sour grapes. They neglected to mention any honorarium, but what the hell. It's enough to savor the novelty of "going legit."

Personal Log, Jasper Kent, Director of ECTO, December 4

I'm fudging on my vow to economize, but that's okay. Unforeseen expense has motivated me to abolish live-in liability once and for all. After the lackluster bust of a cold, quiet, defunct paper mill in Nowheresville, Maine, Evie's Camry followed my LaCrosse into the driveway. I'd convinced her to make a night of it after stop-and-go spooning Down East, but then we couldn't park out back because the tenant's damned junker was embedded in a corner of the house, blocking half the tarmac's width, with single headlight's dim beam blinking erratically at us. He'd been hale enough to exit the vehicle, but too addled to kill the ignition. No blood stained the windshield or upholstery.

Can't blame Evie for shifting into reverse and waving goodbye. She'd been urging me to boot him out for months. The standard protracted hammering on his door retrieved him at his most mumbly and droopy-lidded yet. Maybe I should have strong-armed him to the ER, but he was adamant about suffering no concussion or other injuries; and incensed as I was about Evie flying the coop, I was content to leave it at that.

Whether he was just pathologically spacey or embarking on

drunken joyride, I didn't dare pretend he wouldn't do anything worse. The present damage proved mostly cosmetic, and it's an outlay I'd rather absorb than risk a hike in insurance premiums. But next time will I have to shell out for a whole new house after he burns this one to the ground? The stakes are down to him or me.

And as I'm wont to say, gotta love my entertainment lawyer. He's putting me in touch with a colleague notorious for fast-tracking evictions, as well as foreclosures and repossessions. Not someone I'd include on the side of the angels, but he'll get the job done. I guess I can dirty my hands that much in order to clean house.

Then on top of everything else, that damn speech at the NPL is hanging over my head, Damocles-like. I ought to make a contingency copy here of what I've got so far:

> Ghosts are universally tied to specific locations, most often houses, or if not some form of architecture, to a forest, a roadside, or a graveyard. Even the vampire is obliged to rest on native soil. But what of the ghosts with no place to haunt, who can attribute their ghosthood to being dispossessed, disenfranchised in life? Would they, by default, be endowed with some freedom of movement? We at East Coast Traveling Occultists have learned that, in any event, potter's field has lost its power to hold them.
>
> Some who essentially died of homelessness since perhaps the Kennedy era have come to haunt those who used foreclosure, eminent domain, exorbitant rents, etc., to put them on the street. In death they retaliate by occupying the mansions their extant selves could only gaze upon through iron gates. For this we have the word of the ghosts themselves in multiple cases. These ghosts, however, do not or cannot express their reason for undertaking this mass harassment now.
>
> What would it reveal about the workings of the "spirit world" if ghosts of the homeless acquired a collective intelligence, an ability to strategize and deliberate, when their numbers reached a certain critical mass or tipping point? Or is their activity altogether unplanned and spontaneous, the result of arbitrary trigger, like the species-wide uprising of the birds in the Hitchcock film of that name?
>
> To indulge in yet purer speculation, are life and afterlife as

disconnected as they seem? Can the highly charged emotions in these days of social unrest and income disparity penetrate the "veil" and exert galvanic influence? We at ECTO or any paranormal organization would be thought presumptuous, I'm sure, to counsel dealing with the homeless in their lifetimes, or deal with them unhappily ever after . . .

Odds are the NPL wants a more scholarly orientation, a stiffer dose of jargon, a format in line with technical journalism. Which is to say, not me. I'm not wild about my brainchild at this fetal stage either. Unfortunately, whatever satisfaction I derive from the final draft won't be shared by my listeners. Not my fault they enlisted a media philistine.

Personal Log, Jasper Kent, Director of ECTO, December 11

I had my fingers crossed the eviction notice would arrive after I'd vamoosed to the convention. No such luck. The tenant, for a change, came banging on my door.

"What is this bullshit?" he greeted me, brandishing a document he had evidently crumpled and uncrumpled. "What did I do?"

"You're joking, aren't you?" I stood squarely in the doorway. Like hell was he coming in.

"Look man, I've had some problems lately." Plus he was in worse shape than I'd ever seen him. Whatever he was down with, I was afraid it might be contagious. Another excellent reason to bar him entry. His flourishing, thick, collarbone-length black hair framed his emaciation in stark relief, and his red eyes smoldered vivid against yellowish waxy skin. Conjunctivitis, I diagnosed off the cuff, and jaundice? "You gotta give me another chance to straighten out."

Steady now. No more special pleading. "You've had chances galore, up to the point you took out a corner of my house. You've done nothing here that hasn't chipped away at property values." I shook my head resignedly. "I've shown you every consideration."

"Really? Since when? Don't pretend to care about me, all right? To you I'm just a pile of cash once a month." Not even that, I noted sardonically. He was verging on two months in arrears. "I bet you still don't know what my name is, do you? It's just something you make sure is filled in at the bottom of a check."

Dammit, his name must have slipped my mind in the heat of the moment. He couldn't possibly be right. "I've done what I can. I'm sorry."

"The hell you are. You have to give me more time. Where am I supposed to go in a week?"

"Go crash with those friends, the one who've stayed here over-night. They owe you a few."

"They're not my friends." He'd say anything to drag this out, wouldn't he? Now he was starting to piss me off.

"Whatever they are, they helped get you into this. Maybe remind them of how much they made off pawning my TV and computer. That ought to rate you some gratitude. But I wouldn't mention the stereo. That was mostly reconditioned crap." I swung the door shut and heard no more of his comeback than "fucking yuppie." How dare he? How long would a "fucking yuppie" tolerate a plague dog like him?

Personal Log, Jasper Kent, Director of ECTO, December 18

The applause after my thirty NPL minutes climaxed in the polite smattering I'd expected. The Q&A morphed immediately into a brisk exodus, and I ranked as an untouchable for the rest of the weekend. Was I "too political" for these aspirants to scientific neu-trality, though my data were meaningless outside their "political" context of elitism and exploitation? My findings were as unwelcome in the NPL's scale-model ivory tower as the NPL's findings were in the grander ivory tower of "real" academe.

My lone partisan surfaced, or rather blocked my path, as I was checking out of the hotel on Sunday afternoon. He praised me as "a whiff of fresh air" and exhorted, "Stick to your guns!" An awkward si-lence ensued wherein I sensed I'd somehow muffed a cue. What was I failing to acknowledge? "We met in the performance of my duty," he imparted after a lengthy instant. "In uniform I must look different."

Uniform? Oh, right! He was one of the cops responding to my complaint about the burglary. The big fan of *ECTO Files*. And off the clock, I surmised, an aficionado of the occult in general. Had he been sporting wire rims and a pencil mustache in my apartment? We shook hands and lamented how every speaker had apparently felt honor-bound to embalm fascinating topics in paranormal argot. "Except for you!" he hastily amended. "And hey, sorry we couldn't nail your downstairs neighbor. We both know he did it, right? Maybe next time, if he lives that long."

"What do you mean? Did he tell you he was sick?"

Officer Wire Rims stared at me like I was drooling. "No. I've seen enough junkies. They don't come more obvious."

I nodded judiciously, as if I hadn't been clueless. "Well, the landlord's kicking him out. He should be gone by now, actually." Referring to myself in the third person seemed extemporaneously wise. I'd never let on I owned the building, had I? Harboring a junkie wouldn't exactly redound to my credit, in the eyes of either the law or the viewership. And pleading ignorance as an excuse would only put an ugly dent in my sagacity.

"Sometimes easier said than done," my friend on the force informed me. "But for what it's worth, you can tell the landlord his tenant's already had two priors. One for simple possession, and one from out of state for DUI."

"No kidding." This I had to hear through an extremely chance encounter at a spiritualist convention? It hadn't dawned on the cops that night to come back up and warn me a criminal was lurking downstairs? Pretty damn irritating, but what could I say?

Definitely for the best that our discussion switched gears. From a pouch in his valise, policeman extracted an *ECTO Files* DVD, partly in Chinese and doubtless pirated, for me to autograph. On inside front cover I scrawled, "Thanks a million for the thankless chore of cheering me on at NPL in NY" and scurried off, claiming a train to catch. I declined to harp on lawman's patronage of the black market. Drug addiction had only strengthened the case for ousting my tenant, but I felt more impelled than ever to prove, to myself anyway, that I wasn't turning into some hard-ass Babbitt, and expressly not into a "fucking yuppie." Not that I really cared if the gendarmes trafficked in illicit goods.

I'm writing this on the train, lest things at home get hectic and memories slip through the cracks before I can open my logbook again. Police-blotter details about druggie tenant are of especial value, in case my conscience needs to stave off remorse.

Personal Log, Jasper Kent, Director of ECTO, December 19

If anything, to quote countless cardboard characters, "it's too quiet here." Arrived circa midnight. The tenant's junker was still out back, exactly where he'd rolled it. Abandoned? Ground-floor windows were dark, and his apartment door was locked. Maybe he vacated, and maybe he's opted for passive resistance. Very well then. Our interactions have always involved dipping into my reservoir of patience, and I can tap into it again for a few more days.

And for the duration of that patience, I can marshal my resentment, my frustration, into the language with which to confront entrenched deadbeat, to parry whining or pissy appeals for a grace period, for one more reprieve. If he's still downstairs. My patience hasn't ticked away to the breaking point of having to go beat on his door.

The mere thought of renting to a junkie, of the damage that might do my image, my career, if the wrong people chose to make something of it, has me fuming. To say nothing of the scandal should some drug-related felony lead to arrests under my roof. Officer Wire Rims, by blabbing about me to the media, could inflict the most grief, but he's a fan, a partisan. I don't remember alienating him. He's in my corner, right?

Besides, who does lowlife junkie think he is, keeping me from doing what I want with my own home? What am I supposed to owe him? I want my house back, to remodel it for purposes that are nobody else's business. I want to get on with my life. My rights are as sacrosanct as anybody's, and the expensive leverage of the legal system is on my side.

Personal Log, Jasper Kent, Director of ECTO, December 22

To cite Gospel, "the poor you will always have with you," but postmortem till doomsday? This dilemma has acquired a personal resonance for me, and I note ruefully that it will never be addressed at an official level, because no "responsible" governing body will ever concede the reality of ghosts as a cornerstone of setting policy. Not even, for once, to pacify obnoxious millionaires.

I had toiled over some of these logbook passages with an eye toward pitching a book to publishers. It would have combined a tabloid-worthy narrative of hauntings among the greedy rich with a muckraker's interpretation of those hauntings, moreover affording me an opportunity to recycle that unacclaimed disquisition for the NPL. But I just don't feel like writing it anymore.

After three days without a peep from below, I was peevish enough to rummage up the master key. ECTO had a weekend excursion at a sinister brewery in Delaware, and I didn't want my tenant's unresolved status weighing on me throughout. My judgment tilted toward marking him as absent, foremost because from under his door flowed the fug of bursting garbage bags, with a puzzling trace of adult diapers. Since the concentrated stench inside must have been unbearable, I took it that the tenant had slunk away, bequeathing me this rank token of esteem.

Or had he? My three mugs of French roast for breakfast were basically calling the shots as I sought for a foil against contingencies, a ticket to tactical superiority. But a bellyful of coffee never cured anyone's naïveté, has it? Smack-addled loser, I worried, may not be above shredding the eviction notice he'd already ranted at me about and insisting he'd never received it. In deference to Murphy's Law, I had run off multiple copies. I snatched one from secretary desk drawer, and with paper and master key in respective upheld hands like some two-gun sheriff, I sallied out. Caffeine lent a jittery spring, a French roast courage, to my steps.

My knuckles smarted from rapping on tenant's door too sharply. Patience evaporated in the course of inhaling and exhaling. What the hell. Supposing he were in, I refused to invest the time he always wasted before opening up. With an aggressive twist of the key, I shoved ahead. The tenant was right there. Lucky the door hadn't clobbered him. I'd have been more startled, had I not been fighting sudden urge to upchuck at miasma much worse than I'd imagined. It didn't seem to bother him, but milky pale complexion implied he was operating at reduced capacity, senses blunted, wits dull. He squinted vacuously, as if slow to recognize me across a vast distance.

What to say? My treacherous brain had gone blank, and sickly addict wasn't about to break the ice. He also hadn't lifted a finger toward quitting the premises, had he? Ratty Dacron rugs and Salvation Army furniture remained in defiant place. He had yet to get my message on a level that translated into action. Ah, but tongue-tied as I was, I had the xeroxed eviction notice to speak for me. With self-congratulatory flourish, I thrust the sheet, limp with the damp of my palm, at him. "Here!"

His sluggish reflexes weren't up to intercepting it, but that would have made no difference. It slid straight through his underperforming arms and fishtailed swiftly to the floor behind him. He protested, without appreciable irony, "I can't take that, man!"

In the face of this stunning development, I had less to say than he did, and he was dead. The back of my throat was burning as it had when I was a ten-year-old in serious trouble. Couldn't be plainer what had become of the tenant, and what was causing that foulness, and what would come of my pretty plans for house and relationships and life in general.

Still, a perverse urge for ironclad proof made me sidestep him and survey the squalor till I spied his corpse on kitchen floor, head propped against cabinet below the sink, the skin of bare feet glossy blue in the patch of sun through a window. On one pleasant note, ghost tenant was wearing the same T-shirt and jeans in which he'd died, but only the corpse's shirt was plastered in vomit. Meanwhile he mutely abided as I drank in my fill of his defunct body, as if he had all the time in the world, which he did, didn't he?

"What happened here?" I finally croaked.

The corners of spectral mouth sank in pantomime disappointment at my cluelessness. "I ODed."

"Yeah, but why am I talking to you?"

"I ODed after the date to move out, so I was here but I was homeless. Legally. Because of you. You're the ghostbuster. You ought to know how it works," he reproached me.

Though none of this was news, it needed expression aloud to achieve full-fledged reality. No matter that the speaker no longer existed.

To be lumped with the bureaucrats and plutocrats who deserved their ghostly tormentors was galling, as well as grossly unjust. But with whom was I to file a grievance? I'd done nothing more odious than look out for myself, and for that I was to be punished forever?

"Talking to you makes me tired," my once-and-future tenant murmured sepulchrally. "Not used to this afterlife. I have to rest up, but I'm not going anywhere." And then he unceremoniously ceased to be there, leaving me with his decomposing cadaver and its disgusting effluvium.

I've opened all the windows and the back door, but I fear the odor, like the presence, is here to stay. I've phoned the police and I'm writing this while waiting for them. Am I the first ghost hunter to be haunted himself? What will Officer Wire Rims make of that? Frankly, I'd rather not have to face any of my fans right now. That brewery in Delaware, on reflection, may deserve a much lengthier investigation than originally scheduled. Hell, maybe the brewery's hiring. Maybe my nemesis is too much the slacker to follow me.

A Retouch in Camonica

Third-floor hotel window overlooked the village piazza, from Romanesque church at one end to Romanesque town hall at the other. On casual inspection, Vic could only distinguish between the two because a modern clock glowed moonlike under the town hall gable. It read midnight.

In front of the church was a much larger-than-life crucifixion, whose baroque wrought-iron cross made him think of New Orleans balconies. Quite disorienting! And crowding the square were even more disorienting bumpum cars and tilt-a-whirl and carousel and open-sided big rigs hawking greasy snacks and games of chance, floodlit under metal Christ as if to celebrate, to mock his suffering. That couldn't have been the sentiment behind this feast day or carnival or whatever it was, and though Vic considered himself correctly irreligious, he still felt disinclined to venture among the citizens in their unwittingly heathenish revels.

If only Darcy were here to share this, he brooded with pangs of loneliness. That was the fun of travel, wasn't it, to share oddball scenarios with someone dear? How much quality of life could she enjoy sticking with agoraphobic boyfriend, about whom she complained constantly and bitterly to Vic, to anybody with ears?

Vic had talked her into joining him as wayfaring friend, and then nature, he was confident, would have taken its amorous course. But she'd reneged out of loyalty or timidity or masochism, goddammit, after he'd fronted her the tickets. Plenty of guys had poached girlfriends of his, so why not dump self-defeating ethics and play the cad at last? Sadly, embracing his dark side hadn't worked any better than taking the high road.

On the other hand, even if going it alone cast a few melancholy shadows on this tour of ancestral Lombardy, he had only himself to please. He'd made split-second decision to hop off the bus in Serio because its name in Camunian dialect was Zero, and who could resist biding a while in Zero, the self-proclaimed middle of nowhere? Well, Darcy, perhaps, in light of her disdain for Edward Lear and Lewis Carroll and other masters of whimsy. She might also have disdained Vic's modus operandi of finding hotels at the height of tourist season by winging it and hoping for the best.

But as usual, fortune smiled. This *albergo* in eccentric pine-green stucco was full, *però scusi, uno momento!* The manageress liked his looks and offered Vic the room of her daughter, off on holiday. There in itself was an experience unapproachable via standard channels. The girl was apparently smitten with Coca-Cola, which figured as motif on bedding, airbrushed posters, inflatable pillows, cookie tins, area rug, and best of all for local boosters, a shelf of unopened bottles shaped like soccer balls bearing the logo "Coca-Cola Zero."

Vic knew of no Americans so shamelessly devoted to corporate fetishism, especially not rebellious teens. But here, he mused, such vulgarity amounted to mere veneer, because unlike the callow Yanks, Europeans could take millennial continuity, some bedrock of heritage, for granted. Beneath the electric glare and clamor in the piazza, what drew townspeople together on this date every year? And if it were some saint's day or seasonal milepost, what Christianized pagan festival, lost to conscious memory or written record, still functioned at the heart of social cohesion?

Vic was here to plumb that depth of continuity in his own half-Italian background, to graft himself onto it somehow. Funny how this room's young decorator sought New World façade where he was eager to fabricate Old World foundations. Never mind that midlife quest so far had only reinforced his gloom of isolation. Self-respect required he go for broke immersing himself in lifeways disengaged from consumerism, upward mobility, mass media.

Had Darcy appreciated or even understood what this spiritual argosy, this psychic reconfiguration, meant to him? What it could have meant to her? If she had, she wouldn't have bailed on him, would she? The hell with Darcy. Tall, bodacious, platinum-blonde Darcy with the ice-blue eyes. Yeah, the hell with her.

She might even have scoffed at his primary motive for visiting

Val Camonica, its most renowned feature of continuity. For instance, in the Parco Nazionale on the alpine slopes above Zero, several hundred of the valley's roughly 300,000 petroglyphs were accessible to the public. Camonica, in fact, boasted the highest concentration of folk art on stone throughout Europe. The tradition had endured from the Neolithic right into the nineteenth century, despite the influence, invasions, and interbreeding foisted on native culture by Greeks, Etruscans, Celts, Romans, Lombards, and Catholics.

Hell, medieval witch-hunts had twice scourged the region, but here in Zero, with iron Christ as their witness, the people had clung to their legacy and turned a touristic profit from it. Had he been too quick discounting that the merriment out his window was at the expense of oppressive savior? Irreligious Vic felt ill-qualified to judge and consigned himself to lie between the Coca-Cola sheets, pretending that the unremitting ruckus was surf to lull him to sleep.

On foot in the torrid morning, Vic wished he'd breakfasted on more than black coffee and porous white bread with fig jam and butter. A quart of orange juice or Pellegrino would have been smart. Two winding, uphill kilometers through arid scrubland were maddening torment under the baking sun, and hatless Vic was feeling parched and shaky. Temperate night at this elevation hadn't prepared him for tropical day.

The dust had seemed to fuse indivisibly with the paving underfoot till the rare car chugged by and chalky clouds billowed at him. Finally the road forked where a woodsy dell opened up on the right. A multilingual sign for the park pointed along the byway into the dell. Grateful Vic, febrile seconds away from giving up and slinking downhill, followed the arrow.

The cooling shade of roadside maples was a godsend, and he resisted temptation to gulp from a gurgling brook beside the lane. During this leg of gradual ascent, the forest changed from maple and cypress to birch and pine, from temperate to montane, encouraging the illusion of hiking back in time to postglacial 8,000 B.C.

At the park's frontier, a crenellated stone wall some ten feet high conjured the Middle Ages rather than prehistory, and theoretically repulsed nonpaying riffraff. To both left and right it disappeared among evergreen fronds and scaly white trunks. The pavement in front of ponderous, yawning double gates widened into a car lot, presently accommodating only a German bus and a few Italian and Swiss jalopies.

On circular welcome sign above the rounded gateway, the park's apparent mascot, as cribbed from ancient petroglyph, predominated. Birdlike head surmounted a stocky human silhouette, whose arms each held aloft a hammer. It was the closest Vic would come here to a greeting from a local friend, for he'd made the acquaintance of this image, uncharitably characterized in a guidebook as "a beaked monster beating itself," during pre-vacation research. Nice to see it enjoying pride of place in the environs of Zero, and it reassured Vic his pilgrimage had the blessings of nondenominational cosmos, or anyway of a cryptic avatar.

The attendant behind Plexiglas who exchanged euros for a ticket, and the counterperson who sold exorbitant liters of Acqua Panna, were no cheerier than bank tellers, as if they didn't work anywhere extraordinary. Nor did this uninspired park show off its attractions to any advantage. Instead of landscaping that emphasized scenic vistas, dirt paths with rusty iron rods for railings wormed through green tunnels of dense bushes and undergrowth, overall obscuring as much as directing perceptions. When trails spewed him into the blinding sunlight, they became boardwalks alongside beetling outcrops or straddling defoliated tableland.

Pictographs on these rock expanses were not only well beyond reach of grubby fingers, but also out of comfortable focus, especially in noon glare. Because he'd schooled himself beforehand, squinting Vic was able to identify stick figures in procession behind a ceremonial ox-cart, other stick figures hunting elk, cross-sections of Bronze Age houses like chalets on stilts, solar discs like archery targets, and blocky, horned, ithyphallic gods.

Where boardwalk skirted the base of a sheer flint cliff, he overtook a sixtyish couple in matching Aussie slouch hats and ill-advised shorts. They were forlornly goggling at spiky-headed warriors dueling with spears and shields, as if blind to what the signage welded to guardrail was describing. Vic thought better of cluing them in when he cleared his throat and they regarded him askance in unison. Besides, no telling what language they spoke.

He soldiered on into green tunnel again, with smoldering exasperation at this game of topographic peekaboo, this obnoxious concealment of the general landscape. He had access only to disconnected points, with no map to unite them, retaining no impression of traversing a park per se. What kind of memories would survive, especially since the camera around his neck was useless in the blanching sunshine? He'd have to stock up on pamphlets and postcards back at the entrance. Maybe he'd air-mail Darcy a *vista panoramica* of what she was missing.

Worse and worse, claustrophobia was assailing him when that German busload came trudging around the bend, projecting no more geniality than the clueless twosome. Bad timing had released a sluiceway of ill-humored humanity upon him. Outbursts of nattering were brief and sporadic, and their inflections were petulant, demoralized. Must have been the heat. Many of these wilting fifty-somethings were fanning themselves with fliers from the visitors' center. They seemed of neither a mood nor a disposition to part ranks for him graciously. Vic dreaded an unsporting gauntlet of jostling and elbows as much as he resented the prospect of doubling back to wider boardwalk. What right did these damn Germans have to push him around?

Almost from the get-go, Vic had bridled at huffy warnings, also welded to the rails at random intervals, to stay on the railed paths. "Trespass in the Land Disallowed!" The journey here had imposed frequent hassles, from jetlag right up to this morning's dusty, dehydrating hike. He'd paid *molto* euros to enter these dubious precincts, he was feeling distinctly shortchanged, and now an ideal excuse to "Trespass in the Land" was bearing down on him. Stony, overgrown tracks into the wooded heights, little more than erosion runnels, had beckoned every so often, and one emerged between him and the impending phalanx.

Vic hustled ahead and ducked into leafy recess scant yards away from ugly collision. The Germans at arm's length trooped by, in two tones of sallow thanks to complexion and sunblock, and none turned sweaty heads to acknowledge him with a frown or, God forbid, a polite nod, as if he'd never existed. But then, hadn't he disappeared into metaphorical rabbit hole to parts unknown? So what if the crazy rabbit had contrarily burrowed upward? Fun at last! He fairly sprang into delinquency.

Steep channel had become more overtly a trail by the time Vic's knees began to ache. It was still a tough 45° slog as forest abruptly transitioned to rugged, patchy meadow, and Vic soon took a breather to survey the terrain he'd covered. It remained terra incognita because the forest spread its canopy over the dell, hiding all except the treeless boardwalk areas from him, and fortuitously hiding him from tourists and park personnel. Around him towered the hazy, sublime ring of mountaintops primeval. In terms of memorable scenery, this was more like it, and whatever petroglyphs awaited were his to examine close-up and photograph and even manhandle with impunity. Not that he'd court the bad karma of abusing anything touted as sacred.

On the slopes above, black creases of several paths crisscrossed and spanned the mineral gray and sparse pale green. Someone's feet had to be maintaining these literal folkways, whether shepherds or hunters or the Camunian version of hillbillies.

Vic's route continued its straight ascent, intersected another trail at right angles, and terminated among some boulders. Aha! A destination for the locals, he reckoned. A repository of sacred carvings? Or a hide from which to ambush moose or goats or lesser game? Captivated Vic scrambled skyward, his amateurish footwork loosing mini-cascades of scree. Without pause or lateral glance he brazened past the crossroad as if it represented a barrier, a borderline.

On the rockbound terrace at the head of the trail he was panting for oxygen. Was he that out of shape, or already at an elevation to induce altitude sickness? He shelved this no-win choice in favor of snooping among the scraggy crescent of boulders. Nope, no engravings, and no spent shells or ashes of campfires. Nothing so clear-cut.

Toward one end of the crescent, a crinkle in the mountain's flank deepened into a triangular cleft, high and wide enough to sidle into with hunching shoulders and bent knees. The crooked row of glacial erratics perfectly screened the cleft from onlookers below. And though daylight was brightening its interior for now, the sun hadn't far to sink till the boulders blocked its rays.

Well, was it or was it not this cave he'd traversed ocean and continents to explore? Or anyway, this kind of doorway to restorative experience? He clenched his teeth and squeezed inside, taunted by the possibility of permanent regret if he shied from this veritable high point of his adventure. To his relief, the temperature dipped refreshingly, and the tight entrance led to a comfier pocket, the first in a series of chambers and puckers receding into the black heart of the mountain, like geologic pleats wrought by eons of quakes and rockslides.

The riot of markings on the seamed and scoured walls was obvious before his vision adjusted to the soupy twilight. Did deeper chambers host more artwork? This one was adorned to repletion and then some. Centuries of bone and bronze and steel chisels had cavalierly incised symbols and people and animals on top of cracks and each other. Sculptors had conjoined or juxtaposed leaping deer and stylized shoeprints and priapic swordsmen and spiraling labyrinths and relatively recent upside-down crosses and broken church keys and popish silhouettes, in miter and cassock, skewered on spears. Voodoo-wise, at least, the natives hadn't taken witch trials and Inquisition lying down.

Though Vic carried no brief for the papacy, its impalement in effigy made him uneasy and reminded him of last night's carnival laughter under the suffering Christ. On the other hand, what was this? He detected color in a random assortment of older and newer images, sometimes faded flecks, sometimes full coverage in white or blue or ocher.

No rationale occurred to him for particular colors in particular pictographs, or for the coloration of some and not others, but that hardly dampened his pride in discovering this mother lode of a gallery, even if "discovery" was a relative business. Seemingly secret site may have been common knowledge to park officials or archaeologists or everyone in Zero. Someone had been sprucing up the contents of this cave within the shelf life of modern paint.

But was that any reason not to document like mad in here? Someday he might luck into a coffee-table book about this very chamber. Till that doubtful hour, he could make this place a little more his own by photographing it from end to end. Hell, maybe he'd be the author of that coffee-table book. From a distance, his rapid-fire automatic flash may have read as gunplay or the Fourth of July. As if this wasteland attracted enough traffic to worry about.

The room narrowed toward the rear, and two massive slabs tilted together to form both the back wall and the pointy archway into the next chamber. They struck Vic as ominous, like gigantic poised mandibles. Alongside the left slab, a gap prevented the side and back walls from meeting. It contained the meager dimensions of a voting booth or a changing stall at K-mart.

Vic padded warily into the breach, as if doing so fulfilled a fated progression from open countryside to park to cave to this pitch-black cranny, all in the direction of epiphany. Dammit, he'd hoped the dark would be less absolute on the inside, but it wasn't. Giving his eyes a minute to adapt made no difference. He'd get his only glimpses of whatever surrounded him by taking snapshots with the automatic flash.

He hoisted viewfinder to his face and was about to shoot when something barely audible made him hesitate. Maybe a bead of condensation on the ceiling had plunked against the floor. Maybe someone had put down a leather sack. It might have come from the mouth of the cave or the next chamber or right outside his niche. It might have been his imagination, which felt more plausible the longer he waited in silence.

He was on the impatient cusp of firing away with camera still pressing up to eyebrow when faint rustling and clatter stopped him, along with what he identified as the sound of dabbing, if there really was such a sound. Gradually these were supplanted by the snuffling, wheezy respiration of a man deaf to his own noises, lost in concentration.

Should Vic announce himself? Try his Berlitz Italian on this putative local who might impart priceless lore about these petroglyphs? He opened his mouth and let it hang open as the raspy breathing erupted into guttural, self-absorbed chuckles. This wasn't nice clean laughter, as Vic's grandma used to say. And Vic was not only trapped in this black cubbyhole, but also facing inward, blind to hostile movements, like a sacrificial calf.

The chuckling subsided, and Vic prayed no pebbles crunched underfoot as he slowly turned with baby steps toward coarse exhalations. Mission accomplished, but then a ballsy impulse hijacked better judgment. Thanks to the angle of weak sun infiltrating the cave, nothing in his alcove was visible from without, right? He hazarded one step heel-to-toe, and another, and another, gambling that the heavy breather would impinge on his line of sight.

He peered down into the pure black and forced himself one more inch forward. If he couldn't see his shoes, nobody else could either. This was the limit, though. The width of a doorsill separated him from exposure. He raised his eyes. His teeth would have clicked in alarm as his jaws clenched, had he not bitten his tongue.

In euphemistic terms, here was simply an artist in the middle of the creative act, a mere pitchfork's length away, between Vic and the entrance. At the painter's booted feet was a silver flashlight propped on a stone, illuminating the wall in front of him and casting his features into stark chiaroscuro. From a bag of sewn hides he must have fetched the palette of birch bark in one hand and the double-headed brush in the other. He was dipping one brush end into a gob of sulfurous pigment that smelled almost as acrid as the artist, and expert hand had needed no visual guidance to find the paint.

Ghoulish lighting from below, Vic conjectured, might be doing this rough-hewn *paisan* a disservice, might exaggerate his balefulness, his brutality. Craggy exterior may be shielding a gentle soul, sociable, wise. Vic searched leering expression for any hint of redeeming traits and decided to err on the side of caution.

Tiny eyes like single currants at the bottoms of bowls glowered at the task before them, and fleshy lower lip protruded in abstraction. The nose would have fit more happily on a Boston terrier, and oysterish ears stuck out like trophy handles. Thick blond hair was spiky, like boar bristles. The fist gripping paintbrush thrust violently at the wall, as if violence were a ritual part of this activity, halting at the last instant to daub carefully. Here was someone so unlike anyone Vic had ever seen that he might well have clambered from the bowels of a cavern. Was he atavistic or inbred or relict, as if those labels were mutually exclusive?

Meanwhile, despite harrowing situation, Vic harbored a spark of wonderment at spying on a breed of continuity wholly unexpected. Aboriginal Australians, with a cultural stability unthinkable in the

West, had revered the same outback sanctums for 40,000 years and took occasional initiative to retouch mythic scenes within them using a mix of ash, clay, and blood. This never failed to awe Vic, who couldn't even sustain a relationship much beyond three months. To find similar tradition on a millennial order in his own ancestral homeland was likewise awesome, perhaps more so because of its personal resonance.

Yet he couldn't be related to this throwback. And where the Aboriginal custom always came across as benign and sympathetic, this version smacked of the sinister, the feral, of clannishness or secret society. But such cultish aura was understandable. Maybe this strain of the population couldn't have survived otherwise, after centuries of persecution by the Church and whoever else. How could family lore of forebears burned as "witches" not exert an embittering effect?

An outbreak of shrill whistling restored him to the moment. The unsavory artist was gone, and wherever he had come from, he was now twittering down the hill, in a style reminiscent of those indigenous Canary Islanders who communicated across valleys by warbling in ancient code. The Camunian tune was melancholy, uncommitted to one time signature, somehow unnerving, and no doubt archaic. Vic didn't dare budge until the tune dwindled away and then a while longer, to let a stray fidget or cough betray any lurking confederates.

The bag of art supplies was also gone, but the sulfurous reek and the flashlight remained. Anemic beam still hit the wall, encircling new handiwork. Could the painter, throwback or not, really have been so forgetful? Vic resolved to take a gander, and a snapshot, and then vamoose in case absent-minded owner had reversed course to retrieve his lighting source.

Later, however, Vic wasn't sure how long he'd stood there gawking. First, within the chaos of engravings, he had to home in on those few with wet paint, to the exclusion of the rest, and treat them as a composition. Then he had to figure out what each of them depicted, which brought him no closer to understanding their collective meaning.

To the right were three of the so-called paddles, two whitewashed and one blackened. They were rectangular with knobbed handles, like mirrors or cardboard fans, but whatever object they'd actually represented, according to online informants, was a prehistoric riddle. Rather, they functioned symbolically to confer influence or control or victory or simple luck. These paddles radiated, handles outward, away from a polychromatic stick figure with arms raised in supplication or prayer or self-defense. To his left, the point of a relatively giant dagger menaced him, of the venerated type dubbed "Mycenaean," though its design had graced ancient monuments everywhere between Stonehenge and Karnak.

Poor stick figure, hemmed in at knifepoint! Vic examined its colors more carefully, and suddenly his compassion was a far cry from academic. The cranium was brown, the torso was yellow, and the legs were blue, just like Vic's hair, shirt, and jeans. Coincidence? Or no less unlikely, an extrasensory appraisal of what should have been his invisible, unsuspected self? Or would a lateral glance down at the crossroad have shown him this daunting character en route? And if the daunting character had spotted him, which seemed altogether feasible, then the flashlight must have been aiming at something Vic was supposed to see.

Now that knife and paddles were endowed with more personal connotations, they could be nothing but diabolical. Was he under Bronze Age curse for a trespass graver than he'd realized? Had he set that curse in motion by viewing graven imagery of himself? Or did a mean-spirited prankster want him to believe that? Yeah, that was it. The underemployed around here must have made a sport of fucking with the damned Americans.

Still, his effigy in the crosshairs of malice was more disturbing the longer he gaped at it. He had to go, show it his scornful back, deny it any power over him. And he felt obliged to exit in haste. He had yet to photograph the entire wall behind him, but the sun was already half-hidden by one of the boulders out on the ledge, and to grope through the worse impending darkness would be plain reckless. Besides, he'd imbibed more than his fill of tradition and revelation for one afternoon.

A pregnant hush, a somber ambience invested alpine meadow, tangled forest, and unpeopled boardwalks during his descent. It had to be in his head. The environment would not be unnaturally quiet just because he'd entered a secret cave. True, he'd crossed more than one forbidden line, but no park authorities popped out of nowhere to clap him on the shoulder, no blond primitives waylaid him.

On the road into town he invoked a favorite mantra, that guilt was for idiots. Therefore remorse couldn't account for his subdued mood. And he'd already concluded he wasn't cursed. He tried to relax, allow his thoughts a looser tether, dwell more mindfully on himself.

Aha, it finally got through that he was hungry. How long ago was breakfast? What time was it now? Especially hard to pin down during European midsummer.

Underneath the iron Christ, the carnival scene had vanished without trace, like ancient history. Or hereabouts, more completely than ancient history. This was his first unobstructed look at the piazza, and where yesterday a kiddie-scale Ferris wheel rattled and creaked, the green awnings of a trattoria telescoped well into vacant space, like a canvas arcade.

The clock in town hall gable read 4:30. Could that be accurate? Had moments in the mysterious cave dilated into hours, like a touch of Rip Van Winkle in the Alps? Vic had yet to get the hang of Italian dining habits and made a beeline for the restaurant in case its kitchen was due to close till eight or later.

Greeting him in the shade of the foremost awning was a plywood cutout of a mustachioed chef, bearing chalkboard announcement of daily specials, mostly involving risotto and polenta and veal. Vic was grateful that the chef was modeled on vapid stereotype and not on vicious hill folk with recessive genes.

The better to be noticed, he chose a table next to that of the other customers, a pair of sunburnt pensioners nursing goblets of red wine. A dark, plump girl in black knit slacks and starchy white shirt, an outfit perhaps intended to complement the black-and-white checked tablecloths, brought him a menu and smiled pleasantly, leading him to believe he wasn't putting everyone out.

The bill of fare was on a single xeroxed sheet within clear plastic and a metal frame, which apparently hung upside-down from a peg hole in a long wooden handle when not in use. As Vic tested his language skills on descriptions of Lombard delicacies, he did his best to ignore the similarity of the menu to a paddle.

Out the corner of his eye, the black knit fabric of wait staff uniform had already rematerialized at tableside. It startled him a little, and he raised his sights toward white shirt and beyond, and found it wasn't the girl at all. In the cave he'd speculated that the flashlight's placement might have exaggerated the painter's freakishness. Now he could verify that it hadn't. A couple of desperate blinks failed to normalize that monstrous face.

To the pensioners' astonishment, Vic's upended chair was clattering upon the cobblestones, and before the waiter had spoken or moved, Vic was up and running across the square to his hotel. Was he a victim of hallucination after too much sun? That was a possibility to address at leisure, not when vengeful savage might be at his heels.

A block of flint propped oaken hotel door open during the day. Vic dashed blindly past the reception counter and up the steps, two at a time, to his room. He locked himself in and panted for breath. Was he in a refuge or a trap? Should he hole up or hightail it? Since he never unloaded his backpack, he was always primed for quick getaway, so that was in his favor. And then the half-length mirror on the wall made the decision for him.

In keeping with the rightful occupant's decorating scheme, the mirror celebrated Coca-Cola, with logo in bold red spanning the width of rectangular glass, and a black and red mosaic frame from whose bottom edge projected a Coke bottle, approximating the outline of a pestle or a wooden spoon.

Maybe Vic shouldn't have slammed the door so vigorously on his way in. While staring bleakly at his reflection, he began divining mirror's resemblance to a shape he'd already come to dread, when it plummeted straight down and burst with a racket like a car crashing into a storefront. He instantly squinched his eyes shut, but felt no flying shards or particles. His reaction was visceral, galvanic, out of his control, and his vision was still a bit bleary as he scooped backpack off the floor and fled the room, letting the doorknob bang into corridor wall.

He staggered over to reception and slapped down his key. The manageress sat dumbfounded, at an understandable loss for what to think yet. "There's been an accident," he blurted in English. Should he squander precious seconds and translate that into Italian? Would that really help? He'd paid for two nights in advance. Let her keep the money for tonight to make up for the busted mirror. Yeah, that ought to appease his temporarily shellshocked conscience.

He bolted into the daylight and down the first street off the piazza. The houses looked kind of familiar. He might be backtracking toward the Plexiglas-and-steel bus shelter where the name Zero first caught his fancy. Then again, these hulking, stuccoed houses were all pretty much alike.

Dammit, he wouldn't be in this mess if Darcy hadn't flaked out on him. She'd have put her foot down when he tried sneaking off the designated trail. Hell, she'd have put her foot down at his impulse to disembark in Zero. With her restraint to balance his spontaneity, they'd probably be having fun together in some other town right now. Fucking Darcy.

But then, Vic's legendary luck was on the rebound! Up ahead where the street took a dogleg turn, the bus stop's tubular struts threw mannerist afternoon shadows onto narrow sidewalk and a mustard-yellow wall. His shirt might even blend well enough with that yellow to pass for camouflage. Without removing his backpack, he plopped onto faux-wood plastic bench and let the burning in his lungs recede.

Of course, no schedule of arrivals was posted on the Plexiglas. And as idle minutes ticked by, Vic more keenly felt his need for food and bathroom, both of which he'd forgone since breakfast. He anxiously padded farther along the road and strained his eyes in vain for a corner store, with frequent glances backward. A coach could pull in from either direction.

The townscape henceforth became more suburban, with alleys and weedy lots between buildings. From the alley beside him, warm breeze was rank with stale piss. Others waiting for a bus, he theorized, had set a precedent for him to follow. Well, didn't fortune favor the brave? He strolled on in, wrinkled his nose at the added pungency, surveyed a claustrophobic wasteland of rubble and parched vegetation, wondered where curving stairs at the far end led, listened to the dead silence, and let fly into a clump of brown grass in a crack of masonry foundation.

He went off-target when his roaming eyes met an old acquaintance. The "beaked monster beating itself with hammers," the mascot of the Parco Nazionale, was looming above him, as reproduced with stencil and magenta spray paint. Vic was fond of this quizzical pictogram, and was sorry he hadn't happened upon it inside the park, but finding it in piss alley was off-putting. What's more, beneath it was a freehand inscription in an alphabet strange to Vic, superficially like runic crossed with Greek. Again he felt he was encroaching, this time upon a gang marking turf with spray cans and urine.

He zipped up, and a noise from the mouth of the alley lodged his heart in his throat. A bus engine! He raced to the street, flapping his arms and hollering, and could scarcely believe his luck, now verging on the fantastic. The bus was approaching from town and was not quite abreast of the shelter as Vic scrambled into the driver's line of sight. Brakes whined, engine downshifted, bus jerked to a standstill, and door whooshed open. Ecstatic Vic boarded. He handed the doughy, grizzled driver a bunch of euros without counting them, or saying anything, or giving the least thought to a destination. Glum driver counted the money, nodded, and arm-wrestled the gearshift.

Vic stumbled into one of many empty seats as his rolling sanctuary lurched onward. His half-dozen fellow passengers evidently found him less interesting than their tabloids or crossword puzzles or window views. He wriggled out of his backpack and left it with straps akimbo on adjacent seat, and all the exertion and stress since he'd fled the hotel overtook him. In the air conditioning, his sweaty clothes stuck to him like cold, clammy plaster. And when he tried to rest his eyes, the spectacle of Coca-Cola mirror dropping like a guillotine blade repeated, with the perseverance of midnight ruminations.

Okay, he'd slammed hotel-room door. That, he tried convincing himself, would logically shake a heavy object from its wall hook, or detach an overtaxed nail. But with every replay, he recognized more vividly the occult repayment of intrusion with intrusion, the unfolding of shamanic curse. He'd escaped it, though, hadn't he? Or had it succeeded in flushing him from under cover? He curbed these flights of unreason and minded the scenery. He'd slammed the door and down came the mirror. Period.

As escapes went, this one was vexingly stop-and-go. Labyrinthine bus route included every minuscule hamlet and all too many roadsides in the middle of nowhere. No more than a single person ever shambled on or off. At some shelters the driver paused a while without gain or loss of riders, and others he sped blithely by. Vic debated whether they were still in Camonica Valley and took it in stride that no locales on signs were familiar. In three thousand years, almost as many names could have piled up for every point in the topography.

He hadn't planned this exodus past getting on the bus. In his beleaguered state, an indefinite circuit of the countryside was fine. Hunger pangs no longer plagued him. His stomach must have shrunk. So why not travel in comfort till the driver kicked him out when he'd used up his fare, or when they reached the terminus, somewhere major enough, presumably, to boast multiple hotels and restaurants? What's more, sun slid behind peaks and imposed abrupt nightfall. Soon the headlights were boring through inky black, and Vic was loath to hop off anyplace without streetlamps.

In anonymous moonlit jerkwater, he watched indifferently as the bus switched drivers. Good news, initially. The new guy had no idea where Vic had boarded and might well let him ride around forever. Good became bad in a heartbeat, though, when dashboard lights starkly etched the replacement's protruding lip and terrier nose and cavernous eye sockets. Yes, Vic decided, they were still in Camonica.

He hunkered down and pressed boggling eye to the gap between the seats in front of him. Was this the same individual in yet another guise, or a fellow inbred tribesman? The distinction was irrelevant. The whole fiendish cult likely had it in for him, and changing out of telltale yellow shirt now would only draw unfriendly attention. Or had the driver IDed him already?

The bus rumbled into the rural night. Vic's strenuous day minus food and water might well be distorting senses and judgment. Hallucinogenic agar may have tainted bread and jam at breakfast. But did he dare buy into those hypotheses? No, he had to play it safe, and his sole safeguard was the ongoing presence of other passengers. Furtive head count fore and aft apprised him of three drowsy yokels, too unobservant or tipsy to balk at the ogre chauffeuring them. Yet that ogre wouldn't pounce on him amidst even a groggy audience, would he?

At every shelter the bus jolted to a halt, at every sharp turn the tires squealed, and at every pothole the chassis bounced, till Vic heard himself grumbling, despite dire predicament, What the hell kind of Neanderthals do they hire out here? Even that poor vestige of humor dissolved when no further riders climbed on, and one, then another trundled off. He fixated on the brown leather newsboy cap, half-eclipsed by the headrest, of the final passenger. He could feel his inner mainspring tighten as the minutes slowed to a glacial pace. Eventually he was seeing only the cap, like the center of an iris-in surrounded by darkness, and he wondered if he were mesmerizing himself. Then the cap was gone. Fuck! Would he ever learn not to zone out?

He blinked and there was the passenger, bobbing down the aisle as the vehicle shuddered into park. Vic leapt up, seizing backpack by the strap after very nearly forgetting it, and hustled within inches of shuffling heels so that the door couldn't slam in his face. He shunned any glance at the driver as foolhardy.

Luck may have smiled again after all. As he hit the pavement, his spine stiffened in readiness for blunt object to strike it. Instead, the bus door wheezed shut, and with a clumsy stripping of gears the bus roared benignly past him and away. And hallelujah, he could make out the glow of streetlights beyond the end of this piddling lane where the bus had dropped him, the promise of a real town with hotels and restaurants, not just three ramshackle hovels around a well or a gas station.

His footsteps echoed as if in a tunnel, and the way forward, with no alleys or side streets between houses, reinforced his impression of skulking through an underground passage. Every window but one, in a third story just ahead, was shuttered and dark. A silhouette, backlit by low wattage, was framed in that window's pale rectangle. For a second he dreamed it was Darcy, or somehow an Italian equivalent, with whom destiny ordained he'd live happily ever after. Wouldn't that be his luck in spades?

But below that rectangle hung the faint outline of long teardrop-shaped latch for fastening the shutters. Vic, though too overwrought to articulate why, suddenly wanted to give that window wider berth than the lane allowed.

He also had to choose whether to fall back or push past the plodding codger in the leather cap. Why not slow down, take it easy? He'd be out of this tunnel soon enough.

Then before Vic could fall back, the man whipped around, sized up T-shirt, jeans, and deck shoes, and snarled in gravelly English, as if eager for pretext of self-defense, "Are you following me?" The breath clogged in Vic's throat at deep-sunk eyes, knobby nose, and wicked underbite in immediate range. The trophy-handle ears should have been funny, but weren't. From a sheath on his belt, concealed by tweed jacket, Vic's nemesis pulled a dagger whose half-moon pommel and triangular blade were typically Mycenaean. Who the hell still made those?

Vic only had time to gape in despair toward the piazza, a scant stone's throw away. Roughly half of the backside of huge iron cross showed from here. And into his head flashed a final, uncomforting insight—that all blood sacrifice was offered in self-defense, really, wasn't it?

The silhouette in the window bore witness to everything without twitching a muscle, as if resigned to an iron continuity, a force of custom, as old as the land. After it was all over and the camera had been pulverized under boot heels, the silhouette pulled the shutters together, and the pale rectangle went black.

Election Roundup

Candidate Whitman wasn't stupid. He only cultivated that down-home, unschooled persona to fool some of the people all the time, to pass for one of the rubes and disguise his Ivy League frat, Fortune 500 underpinnings. It had defined "presidential" for more than one esteemed predecessor, hadn't it?

Therefore he understood immediately why Mephisto made an entrance by popping into goat-horned, goateed, black-and-red silk operatic splendor beside him, where a second ago his campaign advisor had sat, in the backseat of speeding limo on southbound 95 between Aberdeen and Baltimore. Why invest tedious minutes proving that Lucifer and not flamboyant loony was accosting him? Basic infernal legerdemain nipped argument in the bud. Whitman did hope that Hank, despite their differences, would be restored to him minus charring and the reek of brimstone.

And where lesser men, such as Hank, may have panicked at supernatural incursion, Whitman refrained from visible response, in part because he refused to rank himself among lesser men. Moreover, what if a mere hallucination sat there, generated by election-cycle stress and fatigue? How then could panic not be counterproductive? As for the reality of Satan, Whitman had always accorded it minimal thought, but those months of campaigning had softened him up to believe pretty much whatever at face value. The chauffer, with one-way glass between front and back seats, wasn't an issue.

No slave to convention, the devil leapt right to the point, leaning toward Whitman for emphasis. "I, the Prince of Everything Material, beg leave to borrow your soul, nothing more."

Whitman reckoned he'd gain nothing playing dumb with the Prince of Everything Material. "Borrow? Since when was that your modus operandi?"

"Live and learn," Mephisto shrugged and sat back, with an air somehow both florid and blasé. "Commitment is hardly the watchword of this era, is it? To drum up any worthwhile business, I've had to limit the scope of my contracts." Diabolical green eyes stared at the leather upholstery before them as if applying X-ray vision to the minibar behind it. "So aren't you going to offer me some refreshment? Knob Creek and branch water? A martini? Laphroaig neat?"

"Am I supposed to?" Whitman arched an eyebrow. "I always took for granted you could hocus-pocus whatever you wanted."

Satan sighed. "What do they teach at Harvard these days? You might at least have absorbed Mick Jagger's advice blaring from stereos at a hundred campus parties. If you meet me, have some courtesy, some sympathy, and some taste? I paraphrase, but even your dull Puritan forebears had the horse sense to euphemize me as Robin Goodfellow or Old Nick. I'm to be propitiated."

"Sorry. You want a drink?"

"Not thirsty." He pouted, but with a mocking gleam. "It's the principle of the thing."

Whitman never rose to bait. He prided himself on that as much as anything. Still, he couldn't help concluding, *What a devious bloody fop.* "Would I be discourteous asking how this transaction would benefit you? What you would do with a soul on loan?"

"Maybe I like the way they sing in their cages. Maybe they liven up my gloomy den, swimming around in an aquarium. Maybe they make whimsical chess pieces. Maybe I pad the inventory with them to aggravate the heavenly busybodies." He gathered breath to expound some more.

"Okay, none of my business. Fine." Devilish cologne that seemed somehow distilled from clove cigarettes had become cloying, but Whitman held off on the potential tactlessness of cracking a window.

"Yes, that's right. Not your business. Here's what you do need to know." The beatific sincerity beaming at him Whitman recognized from every politician's face, his included, when spouting pre-election vows. "I'm as bound by my name on the dotted line as you are. If you choose to reclaim your soul on the expiration date, I reunite it with your body, no questions asked. And till then, your every wish will be granted in a straightforward, guileless manner." His smile grew pathologically unctuous. "Think of this as a trial offer. A special getting-acquainted deal. You surely won't be damned for dipping your toe in the water." Then again, Old Nick was also dubbed the Father of Lies, wasn't he?

"What makes you so convinced I can't win without you?" Hank never wearied of listing Whitman's stumbling blocks, but the candidate wasn't about to concede those and make Satanic job easier.

Disappointed Satan tsk-tsked. "Really, you can't afford even to pretend naïveté at this stage. Beating the incumbent is always an uphill battle. Do you want a roll call of all the hopefuls who profited from admitting that to me?"

Yes, he did, though that would have amounted to another form of bait, of losing valuable ground in their conversational tug-of-war. Don't give an inch! "I'm afraid I have to be blatantly P.I. here. Whoever they were, I'm whiter than anybody in the history of American presidential hopefuls, and it's a dazzling, charismatic white. Forgive my honesty, but that's what put me over the top in every local and state race. Not my fault if the voters swing that way, and it's not a quality, however you define it, that requires your helping hand."

Lucifer felt around on his armrest and toggled his window halfway down, which, Whitman realized too late, was a ploy to make him self-conscious. He couldn't pin down definitively why it did, but it put him off his game when urbane Satan expounded, "Now Monty, if you'll pardon my informality, I'd never presume to improve upon your whiteness. I simply ask you to consider its double-edged nature. Your detractors refer to you as 'Whiteman Whitman.' That doesn't play in your favor. It can't come as news to you that complexion no longer equals carte blanche, and I sympathize, at least to the degree I doubt you're serious. Without luck, on the other hand, there are no sure earthly bets, unless we reach an accommodation and luck becomes irrelevant. Wish wisely, and the White House is yours, and none will suspect my helping hand."

Intrigued in spite of himself, Whitman countered, "And what do you suggest I wish for, since my future's such an open book?"

The devil coyly shook his ruddy head. "Am I your campaign manager? Is that in your budget?"

As for Hank, Whitman decided, best not to mention any of this. In fact, he couldn't conceive a single reason why he should, provided, of course, he ever saw Hank again.

And speaking of opinionated campaign manager, what was that *idée fixe* of his? That Whitman had to loom large among homogeneous rivals, stake out an edge, promote his individuality, go out on a limb, as long as it was a solid, unassailable limb? Monty didn't often sport a mordant grin, but then again, how many candidates had occasion to interpret their handlers' advice as incentive to consort with the very devil?

That devil, meanwhile, was sniffing haughtily at fumy, humid Baltimore air streaming into his half-open window and buffeting the curly locks of his dangling goatee, the kind that dared you to pull it. Smug bastard, bristled Whitman, but as he stared out his own tinted glass at the ramshackle sea of brick and tarpaper tenements and rundown office buildings, he had to admit, Yeah, his signature had been a foregone conclusion all along. An eyeful of urban blight usually hardened him to the human condition and made a franker pragmatist of him.

Mephisto cleared his throat. His airways sounded gritty. "Always had a soft spot for Baltimore, myself. Glad we didn't take the tunnel. I'm underground too much as it is." Whitman resented any onus on him to acknowledge purposely lame wit and pondered whether everything out of the Great Deceiver's mouth amounted to cryptic manipulation. "What say we start with a three-week lease? That'll secure you the party nomination, and then we can discuss another short-term stint. No pressure. I'd never dream of adding to the stress of election season. Done and done?"

Mephisto extended a leathery maroon hand with the impeccably manicured long nails of a month-buried corpse. Whitman took hot, abrasive hand without hesitation. He'd shaken uglier.

"So where's the paperwork?" Somewhere off in the landscape, an antitheft alarm doubled as an echo of warning bells in his head. "We need to get this in writing. You did refer to a 'dotted line,' as I recall."

"No cause to be suspicious, Monty. A hand seal has been legally binding for millennia. See?" From a fold in black velvet cape, His Infernal Highness drew a book. The cape was adorned with a scarlet flamepoint design that made Whitman think of drag strips. The book was slightly worn at the corners, in octavo format, bound in creamy leather, edged in ox bile. "You gave me the idea yourself when you likened your life to an open book."

He leafed briskly through initial spotless pages that picked up stains and flyspecks as he went along, till he stopped about two-thirds in and jabbed scaly index finger at dense, tiny print. "Here. It says right here we validated this pact today in the back seat of your limo." He treated Whitman to the ghastly rictus of a smirk. "You've heard of the word made flesh? This is the spirit made word."

Whitman was briefly speechless, not because his soul had been converted to a pocket edition, but because the page in question implied he was somewhat more than halfway to his grave. Never had he had to confront mortality in such graphic mode. Do not, repeat, do not accept the book if Satan offers it. Indulging temptation to peruse the ending would absolutely not conduce to his happiness. Rather, he belabored the self-evident. "You're telling me that's my soul? You removed it already? I get nothing for my records?"

Satan pursed his arid lips. "You are a stickler for the technicalities, aren't you? Fine, if we must." From another velvet fold, he drew a variation on those oblong doohickeys for credit card or UPS transactions, with a liquid crystal display for inkless signatures. His cadaverous fingernail scratched something across the display, and he tossed the doohickey to Whitman, who found Satanic penmanship as illegible as anybody's on those devices. As an afterthought, the devil plucked a plastic stylus from his bountiful cloak, and Whitman received it from maroon fingertips. His scrawl was no more legible than Satan's.

"How do you print out this contract?" Whitman started handing the device back, but his new associate waved it away.

"Keep it. The hard drive holds a copy of what's in the book. It's purely for your peace of mind." Peace of mind? Whitman haplessly ogled the two black scribbles on the little green screen. Though he hadn't a clue about operating the doohickey, the grievous details and date of his death were in there, and how was he supposed to coexist with that? Lucifer may as well have chucked him a ticking bomb.

He looked up, meaning to say as much in flustered, uncertain terms, but Hank and nobody else was sitting beside him, blinking at half-open window and remarking, "Baltimore already? Y'know, I've always had a soft spot for this town." Not even his damn fool side-burns were singed. Before the exit for Glen Burnie, Whitman had managed to stash the doohickey between the seat cushions with Hank none the wiser, and Hank had resumed his irksome song-and-dance about aspiring to more than the standard pandering this noon when Whitman addressed the American Nurses' Association in Bethesda.

Whitman, for the nonce, debated his sanity, and who but a madman would not? Then he experimentally "dipped his toe," in devilish parlance, at the ANA banquet, partly for the petty pleasure of showing Hank up. Poor Hank could only roll his watery eyes when explosive applause rewarded the "standard pandering" of hollow flattery and platitudes.

Afterward, to avoid any whiff of complicity, however far-fetched, in events serving his interests alone, Monty framed wishes of such indirect benefit that he questioned whether his influence had actually been necessary. He plodded steadily ahead in the polls. No riptide surges. The Dow underperformed woefully, despite business headlines that normally reenergized it, but the market always was an irrational beast, wasn't it? Unemployment numbers stubbornly hovered in the double digits, flouting federal incentives and Pollyanna forecasts. Blame unfairly fell on the incumbent, with nary a twinge of remorse from Whitman. Since when was power the game for a tender conscience?

He likewise lost no sleep over the more widespread human toll of making his dream come true. On that score the devil's involvement was entirely extraneous, and Whitman's attitude was no different than during his salad days on Wall Street. In fine, how many customers at Wendy's contemplate the slaughterhouse while chomping on a hamburger? Fuck those liberal hypocrites with the gall to lay guilt trips on him. People would go hungry, broke, and homeless with or without Whitman shifting the goalposts.

Obligatory Sunday churchgoing continued, with no apparent perception by man or deity of his soulless state. Lightning didn't fell him when he set foot on the portico, and nobody, from his wife to the minister, treated him any differently. Whitman certainly felt no more the infidel than usual.

And come the convention, despite unbeatable lead as party front runner for weeks before Mephisto's involvement, he explicitly wished for the delegates' endorsement, just to be on the safe side. Beyond that maybe he did go a tad overboard, magicking up his choice of VP running mate, golden eloquence for his acceptance speech, one-night celebratory extramarital fling, and those were only the memorable recourses to diabolic hoodoo.

But jubilant as he should have been at ambitions fulfilled without effort or strings attached, inexplicable malaise, a blunted satisfaction haunted him. A pragmatist on his scale couldn't have cared less that his success was "unearned." What was he, a Sunday school teacher? That devilish contraption with his complete vital stats, currently ensconced in bedroom wall safe, must have contributed to his impaired affect. Nothing to do for that, however, except wish to forget devilish contraption whenever it sprang to mind. Why not? Wish-wise, the sky was the limit till his contract expired.

That termination date coincided with woozy day after closing ceremonies. Monty anticipated smartass or theatrical Satanic reappearance around every bend. Just the same, Lucifer managed to blindside him. Not for nothing did his aliases include Great Deceiver, and he'd been honing his chops for how many centuries?

To minimize chances of staff, handlers, or security bearing witness to Whitman's unholy affiliation, he'd sent them all home, except for diehard Hank, who insisted on a brunch discussion of Hank's interviews tomorrow on the network morning shows. As usual, campaign advisor arrived first in the hotel coffee shop and grabbed a secluded booth.

Eagle-eyed advisor homed right in on Whitman's midriff. "You skipped a loop on your belt." No need to explain how the press could inflate minor carelessness into a major embarrassment. Whitman didn't even slow down before continuing to the men's room to rectify his wardrobe malfunction.

He'd have sworn he was returning to the correct booth, but there sat a pungent homeless guy, huddled to one side and reading by the sliver of sunshine between curtain and window frame. For the rates this hotel charged, you'd think they could do a better job patrolling for riffraff.

Without laying eyes on him, the homeless guy wheezed, "Y'know, you could've just wished the belt into the loop and saved yourself a trip to the bathroom."

Yes, vagrant malodor did contain a telltale whiff of cloves. Disgusted Whitman sat across from fallen angel. "I hope you ordered us some coffee," Whitman said as if still addressing Hank.

"Damn waitress is ignoring me," Mephisto grumbled. He had yet to tear himself away from whatever preoccupied him below table level.

"I might wish you were more presentable," Monty commented, "but as you remarked, our bargain has run its course."

"Would you really prefer the public observed us together in my more traditional guise? Easy enough to hocus-pocus it for you." Green eyes sparked roguishly at the candidate's loss for words. "But since you're on your own again, Whiteman Whitman might do worse than a photo op with a bum. The pundits say you lack people skills, the empathy to connect with the great unwashed."

Cunning eyes flicked hither and yon from under shaggy brows. "The Secret Service detail, the boys you can't dismiss because they work for Uncle Sam and not for you, might be good at deflecting harm and harassment, but trust me when I count a dozen electronic gizmos immortalizing our chat, even filming it for YouTube with comical soundtracks attached. The Feds, in fact, are uploading with the best or worst of them. And sadly, the repercussions of those videos are out of your hands, at least at our present pass."

You son of a bitch, Whitman fumed, not caring how telepathic the archfiend was. He snatched the laminated one-sheet breakfast menu from its silver clip amidst the salt and pepper and sugar packets. He glowered at it as if it were a subpoena.

"Meanwhile, what have we here?" From off his lap the Prince of Everything Material scooped a white book lying open and facedown. He tossed it carelessly over to Whitman. It landed on a previous customer's crumbs. "All yours. That is, if you really want it back."

What the fuck had irresponsible devil done to Monty's borrowed soul? He was hard pressed not to sputter, but that was no spectacle to share with the world, let alone this infernal slob. The creamy leather was scuffed as if dragged behind a truck, circular stains implied misuse as a coaster, the spine had endured multiple cracks, the corners were blunted from numerous impacts, and a few loose pages were sticking out. "In its present state, you might feel better without it," Satan suggested.

Grungy fingers may have flexed in preparation for cracking knuckles, or had they started creeping up to repossess the book? Oh no you don't! Whitman, with vestigial reflexes from college rugby, made a protective grab for his property. No sooner did he register its warmth, whether from Satanic lap or its own innate vitality, than it was gone. "Well, that's settled," intoned the squalid Prince.

At Whitman's touch, his soul had darted to its fleshly nest, as he well comprehended because Satan, confound it, had been telling the truth. Whitman didn't fit together quite right anymore, as if giant ultrasharp scythe had swung down and split him in two or possibly three, and the planes of his divided self had slid apart a little. Each least movement stung, too, as if it triggered interior paper cuts, though a healing second later he couldn't say where exactly it had hurt. This was not what he needed while haggling with the Great Deceiver. And where the hell was the waitress?

Like the fulfillment of a bonus wish, there she was. Six feet tall, the build of an Olympic gymnast, auburn hair down to her delectable ass, and the bone structure of a goddess. The secret service youngster who hovered behind her in case she was an anarchist or a suicide bomber was as good as invisible. Whitman's impure thoughts inflicted a shooting pain, which he attributed to disheveled soul acting up. "Are you all right, sir?" the waitress asked.

Whitman ignored her concern and ordered. He avoided additional distress by training eyes on the menu. Then her lithe arm entered his field of view, and the long crimson nail of a slim finger was languidly encircling a line under Monday Specials. "For fifty cents more you also get orange juice and a slice of melon."

Beholding that much of her was enough to send pangs like a needle doing stitchwork down his spine. But already, to his dismay, he'd mechanically glanced up to say, "No thank you." Oceanic violet eyes and lascivious smile enthralled him, despite her slightly overgrown canines, for the instant before vertigo set the coffee shop gyrating. Through kaleidoscopic nausea he heard the devil command, "The usual for me. And don't forget the bottle of Tabasco."

"She's one of yours, isn't she?" croaked Monty through the vortex. He'd also decided he could weather no more of this spiritual turbulence, that he couldn't wait for body and soul to reintegrate eventually if ever, and why put himself through further torture when a follow-up deal was inevitable? He was perhaps literally hellbent now on clinching the election.

"I dare not entrust service positions to just anybody," Lucifer explained. He essayed the sleazy leer of a procurer. "But do you want her anyway?"

"If I do, I'll wish her into bed myself, thank you." Whitman's dizziness had subsided to midtempo seesawing, and he had no idea how long he'd been gripping the edge of the table for dear life. Sexy demoness had withdrawn to the kitchen or to Hades with their breakfast orders. The Secret Service dude, though his mirror shades made it hard to be sure, seemed to be gawking around as if she'd evaporated.

"By that I infer you'll not waste this morning shilly-shallying. Minus the specifics, we have an agreement. I commend you!" Derelict Satan undercut his elegant diction by scratching his balls. The room meanwhile had come to rest, perchance as soon as Whitman found the presence of mind to want it to, and it had, after the fact, entailed no more exertion than planting his feet to stop a rocking chair.

"Yes, about the specifics. Again, we're finalizing a loan, not a bill of sale."

The devil nodded deliberatively. "Till Inauguration Day. How about that? No worries that we'll have to renegotiate before you win your heart's desire." Grizzled, seamy visage flashed that same beatific show of sincerity as during their first parley.

"I'll also need your guarantee my soul will be returned intact, with current damages repaired." Whitman watched in vain for cracks to spread in devilish show of sincerity.

"Please, your hostility is misplaced. Those were all acts of God. You have to make allowances for normal wear and tear."

Wheedling always rubbed Whitman the wrong way. And pawning off acts of negligence on God? Hiding behind the Almighty's robes? Really? He cast up his hands as if to deal himself out. "Okay, I'll have to quit while I'm ahead. My prospects are in better shape than they were before you happened along, so thanks for that." Monty was contemplating the histrionic flourish of standing up and stalking out, but thought better of courting another round of psychic lacerations and vertigo.

"All right, all right." The archfiend waved a dirty paw in surrender, but his air of candor had become less convincing. "Let's go outside." Huh? Was he challenging his client to a brawl? "See what I've rigged up for you. We won't seal this bargain unless you're content." Infernal vagrant raised a puff of sulfurous dust as he lurched from the booth. Whitman tentatively followed suit, stepping livelier when no metaphysical vertigo ensued.

The federal agent still loitered on standby, mere heartbeats away from the next President. "Keep my seat warm," Monty instructed him, "and tell the waitress we'll be right back." He gave the kid's shoulder a fatherly pat.

Out on the street, Lucifer maintained his homeless persona as he bowed and grandly gestured toward a shiny black Lincoln Continental at the curb, its right front whitewall aligned with a Loading Zone sign. Whitman intuited it had been the model the year he was born, a sleek, atom-age masterpiece of a juggernaut. "An *objet d'art* to cherish, to pamper, to treat with kid gloves till the end of the world, *n'est-ce pas?*"

Here, then, was Whitman's soul, illegally parked? Pretty damn flattering, he had to admit. Plus, it hadn't a ding or a scrape. Satan had manifestly restored his battered soul to pristine status in changing it to a luxury sedan.

"I imagine you've safely squirreled away our previous contract?"

Whitman was not insensible to the implicit sarcasm. How could the most impregnable vault be safe from the Prince of Everything Material? He gamely nodded anyway.

"Well, this supersedes it." Lucifer reached in through passenger window that hadn't been open a second ago, popped the glove compartment, and fished out a lease in the style of Hertz or Avis. "You're more comfortable getting it on paper, you'll get it on paper."

Whitman skimmed the text, which spelled out more verbosely, but without fine print, the consensus both parties had achieved. Only the words at the bottom of each copy gave him shuddering pause. The white top sheet was the "Dark Lord's Copy," whereas the canary sheet beneath was the "Copy of the Provisionally Damned." But why get worked up? It did say "Provisionally."

Whitman signed with a ballpoint from his pocket, using his associate's cruddy overcoated back, hard as chitin, for a writing surface. The devil requested Whitman's pen and made do with his right palm for a clipboard. "Dark Lord," he scrawled, and palmed the pen.

The two 8 × 14 pages he rolled up and thrust at Whitman. "Keep 'em both. Double the reassurance. That way you'll know I haven't tampered with mine, and besides, it's easy to be careless with flammable items where I'm headed."

Archfiend held out his right for the official handshake. His sullied mitt felt exactly like the hot and scaly flesh of the more "natural" Mephisto three weeks ago. He squeezed right up to Whitman's threshold of pain, Whitman blinked, the pressure let up, and unholy ally was in the driver's seat, soiling the upholstery with his ragged garb. He leaned over and called out the passenger side window, "Monty, the keys!"

What keys? Whitman automatically fumbled through his pockets and located them in his jacket, between his handkerchief and his heart. Satan wagged his hand impatiently out the window. "If you please. We both have a lot to do. And I wouldn't want your soul to get a ticket." Whitman had to swallow some remorse when vintage Lincoln's lessee revved the engine and peeled out, trailing a bouquet of burnt rubber.

Reckless fiend was right, though. Tons to do. Right off the bat, before it slipped his mind, Monty consigned all cellphone footage of his breakfast with filthy devil to oblivion. He then about-faced into the hotel coffee shop, and en route to the booth quashed his misgivings like the seasoned barnburner he was. Was the Oval Office his top priority or not? He hastily folded and stuffed blasphemous lease into the pocket where those keys to his soul had solidified.

Hank was back, and the Secret Service rookie had departed. Breakfast awaited, and Hank's wrinkled brow signaled his disorientation. The bottle of Tabasco rated more perplexity than anything else. "While I was up, I ordered for both of us," Monty explained, "thereby saving us a couple of those minutes you deem so precious. Okay?"

Hank shrugged philosophically, and they buckled down to business. Or rather, Hank did, cleaving fast to tiresome question like a schnauzer with a rat. Why, in twenty-five words or less, was Whitman the better man to lead the country come January? They needed consensus on some sound bytes before Hank went on tomorrow's morning shows. Whitman humored him with better grace than usual, though in light of diabolical assistance, any public statements by or about Whitman hardly mattered now. And wasn't a host of media professionals already crafting Whitman's message?

He might have wished Hank would just go away, except he fancied himself the opposite of an ingrate, whatever that was. Expert advice had simply become as irrelevant as luck, and Monty heeded Hank's directives as offhandedly as he knocked on wood or gave ladders wide berth. Party bosses, PR consultants, and corporate donors were also struck by Whitman's compliance with their recommendations, as if he were devoid of the ego once wont to put its two cents in. He just nodded deferentially when his minister had the gall to whisper counsel while shaking his hand after Sunday service. Behind bland smile, he was in no wise complacent, but why spoil everyone's fun by throwing a star fit?

Instead, he wished bigger and bolder as the race hurtled into its most hyperbolic, bloody-fisted home stretch. He, like any remotely competent student of history, could list those intractable circumstances that won a challenger votes. Or more aptly, that lost votes for incumbents. Ruthless Whitman whistled up chaos and reversals for the perennial troop deployments in the Middle East and Central Asia. He sabotaged emergency responses to wildfires in the Southwest and floods in the Southeast and tornadoes in the Midwest. Investment firms and banks crashed and burned, with a million mortgages and pensions for fuel. Yes, victory meant tilling Mephisto's rows for him, and while he hated helping his odious associate, he couldn't let that stop him.

By the first Tuesday in November, the flimsiest promises of relief from the crises ravaging his opponent's credibility pretty much guaranteed Whitman a landslide. He'd hardly needed to wish gaffes into opponent's mouth during televised debates, but couldn't find a reason not to. To wish for votes was gilding the proverbial lily, but by then he'd become habituated to concocting wishes as supplementary insurance. Why stop when it counted most? He also succumbed to the temptation of a fling with the athletic demoness, who was terrifically seductive and submissive, but she somehow exuded a dearth of enthusiasm that soon cooled his passion.

And so Wednesday morning's headlines brought him the thrill of a lifetime, but with an anticlimactic undertone, an extension of the malaise that dated from his first diabolic handshake. With hell in his corner, the outcome had been inevitable. He also entertained recurring doubts about the devil's vow to keep the Lincoln of his soul in tiptop shape.

What's more, that oblong doohickey retailing his deathbed scene was as troublesome as ever, and damn it all, he could have wished anytime for the skills to control it, couldn't he? Bestowing on himself the nut-and-bolts mentality of, say, an engineer might have been a smart move, but then with that mentality he might not have hankered for the Oval Office anymore, and his Faustian commerce would have been for nothing. Meanwhile, if only to make pending presidency easier on himself, he wished away all the calamities he'd created.

Hank was off the payroll and their paths no longer crossed. Of course, that was no excuse to leave him off the guest list for inauguration ceremonies. Hank was supposed to maintain the proper distance, though, as a face in the crowd, at arm's length, and not burst into the Whitmans' hotel suite after the wife had toddled off to the makeup crew down the hall.

"Hello, Hank." Whitman invested a mediocre effort in suppressing his irritation. "Kind of busy here this morning. Didn't security give you a hassle?"

"Me? In some areas, I always say it's better to give than to receive." The body and face were Hank, but the green eyes and feral smile were pure Satan, as was the insidious pall of clove tobacco.

"I didn't think you were due till tomorrow. Not till after the swearing in, anyway." Whitman sat on the edge of his bed, which he'd always defined as a position of offhanded superiority. "But I might as well inform you now as later, I won't be renewing our contract. Thank you for getting me this far, but I'll have to tackle the next four years on my own."

Hank placed his chubby hands on his hips and arched a gray eyebrow. Maybe Whitman had been remiss again in propitiating Old Scratch. Should he offer Dark Lord a seat? A treat from the minibar? Why bother? "Fact is, Monty, I'm here to inform you of something. A twenty-four-hour notice, if you please. Go to the window and say goodbye, why don't you?"

Whatever he was up to, the infernal S.O.B. would have to ruin this of all days, a gross malfeasance no matter how much credit in it he could assert. Whitman couldn't calm the fluttering in his stomach, but did reach the window without attempts to second-guess what he'd find. The Lincoln at the curb looked okay aside from a dent in the fender and black scrapes on the whitewalls. "You're changing my soul back from a car already? Would you mind fixing that dent and whatever else? Like it says in the contract?"

Hank wearily shook his head. "Must I spell it out? I don't have to fix a thing. And it's not your problem anyway. Your soul is forfeit, Monty."

Bushwhacked by Satanic guile once more, Whitman mouthed several false starts in search of the best way to cry foul.

Lucifer heaved a dismal sigh. "No, I shouldn't expect you'd take me at my word. Maybe a favorite Irish legend of mine will put your case in perspective."

Whitman's soul had rated no solicitude while it was his, and he'd never missed it, but he hated dwelling on slovenly archfiend behind the wheel of that gorgeous automobile. And what the hell was this about an Irish legend? Further bids at protest came to nothing. Embarrassing to be so egregiously tongue-tied, he who would be leader of the free world in a couple of hours!

"A youthful hero, whose name I'd best render as Angus, set out to win a kingship," the devil recounted. "On Halloween, a high holiday back then, he ambushed the king, whose name we'll simplify to El, at Newgrange. El was unarmed and had a simple choice to make:

fight for his crown with the odds greatly against him, or let Angus rule in his stead for a day and a night. El consented to the temporary handover, but when he went to reclaim the throne, Angus reneged and convened the royal counselors to arbitrate. They awarded Angus the kingdom because defending it had meant less to El than his well-being, and therefore he deserved it less than Angus. Do you understand?"

"No." Beleaguered Whitman was incapable of saying more.

"The Irish had never heard of me, and wouldn't for centuries, yet how aptly they dramatized the rules of my game. To trade away something is to betray your sovereignty over it. The terms of that trade are secondary. You were damned forever, Monty, for agreeing to part with your soul in the first place. Whether or not I restore it to your body is immaterial." Satan flashed the smug little grin of the card sharp, the compulsive trickster. "Though I wasn't the one to write that rule, I'm eternally grateful for it, of course. Ultimately, my jurisdiction doesn't transcend anything material."

Whitman, in the midst of Satanic blather, began to experience the renewed calm that came with entering familiar terrain. Rigging laws in his favor, manipulating the ignorant, making virtue of vilest expedience—these practices he could relate to, and he'd always more than held his own. In fact, he tingled with a surge of youthful energy. He hadn't been obliged to apply the instincts of a scrapper with such aplomb since his ward heeler days, and now he glared contempt at his opponent and sought an opening. He had to take this duplicitous, smarmy bastard down a peg. It didn't hurt that he could also use Satan's present form to flush numerous petty digs at Hank out of his system.

"Are we really that different, Monty? Before you complain you've been a victim of less than full disclosure, let me ask when last you announced a decision or a policy or a proposal with full disclosure of your motives or the benefits to you." Dammit, even when the devil was under that pasty skin, Hank always seemed to be arguing ethics with him. Strange to say, though, Hank had never sounded so sanctimonious.

"On the other hand, Monty, I'm not out to shortchange you. I preferred you recite the oath of office without misunderstandings between us, but till then your wishes will come true, pursuant to the letter of our contract. Though what you'd wish for I can't imagine. You are, after all, about to become president."

If only Whitman could keep a cool head, he'd have a clear channel to receive the idea that could save him, or at least give the devil his due, show this pompous clove-tainted clown what he was made of. Whitman summoned his best pokerface.

"Go on, Monty. Wish away while you can. I'm beside myself with curiosity. What will the man who could have anything, at least in the short term, demand of me?"

Whitman, poker face intact, had to resist wishing for the devil to shut the fuck up.

"One word of caution, however. It may strike you as clever and original, but you're not allowed to wish we'd never met. The wishes you make can only come true on the condition that we have met, so it wouldn't work. Those are the rules of logic, not mine, and not even my powers can prevail against them. Sorry. Likewise, dare you commit yourself to living forever after the power to wish for anything else expires?"

Oh, but to wipe that canary-eating grin off Hank's fat lips. Hah! Inspiration had blossomed in the middle of Satan's caveat. Beside himself, eh?

"Fine. Going back to square one hadn't even occurred to me." Whitman examined Hank's pirated features closely. He wanted to recall them always, in detail. "I want to be you, the Prince of Everything Material. We trade places. Forever."

Done and done! Whitman was a little surprised. Had nobody in human history ever thought of this before? Or had the fallen angel now stuck in Whitman's body formerly been Franklin Pierce? Whitman was especially glad he'd appended that afterthought "forever."

"Monty, you poor fool, you have no idea what you're biting off here." The devil tried composing his new physiognomy into Whitman's poker face. He somehow conveyed the pain of constipation instead. Or had that been Whitman's actual expression all along? Yikes! "Have some pity on yourself and change us back. We don't have all the time in the world here."

"Au contraire," Whitman replied and, sick of Hank's crass Long Island accent, discovered he could shed both voice and physique at a whim. Yes, that was more like it. Horns and cloven hooves would take some getting used to, and his throat seemed partly clogged with ashes, but these were hardly excuses for self-pity. "I, for one, am looking forward to eternity."

Whitman readily saw through the Father of Lies. If ruling hell had been 100% onerous, why be so steadfastly attached to it? "You know what they say about kidding a kidder, don't you?" Like any politician worth his salt, Whitman was a realist first and foremost. Granting he was damned till the end of the universe one way or another, he was bloody well going to be damned in the driver's seat.

As for how he'd deal with the patently mutinous spirit in his erstwhile flesh when that flesh gave out, Whitman considered himself a problem-solver. He relished a challenge. And in retrospect it was funny, but he should have gone ahead and mastered that doohickey, still in townhouse wall safe, with his dying day in it. He'd then have known exactly when to unroll the red carpet for his ex-associate.

A discreet knock on the suite door turned both their heads, but the tenant in Whitman's body was far from his classic cocky self. Grimacing, no more than poker face, suited Whitman's features.

"Sir? We should be going." Neutral tones from out in the hall conveyed no awareness that the man of the hour had been nattering with parties unknown or, perish forbid, with himself.

"Word of advice," Whitman warned. "Exercise some caution with the wife. Under that demure exterior, she has a way of settling scores. You may learn a trick or two." He tried on his premier diabolical grin. "Best of luck with that, and the rest of it."

At the repetition of the discreet knock, Whitman chose to vanish and skip ahead to the swearing-in, which he watched as a literal fly on the wall. The devil uncharacteristically stammered through the oath of office, maybe on account of that hand on the Bible routine. But where was Hank? Preposterous, after months of grueling effort, that he'd blow this off.

Whitman wondered if maybe Hank hadn't been a guise of Satan all along. How had Hank referred to himself sometimes? "The Great

Enabler," wasn't it? Quite the novel sobriquet for an advisor. Whitman would have to see about that when he and deposed Prince next conversed.

Afterward the demands of learning the infernal ropes overwhelmed Whitman's schedule. However, it wasn't the most byzantine or corrupt setup he'd ever tackled, it was the second most stable in the universe, his underlings gave him no guff, and nobody down there was his superior. Quite the extraordinary trade up, actually, from riding herd on one measly, polarized country for a maximum eight years. Ruling in hell definitely beat serving in Washington. But in stolen moments he cringed at that administration blackening his name, whose callous, capricious policies he alone could have explained. And whatever it said about the divine order, Satan kept up with the mandatory churchgoing with no outward repercussions.

If shrewd, mousy Mrs. Whitman noticed altered personality and defective memory in her husband, she never mentioned it. A firm grip on the reins of the world's greatest superpower was bound to exact some psychological toll. Even those hoarse, one-sided exchanges with inaudible tormentor that penetrated the wall between their separate bedrooms she dismissed as the vocal outgrowth of a nervous tic. What, in his position, could he possibly want anyone to give him back?

Swedish-American Triptych

Missing the Boat (The Promised Land)

"With what a hunger wild oblivion swallows fame!"
—Ambrose Bierce

"Down among the dead men!" my cheerful driver announced. Maybe he was only airing a fondness for the verse of Ambrose Bierce or William Morris (or both?) by quoting it in some highly personal context. But how could I not regard neo-hippie Swede askance?

"It is just an expression." Ralf nodded toward the twisty two-lane blacktop into the uplands. "It means we're going back in history. As you requested. Nothing to fear!"

"Famous last words." My wits, slowed by lingering jetlag, framed this rejoinder a few seconds too late. It probably came off as loopy American's non sequitur. Anyhow, Ralf let this exchange die in lonely silence.

Nothing to fear, eh? For all I knew, Ralf was smarter than me, but I was senior enough to mistrust such unconditional statements. In my case, after two decades of press and playlist limbo, I'd assumed my musical career was dead in the water, not that "career" ever transcended a flash in arbitrary pan. My art school combo had never courted popularity in those happy-go-lucky 1990s, but then Norn accidentally nailed some sweet spot amidst Acid Folk and New Weird America and Neo-Prog and New Traditionalism, those vague, transient pigeonholes in which to bury the 1980s.

We multi-instrumental dilettantes who'd never set eyes on a dolmen or a runestone became darlings of college FM and NPR and BBC and the tour circuit of campuses and midsize clubs and European festivals, thanks to quirky pseudo-broadsides about mythic heroes and Vikings and pagan gods. Go figure. Maybe we appealed to fans of T-Rex and Incredible String Band born a generation too late. In our heyday, we must have ventured close but never did behold a genuine runestone or dolmen, before the standard substance abuse and interpersonal chemistry split us up.

I'd pronounced Norn unconditionally kaput without reckoning on the whims of revivalism and reissues, downloading and online radio, the appetites of a new century. And when, shock of shocks, a promoter tracked us down to offer a three-month Northern European package, mostly of festivals organized in tribute to those we'd played pre-1994, I alone among the septet had nothing better to do. But as chief songwriter, front man, and lead guitar, I retained proprietary interest, didn't I? Why not recruit some twenty-something fans who'd honed their chops on Norn CDs and hit the continental road?

Mere days along, I already had a handle on why not. The youngsters were quick studies all right, tractable, deferential, virtuosic. But lordy, how they drank and chain-smoked till way past my bedtime, and buried their noses nonstop in iPads or Netbooks or whatever it'll be next month. In other words, their behavior matched that of the original Norn to a T, which is why we'd never managed to visit the ancient monuments I sang about. Thus as middle age loomed for me, further delay in paying my respects to Europe's remnants of the Middle Ages began to feel inexcusable. Why not give the boys some space for a while?

We had two days of downtime after playing in Stockholm at the Culture House, which assigned us Ralf as gofer, guide, and chauffeur. With bandmates' blessings, I commandeered him to show me antiquities in the countryside, and he acted thrilled that I was interested. "Maybe you will be inspired to write something new!" he enthused, leading me to wonder whether he secretly thought us lame for confining our set list to "old stuff." I didn't pursue it. One of us had to make sure we didn't get off on the wrong foot.

I sprang for Ralf's vegetarian lunch at a falafel stall in a subterranean shopping complex, down an escalator by Hay Market Square. Then half an hour in his trashy golden Peugeot transported us from major EU capital to pastures, red barns, and woods, and he let spill that gleeful quip about "the dead men."

A minute later he briefly unclenched one hand from the wheel to gesture toward the windshield. "See there, you want to know how far we've come in a few miles." Blue triangular road sign contained the silhouette of a trotting boar. "These wild swine, you are familiar with them? They are becoming a problem all over, except where they are welcome on the menu." I'd also glimpsed a bunch of white scratches across the black image, like the ritual wounds Cro-Magnon hunters inflicted on cave paintings of their quarry. Yes, just how far had we driven?

While Ralf focused on steering I vetoed sharing these esoteric reflections, even if the kernel of new lyrics was in them. The road was rarely straight, curving around every hillock and hollow to traverse level ground with diehard constancy, a telltale sign of its substantial age. But I'd no idea how substantial till we approached a crossroad and Ralf called, "Here's something for you!"

My mouth hung open and I gawked, as if at otherworldly vision. Ralf parked the Peugeot on a dirt shoulder and I was out the door ahead of him, barely able to refrain from racing across the highway first. In the clay and scruffy grass at one corner of a rye field stood an actual goddamn runestone, rooted to that ground for upward of a thousand years, no higher than a pedestal but beacon-like with bright red paint accenting its engravings. The central motif was a cross whose arms of equal length resembled petals, surrounded by a convoluted ribbon of runic text with the head and tail of a serpent.

This wedge of rock exerted a pull of gravity upon me grossly out of proportion to its unimposing stature. Stubborn survival of Viking culture had greeted wayfarers since before the Norman Conquest, meaning this road had also existed for at least a millennium. At home, nothing manmade preceded the 1700s and might yet fall victim to the wrecking ball.

"Well, how does this one measure up?" demanded Ralf, reminding me I wasn't alone. If Norn's repertoire of "old stuff" had already incurred his disapproval, why push it by confessing I'd never seen a runestone till now, despite songs to indicate otherwise?

"It's gorgeous," I opined. "What it lacks in size, it makes up in elegance."

"In Stockholm there's a bigger, fancier one on public land ten minutes from where you're staying," Ralf informed me, "although I think this kind of setting is more natural and sympathetic, don't you?"

I'd have countered by asking why he hadn't previously mentioned a prize runestone practically on my doorstep, had he not gaped earthward and shrieked. Holy shit, was there such a thing as cursed runestones? Ralf skipped backward onto the blacktop, swatting at his legs, and I briskly retreated too.

"Ants!" he caterwauled. "Piss ants!" They were red and little and crawled too fast to guess their number, especially while Ralf was repelling them. Funny, we'd been right next to each other, but me they ignored. My extra coverage must have helped, as I was in ankle-length denim and desert boots, versus his shorts and sandals. Still, I unpocketed pen and paper napkin to scrawl notes about capricious Nordic curse involving bugs. Poor Ralf was already worth his weight in inspiration.

I finished scribbling to find him catching his breath, composure on the mend. "No harm done!" he wheezed. "One second they weren't there, and the next a hundred were almost in my pants. At least they didn't bite. I read somewhere they wait for a chemical signal and then all attack at once, so I must have killed their squadron leader."

I doubted Ralf would appreciate hearing he'd more or less reinvented that quaint English expression "ants in your pants," so I nodded agreeably and took photos of booby-trapped monument from a safe distance. Amidst the scruffy grass, a plaque on a stubby metal post converted the runes into modern Swedish, but far be it from me to play the ugly American and request he wade back in and translate for me. Besides, barring info to the contrary, I was free to believe the placard described an Old Norse curse.

Underway again, I conjectured Ralf and I were on divergent journeys. In the wake of the same incident, medieval fantasy brewing in my head had reinvigorated me, whereas Ralf hadn't quite rebounded from the harsher reality. His grip on the wheel was too shaky for comfort on roads as rife as ever with dead men's curves. How to put this tactfully? "We can go back if you like. Quit when we're ahead."

Ralf looked hurt, and disappointment weighed down his voice. "So soon? I had more for you to see. You are not happy?" His eyes swerved from the white dividing line to me, and the vehicle swerved a bit with them.

"I'm happy!" I hastily affirmed. "Ants didn't swarm all over me."

He snorted. "It was nothing. Like I said, no harm done." His twitchy thumbs hinted differently, making me choose between trusting his word or his extremities. I gamely asked about our next objective.

He had to repeat his answer, but only drew a blank again. Louder, more deliberate enunciation of "fwepsetning" implied I must have had a mental block. "A prehistoric grave. Boulders arranged like the outline of a boat. A stone ship, in English?" I nodded knowingly. To confess "fwepsetnings" were news to me could hardly have enhanced my luster. "People say one is near here. We take a left, and it should be coming up on the right. I am told it is impressive."

That left turn was a little hard for my taste, and single lane was bumpy with loose pebbles and rattling gravel. Overhanging birch and linden branches cast alternating bands of sun and shadow, and I worried about their hypnotic effect on my borderline wobbly driver. I also harbored growing doubts about his navigational skills. This road felt wrong. Would impressive archaeology languish in dense, untended forest? We'd never see the "stone ship" for the trees, unless it loomed on the scale of Stonehenge.

"Oh look, more proof of how far we've come in a few miles," I chimed, in case Ralf hadn't noticed the tractor idling dead ahead. Nobody can ever say for sure what someone else perceives, right? In fairness to Ralf, he was plying the brakes before I was halfway through my sentence.

The tractor was a dusty red hulk from the '50s or '60s, of ideal dimensions to barricade our path. The farmer astride it eyed us sharply, perhaps challenging us to yell or honk at him. He rewarded our patience by chugging forward into his front yard, which didn't actually help because a chain now stretched taut across the road at headlight level. One end was fastened to the tractor and the other encircled a hassock-sized rock, which the farmer had tried to drag from the left-hand verge to nowhere obvious. He descended from his rumbling leviathan, unhitched the chain, and walked it over to the rock.

Ralf called out the Swedish for "excuse me," and the next word I distinguished was "fwepsetning." The farmer relaxed his stance, and his reply seemed civil and specific. He might have been roughly my age, with incipient paunch beneath white T-shirt and dungarees, off-set by a youthfully black droopy mustache and hair parted down the middle, as long as Ralf's.

I concluded he if anyone would be well-versed in pagan places because of that chunky Thor's hammer pendant, hanging from a triple loop of silver chain heftier than the one hooked to the tractor. The hammer's proportions lent it some resemblance to a dreidel or a mushroom, though I kept that to myself and via Ralf simply conveyed my compliments on its craftsmanship. Where had he unearthed it? The farmer regarded me coolly while telling Ralf he'd purchased custom-designed talisman from a Stockholm jeweler, apparently two blocks from Ralf's apartment, though much less expensive tin versions were available in the tourist quarter of Gamla Stan.

As for our "fwepsetning," of course it was back the way we'd come, and with an economical gesture the farmer bade us do a U-turn on his lawn. A scant hour out of town, and we'd met up with flesh-and-blood as well as stone outcrops of the archaic past! And such a nice obliging devotee of Thor, too. "I kinda wish I'd gotten out of the car and posed for a photo with him," I lamented.

Ralf fixed his eyes on the road and warned that a lot of these neo-pagans also had Nazi leanings. Furthermore, since artifacts from Swedish soil were automatically state property, to presume the farmer was sporting an archaeological find amounted to a criminal accusation. Yes, we did seem to be on divergent journeys together, or viewing it through different-colored lenses.

We'd allegedly gone wrong in taking that left instead of continuing straight and watching for stone ship on the right. But to our frustration, acres of tawny grain monopolized the landscape like a revolving backdrop till we had to face we'd overshot our goal. Or was "impressive" Iron Age gravesite overwhelmed by rows of cereal? Second thoughts about our cooperative pagan ensued. Had he purposely misled us, or had Ralf no talent for following directions?

The roar of jumbo jets and airbuses at jarringly low altitudes created further annoyance, for me anyway. Ralf explained we were in the vicinity of the airport where I'd landed. Hadn't I seen the signs for Arlanda? What could he say when I shook my baffled head?

We gave our pagan every benefit of the doubt. Ralf cruised back and forth while I squinted into the wall of forest beyond the fields. He pulled over several times for me to hop out and survey the terrain more closely. Neither of us proposed additional consultation with the farmer. The search was tabled indefinitely when Ralf remarked the tank was almost empty.

His claim of recalling a gas station nearby inspired limited confidence. I entertained scenarios of returning tired and dusty to the farmer and begging a gallon of fuel, especially when the engine sputtered ominously. But I suppose we were due for a miracle.

We'd been coursing downhill so gradually that I was none the wiser till a lowland vista spread before us. August sun bestowed uniform sheen on pastures and groves and tracts of gray loam and Romanesque steeple on the horizon and, to the immediate right where our road merged with busier thoroughfare, a convenience mart with gas pumps in the middle of desolate tarmac. Minor-league déjà vu kicked in at the sight of a stop sign ahead of us just like any American stop sign, down to the word "Stop."

Ralf refueled and then refused my cash donation. "Culture House will honor the receipt," he insisted. He went inside to pay, while I lounged against the car and assessed this outpost of the retail sector, a franchise of the ICA chain in as nondescript a bunker as a gas'n'go anywhere. This one, though, was more forlorn than average, as shown to starker disadvantage by the bright sunshine.

I was particularly drawn to the row of banners flapping on the roof. They'd formerly proclaimed the name of the shop and a slogan, but seasons of exposure had truncated them to lozenges of fabric with tassels of frazzled threads and the same meaningless fragment, "IC nä." I might be forgiven for suspecting the dull present around here had given up competing with grander yesteryears.

Meanwhile, why was a simple cash transaction taking forever? A blue Ford compact drove up behind the Peugeot and, at my despairing shrug, revved around to the pump in front of ours. I avoided eye contact with rightfully irate motorist, trying instead to i.d. the logos on planes overhead. When Ralf did come sprinting out, he carried a blue cellophane sack, almost the proportions of a brick, with red lettering. He plunked his purchase between us and shifted into reverse, and our argosy resumed.

I was flummoxed when he exclaimed he'd bought us a "dime bag" to share, a "typical Swedish" treat. Had Sweden, unbeknownst to me, radically liberalized its drug laws, or was this young stoner humor at its goofiest?

A glance at the red lettering disabused me. The candy was spelled "Daim," and the bag contained some fifty bite-size specimens, individually wrapped. I sampled one. It was hard toffee with a milk chocolate coating. "They're like little Heath bars." I must have sounded underwhelmed. I also wasn't positive he hadn't been perpetrating stoner humor.

"You don't approve?" It was Ralf's turn to look flummoxed. "Who doesn't like Daim?" I didn't ask if he was parroting the manufacturer's catchphrase. Au contraire, they were great, I remonstrated, and they did prove pretty addictive. In short order I'd littered the floor with wrappers. And maybe Ralf had just been hypoglycemic after battling piss ants. A handful of Daims later, his grip upon the steering was more vice-like.

Through a mouthful of crunchy toffee, Ralf apologized for faulty research on the "fwepsetning" and urged me to be happy. We were en route to the outstanding ruins of a castle, "much more difficult to hide than a stone boat." He could vouch for the existence of this locale because he'd been there once, and it was on the National Historic Register, which meant official signs would guide us.

All fine and well, but none of this guaranteed Ralf's pathfinding acumen. The car was soon neck-deep in testy silence as we meandered, backtracked, and bumbled down more roads than should have fit into this amount of geography. I was already reconciled to a low-interest range of scenery for the duration, of farmhouses, haystacks, and livestock grazing on meadows. How electrifying, then, when Ralf cried, "There it is!"

I tore my stolid gaze away from sheep drinking at a muddy pond and barely glimpsed a sign depicting a square with a loop at each corner, like a stylized aerial view of a castle with four turrets. It signified an ancient architectural treasure, according to Ralf.

I was on the cusp of regretting my pessimism about Ralf the navigator. He heeded further signage for the word "slott," which shunted us down lesser and lesser byways. At last a gravel lane, flanked by gigantic oaks, petered out at the edge of fallow acreage. On our right, a retaining wall enclosed a baroque-era church and graveyard.

The castle was situated on the slope of a knoll across the field and, to my inexperienced eyes, was amply diverting, though too little survived for a clear picture of its primal glory. One section of wall, topping off at a height of three window courses, echoed the contours of a line graph charting a company's boom and bust, or just as readily the rise and fall of feudal society. Another section, of greater elevation, resembled a stack of horseshoes. I started asking Ralf how we'd proceed in the absence of marked trails, till his cloudy brow stopped me.

He was frowning at a message board under Plexiglas on the edge of weedy expanse. Damn, I hated having to downgrade my better opinion of him already, but he'd manifestly failed us again. He tapped upon the word in biggest print, "STÄNGD." "Sorry, it is closed. I was here eight years ago, but public access ended last summer." He waved glumly at a strip of thicket and wildflowers, twice as tall as the surrounding flora, between us and the castle. I'd taken it for a property boundary. "That was the path, which they seeded with nettles to discourage trespassers."

I had to vent skepticism at the basic concept that a ruin could be closed. It wasn't like a theme park behind fences or a condemned warehouse, but part of the topography, wasn't it? Ralf patiently elaborated, "It is not safe. People were hurt by loose masonry." Closed, though? Granted, I was harping on semantics, and out of peevishness, not defiance. I wanted no more than the next tourist to brave ticks, snakes, and thorns among the verdure. But the shortage of exciting destinations on this trip was getting to me.

Ralf sheepishly invited me to check out the baroque church and its cemetery.

"Unless you really want to, I'd prefer to move on." I was working the passenger door handle as I spoke. "They don't exactly measure up to archaic monuments as promised, do they?"

Pangs of conscience needled me the second I fastened my seatbelt. Anyone might have been upset at this afternoon's series of missteps and letdowns. But as a pointedly more subdued Ralf hunkered into the driver's seat, I reflected on how much I was behaving like a rock star, ill-qualified for that role as I was or ever had been. Still, how damnably easy to act the part in response to the mildest deference.

Ralf jiggled the key into the ignition, and before he could launch into self-reproach or self-defense, I babbled, "Listen Ralf, I can't thank you enough for all your trouble on my behalf, and at some risk of injury. Things didn't go as planned, but do they ever? We were victims of circumstance. I say we cut our losses, call it a day. I have to be back anyway for some big crayfish dinner or something for the band. But first I'd appreciate it if we swung by that fancy runestone you were talking about, in the middle of town."

"Sure." Ralf was hardly chipper, but I'd prevented our rift from widening, hadn't I, and aimed us toward rapprochement? After a good while, though, Ralf was no less taciturn, and we appeared no closer to Stockholm.

"Should I be watching for any particular highway numbers or place names?" I'd suddenly become the deferential member of this expedition.

"No, it's fine." Fine? Okay then, I should just relax and accept that we were definitely on two separate journeys in the same car.

The rank monotony of staying lost triggered flights of elaborate fancy. Once our hunt for the "fwepsetning" had commenced, or perhaps once the farmer had rerouted it, I envisioned we'd entered a colossal, or perhaps merely figurative, version of a more venerable, archetypal structure than stone boat or a castle. "Ralf?" With some trepidation, I broke into his rigid brown study. "You ever hear tell of prehistoric labyrinths in the Scandinavian landscape?"

"Oh yes, there is a beautifully restored one about two hours west of here."

"How big is it? Like a hockey rink or a football stadium?"

He chortled at my naïveté. All right, I had that coming. "No, no. More like a patio. And it's made of small stones, about like your fist."

"So they'd never cover miles, like a project by Christo?"

"No, never."

Figurative this labyrinth was, then, or else implanted on the terrain, created as we went along, by our own lackwit inability to get anywhere. Or was there a preternatural influence in it? White-knuckled Ralf was plainly in no mood for such outré speculations, so I meekly jotted them on paper napkin as further lyric fodder. Simultaneously, I wished Ralf would notice me enlarging the Norn songbook, in case he thought I was touring strictly to cash in, minus redeeming artistic impulse. Still, had he not put the bug in my ear, I'd never have started penning new material, would I?

Subjective ages elapsed, but what did the clocks in Stockholm say? I had neither watch nor cell phone out of chronic refusal to let them compromise my leisure. To pester Ralf struck me as tactless, and protracted subarctic days made the sun impossible to gauge. And was Ralf too fixated on making headway, or mulishly unwilling, to acknowledge our weird predicament? The sporadic oncoming car or low-flying aircraft felt like mirages from another world.

This boondocks maze, I wrote on my napkin, had enfolded us like a hermetic microcosm. We were trapped in a Möbius trip, a pastoral M. C. Escher poster. Tortuous roads to nowhere had to intersect with roads to somewhere eventually, didn't they? But no, they always emptied onto other nowhere roads. Straight and narrow sidetracks that gave Ralf "a good feeling" penetrated new countryside, yet curved deviously to redeposit us in sight of where we'd turned off, many wasted minutes later.

Signs and landmarks proved useless or worse. Along the same stretch of highway as before, I'd have sworn, was that same silhouette of a boar inside blue triangle, except those long white scratches had vanished. And uncanny that our runestone and the ICA never reappeared, however often we must have crisscrossed the map. What would happen when we ran out of gas and Daims? Or would we never run out of gas and Daims, in this jalopy version of the Flying Dutchman?

Damned if this onerous afternoon didn't encapsulate my whole adulthood of false leads, going no place fast, waiting in the passenger seat for something always beyond the next corner. Missing the boat, be it stone or metaphorical, had defined me for decades, hadn't it? After Norn, I could have maintained a toehold in music, for recreational purposes anyway, instead of delaying my reentry till now. Meanwhile, poor Ralf! Technically he had the wheel, but metaphysically this trek was mine, and he was purely along for the ride, a hijacked innocent bystander.

"Sorry, Ralf." The depth of my contrition surprised both him and me.

"Excuse me? What for?" In earnest confusion he goggled at me, rekindling my fears he'd blindly career into a ditch. But yes, why penalize Ralf for my underachiever's résumé? Why penalize me, for that matter? And who the hell was meting out this punishment?

I racked beleaguered brain for any convincing *mea culpa* short of blurting out I'd somehow consigned us to endless joyride in the Twilight Zone. That kind of talk was for my paper napkin alone.

Then sudden crisis compelled me instead to shout, "Watch out!" We rounded a bend on a gravel lane, in the shade of birches and lindens. Ralf had to slam on the brakes or we'd have rammed hulking red tractor and long-haired farmer astride it. Since we were approaching from the opposite direction, I'd had no idea where we were and was doubly befuddled to be here again of anywhere today. Our pagan, conversely, beheld near-collision without raising a black eyebrow.

In one respect it was like we'd never left. The farmer was still trying to drag gumdrop-shaped rock from the roadside, to no avail. What the hell was he doing wrong, for a humble chunk of basalt to resist steel chain and horsepower?

Ralf let the golden Peugeot idle while he got out and presumably apologized for this second brush with vehicular assault. I also stepped out to stretch my legs. The farmer mumbled a few non-threatening syllables, killed the chugging engine, and dismounted. He betrayed no umbrage at detaching the chain again and walking it over to the unyielding rock. A Nazi he was not. His vibes were patently not of master race.

The Thor's hammer glinted in a sliver of sunshine through the trees as its owner addressed me in mild-mannered English, "I see the roads to the stone boat have brought you back to me."

"It's been that kind of a day." I didn't anticipate how shy, how diffident I'd feel relating to this salt of the earth. "It might not hurt if I rewrote your instructions in English. We seem to need all the help we can get." Not till the words were out did I realize my native guide might find them disparaging, but hurray! He was staring into the distance behind the ramshackle farmhouse. I was too relieved at averting awkward incident to care what was so fascinating.

"If it's help you need, I may have just the thing." The farmer, fingering his pendant, sauntered close enough for me to smell his honest sweat and musky clothing. Ralf still squinted into the indefinite yonder. "Thor had a reputation for aiding travelers and sailors. You were admiring this hammer of his. It might serve you as well as it has served me."

With both hands he delicately hoisted triple loop of heavy-duty silver chain over his head and hefted it toward me till I had to receive it or let it thump against my diaphragm. The hammer shiny in the sun was bedazzling, almost hypnotic. It would make one hell of a gorgeous memento, especially for the front man of Norn. My eyes must have said so, but the hammer shone like solid silver, and how could I afford that? The bulky chain didn't even enter into the equation.

"You can have it for fifty crowns. The chain comes with it."

"Ralf?" I barked to pierce his distraction. "Is fifty crowns a good price?" The pagan didn't seem the type to resent token haggling.

I jangled the necklace at spacey Ralf, who deigned to blink in my general direction. "Yes, good, good. Fifty crowns is nothing. The Daims cost that." He then reset his sights on nowhere obvious, perhaps that same nowhere obvious to which the rock was theoretically bound.

"Sorry to quibble," I told the farmer while digging out my wallet. "I haven't gotten the hang of the exchange rate yet." And in that exchange rate, was a kilo of silver equal in value to a bag of candy? Outward brilliance must have belied electroplated lead.

He shrugged nonchalantly and pocketed my fifty-crown note. Actually, between necklace, wallet, and currency, I had my hands full, and when I inadvertently thrust the necklace back at him, only then did his poise falter a little, with an unquiet flicker in his gray eyes. Courteous heathen, I surmised, simply didn't want me doing anything I'd feel foolish about.

"We should go," Ralf butted in. He shot me a grimace that implied readiness to shove off with or without me, ducked into the car, and slammed the door. Our pagan rated neither wave nor word of farewell. I wasn't displeased that gumption lay somewhere under the mellow skin of hippie chauffeur. Good for him, except he hadn't spared me the chance to learn why the backyard had drawn and then repelled him while I'd been dickering over neckwear.

"My friend's anxious about a dinner reservation," I kind of fibbed, and reached for the passenger door handle.

The farmer threw up his hands, palms forward, like a gesture from an illuminated manuscript, as if I were about to paddle over a waterfall. "Put it on!" he admonished. "It won't work unless you put it on!"

My door was wide open, so I wagered Ralf wouldn't speed off in the trice it took me to humor impassioned request. As the weight of the chain fell upon my collarbone, the pagan was climbing into the seat of his tractor.

And a dizzy instant later, the red steel seat was under my ass, and I peered mystified at myself in the car for that speck of eternity before it accelerated away. The mood in there had brightened considerably. Insofar as I was sitting slack-jawed atop the tractor, I had to infer that behind my face, the body-swapping farmer was chatting more vivaciously with Ralf than I ever had.

Chuckling Ralf was grabbing a Daim from cellophane bag at my ostensible urging, and then the Peugeot was forever around the bend. Were they joking about the hayseed's ineptitude at moving rocks, at pricing jewelry? What a good sport the hayseed was, to join in at lambasting himself. Then again, he could afford to, as he'd scored the last laugh on me and clueless Ralf. Surely Ralf had no knowledge, no part, of this unholy switcheroo, right?

I clambered nerveless, despite new and improved muscles, off the tractor. I had no inkling how to start, let alone operate vintage heavy machinery. Or would the same sinister agency that had saddled me with this flesh instill that knowhow? Meanwhile, the pressure on my shoulders hadn't lifted. Should I have been amazed at hammer and chain restored to the body they'd just departed? I wasn't. They did belong to the person inside this body, after all. My psyche had room for no more amazement, for nothing beyond numb acquiescence.

Giving scary red juggernaut a slow, morose once-over accomplished nothing. I had to master at least the rudiments of shifting into reverse and blocking the road, to impede future daytrippers, strike occult bargain with them, and steal their car. Yes, that must have been the fiendish setup here. Was there a Mrs. Farmer to teach me Tractor 101? Tires, rusty oil barrels, and circular piss burns across the lawn argued against a woman's touch.

What further assets were in store for me here? Foremost priority was the target of Ralf's fascination, certainly, but I couldn't very well get a bead on that and walk at the same time. In the grassy side yard between house and woods, I had to keep eyes downcast or else gash shins on iron debris and derelict equipment, or blunder into spiderwebs slung from faded yellow walls to stalks of ragweed and thistle. The technology aged dramatically as I forged along till I was skirting rusty plowshares and skeletal wagons.

Adding to the difficulty, my alien legs had their own ingrained tendency to lope headlong, nearly pitching me into obstacles I thought I'd already avoided. And thanks to unaccustomed myopia, whatever Ralf had been ogling was still a blur to me. I wondered how many of my ex-body's defects would perturb its new tenant. To what degree did he plan on stepping into my shoes? Could he even play guitar? Sing?

It'd be a pity if he blew his nose on paper napkin instead of developing my kernels into songs. Right this minute, was he reciting that nonsense blaming runic curse for Ralf's problems with ants and Möbius roads, and were they sharing a good laugh? In any case, more was the pity if this evening's guest of honor hated crayfish.

Behind the house, messy side yard broadened into a litter-free, neatly mowed field within a ring of pines. At first I smiled at this prettier view, but then realized why an apparently random assortment of geology amidst the grass had sent Ralf packing. The arrangement was less than obvious because it was unfinished but, like the runestone, was more imposing than height and length warranted. In connect-the-dots fashion, squat stones outlined three-quarters of a stylized eye or boat that would fit inside a one-car garage.

I'd discovered my "fwepsetning" at last, along with intimations of a fate I couldn't flee in a stolen car. So I hadn't really figured out the fiendish setup here, had I? To reframe the situation, I'd missed the boat, and now I'd found the boat, and how long would I have to labor on it before I disembarked?

I never used to care where my life was going, so why start today? Why not give this existence a go and see if it didn't suit me as well as my unthrilling existence back in the States? As if I had a choice. Anyway, this was a golden opportunity to catch up on some of those songs I hadn't been writing for twenty years.

Yes, that held much more appeal than trying to maneuver a tractor with rock in tow through the maze of detritus alongside the house, for that rock by the roadside must have been ordained as the next dot to connect in the outline. And worse, when I strained myopic eyes back at that rock, it looked mockingly, irrationally bigger. My life had become the most outlandish Norn song yet, and I felt woefully unqualified to say whether that would ultimately prove a blessing or a punishment. "Nothing to fear!" Ralf had professed at the outset of this excursion, and now it seemed most needful to believe him.

Harm Like Water
(The Undiscovered Country)

They haven't decided what to do with me. Though I can't understand a word, I gather from the gravity, the painstaking ebb and flow of campfire debate, that I'm their worst moral dilemma ever. Their dedication to conscience is admirable. Only too bad my chances aren't much better than their butchered deer's, whatever they decide.

Putting myself in their Timberland shoes, the gist of their discussion poses no mystery. Do they handle me like a mad dog or a victim of malady? My captors could avenge their friend and bury me out here, to ensure a modicum of justice. Or they could submit me to the rule of law, but unless I'm sentenced to life without parole, unable to harm anyone ever again, their friend will have died in vain. The jury will have cheated him and society.

Meanwhile, my captors aren't inhumane. I've had my fill of venison and I'm as comfortable as possible sitting against a fir trunk, wrists tied behind my back, legs outstretched and bound at the ankles. Or am I stoically enduring Stockholm syndrome in its country of origin? This nippy October night, I could stand languishing closer to the heat.

The hell of it is, I came here to make myself scarce, to stay off lawbreaker radar. It's all backfired at every stage, ever since my eighteenth birthday. A stint in the military to help cover college sounded reasonable till we invaded yet another oil-rich dictatorship. Applying for conscientious objector status earned me short shrift, derision, and hazing. Barracks life became unbearable, and from there? Help "spread democracy" at gunpoint, to the dismissive tune of how much "collateral damage"? Oh fuck no.

Next stop, Sweden and political asylum. Unfortunately, to quote

Bogart's immortal Rick who moved to arid Casablanca "for the waters," "I was misinformed." If nabbed, according to English-speaking hipsters at more than one bistro, I'd face summary extradition. Deserters apparently wore out their welcome after Vietnam.

In the wake of that info, I was planning to come up with a plan, and that's how pitifully far I'd gotten. I avoided using credit card or ATM, on the premise I'd take longer to trace redeeming traveler's checks, hoofing it from hostel to hostel, paying cash for everything. By days I intended to travel back roads or preferably nature trails. Have backpack, will straggle.

Therein lay the rub. Beginner's luck in the vagabond lifestyle would have been nice, but no. One mere province along, in unpronounceable Östergötland, I studied a spaghetti-tangle map of trails on a wooden sign at the lakeside entrance to vast evergreen woods. I redrew the relevant sections of map in my scratchpad, noting approximate distances of each branch between intersections, to bring me by 5:30 dusk to a hostel near the likewise unpronounceable Ljusfallshammar. Yet for all my forethought and mindfulness, the paths I hiked soon had no connection with those on paper. I couldn't have been more lost in purgatory.

Surprisingly, hours of futile wandering never penetrated what I'd call forest primeval. Human influence, ancient or recent, was as pervasive as in a townscape. In addition to footpaths, there were dirt roads wide enough for cars or logging machinery. On one such serviceway I'd compiled a sticky patina of dust and sweat in the humid sunshine, and then had the temerity to flag down a couple of yuppies in a brown Range Rover.

The passenger slightly lowered tinted window and cell phone, and I asked in English if Lee-us-false-hammer, as best I could express it, was down the road. Without pause she said to just keep going, and as if I must have been a crazy drifter, the SUV sped off. Only sometime later did I realize she was lying because Ljusfallshammar was due west of the park entrance, and the afternoon sun over my left shoulder meant I was northbound. So much for the good it did that every Swede spoke English.

I encountered no more people that wayward day. All the same, I never felt especially alone amidst reminders of chronic exploitation, as if this were hardly a "real" wilderness compared with, say, the Yukon or Siberia, not that I'd seen either firsthand. Around the shores of ponds, trees were markedly fewer and younger, thanks perhaps to culling for the sake of flycasters and boatmen. Unnatural order was strictest among the tallest firs, slated for harvest like any other crop, in precise rows like cornstalks among the ferns and mossy rocks.

And though I hadn't glimpsed so much as a squirrel, manly dominion plainly included edible fauna. Hunter's blinds sprouted like mushrooms a stone's throw from trails or roadsides, and several often lined up in sight of one another. Some were more weatherbeaten, some hugged the ground, and some commanded a fire warden's view. All were boxlike structures that could accommodate two recumbent marksmen. The walls were a shaggy camouflage of hay or rushes, reminiscent of hula skirts.

No spent cartridges, no litter, nothing underfoot suggested these blinds were in current use, and no gunplay had spoiled today's lonesome serenity. None of this cured worries I'd be mistaken for a deer or moose, beyond baseline worries about reaching Lee-us-false-hammer before dark.

Best efforts to slog westward met with repeated frustration on swerving paths. I could have fixed my gaze on the sinking sun and struck out across trackless country, but damned if I was desperate enough for such foolhardiness.

Twilight fell as if someone had twisted a dimmer switch, and too late then to wish I'd been more foolhardy and overruled my treacherous common sense. Be that as it may, foolhardy options didn't extend to groping onward in the dark, where I might sprain an ankle or worse, and where hunters or other carnivores might mistake me for dinner. My own dinner would be down to snacks from a suburban minimart, untouched so far because disorientation had killed my appetite. Hunger was MIA for the foreseeable duration.

I had to find shelter fast before backwoods night blotted out the ground at my feet. Beneath the trees, fitful gusts were rattling fallen leaves, which I took as a signal of approaching dark. On second thought, though, these evergreen woods had no leaves to rattle, and no wind swayed the sagging boughs. Something besides the dark was approaching, wasn't it? True, I hadn't felt altogether alone earlier, but that was an impersonal, socio-historical presence. This rustling with some specific origin had me spooked, whatever its unspooky explanation.

I quickened my pace, and straining eyes probed left and right for any sanctuary. Though a quarter-hour at most had ever elapsed between hunter's blinds, when I happened on one at this crucial juncture, it smacked of the miraculous, almost too good to be true. And it was the optimal kind for surviving the night.

It dominated a modest clearing and was perhaps built of the pines that formerly lorded it over knee-high grass, yellow and limp in the heavy air. At twice the height of a lifeguard platform, it promised safe refuge from dangerous beasts and the sportsmen stalking them through infrared scopes. I also had to believe it would debar whatever was skulking in the understory.

Square enclosure in its hula skirt balanced atop four skinny, unfinished tree trunks, reinforced from corner to corner by X's of crisscrossed poles. A diagonal pole from the grassy sod to the lip of the platform lent an appearance of extra stability, but I braced for a shaky climb up rough-hewn ladder to a gap in the wall. The carpentry proved less rickety than it looked, and the plank floor was clean and snugly fit together.

Lucking into this haven revived my appetite, and I celebrated with chocolate, an orange, and some bottled water. Just before dusk faded to blackout, I pissed through the gap in shelter wall, and mostly missed the ladder. From backpack I grabbed extra pullover layers and overcoat and Army blanket and settled in, wedging my back into a corner to conserve warmth. I might wake with chattering teeth and numb toes, but as roughing it went, this was utopia compared with Middle East inferno. I nodded off with the soothing reflection that at least I wasn't one more combatant helping to ramp up civilian death toll.

It must have been the nearby rocking motions that awoke me, flickering across my eyelids. I was expecting the same zero visibility as at bedtime, but by grace of moon and stars the world was uniformly bleached and murky, actually making for a less charged ambience in which to learn I wasn't alone. Also just as well I was too stiff and groggy to budge, because my first panicky suspicion was of Swedish or U.S. investigators tailing me here. But that was irrational, wasn't it, to fancy myself public enemy number one, dogged by latterday Sherlock or Inspector Javert?

Instead, a hulking brute who took no notice of me was performing a manic pantomime. The intensity of my pins and needles, the gamut of muscle cramps, convinced me I wasn't dreaming, and in the milky gloom this woodsman seemed as solid as anything else, whereas I, huddled inert under a blanket, may have passed for a sack of potatoes. My bivouac had become a lot less spacious.

I could have poked his cleated boots with a yardstick, but I'd fled America to escape mayhem, and he didn't appear the type to suffer interruption gladly. His profile roiled with cruel glee, or possibly ecstatic rage, projecting more feral menace, perhaps, than whatever was prowling below us. Mouthing venomous expletives, literally frothing, he imitated blasting away with his shotgun into the night, giving way a pace or two at the recoil and snapping double barrels open to reload as he advanced to fire again.

In his bloodthirsty zeal he was almost pixilated, and his outerwear, and the elongated proportions of his fowling piece, reinforced cartoonish but nowise comical image. Knee-length greatcoat was trimmed with fur at hem and cuffs and collar. No gloves coddled his ogre's paws. Bulbous sheepskin cap in soupy light was hard to distinguish from a toupée and was jammed down over his ears, to overlap prodigious beard. He could have been the archetype incarnate of crazed backwoodsman from silent movies or dime novels.

By the time I'd regained the wherewithal to wonder how any target could evade or ignore such a punishing barrage, my impression of the shootist as mime had to undergo revision. Garbled, grating, isolated snatches of speech began fetching up in my ears as if I could only tune them in after prolonged exposure, or as if I were under water or some other distorting, turbid medium. Even with clearer reception I'd have understood nothing, and the couple of words that did spew out intact sounded inexplicably like "fan" and "grease."

Then another inchoate layer began to gel in the soundscape, further muffling the audible bits of verbal torrent. Consistent with the smothered vocalizing, each eruption of sparks and puff of smoke from vintage breechloader was accompanied not by deafening bang, but by something like the swooshing of a cupped hand through water, replete with psychedelic flanging effect.

My mental disarray made the notion of spying on some unearthly regime less absurd. Unfortunately, that regime seemed no less vicious than the one I'd gone AWOL to avoid, and the longer I dwelt on it, the closer I came to bridging transworld gap.

If I'd thought to shut eyes and ears, that might have severed contact with the phantom country. Thus far I'd managed not to freak out, but then a third tier of noise impinged from below, rising like a tide upon protracted listening. I couldn't articulate why I began quaking at the renewal of leaves rustling in a place without leaves, and my alarm grew tougher to contain as perception honed the clatter of dead foliage into the scampering of animals.

I still heard everything as if through warping, reverberant funnel, and so couldn't tell whether paws or hooves, a herd or a pair, were racing back and forth. After it hit me that the scampering wasn't a bit discouraged by steady fusillade, my hold on champing nerves finally gave out. I wasn't aware of venting hysteria aloud, though I'd bet it radiated from me like a neon aura. Had I almost come unhinged at prospects of bulletproof beast climbing up the ladder, or were the last several minutes *in toto* taking their toll?

The fiendish huntsman froze while trying to get a bead on nonchalant target. Maybe he'd smelled my fear, or maybe I'd let slip a few stricken syllables. In any case, metaphysical veil between us had thinned to where he could damn well see I wasn't a sack of potatoes. Whirling toward me, he hoisted gun barrel to aim above my head. This chivalrous gesture aside, he glared the same deranged ferocity at me that he'd focused through the crosshairs.

I'd staked my claim here hours ahead of him, fair and square. He had no call to resent my unobtrusive body, but he patently didn't see it that way. More fool I, to expect our interactions would be more rational than anything else in this situation. Rearing up like a grizzly to even greater stature, making the heavy-duty shotgun in one upraised arm look more like an ice scraper, he opened his mouth to bellow at me. I can't describe how raggedly his rant came through that metaphysical veil because I have no memory of a single decibel, only of an impact like a sonic boom, blowing out my consciousness like candle flame.

Then my eyes were fixed on white dawn sky. My position in the corner hadn't changed, except my muscle cramps and aching joints had multiplied since the dead of night. As for mad shootist, like a nightmare he was gone without a trace. No shotgun casings or scuff marks blemished the floorboards. And despite his wrathful display, he hadn't tangibly manhandled me.

Psychically, the story was different. The oppressive funk that lingers after bad dreams was casting a pall over the sunrise. Or, recalling how certain I was of being awake, had I trembled at ghost or omen or other visionary species? That was something to debate at leisure. Thawing out and regaining motor control were higher priorities, especially as today's push westward had to put haunted hunting blind forever behind me.

But first I had to crack the cruel ice in knees and elbows and hips, bring sluggish circulation up to speed. Wan, daybreak woods were flush with sunshine before I was on my feet. From there I was still in no shape to brave the ladder till I'd limbered up by pacing the enclosure over and over, and for that nebulous duration I had nothing besides brooding to occupy me. That might have been okay, had I something other than uncanny visitation to brood about.

Abiding post-nightmare funk didn't help. It filtered the cheerfulness right out of a bright morning and primed me to contemplate the worst. For openers, unless trigger-happy entity were simple mirage, shouldn't I be on my guard for aftereffects of an outburst whose vehemence instantly put me under? He hadn't seemed the sort for empty gestures.

The pall persisted after I'd vacated the tower and sat eyeing it while breakfasting on crispbread dipped in peanut butter. Maybe that pall was in itself a symptom of whatever the entity had inflicted on me. Would I really be rid of him just by taking a hike?

Yes. I couldn't afford answering otherwise, any more than I could afford to doubt my course of action since bailing on boot camp. On deeper thought, why not blame present difficulties on greedy deans who put college tuition out of reach for anyone without trust fund or military benefits? I entertained these ramblings while squatting over pine roots, surrendering to necessity. And because nothing and nobody ambushed me in my supremely vulnerable position, with reinforced confidence I wiped my ass using fistfuls of crumpled fern and lit out.

Yesterday's foolhardy urge to cross trackless country had become today's best bet. No more devious trails, I vowed, no more vacillation. Go west, there was my mantra, exploit the eternal verity of morning sun in the east, of every forest shadow, mine included, pointing forward, and by lunchtime I'd be unwinding in a café. This was only a national park, dammit, not the back of beyond. All I had to do was advance like an arrow.

For a pretty good spell, I saw no reason not to give my bold and simple tactic high marks. No end to the forest was ever in view, but the farther I tramped, the closer to the edge I must have been, right? Such optimism pathetically crashed and burned at the shore of a lake whose manifold inlets and mudflats were going to frustrate travel in a straight line for the indefinite future. Thanks to headlands and islets, I couldn't even tell whether more water lay to left or right.

I was about to flip one of those Swedish coins with its portrait of a real live king. Two fingers had latched onto cash in hip pocket when an outbreak of guttural snuffling stopped them. Where the hell was it coming from? From behind every tree, according to forest acoustics, from behind every boulder. The next whiny bout was more piercing, but equally impossible to pinpoint. My pivoting, bug-eyed search from compass point to compass point grew more urgent as unseen squealing body brushed apart fronds and scrub, and hooves clacked across stone.

I reeled to a standstill upon twisting 180° the second time, at movement I'd been too overwrought to catch at first. Cutting a swath toward me through the ferns like a torpedo through white-caps was a boar as big as a mastiff. And noting how he'd followed in my footsteps, I made the illogical but irrepressible leap he'd picked up Yankee scent at my overnight accommodations.

Agate eyes were riveted on me as he vented contrarily soft, idle grunts, like a codger doddering over a menu. He manifestly meant to gut me with his tusks, but he was only doing his job. No cause for excitement or haste. Did he really expect I wouldn't bolt? My fingers flung coin in the air as they tugged free of hip pocket.

I sprinted toward the lake, seeking haplessly for some smarter re-sort than the water. The hoofbeats and oddly placid snorting were louder, warning that the beast was gaining on me, but I'd swear he wasn't trotting any faster or breathing any harder, as if my bid to out-race him didn't matter, was a foregone conclusion. That coldblooded self-assurance unnerved me the most. Stupefying fright almost goaded me past the opportunity presented by boulder smack against fir tree.

Maybe hardwired instinct, or maybe basic training, sent me scrambling up the boulder. I can only affirm my wits were unin-volved. I flicked backpack straps from my shoulders and shrugged off all my worldly possessions. My arm swung overhead to clutch a low dead bough that broke off rather than support an ounce of my weight. Straining fingers clamped around another branch, almost out of reach, and incredibly, it held.

With boot soles winning traction on the trunk's furrowed bark, I boosted myself into clumsily wrapping my limbs around the branch and inchworming to the trunk and up to the next branch. I sat down on it, leaning into the trunk and encircling it with one arm, legs dan-gling into space, to minimize the burden on my perch.

I performed these maneuvers minus the middleman of volition to slow them down. They were still underway as the boar slammed with brash momentum into the boulder, tusks resounding harshly like chisels glancing off boilerplate.

Murderous ambition withstood the impact unscathed. The drop from here was enough to crack my skull, but gaping earthward, panting for breath, I was tempted to climb some more, or at least pull up my feet. Ebony eyes fastened on mine as if I were nothing special, another mere nuisance to destroy. Meanwhile, spindly fore-legs scrabbled at the rock face and, independent of them, hind legs bounced madly.

A boar wasn't built for scaling sheer slate, though I was coming to accept this one might have a prayer, if God rewarded OCD. Overheated antics would have been laughable in any other context. From my grim vantage, they were petrifying.

He persevered till I had to question whether I'd have adequate daylight to exit the forest once he finally desisted. And at arbitrary length he did about-face and saunter away, wagging his tail like a good sport, as if resigned to sniffing out amusement elsewhere. To play it safe, I waited for him to dwindle into the distance, not that my body consented to budge yet in any case. And suppose my nemesis had a yen to renew campaign against me ten minutes after I descended?

He nipped this concern in the bud by making a U-turn while his hooves on rock still rang out sharply. He lowered his head, snout almost touching the ground, as he accelerated to a gallop and I hugged the tree tighter. The game plan was all too obvious.

Boar skull slammed into evergreen trunk, and the shock wave was like a 2 × 4 bashing my arms and ass, but I held firm and the tree remained upright. The beast may not have expected anything more because he was already withdrawing to charge again. Businesslike killer seemed ready to invest whatever effort produced results.

Second and third offensives didn't noticeably weaken the tree. They exacted a toll on me, however, shaking more and more of the strength from me to retain grip and balance. I kept my sights glued to the beast during its next onslaught, to steel myself for the crash, but it was no use. At the merciless thud, stabbing pain flashed across my temples, and dizziness set the branch to seesawing, as if I'd been the one to carom into the trunk. If upcoming attack succeeded, would the fall or the tusks do me in?

Unprepared as I was to die, I also wanted, to the exclusion of all else, for this ordeal to end. The beast had arrived at the end of his lane of trampled fern, at the apogee of outbound trot. He turned around and bowed his mallet head, and at that split second deafening gunfire exploded, and so did the boar, atomizing in midstep into a spray of pink gore that hung briefly in the air and dispersed like dew. What the hell had hit him, a rocket-propelled grenade?

There was a homicidal beast, and then there wasn't. I should have been relieved and elated, pulling myself together to fumble down to terra firma. My noncompliant body disagreed. Whoever had blown up the boar might have saved me inadvertently, with no inkling I was nestling in the greenwood. Yesterday's worries about big game animals were in literal smithereens, which only created more room for yesterday's worries about hunters mistaking me for big game, particularly if they had armaments better suited to a warzone.

Maybe it was forest acoustics again, or lingering tinnitus from that gun blast. Why else would snatches of chatter echo and buzz like a broadcast from another dimension and suddenly loom near and clear? No Swedish was necessary to parse upbeat mood, perhaps the unique jubilation of sportsmen bagging, or in this case annihilating, their quarry. I was no expert, never having shot a living target. My deserter's conscience was stainless in that department.

Hazy glimpses of orange vests and camo wear directed me toward the southwest, where four guys trooped into the subjectively blanched sunshine. Cynicism led me to predict unwashed, inbred yokels from *Deliverance*, but lose the rifles and outfits, and they could have been on midcareer sabbatical from a cover band or magazine staff or TV crew. They were almost in spitting range, en route, I reckoned, to inspect the remnants of their marksmanship. And they were totally oblivious to me.

But save me they had, and apart from their love of firepower, they came across as sympathetic, approachable characters. The sunshine shed its somber tinge. Tension I'd been harboring till I'd become unconscious of it wheezed out of me, and after my emptied lungs reinflated, I was mystified to hear myself shout, "Don't shoot! I'm an American!"

I had no cause to presume these guys were trigger-happy, but even if I had, why would those words pop out of me? My brain, left to its own devices, must have concluded I really was in a warzone, susceptible to friendly fire. The hunting party was gawking around, confused into inaction by disembodied plea.

I waved and whistled. The first to spot me had the weedy physique, sculpted Nordic features, and bristly blond hair of a pop star during the heyday of the Police, and all four looked to be about that age. "Why should we shoot you?" he yelled.

I had no better answer for him than for myself. "I'm coming down, okay?" Nobody objected. Resting guns on forearms, they impassively witnessed my wobbly descent. They seemed unsure yet what to make of me, suspending judgment with the same neutrality that had steered them peacefully through the Cold War. I retrieved my backpack and slipped it on before sliding off the boulder, anxious to quit any elevation from which they might picture me pouncing on them.

"Thank you. Thank you." I was still a tad short of breath. "I owe you people my life. I hate to think what would've happened if you hadn't nailed that boar."

Their brows wrinkled as if a language barrier separated us after all. Big slab of a dude with a ruddy, full-moon face and acne pocks explained, "One of us shot a four-point buck. Killed it instantly, which is quite rare. We're on our way to collect it. A boar, did you say? There are no boars on this land."

Did I truly care to argue? I'd seen a boar and not a deer bite the dust, but I was unanimously outvoted. I'd already made a weird first impression, and raising graver doubts about my sanity among gents with guns would have been impolitic. Besides, any evidence in my favor had been reduced to flesh confetti. "You're right. The deer chased me up the tree. Sorry. I misspoke because I'm so flustered."

Somewhat elfin fellow with blond goatee, a circlet of collar-length blond strands, and nothing on top remarked in slow bass tones, "A deer with antlers can kill you just as dead as a boar. You were correct to be frightened."

Was this meant as solicitous, a verbal pat on the shoulder? As opposed to what else? For the sake of tact, I nodded appreciatively.

"What are you doing in these parts anyway?" asked the fourth huntsman, the sturdiest and most outdoorsy, with a salt-and-pepper ponytail, prominent brow, practically no eyebrows, and cross-shaped ear studs. "You are some miles from the nearest path."

"I was heading for Lee-us-false-hammer."

"Where?" The full-moon dude shook his uncomprehending head. I had to repeat the name twice more.

"Ljusfallshammar?" Weedy pop star expressed the shared bewilderment. "Why?"

"I was going to stay at a hostel there. I went off-trail yesterday when it got dark earlier than I'm used to, and I had to spend the night in a hunter's blind. This morning I was trying to reorient myself when your deer chased me up the tree." My run-in with nocturnal fiend was nothing to bring up among new acquaintances. Nor was my international fugitive status.

They might well have pondered how I could have gone astray when those blinds always flanked roads and trails. But a more apposite topic had occurred to the outdoorsman with ear studs. "You had to be in that tree a long while for the deer to forget all about you. He was calmly chewing his cud when we sighted him. We caught him completely off guard."

"It felt like a long while, yes." Were Swedes attuned to the inflections of hedging in English?

The balding elf was becoming fidgety. "If you still want to stop in Ljusfallshammar, we are passing that way after we finish here. Right now, though, we should be dealing with that buck before crows find it."

With murmurs of agreement, the posse shoved ahead, and I tagged along, effusively grateful. I was as good as out of the woods, too rapturous even to consider I might finagle a ride somewhere better than Ljusfallshammar.

Their every footfall supplanted my frames of reference with their own. They tromped alongside the lane of trampled ferns as if it didn't exist, and I didn't call it to their attention, for what would it prove? Likewise, to show them where they'd annihilated the boar would serve no purpose, for its substance had been aerosolized, reduced not to confetti but to reddish stipples indistinct from spores on fronds, or lichen on rock.

I was on the cusp of conceding my informants had their facts straight. Wild swine didn't really belong to local earthly bestiary. My attacker hadn't gone the way of normal flesh, leaving less behind than a balloon, giving me to believe it was of the same realm as last night's deranged gunman. He, and not these spare-time sportsmen, must have obliterated the boar, after remedying whatever had spoiled his aim earlier.

Did his deadeye shot coincide with that of the deer hunters, or were they synchronized as part of this connection between worlds? And wouldn't I be rash to assume he'd already gone home? I wondered if I could get shut of him, since I was somehow keyed in to his alien wavelength, the virtual keystone of this interplanar bridge. No, I wasn't halfway out of the literal or figurative woods yet.

A general halt disrupted my cosmic wool-gathering, a few steps away from blundering into big, dead deer. This animal certainly could have killed me, but his splayed legs, oozing hole in the throat, and tongue lolling in the dirt were sad all the same. The responsible party also spent a somber moment contemplating their victim.

The funereal hush broke when silver ear-studs declared, in English for my benefit, "Well, the sooner we butcher him the better."

Team deerslayer had definitely done this before. Pooling the contents of their leather rucksacks, they laid out a gleaming array appropriate to Victorian surgeons or Grand Inquisitors. I wavered between marveling and shuddering at the mechanical efficiency that positioned the body on downslanting stone surface, bent the head backward by its antlers, and sliced the neck open to release the blood. At the dark red gush I flinched away, with an unsoldierly wave of nausea, and kept my eyes glued to the space between two trees. What a joke to pretend I'd ever have been fit for battle.

Telltale bass tones of the goateed elf invited me to retire upwind if I was unaccustomed to such graphic activity, which would also shortly produce unpleasant noise and odors.

"It's all right," I fibbed without meeting his eye, and added more shamelessly, "Anything I can do to assist?"

Somebody let fly a skeptical chuckle at that. A more generous spirit tried distracting me from the carnage. "What was your purpose in coming to Sweden?" Generous or not, was this guy a customs officer back in civilization?

"I'm just exploring my options," I blurted. "To see if moving here might be a good idea." One little question, and I was about to spill the whole can of beans.

"By getting lost in this forest?" At a guess, my interrogator was the stocky, pock-faced dude, accompanied by a hatchet chopping through one bone, and another, each followed by a clatter of detached hoof across stone, and then by sawing into muscle and something squeakier, and a spattering cascade.

My pasty features may have contained less blood than the deer by now. To deflect this palaver away from me was imperative, but the sound effects weren't conducive to linear thinking. "What's the opinion here about the U.S. president?"

"A clown." Whoever this was, the rest didn't dispute him.

"Though after starting the war, a very unfunny clown."

I mistook quiet behind me for a pause in the abattoir procedure. I turned only till I registered that silver ear-studs and the stocky dude were pumping the buck's hind legs like an elliptical trainer, to force blood glugging from the neck incision. Gory tableau must have addled me into spouting, "Would you say then that soldiers were within their rights to desert rather than fight in an immoral, unprovoked war?" Why not just fork over a signed confession?

"No, once you join the military, you make a commitment. Dishonoring that, it is not exactly patriotic." Could that be the pop star talking like a Red State reactionary?

"Is that the primary issue? When patriotism trumps conscience, isn't there something wrong with patriotism?" To articulate this sentiment was something of a triumph against the background of gurgly bloodletting.

"Or is there something wrong with your conscience?"

My God, were they on to me? Was that a rhetorical, generic "your," or did it refer specifically to my conscience? I was racking my brains for some casual rejoinder that admitted nothing, acknowledged no accusation. Staring into space, I couldn't confirm which of the others reprieved me by stating, "Nobody in my experience has been qualified to see what's in another person's conscience."

"And that is why we can only judge a person's actions, which is complicated enough," droned the balding elf. I'd prematurely concluded he was on my side. Or was he fundamentally a partisan of "the truth and nothing but the truth"? The discussion switched over to Swedish, maybe because its nuances had become too subtle and abstruse for English as a second language. I had fallen in perchance with a klatch of moralists, unless philosophic deliberations were standard fare on Nordic hunting expeditions.

At least they'd dispensed with me as subject matter, or if not, eavesdropping would accomplish nothing. Why not take advice to stroll upwind? Besides, the more conspicuously I loitered, the likelier they'd resume interrogating me. I leaned against a scaly pine trunk, off where boughs heaving in the breeze would mask the dismemberment, gutting, and discourse. The sporadic carving, hacking, and hammering that harassed my ears, and the vagrant whiffs of half-digested gunk and glandular musk and shit, almost made me turn again to see how anyone could stand it.

Instead I homed in on an encore of yesterday's unreal rustling of leaves, down toward the water's edge. It was a blatantly mismatched soundtrack to the leafless, sunny ground, the naked rocks, the sparkly lake. A shadow, like the recollection of a bad dream, again grayed the terrain, except no cloud was blocking the sun.

Prolonged exposure to the autumnal white noise clarified details within it, of feet trudging back and forth, swishing through leaves as if through shallow surf. I intuited impatience for a bell to clang, a door to open. With subpar results my concentration shifted to the less ominous racket of dismantling an animal.

I leaned upon the pine for an imprecise period, as good as catatonic, my spine and one foot flat against the bark, posing for a shutter that never clicked, a miserable antenna tuning in one traumatic set of signals or another, until a tentative hand on my shoulder startled me. "Did I scare you?" silver ear-studs asked, not outright apologizing, not waiting for an answer. "We are returning to the campsite. Join us, and we will give you a ride tomorrow."

"Tomorrow?" I tried suppressing my alarm, and probably came across as petulant. My alleged godsends had trapped me into a second night in haunted wilderness, hadn't they? Or, since nothing uncanny had happened to them, would they function as buffers between me and the hostile supernatural?

"The meat has to cool before we can transport it, and we're soon losing light. We would be groping around in the dark before we got back to the car. You understand what that is like." So there was the deal, take it or leave it.

I resisted an urge to poll him on whether he too could hear those invisible leaves. Simple thanks were all I dared voice as I stretched the kinks out of my joints and fell in with him. And he didn't hassle me about my furtive, birdlike squints into forest depths, as if anxious that another dangerous beast might yet ramp out.

During our march upslope, the other three safari members were wiping fluids and tissue off steel edges with rags, reapportioning implements into rucksacks, and peeling off latex gloves and chucking them into plastic trash bag. The butchering rock was bloody as any pagan altar. Dragging inedible portions into the semi-concealment of fern beds made scant dent in the dizzying stink of innards, waste, and just plain death. Stone Age chunks of meat distended sleeves of fabric resembling camo spandex.

The men conferred in sotto voce Swedish, punctuated by discreet pairs of eyes flicking unreadably at me. To endear myself by a better-than-nothing effort, I volunteered for a share of the heavy lifting. My lot consisted of their garbage bag over one shoulder and pop star's rucksack over the other. Long afternoon shadows coalesced into dusk as our jaunt began to feel like a marathon.

It still wasn't enough to dispel the pungency of slaughter from my nostrils. That scent, meanwhile, was luring my thoughts down a path these Swedes had certainly never explored. I'd infiltrated their country to dodge a shitstorm of mayhem, yet what was I smelling now? What had been harrying me since yesterday, converging from not one but two worlds? I'd sidestepped oil-fueled war machine, only to bungle into the machinations of karma, fate, or murkier powers. In this suddenly madder universe, was I accountable for some preset quantity of violence, some inborn quota, wherever I went? Maybe harm, like water, always found its relentless way.

Listening to myself, I had to commend Swedish wisdom in assigning me rubbish and not rifles to carry. I also inwardly applauded their campsite of two tents on a grassy patch, and not a hula-skirted platform. With the same laconic coordination that had demolished a deer, they proceeded to light electric lanterns, build a fire, distribute beer and snacks, and unsleeve some meat for dinner. Me they ignored like a classic fifth wheel, beyond treating me to chips and a beverage.

When the sunset activity had died down, everyone surrounded the stone-encircled flames and the haunch roasting on four-legged grill, and benign elf droned, "I hope you're okay with venison. You're not vegetarian, are you?"

"Oh no," I enthused. "What could be better?" Not that I'd ever eaten venison. "Sure beats two suppers in a row of oranges and chocolate."

"So you're contributing the dessert," moon-faced dude informed me. "Chocolate. Excellent. And the oranges we can use to make the deer more special."

Hooray, they'd accepted me to the extent of declaring my supplies communal property. I rummaged up a civic nod and smile, along with the foodstuffs from my backpack.

The pop star quartered my three oranges and wedged them, rind up, into slots he cut across the top of the haunch. Bald elf and moonface uncapped fresh beers and withdrew into earnest disquisition. Silver ear-studs leaned back and flung out an arm to slide the lid off the cooler beside a lantern. He extracted a pair of bottles one-handed and gave me one.

I saluted him with upraised bottle, and he eyeballed his and cleared his throat with a diffidence at odds with commanding, outdoorsy persona. "Don't worry about these," he said, jabbing a finger at the cross in his left ear. "I know better than to discuss Jesus in mixed company."

"Unless he forgets what's good for him," the pop star interjected while flipping the roast with a pair of barbecue forks.

"As an American, you are so lucky," bashful Christian opined. "You are too young to have seen them, but relative to us here, everything about the Grateful Dead is there at your fingertips." Despite a promise not to preach the gospel, religious fervor shone in born-again Deadhead's blue irises.

"I was never really into the Dead. They didn't do it for me. Don't know why. Sorry." Did my tone translate as conciliatory?

"How can that be?" His frown indicated he was genuinely hurt, crestfallen, incredulous. "That music is part of your heritage, a major cultural phenomenon. And all you say is 'Sorry'?" He swigged beer as if indignation made him thirsty.

Seconds impersonated minutes as I scrabbled after some glib expiation for this new character flaw. Christian ear-studs glanced sidelong, snatched up the lantern as he staggered to his feet, and strode toward the perimeter, glowering like Diogenes opposing the darkness.

"I didn't mean to get him upset!" I addressed the pop star who along with the others was keeping tabs on their friend's tour of inspection. "Am I in trouble?"

Pop star curtly shook his head. "We don't like his ancient hippie music either, and from us that doesn't offend him. But it's different because you're an American, and you're supposed to have better taste."

"However, you're not the reason he took off," the elf interposed. "A twig snapped somewhere, and he's investigating. I heard it too, but to me it was some kindling or fat in the fire." I, the Yankee greenhorn, had heard nothing over the crackle of flames. "Maybe it is for the best he does go check, in case of a moose. You don't want one galloping into camp when everyone is asleep."

"Do you have moose in the U.S. where you live?" inquired the pocky dude, furthering the pattern of conversation since this afternoon. The Swedes asked me about myself; I didn't ask them about themselves. I had more to prove, credibility to establish, trust to earn. They didn't have to prove a thing. I'd been the foreigner perching on a branch and spouting nonsense. To poke into their business might well qualify as pushy.

"Nope, no moose," I answered. "Sometimes a bear knocks over trashcans one town over, but that's pretty common everywhere these days."

Prudent Diogenes had finished his patrol and replaced the lantern beside the cooler. In reply to the unspoken question on every face, he shrugged, and that satisfied the others more than me. A moose was many orders of magnitude less cunning and demonic than the intruders on my watchlist. On the other hand, to grasp at a silver lining, if I weren't alone in sensing these intruders, my sanity was perversely vindicated.

I now observed the interactions among my hosts, and my interactions with them, from more trenchant perspective. Discounting that fuss over a broken twig, they were blithely unaware of baleful surveillance. They might have been less vulnerable had I clued them in, but that might have thrown away hours of effort convincing them I wasn't crazy, and was I absolutely convinced myself? These guys could have been under my baleful surveillance and mine alone.

They prattled solemnly about how long to cook the roast, how much of the meat was done already, how rare was too rare, and acknowledging I had a vested interest, they included me by speaking English. I, throughout, was dwelling rather more solemnly on the likelihood of a massacre before dinner could be served.

When finally moon-faced dude unpacked IKEA plasticware and we dined on the most exquisite game ever, the Swedes were quibbling about the merits of adding more salt or herbs or lingonberry sauce next time. I pondered whether this would be our last meal.

After dead-serious fair parceling made short work of my several chocolate bars, fellow campers rose and ambled around, to loosen up or piss into the dark or generally relax. I hunkered up to the fire till the heat stopped me, as tension mounted in my every fiber, as each heartbeat edged us nearer the inevitable bloodbath.

While I fixated on the blaze, someone removed a lantern and announced he was rinsing our dishes in the stream. Someone else announced borrowing another lantern to fetch an armload of firewood. I almost babbled a cri de coeur about the buddy system, but if they heeded me, I'd be on my own. So I basked in the ruddy warmth, in a guilty silence tantamount to criminal negligence, letting two men skip off like babes in the life-threatening woods.

Two remained in camp. Of that I was fully cognizant, yet the oncoming tread of boots on pebbles jolted me head to foot.

Silver ear-studs loomed over me. "You seem like a pent-up individual."

Once he'd squatted uninvited beside me, I had a half-baked impulse to joke, *Sit down, why don't you?* But he wouldn't have gotten it, and once the impulse faded, I didn't either. What was I thinking? This was his turf. I limited good-humored response to attempting a broad Stan Laurel smile.

His soft-spoken, confidential delivery was hard to absorb over the lively combustion. "I agree, your conscience has to be your chief guide. What would have happened had the early Christians not defied their government?"

Speaking as an agnostic, he had me stumped. I was also dumbstruck because, for all his sincere empathy, he was sitting cross-legged with a rifle across his lap. I was still emphatically on probation, especially when half the crew was absent on chores.

"You guys act pretty comfortable around guns," I digressed. "Were you in the military?"

"I had National Service, right before they abolished it. But pacifists didn't have to do combat training. I was in a conservation corps.

And you? I have a hunch you had armed forces experience."

"Yes and no." "Roomy" would have ill described our grassy patch within its pool of lamplight, but before now I hadn't labeled it "claustrophobic." Reducing our lit circle by two lanterns may have made the difference. I doubted it, though, because my vision was confined to rifle barrel catching restless gleams from the fire. I couldn't tell if the roar of surf was solely in my panic-stricken ears or everywhere, like the Red Sea parted and suspended and about to crash.

"I for one am willing to invest faith in your motives. You should feel free to reveal how your conscience led you here." He laid a brotherly hand on my forearm. "You can rely on our sympathies. Give us your name, at least."

The problem was, I couldn't get past the discrepancy between his benign sentiments and the weaponry on display. And the words to unburden myself wouldn't form till I'd found a tactful way to ask, *So why the hell are you cradling that Winchester?*

At that instant, the mystery became irrelevant forever. With the din of a wave smashing into a jetty, the deranged woodsman, my own personal avatar of violence, burst from the darkness a dozen yards beyond the fire, bathed in a moonlight that illuminated nothing else. He bounded straight for me, a noiseless war shriek contorting his lips, shotgun barrel in two-fisted grip like a batter's, ready to swing iron at my head.

Reflexes of basic training kicked in. I snatched up born-again Deadhead's rifle, went down on one knee, and, with lessons learned too well on the shooting range, pulled the trigger as my bearish target leapt over the campfire.

An earsplitting bang, a blinding flash, and recoil like a thundergust toppled me onto my ass and knocked the rifle from my hands. Time lagged as I squinched into the quick-fading retinal burn, terrified I'd somehow missed. No, frenzied madman was gone all right, like film snapping in a projector.

The pop star had been emerging from the dark at the heels of vanquished enemy. I made that i.d. based on blond coiffure and weedy physique, because my rifle blast had expunged the face, simplified it to a blank pink oval, surrounded by pink cloud that dispersed as a slow drizzle, a variation on the boar's unnatural destruction. Load of firewood rolled from dying arms, and the lantern, whose handle was hooked under a finger, clattered and tossed shards of brightness as the body crumpled.

Pious hunter already had Winchester back in hand and leveled at me, as the elf burst from his tent, rattling off more excited Swedish than I'd have guessed was in him. Neither of them betrayed the least interest or awareness regarding the unique behavior of my bullet's impact. Nor would anyone else find it wry that pop star had initially greeted me, "Why should we shoot you?" and here I'd gone and shot him. With 20-20 hindsight, yes, for his sake, they really should have shot me.

To silver ear-studs, the onrushing maniac was plainly like the boar, invisible, preposterous, a figment doubling as red flag of my psychosis. After I expounded on crazed woodsman in copious detail and swore he'd blocked my view of anyone else, my captor-cum-host could only shake his head and repeat, "Why did you do it?" Did Christianity or the Grateful Dead, I wondered uselessly, blinker him from seeing what I'd seen?

Moon-faced dude reentered camp with wet, clean dinnerware just as his extant friends were binding me at gunpoint. Incredibly, he didn't drop the lantern and the stack of plates while boggling at a recap of the incident in distinctly prejudicial Swedish.

From my seat against the fir trunk where they deposited me, I continued accosting them about my innocence, my attacker, my justification in self-defense, my abject sorrow. Balding elf soon came over and rumbled, "I voted for turning you in as a fugitive at the beginning. Whatever we do next, you will have no say in it. If you keep jabbering, we will gag you as well as tie you up." That was the last English any of them, and I for that matter, have spoken since. The night chill meanwhile has seeped through the ropes, my clothing, my skin.

All my efforts to ensure my freedom, my mobility, have landed me here, with worse prospects than if I'd gone into active duty. Trussed like a turkey, numb to the marrow, and with nothing to do besides stew in my thoughts. What were the odds of that? The dice feel ever more loaded.

When nightmare realm trespasses on normality, doesn't that

normality then become suspect because such trespasses occur there? Why be cocksure this absurd moment is real, that I'm not comatose in desert dune or a field hospital, bound up in bandages, IVs, and traction instead of hemp? Maybe I did ship out and come to grief and can only dream I had the smarts to go AWOL, though even in dreams I can't elude immobility.

Earthier concerns restore me to the moment. Suppertime beers I'd swigged in short-lived fellowship are clamoring for release. I risk a mouthful of rag on behalf of some vestigial dignity. "Hello? I have to go to the bathroom. Can you help me? Might be better all around if I don't soil myself. Please?"

I'm subjected to no reprisals for breaking my silence. The collective attention is elsewhere. Thanks to the oceanic sibilance in my ears, whether from hypertension or mental overload, I can't discern whatever prompted my warders to crane their necks, negotiate gravely, fetch rifles and lanterns, and file into the blackness, consigning me to the pain of urinary urgency, the paltry glow of campfire and one lantern, and the company of faceless supine corpse at the edge of light farthest from the tents.

How childish of me to assume mere point-blank gunshot had obliterated a denizen of afterlife or underworld. I wouldn't even bet against that boar making a comeback. Bladder pressure increases torturously at the concept of sly madman enjoying free access to me after staging decoy commotion to lure everyone off.

But I've drastically misread his intentions. The probing voices, the bouncy white lights of the searchers recede among the silhouettes of trees. Of the people per se I can glimpse nothing, only this shadowplay. No pause or agitation in their talk precedes brilliant flashes of three gunshots devouring one lamplight after another at an almost leisurely pace, and then portentous, vacuum darkness.

That darkness drags on and on till I have to concede my hosts are never coming back. Further epiphany finally dawns that unearthly woodsman wasn't stalking me but rather the hunting party. I quail at picturing what he wants of them. Trophies, maybe? But my role as bait, as Judas goat, is hideously explicit. To him I'm an investment, and can he be done with me already?

I have occasion to answer that after my desperation to piss is dulled by the cold and my encumbered circulation. Or can a bladder, like a soul, become inured to hardship? The painful pressure rebounds when new voices jar me to alertness, and they sound like angelic choristers warbling a roundelay of hellos, based purely on expectations they'll cut the ropes so I can relieve myself.

I bellow that I'm near the firelight, and they respond in kind to my English. Someone had shot out some lights, and am I okay? I simply urge them to hurry.

What colossal luck for me that others were nearby, and what abominable luck for them. But playing dumb instead of crying out wouldn't help, because I detect that persistent, do-gooder timbre right through their singsong accents. They'd stumble upon me eventually. And then what to say, that I'd kept mum to forestall their supernatural doom?

Several flashlight beams rove methodically toward the place of putative ambush. There's a screech, and the beams congregate on one spot, hidden from my location. My rescuers revert to Swedish. Distress and terror require no translation.

To cite an upside at this juncture may be ghoulish, but would it be my worst sin? When these newcomers finally discover me, they'll see I was in no position to commit whatever atrocity has appalled them, and by extension I'll be innocent of pop star's murder too. As for explaining my captivity, I reckon when these ropes come off, that'll free up my creativity as well.

Before this night is out, I may well be complicit in more death and carnage because of facts, far-fetched or not, that I've withheld, guilty by association, like a silent partner. But then again, I may be in a coma dream half a world away. None of this might be real, so it's premature for self-recrimination.

Just the same, I wish those semi-hysterical Swedes would detach themselves from lurid scene and tend to me. Even if I'm hallucinating, to wet myself will be disgusting. Where has all my moral high ground gone? Maybe, like violence, it's doled out in predestined but finite measure. Time will tell if I'm wrong about doing less harm here than in the war.

Taking the Plunge (The Old Country)

There is greater variation within "racial groups" than between them.

—American Anthropological Association

Magic in the air. Sounds like the title of a '60s pop song. Probably more than one '60s pop song. Can't be helped. When was I last carefree? So many ages ago I forgot how it felt. No phone or e-mails to answer, no deadlines or pressure. Just tooling around in the land of my ancestors on a balmy summer afternoon. Not even the need to stop and piss can put a damper on this gift of buoyancy.

I'm blithely unaware of the toponyms that bind or separate these red barns and rambling pastures and forest glades and acres of yellow grain. After today, couldn't retrace this route to save my life. No matter. Wouldn't be the same. The million unperceived and perceived ingredients, from temperature and humidity to what I had for lunch, will never recombine quite perfectly to recreate this happiness. Just have to inhabit golden hour to the utmost.

Where to piss, though? I slow down while passing a church. Whitewashed, with black steeple. Fifteenth century, if memories of guidebooks serve. Empty parking lot on one side, cemetery within flagstone walls on the other. None but the dead on hand. No access to spiritual or bodily solace.

The church is on my right. Coming up on the left is a swatch of woods, the size of a vacant lot between tenements, wedged into a corner where a gravel lane merges with the road. My host Cousin Halvard informed me that pissing into midtown bushes raises few Swedish eyebrows after dark. What onus then in retiring behind trees in the middle of nowhere?

I pull over on roadside dirt and spring from my rented Saab toward relief. But hold on. The acute angle of woodlot in the T-intersection has been defoliated and the grass trimmed, to set off a boulder like a gem on green felt. I have to detour and gawk a minute. Its dimensions are those of a treasure chest, its contours those of a crudely sculpted polka-dot mushroom cap.

On closer inspection, the human artistry is less representational, more perplexing, distinctly prehistoric. A dozen or so indentations, the depth of cereal bowls, plus the ham-handed intaglio of a horse or a deer near the ground are painted red for emphasis, apparently by the same conservators who mow the lawn. Too bad they also couldn't post explanatory signage, not that I'd get half the gist. For now, enough to feast my eyes on ancient monument a forebear may have wrought. Besides, I have pressing business.

I pick my path with care among the rocks that poke every which way from the riotous flora. This must have been a long-term dump for rubble that leached up in the fields of neighboring farms. Back home, at least, it couldn't be anything else. A heap of brown foliage and deadwood like a landlocked beaver dam at the center of the copse supports the theory I'm in a trash area.

Or possibly more. At the base of the pile is a porthole-wide gap, like the entry to a lair. For a fox? A weasel? How common are badgers? I pause warily, staring at the hole, but hear nothing telltale. My burning gaze flushes nobody out. Okay, fine.

I step behind the nearest tree and unzip. The porthole remains in peripheral vision till I'm done. The instant I lift a foot to exit, my entire body tenses. Seems an overreaction to what my ears are registering. Or is it?

I count five knocks after I think to start adding them up. They resound just loudly enough to get my attention. As best I can tell they originate overhead. Beyond that I can't specify. They lack the rapid-fire tempo of a woodpecker or the incensed energy of prudish onlooker, unless the onlooker is feeble or groggy but has managed nonetheless to hide in the treetops. Of course, this apparent protest at public urination might be pure coincidence.

The knocking resumes. This time I'm quicker on the uptake and tally a series of eight. Once more, their tempo matches that of a ticking clock, and their source could be anywhere or nowhere. I decide

I've overstayed when a third set of eight prompts me to observe, It's less like someone knocking at the door, so much as announcing he's in. My halcyon mood has flown as airily as it arrived.

Should I apologize to whatever I've disturbed? I don't. What formula, what etiquette, what language would apply? Beating a spooked retreat should speak louder than words, giving the bird or badger or more miscellaneous witness what it wants, to be rid of me. And when I advance from woodsy shade to direct sunlight, that air of mystery, no less rare and delicate than bygone ebullience, likewise disperses. Nothing's chasing me, so what's my hurry?

Ancient monument deserves a second glance, especially as I'll never pass by here again, will I? Too bad I can't make head or tail of sacred object in any way that doesn't trivialize it. A caveman tribute to Swiss cheese? A geologic case of measles? The chip off a leopard idol big as a Macy's balloon?

At each guess, I relapse deeper into default frame of mind for these two weeks, an attitude of homecoming. Like all else I dwell on here, no matter how foreign or outlandish, I entertain some proprietary stake in it, as if this mineral portion of inheritance belongs to me as much as anyone, as if seeing it amounts to reclaiming it on some, dare I say, racial level. Yes, even while condemning the concept of "race" as scientifically invalid, reactionary hokum.

Well, journeys of self-discovery can't always yield predictable or flattering results. And initially, this junket was simply about discovering the "old country." Not that such an undertaking in itself doesn't say something about me. I bid bemused farewell to polka-dotted relic, this esoteric, primitive part of my heritage, of myself, and slide behind the wheel, en route again to Stockholm.

My golden hour is up, but scenic tracts of forest and meadow and crops continue charming me after I transition from back roads to main highway. All the Swedish-Americans I know, like most other Americans who self-identify as a hyphenated compound, plan a pilgrimage to "where they came from," only to put it off till family ties fray and disintegrate.

Not me. Peremptory great-grandpa never entrusted gramps or dad with his reasons for teenage emigration. Couldn't have been anything too onerous, because letters and snapshots and a phone call every blue moon have crisscrossed the Atlantic down the decades. Still, the entrée to family connections inexorably narrows. Mine was the first generation to learn no Swedish from its elders. Overseas contact is down to Christmas cards I can't read and death notices with the Old World formality of envelopes edged in black. The writing on the wall, anyway, needs no translation. Go now as a guest, or unhappily ever after as a tourist.

I suppose many seekers after roots share delusions of returning somewhere they've never been, a pretext of ownership in other people's territory. A reverse colonialism, in effect, fully deserving of correction, gentle or not, by the natives. But would I want to own these typical city outskirts of car dealerships, light industry, tacky gallerias? Or that monstrous white globe, as easily a toxic waste tank as a civic arena? Actually, Cousin Halvard, with a subtle tic of wounded boosterism, earlier confirmed "The Globe" houses only cultural events and not hazardous chemicals.

It does dramatically underscore, as do the cousin's digs, how much of a misnomer "the old country" is. What had I expected, thatch roofs and oxcarts? The ongoing appeal of prehistoric aesthetic etched in polka-dotted stone? Halvard had warned of detours and delays in his part of town due to major road and subway construction, but GPS shunts me straight into the basement garage of his spanking-new apartment block, one of many with ritzy ground-floor shops and restaurants, on a spanking-new waterfront boulevard where recently "there was nothing," to quote the cousin, "just junkyards and worse."

Halvard's a freelance copyeditor for technical journals, same as me, oddly enough, which means we've at least one thing in common, i.e., an aversion to talking shop. He shuts down the Dell the minute I let myself in. The furniture strikes an IKEA balance between austere and comfy, but before I have a chance to relax on any of it, the cousin, after being cooped up all day, is raring to go for a walk.

If he were only slightly broader-shouldered, he might not seem gangly. Round, plastic-rimmed spectacles intensify an owlish demeanor. He may not be stereotypically blond. I'm not. Everything above receding hairline, though, is shorn down to a five o'clock shadow that betrays no color. Or is it singed away by nervous energy that seems to pack his gestures with propulsive voltage? He may well need to perambulate after each sedentary work shift.

We hit the street, jog over to the footpath beside the water, and adopt the pace of a forced march. The restful, shimmering harborscape has contrarily exerted a tonic effect on him. He's curious about the high point of my out-of-town excursion. I describe Stone Age relic to him. It's nothing familiar to him, and he suggests I pump Uncle Bengt the archaeologist for info this evening. I decline to mention the enigmatic knocking. Since it may have involved imagination getting the better of me, it feels too personal to discuss with anyone of mere days' acquaintance.

I suddenly go a little unsteady, like my inner gyroscope's been bumped. Without slowing down, I listen intently. Yes, it's that damn rapping again, Exhibit A if I did care to let Halvard in on my mysterious interlude. Freaky, how it recommences the moment my memory dredges it up. Same intervals, same pitch, same volume. These similarities deter me from sooner recognizing the slap of wavelets against the underside of a wooden pier, already fading as we traipse away. Still, that frisson of confronting the uncanny lingers. I tell myself to forget about it. Literally walk it off.

The cousin waves briskly at the nearest of several cement semicircles, like mini-amphitheaters, embedded in the manicured slope between footpath and boulevard. "We've reserved that one for the party later." Ah yes, the party. Friends of his and Annika the missus, plus selected relations, will gather in my honor to gorge on crayfish. Annika should be done with the shopping before we get back. Halvard and I will procure the alcohol. When I confessed reservations about the edibility of crayfish, I was advised to count my blessings. A few weeks from now I'd have been up against the rotten herring festival. And the cousin was dead serious, too.

I hope I can muster the energy for socializing after this headlong trek. Our clip is unrelenting through prim pastel-tone neighborhoods, up steep rocky hills and along ledges on stony dirt tracks, across stupendous bridges spanning bays, into an older big-city downtown with a more even ratio of commercial to residential, and with art nouveau brownstone cornices and onion domes atop turrets.

The cousin directs me to a sign of how important this annual crayfish fiesta is, and my outlook of coming home to a foreign country is sorely tested. At a corner quickie mart, he sums up the headlines of the evening editions. Tons of crayfish pawned off as fresh were actually frozen. Front-page scandal!

Thereafter, hyper cousin's a good sport when I mulishly halt to ogle some of the more ineptly surreal expressions of crayfish mania. In a cosmetic boutique's display window, plastic crawdads lurk among the lipstick and nail polish and perfume upon a laminated tablecloth with decorative motif of crown dill and yet more crawdads. The optometrist next door, not to be outdone, has loosed toy crayfish among the spectacles, and up a backdrop of fishing net.

Perhaps tackiest, though, are these five-and-dime crustaceans on fine silver plate, surrounded by silver utensils, goblets, and champagne bucket in a jeweler's showcase. Suspended over this arrangement is a round paper lantern with goofy smiling face that according to Halvard represents the "crayfish moon." Well, to quote the proverb, "The stranger coming home makes home strange." My Swedish kinsman, however, discerns nothing strange in these storefront setups. He's at a loss to understand how any of this traditional whimsy qualifies as laughable.

Luckily, we trot into another park before my giggling mockery of the retail sector sticks in his craw. For undisclosed reasons, he gives wide, shuddering berth to a Bolivian drum-and-panpipes quartet in bright striped vests. This park could otherwise be anywhere in the world. Children in team uniforms play noisy soccer behind a chain-link fence, pensioners doze on benches, dawdling teenage girls whisper secrets back and forth, red-faced businessmen, overheated in suit and tie, hurry home.

One further personage rates no more of Halvard's notice than the rest, but I find her baffling, and the cadence of her locomotion unnerves me. Gaunt old lady is proceeding with healthy momentum from a cluster of bushes flush against a sheer rock bluff. She's evidently emerged from nowhere. Certainly not from the seamless rock. Her bobbed white hair hangs dry and limp, her nose and chin are blunt, and her complexion is pale and pocky. Her reproachful eyes meet mine from under droopy eyelids. She wears a frowzy gray blouse and paisley slacks.

She boosts herself forward with the aid of a ski pole in each fist, as if they comprise a more outdoorsy form of walker, and they clack, clack, clack with the same clockwork regularity as the treetop rapping. And with the same slightly subdued but distracting impact. After eight strokes she rests for breath, plods onward. The poles lend her the look of a clumsy, feeble quadruped. Her eyes roll earthward. Maybe she'd only glared at me because I was staring at her. Can't say I'm sorry, anyway, that tireless Halvard forges ahead, forcing me to keep up, leaving the ski-poling crone farther and farther behind.

Sinister she may have been in an understated, arthritic manner, but once we're out of the park, she's out of sight, out of mind, and fatigue exerts its toll. How many hours have we been circumnavigating Stockholm? According to my wristwatch, it's been a whole 45 minutes. "Are we heading toward the house yet?" I make bold to wheeze.

Halvard acts a little taken aback at my dearth of stamina, but promises we'll be home shortly, after a stop at the "system." He refers to a liquor outlet. The alcohol here is nationalized. Across one more bridge, through one more park, and there we are, one block down from a post office. And the "system" partakes of impersonal post office ambience, though with clean, spacious aisles and, I must admit, a mammoth selection.

We each tote a wire shopping basket, and it's immediately clear this is a two-man operation. If the kinfolk are throwing tonight's bash for me, then they manifestly intend to get stinking blotto "in my honor." Three kinds of aquavit, half a dozen bottles of wine, a dozen of beer, these'll do, not counting what the guests will bring, and we're out on the sidewalk struggling with two overloaded plastic bags each. Only fair we split the tab, but after paying my half, I feel fiscally gutted.

I vent surprise at Halvard's faith in the tensile strength of thin plastic sack, not even double-ply. In America we'd be crying over spilt booze within minutes, subjecting ordinary retail issue to this much strain. Halvard iterates borderline smug pride in the quality of Swedish bags, with implicit derision of cheap Yankee plastic. I'm in no position to argue. Then again, since these are the bags of my ancestral home, that makes them partly mine as well. Funny how cracked that logic is coming to sound.

Anyhow, by virtue of cash outlay, half the drink is actually mine, and I wish in vain for Halvard to acknowledge that when we greet jockish, softspoken Annika in the kitchen. She finishes scraping dill sprigs off a tabloid-sized breadboard into a jumbo blue enamel kettle, an heirloom maybe, definitely older than anything else in the kitchen. She beckons me near for a whiff of steam from the pot. Within the roiling broth I discern tumbling crimson claws and carapaces. A crayfish vision of hell! The smell reminds me of shrimp or lobster, only muckier.

"Our secret ingredient is sugar," she confides, "which is probably the most popular secret ingredient in the country right now."

I thank her effusively for these epic labors on my behalf, and in that respect I'm sincere. No need to broach misgivings about the main course. She smiles demurely and assures me she'd be hosting one of these feasts anyway. I'm spared from navigating a response to that because she and Halvard start conferring in Swedish, and he's gesturing out the window at oncoming cumulonimbus clouds. Her nonchalant tone suggests she's downplaying his worries.

The situation, come what may, is under their control and out of my hands. If there's nothing I can do, I announce, I should go lie down, recharge my batteries, marshal my partygoing resources. Yes, yes, they dismiss me, if you must, you can squeeze in a brief nap. I detect an insinuation that we offspring of expats have lost considerable starch in a paltry few generations. I'm too beat to care. Drawing the curtains plunges the guestroom into uterine dimness, and the white noise of central air masks the clatter of culinary prep work. On contact with the pillow, I nod off as if I've backslid into the valley of jetlag.

I'm next aware of dreaming I'm afloat in pure black void, content as if morphine suffuses my brain, till insistent, resonant knocking grabs my attention. It nags at me, and confuses me because I can't conceive of what there is to knock on in a void. The vaguest outlines of bureau, chairs, and desk begin to compromise the vacuous dark, and a welter of voices presses in to compete with the percussion, two volleys of sound converging from opposite directions.

My ears pop as if I'm in a descending airplane, and the percus-

sion resolves into rain against the windows. The voices I localize to
the room beyond my door. They must belong to merrymakers driven
inside by the downpour. Disorientation drags on as I wonder, How
much of that out-of-body episode was a dream, and when exactly
did I wake up?

Meanwhile, how remiss of the honored guest to snore through
his own celebration. I shuffle to the door, and from my figurative
dusky cave blink at the brilliance of every lamp aglow, of abundant
candle flames, at too many people trying to make themselves heard
to realize their decibel level in aggregate. And tallying the bottles or
glasses in everyone's hands, I infer they've imbibed past the point of
caring. I make my entrance unobserved, weaving like a transparent
ghost around the preoccupied klatches.

Just as well nobody notices the ghost is smirking. Casual, formal,
swank, or frumpy, all grades of attire are united by tonight's common denominator, the mandatory conical cardboard hat, with flow-
ering dill against a broad green band, surmounted by the body and
pointy nose of a crayfish, pincers curving out from the sides. In silhouette it doubles as tawdry parody of a Viking helmet. I can't picture anyone carrying on their clever or deep or fervent exchanges in
these hats tomorrow.

Across the crowded room a yellow paper moon has replaced the
usual overhead lampshade, and it grins down on a table laden with
trays of crispbread and pâté and cheese and pickled herring and
herbed butter, bracketed by bottles of beer, wine, and harder stuff.
The tablecloth is of a *de rigueur* crayfish-and-dill pattern, as are the
napkins and schnapps glasses. On the table and elsewhere are squat
white candles with decals of red crayfish, and resin candleholders
body forth three rust-and-yellow crawdads writhing claws-to-tail together.

I loom over the table, processing these ugliest specimens of
kitsch, debating how potent a drink they call for, when Halvard
claps me on the shoulder, welcomes me to my own shindig, and
thrusts a Carnegie Porter at me. "It is a nice Class III strong beer. You
have some catching up to do."

No sooner have I pronounced a trial swig excellent than semi-
buzzed cousin steers me by the elbow to a shoo-in for oldest and

most professorial invitee. If he's resorted to low-ceilinged balcony for breathing space and fresh air, the posh gaggle of smokers gabbing by the rail must be royally frustrating. Cool gusts muss his white side-burns and thinning gray on top, except where silly hat clamps it down, and he polishes a stray raindrop off his thick wire-rims with the hem of a cotton blazer.

Halvard introduces him as "Uncle Bengt," though what that makes him to me I haven't the foggiest, and I shake Bengt's chill, damp hand in my capacity as "the American cousin." Halvard claps me on the shoulder again, rattles off some Swedish containing words that resemble "archaeology" and "mystery," and solicitously pushes me a step nearer Bengt before loping away. Gambling I've second-guessed Halvard's drift, I preface my description of archaic monu-ment with rough idea of distance and direction from Stockholm. Naturally I skip any reference to spooky audible presence.

Bengt hitches thumbs in khaki hip pockets and nods perfuncto-rily. Sans hesitation he reels off the Swedish name for polka-dotted boulder, and when I entreat him to repeat it, he digs ballpoint pen from left pocket and prints upon his palm. He shows me his in-scribed hand as if imparting a high sign or incantation.

"Skålgropar," he enunciates more slowly. "Bowl pits, or skull pits if you prefer poetic license to accuracy. Association with the carving of a generic animal, as you put it, implies the Bronze Age." His judgmental eye intimates I'd rather be amused than informed. "The evidence is sketchy, but one theory has it the bowls had a votive or sacrificial purpose and people smeared blood or fat in them, maybe as adhesive for their nail clippings or hair." He shrugs diplomatically. "They were up to nothing we would define as rational, so all our speculation is of limited use."

Does he mean ancestral thinking was too unlike ours to recon-struct, or that ancestral thought has no value because it was such nonsense? To organize these fine distinctions into a question is be-yond me at the moment. Instead, at a loss and flailing for words, I rashly ask, "Have you ever heard of these skull pits being haunted? Are they ever located in ancient graveyards?"

Uncle Bengt regards me dubiously, enfolds "skålgropar" within his fist, puts fist to mouth, and coughs up a storm. He excuses himself, claiming it's too smoky out here and he's thirsty.

Well, if he won't suffer fools gladly, can't say as I blame him, so long as he recognizes everyone's a fool sometime. I've hardly managed three swallows of porter when one of the smokers defects from his clique and joins me. He's got sandy hair that shelves off stiffly to one side, a bulbous nose familiar from tintypes of great-granddad, and a cream seersucker suit from the big-and-tall shop. He scrutinizes familial V-shaped cleft between my eyebrows. "We're related somehow."

"Somehow," I agree, no more eager than he, apparently, to disentangle our bloodlines.

"Don't let Bengt bother you. He can be a pill, as you Americans say." He flicks cigarette butt into the rain. "Where's your hat?"

I shrug. "I just got here."

He gestures broadly toward the living room. "Do you know the Swedish for this kind of party?"

I shake my head. "Halvard must have said, but I missed it."

He pronounces three syllables that come across as "krefweeva" and regards me with more avuncular interest than Uncle Bengt had shown.

I parrot the term exactly as heard, but he bites back a smile, and the fashionistas by the rail have listened in and burst out laughing. Right, as if there's nothing funny about dressing to the nines and then donning a cone with pincers.

"It's tricky," he imperfectly consoles me, with an acerbic glance at his friends. "Few of us would fare any better trying to say 'this is thistle' five times fast."

He lumbers past me to the railing at my back and surveys the lawn and rose beds of the inner courtyard. Wooly overcast imposes false dusk on the prolonged subarctic August evening. The rainfall doesn't hinder visibility, but imbues everything with bleakness. My relative nods like a veteran cop at his umpteenth crime scene.

"What is it?" I'm compelled to ask.

"Not a lethal height, unless a person landed on his head." He peers straight down over the edge. "Broken bones, yes, a fractured ankle at least, a leg, some ribs."

"Is that a prediction?" I gaze inside aghast. The attendees are more boisterous, yes. Some chic young thing irately dabs with crayfish-motif napkin at red wine on her velour jacket. No warning vibes of mayhem, though. And the apartment door opens to admit yet more crayfish fanciers.

Kinsman addresses my concern with the particulars he seemed about to deliver anyway. "These gatherings have a reputation for making or breaking couples. Affairs begin, marriages end." I overhear apartment door bang shut, and seconds later I can no longer devote undivided attention to this "krefweeva" expert. Only with maximal effort can my jittery eyes focus upon him. The measured staccato that's followed me since my pit stop has joined the fun.

"So as might be expected, you find fights breaking out, scores to settle, at these krefweevor. Even more than at office Christmas parties. On top of typical injuries from accident and horseplay at drunken soirees." Sardonic grin exposes teeth, and he lights another cigarette with matches from 7-Eleven.

My concentration on these words to the wise, meanwhile, is in tatters, and as if I'm out to derail two conversations in a row, I burble, "Krefweevor, is it? Please, would you mind writing it on your hand?"

Fortunately, this relative takes my nonlinear thinking in stride. "Only Bengt likes to use his skin as a notepad. It's not a characteristic of Swedes in general. But hold on. I'll spell 'krefweeva' for you."

I'm gratified that he and Bengt at least share the habit of carrying pens in hip pocket. As he unfolds 7-Eleven matchbook, I peek into the living room. Flabbergasting! The crone from the park, in the same gray blouse and paisley slacks, is clacking around on her ski poles, and it's obvious from some dozen yards away how wearily she leans into them, how much they sustain her. Still, for my money, the aura she projects is ominous.

Halvard paid her no heed earlier, and no one but me pays her any now. I can't discount her possible connection with somebody here. Maybe she's seeking that somebody, and not really shuffling aimlessly, unseen because people are too absorbed in talk, or she's beneath their snobbish radar, or they're too polite to make her self-conscious by interrogating her. Or are my hackles justified in rising? What the hell have I "come home" to in this "old country" of mine?

Ahem! Kinsman clears his throat, seemingly right in my ear. I whip around. Open matchbook is inches from my chin. "Do you want this?"

"Sorry. I thought I saw someone I knew." Let him assign likelihood to that as he will. I accept the matches with thanks, and scan block letters bisected by crease in flimsy cardboard. Kräftskiva? Really? I try to mask my skepticism, but where in there is "kref-weeva"?

An all-too-American impatience simmers at this last straw of foreign inscrutability. "I hope that clarifies it for you," my informant remarks. Is he kidding? "Just be careful who you kiss, and stay sharp." He consigns another cigarette butt to the rain.

A sloppy cheer and sloppier applause shift our awareness indoors. The trays of appetizers have been shoved toward the table's periphery, in a pileup like wreckage of tidal surge. Pride of place at the center now belongs to a bristly, terraced construction of crayfish, claws outward, with the dimensions of a shiny scarlet landmine. Dill flowers randomly protrude like preliminary, arrested detonations.

My unnamed relative and his stylish pals plow past me and merge with the unanimous jostle toward the main attraction. Or almost unanimous. While Halvard and Annika smile diffidently at compliments, and fastidious diners tie on paper bibs embellished with cavorting crawdads, and more ravenous diners hover in courteous stalemate over who spoils the gorgeous presentation first, I alone loiter on the balcony.

Therefore none bear witness as the doddering crone swivels around balcony doorway, cornering me with loveless, seafloor eyes. She arrived on foot in a downpour, but here she is, bone dry. I'm granted no chance to ponder this. With a burst of speed, of energy she must have been hoarding for ages, she braces her meager weight on one ski pole and swings the other up to thrust at my sternum. I'm also granted no chance to be grateful that old-fogy ski poles lack flesh-piercing spikes. The impact of blunt end slams me off my feet and over the rail like confetti in a cyclone.

Shit! Head first! flashes through my mind. I'm keenly certain this observation will be my last. I've involuntarily begun to holler, "Hey!"

Instead of bone-crushing impact, a bout of vertigo hits me, as I tumble for subjective ages like a barrel down a tunnel, head over heels till I'm dumped upon my feet. I finish hollering "Hey!" Twilight gloom eats the word.

As racing heart slows and eyes adjust, I seek clues regarding my whereabouts. First off, there's a tree in my face, no farther away than the matchbook had been. Good fucking grief! I'm back in the copse from this afternoon, considerably creepier in sepulchral dusk. Miraculous survival may not involve altogether heavenly magic in the air.

Matchbook still grows damp in one hand. In the other is the pull tab of my fly, as if I've been rewound to moment of decision, and yes, my bladder aches for release once more. I haven't seen a bathroom since mid-afternoon, and though overhead foliage provides some shelter from the rain, the dripping from a hundred branches pushes me toward urge incontinence.

Why transport me here if not to bestow a second chance, forgiveness if I refrain from desecrating sacred precinct again? Point taken! I jam matchbook into hip pocket, remove fingers from zipper, and risk parting glance at sullen porthole in the brush pile. Any ghostly knocking is lost amidst the plunk of raindrops.

I hightail it from the glade, into washed-out sunset and steady rainfall. Has occult agency transported my Saab too? Hah! Perhaps I'm not so summarily forgiven. No sinister eyes peeked back from the porthole, but I'm inexplicably loath to survey the trees behind me. The boulder peppered with skålgropar calls to me, and minus any wiser sense of direction, I obey.

I wonder then how long I'll have to repent at leisure. Weak light is more than adequate for viewing the "skull pits," but I can't for the life of me find that "generic animal" beside them. I can contrive no explanation that isn't ridiculous. All the same, a backward glimpse is henceforth strictly forbidden.

To misquote bartenders everywhere, I've no home to go to, but I can't stay here. Moreover, my bladder's fit to burst. I pad up the road toward medieval church and idly speculate on how many crayfish Halvard's friends will devour before anyone remarks my absence.

The church, of course, is locked up tight. Not a living soul around. Best to act fast, lest I miss sympathetic motorist who might offer pitiful me a lift. I cut across parking lot toward the rear of the church, in a reflex quest for privacy. Am I being followed? The patter of rain continues to hide the clacking of anything solid.

On the bright side, simply setting foot on consecrated ground might deter unholy pursuit. Or will pissing on Christian property put me in better with indigenous spirit force? I'm agnostic at best, so why the hell not? Funny, in a non-mirthful way, how I came over to stake my claim in the "old country," with never an inkling the "old country" might claim me right back.

Dammit, the downpour only gets worse. At the behest of paranoia, I listen in vain for God knows what. I pull down my zipper, in range of whitewashed plaster. What with this deluge, will I even leave a stain? Okay, let 'er rip! Where's the harm?

Lightning Source UK Ltd.
Milton Keynes UK
UKHW010719160223
417123UK00005B/222